The Town of Jasper

JAMES GIANETTI

A Novel

ELEVATION
BOOK PUBLISHING

All Rights Reserved © 2016

The Town of Jasper

No part of this book may be used or reproduced, stored in a retrieval system or transmitted in any for, or by any means, electronic, mechanical, photocopies, recorded or otherwise, without the permission of the publisher except in the case of brief quotations and embodied in critical articles and reviews.

Published by: Elevation Book Publishing
Atlanta, Georgia 30308
www.elevationbookpublishing.com

The Town of Jasper

by

James Gianetti (1991 -   )

p.cm.

ISBN 978-1-943904-07-5 (pbk)

BISAC FIC030000
BISAC FIC031000

Copy Right 1-4074591081

ELEVATION
BOOK PUBLISHING

James D. Gianetti

Thank You

A big thanks to my older brother, mom, photographer Alaina Sacci, long time friend and professor George Elian, the wonderful editor Benjamin Smith, and everyone at Elevation Book Publishing.

"And many of those who sleep in the dust of the earth shall awake, some to everlasting life, and some to shame and everlasting contempt." Daniel 12:2

James D. Gianetti

Table of Contents

How It Was. Who I Used To Be   10

Nail in the Coffin   21

Gone   28

Would You Like To Talk About It?   42

The Council   53

Monster   65

Men of Science   83

Heroes   96

To The Place Where No One Goes   112

Hole   121

Us, Who They Will Thank   142

Behind the Big Brown Door   151

The Things They're Going To Do   161

Pseudonyms & Conundrums   168

The Rich And The Rags   179

Two Cops Walk Into A Biker Bar   198

And Deliver Us From Evil   210

Why   224

Faces Like Coal   229

The Table With The Note   237

The Town of Jasper

Men With No Shadow   245

Tomorrow   255

The Pink House On Gansevoort Street   260

The Plea   277

The Fourth Little Pig Built A Safe Zone   282

Straight and True   294

Silent Night   299

Precedent and Potential   313

The Safe Zone   321

Anonymity of Sin   336

Leave of Absence   344

Persona Non Grata   350

Proditor   357

Crossfire   366

Things Always Turn   387

Prologue

When a disease or illness arises in larger numbers than expected in a specific community or area, during a specific season, an outbreak has occurred. Outbreaks can be very unpredictable in duration and how far it extends geographically. It can spread throughout the world or remain in a single town. Outbreaks tend to last anywhere from days to years. A sole case of an infectious illness can sometimes be deemed an outbreak.

When a disease or illness spreads rapidly, infecting numerous people in a given period of time, it is known as an epidemic. Epidemics tend to spread in short periods of time, usually in less than fourteen days. Some of the most widely known epidemics include Smallpox in New England in 1633, Yellow Fever in Philadelphia in 1793, Polio in 1952, and Whooping Cough in 2010. Infected individuals undergo bodily changes, which help identify the fact that they are the victims of an epidemic illness, which include increased virulence and changes in the host's susceptibility to the infectious agent.

While an epidemic may be restricted to one location, if the disease does in fact migrate to other continents, it would be considered a pandemic. A pandemic is a global disease outbreak that affects a great number of people. Some commonly known pandemics include both HIV and AIDS. In years past, Influenza pandemics have occurred on more than one occasion. The Spanish Influenza killed more than forty million in 1918, and the Asian Influenza killed more than two million in 1957.

What is it when something unimaginable occurs? Something beyond the realms of science and discipline? Something you can't explain. Something you can't talk about. What happens when you are isolated from the world? What happens when you want answers? What happens when it's been a year? What happens when it's been two? What happens when it's been five? When you're alone in the dark with yourself and your questions? When you realize there is no one coming? When you get hungry? When you get desperate? When you sin? When you kill? When there is no light at the end of the tunnel? When you lose everything? What happens?

    Jasper is the kind of place that couples would drive through and tell each other, "This is the kind of place I want to raise our family." Enriched with the conventional feel of a perfect suburban town with family friendly neighborhoods and a town square suited for the affluent, Jasper is the ideal community to the eyes of the oblivious. Its colonial style pays a lovely tribute to early America, while also complimenting the status quo of the middle class. Some outsiders consider the aged town to be haunted, given the local stories and tales regarding the mysterious race that are said to live deep in the hills known as the Fillmore Whites. However, despite the community's tranquility and graceful architecture, it also has its flaws. Flaws that cannot be seen in a brief drive through in a hatchback. Flaws that the residents hide and the visitors question. A book again and again judged by its cover, Jasper is divided into an East and West side, with the train tracks acting as the divide. The boundary between them has created a more than mild rivalry among the townspeople that often results in offensive stigmatizations and occasional physical altercations. The odd thing about Jasper is that despite the town's covert imperfections and diversity, those who settle and consent to live there are almost meant to. Each of Jasper's residents tailors their beliefs and values and molds them in such a way that, over time, *they become the type of residents Jasper attracts. Necessary Sinners.*

Albeit the likes of these necessary sinners live in a unique and established community, nothing can prepare them for the happening that will be known as "The Incident". The aftermath of such incident will create a foregone conclusion of disorder and anarchy.

Not all of Jasper's residents are bible studiers and believers in divinity or higher powers. Some have adopted a more methodical faith. A faith proclaimed far more tangible than ancient scriptures and tales of once wise men. The principles and ideologies of these very same residents will soon be turned upside down. Soon, things will change. All it will take is a descent of the Moon and rise of the Sun. Then, things will change.

The Town of Jasper

How It Was. Who I Used To Be.

Present Day, 2016
Five Years After "The Incident"

Detective Sutherland sat in his car with his right hand on the wheel. It was completely silent as the windshield collected the light drizzle of rain outside. The detective rested his notepad on his lap as he looked at the exterior of the house. His eyes often drifted at the cul-de-sac to his left and then would return, fixed on the house to his right. He did this several times. He remembered how his ex-wife always wanted to move into a house on a cul-de-sac and on a hill somewhere nice. He looked down the road and bit his lip in disgust as he thought about how things ended with her. The stress and strain of thinking about it made the diagonal scar on his left cheek tingle. He rubbed it delicately with two fingers. He looked at the house again as the drizzle turned into a mild shower. His eyes averted from the house, but this time he looked down at a small object on the passenger seat. A small orange vial rested on the leather seat beside him. It sat there, tormenting him. The rain got heavier as the detective recollected on his recent interrogations. Tasked with conducting informational interviews of the people within the wall of Jasper and to acquire sound and concrete information on the town's alleged leader, detective Sutherland felt like a mouse sprinting on a wheel. He has made little to no progress on the case since he started it years ago, and his ignominy became subordinate to his now innate feeling of frustration. Words and phrases flashed into his head as he clutched his notepad with both hands and squeezed his eyes shut. He remembered their voices. The countless people he'd interviewed to no avail. Their voices had been engraved in his head.

    "Things got out of control"

    "Everything started out okay"

    "He made believers out of us"

    "I don't know him. I swear"

    "Things aren't going to get better here"

    "We need to keep holding on. It's all we can do now"

    "Their absence will make us define ourselves"

    "I just want

    "There's nothing you can do to make this turn"

    "I've lost hope"

    "I don't know anything about him."

    "We are being punished"

    "Things won't go back"

    "Maybe this is the way"

    "I've never seen him before. Ever."

    "This place is dark"

    "If they wake up. They're going see me. But me is someone completely different now. I don't remember how it was or who I used to be."

The detective opened his eyes as some precipitation built up around his temples. A hefty swallow and a few hard blinks made him remember he was in the present. He released his deathly grip on the notepad and felt a degree of remorse and somber as he gaped down the road of the cul-de-sac again. He tapped his forehead against the glass window for a few moments as the rain poured down on his car. He removed his forehead that was stuck to the glass from his sweat and grabbed the little orange capsule next to him. He popped off the top and sprinkled three capsules onto his hand. His hand shook as he placed one back into the tube. He threw the two back and swallowed heavily. He looked at the bottom of the orange tube and saw he was running low. Displeased with himself, and the fact that his "medication" was running dry, he banged on the steering wheel. He threw the vial on the seat next to him and stormed out of the car into the rain. As he marched up to the door, he placed a grey ski mask over his dirty blonde hair and oblong face. He knocked on the door several times and waited for an answer.

"I am going to ask you a series of questions. Try to answer them in as much detail as you can. If you are unable to answer a question, you can skip it and come back to it, or just not answer it. However, I urge you to answer every question, as it is vital to my research and your compensation."

The couple, Ron and Kathy Carlisle, both in their mid forties, held each other's hand. Both of them started to slightly tremble. Ron was a well-built man with an innate toughness to him. His tattoos and Mohawk style haircut gave off a bad boy biker type. Kathy had an oval-structured face, with perfect white teeth, and brunette hair. She often fidgeted with her fingers and her feet.

"Before I begin, do either of you have any questions for me?" asked the detective.

Kathy looked at Sutherland gently in wonder. There was a slight degree of optimism and curiosity in her eyes.

"Are you here to save us? The community?" asked Kathy.

Detective Sutherland looked into the eyes of the couple and detected a great deal of concern. It seemed as if they were lost.

"Um. No," said detective Sutherland with sorrow.

The detective opened up his note pad and clicked his pen. Jack Sutherland, a graduate from the University of Chicago with a degree in criminal justice, fifteen years on the force, and promoted to detective on his thirty-first birthday. Now, thirty-seven, nothing from his relevant coursework, experience in the field, hours up all night studying cases, countless close calls, shoot outs, or mentoring from the most notable in the business could prepare him for this assignment. He wore the ski mask to preserve his identity. He wanted to remain anonymous.

"Let's begin," he said.

Both of them exhaled deeply, ready to begin the interrogation.

"Can I get you anything before we start, detective?" asked Kathy.

"No, ma'am. Thank you," said detective Sutherland. "Where were you on the morning of 'The Incident'?"

"We were here. At home," replied Kathy.

"What were you doing?"

"Preparing lunches for my children. It was a Tuesday. The kids had school."

"And I was also in the kitchen. Reading the paper," said Ron, chiming in.

"Do either of your children have any health conditions? Allergies? Handicaps?"

"Our daughter is blind," said Ron uncomfortably.

The detective jotted the piece of information down.

"And our son has a nut allergy. Not sure if that's of any importance."

"What do you both do for a living?"

"I was a bank teller at the Liberty Bank in town here," said Kathy.

"I owned a small tool store a couple of streets from the bank," said the man.

"Owned?"

"Owned. After what happened. I couldn't…I was *incapable*…I just couldn't go there after '*The Incident*'," said Ron.

Sutherland sloppily jotted some notes down. He looked up at both of them with a calm yet serious expression.

"Describe that morning," asked the detective as he leaned forward.

The woman looked down, upset. She sighed as her husband also turned his eyes towards the floor, hoping to never have had to talk about the day ever again.

"I had just finished making lunch for the kids. They were running late. I kept calling to them, and I didn't hear a response," said Kathy. "I thought nothing of it…just a couple of teenagers getting ready for school who didn't want to be bothered."

Kathy's voice began to crack. Explaining the story was not an easy task for her.

"I remember walking to the bottom of the stairs and shouting their names," she said as she looked at the detective, horrified. "Nothing," she practically whispered.

The detective adjusted his posture on his chair and sat up straighter. The couple's discomfort began to wear off on him.

"Again. I thought nothing of it. Just a couple of teenagers getting ready for school, who didn't want to be bothered."

Kathy cracked a fake smile in an attempt to hold back her emotion.

"I walked up the stairs and into my daughter's room. Her name is Alyssa. My first reaction was anger. I screamed, GET UP! HOW ARE YOU STILL ASLEEP? When she didn't respond, I shook her."

Kathy's lips quivered as she looked to her right. Again, she looked into the detective's eyes and whispered.

"Nothing".

The detective studied the woman as tears trickled down her cheeks from both eyes. He was anticipating for her to break soon.

"I remember shaking her and shaking her. Her eyes wouldn't open. I got worried. I screamed her name. *Alyssa*. I checked her pulse and…"

Kathy struggled. She swallowed hard as her husband clenched her tightly.

"Then I ran into my son Zach's room."

She began to cry. Ron also struggled to hold in his emotions as he squeezed his wife's hand.

"I'm here. I'm here. You got this," he told her.

Kathy sniffled as she allowed her husband to hold her and comfort her.

"My son. The same thing," Ron said.

The detective felt a wave of emotions crash into him as he felt the degree of pain and suffering these people had gone through that morning.

"I called to Ron and shouted, 'Call nine-one-one.' I kept shaking my children. *Begging* them to wake up," she continued.

"What happened when you called 911? What did they do?" asked Sutherland.

Ron sat up straight and adjusted his overall posture.

"Nobody answered. The phones were dead," he said. "I ran outside to the neighbor's house and knocked on their door. Nobody answered there either."

Ron struggled to speak. He cleared his throat and looked troubled. As if the sheer reminder of the day traumatized him. He looked down and explained the rest of the story.

The Town of Jasper

"I remember people…running out into the street. Calling for help. Screaming that their children, husbands, and wives…"

Ron looked up at detective Sutherland with glazed eyes.

"They were not waking up."

Sutherland became fascinated by the story. He was too distracted by Ron's explanation of the incident to write anything of value into his log. He had heard stories of the incident before. But none this detailed.

"I ran down the cul-de-sac in front of our house. I remember hearing a gunshot as people sped down the road towards the hospital. Everyone was in a panic. I saw a little girl at the end of the street. She was standing at the end of her driveway. She said she was waiting for the bus and that her parents were still sleeping."

"What did you do?" asked Sutherland.

"I took her with me," said Ron. "After that, I ran back into my house with the little girl. I rushed upstairs and saw my wife holding my daughter in her arms, crying. I rushed into my son's room, pulled the covers off of him to give him CPR. Before I tried to revive him, that's when I realized."

"What?"

"That he was breathing."

"What happened after your son started to breathe?" asked the detective.

"It wasn't just my son," Ron said. "The next day, my daughter's vitals came back. It was the most extraordinary thing I've ever seen. It was like some twisted joke."

"What about the rest of the victims?" asked Sutherland.

"Some took longer than others to come back. Some took hours, others days, some even weeks," Ron said with sorrow.

The detective looked at Ron, who was clearly bothered by having to answer the question. The interrogation made the two of them look haggard, as if they hadn't slept in days. Sutherland reviewed his notes over, trying to cross check and find patterns anywhere he could.

"What happened to the girl? The one you carried?"

Kathy spoke promptly as she reestablished her stable mood.

"She stays with us. Her parents. They're safe."

"Safe?"

"Yes," said Ron.

"Where are they being kept?"

Katherine and Ron became uncomfortable. Ron cleared his throat, knowing it would be best to not discuss things further.

"None of your concern, detective," said Ron.

"I don't understand," the detective stated in baffled tone.

"How could you?" asked Kathy.

"Honey…" said Ron.

"Please disregard my rudeness, detective."

Detective Sutherland looked at Kathy and Ron, who both stared eerily back at him in an interrogative way. The situation now became odd, and the detective felt like he was getting nowhere with it. The pen dropping on his notepad made a quick popping sound as he made sure his handwritten notes were legible enough to comprehend.

"One last question," said the detective as he looked at the two of them solemnly. "Who is Richard Morrissey?"

The Carlisle's looked upon him with a completely different gaze. They looked at him sternly and with obscurity. It frightened the detective. They did not answer the question, but rather remained still as stone. It was if they were there were forbidden to comply with the question.

17

The Town of Jasper

"Would you like me to repeat the question?" asked detective Sutherland.

They both said nothing. They had a look of trepidation painted on their faces.

"Who is Richard Morrissey?"

Silence ensued for several moments, and the detective grew impatient.

"Who is…"

"It's getting late, detective. I think it's time you leave," suggested Kathy.

Sutherland looked up at Kathy. He knew she was hiding something.

"Do you know where he is? What aren't you telling me?"

The couple stood up off their sofa, and the detective copied them.

"We thank you for stopping by," Ron said.

The detective's voice intensified as he became relatively angry at their defensiveness to the question.

"Please. You have to tell me who he is. What does he look like?"

"Detective, please".

"Anything. Age, height, hair color. Just give me something," the detective requested quickly and loudly.

"We can't," said Kathy.

"Why not?"

"You're wasting your time," said Ron.

"I need to know."

"Please leave," Ron demanded.

"Mr. and Mrs. Carlisle, let me help you. Tell me where he is. Tell me. Where is *he*?"

"Get. The hell. *Out*," stated Ron firmly.

The detective licked his finger and flipped quickly through his notepad of recent interviews and analysis.

"I know he's in charge here. I have dozens of people who swear he's your savior, but *no one* knows who he is? You're hiding something. And I won't leave until I find out what."

Ron Carlisle walked into the kitchen and opened a drawer. Detective Sutherland walked away from the couch and followed Ron into the kitchen. Inside the drawer, under a Chinese food menu, Ron took out a pistol with a silencer attached.

"Where is he?" asked the detective. "WHO IS RICHARD MORRISSEY? WHO IS RICHARD MORRISEY?"

Ron cocked the gun's lever back and aimed it at the detective, who dropped his notepad and drew for his side arm instantly. Before either man could fire off a shot, the sound of a girl broke the tension in the room.

"Dad?"

The little girl who Ron carried home the day of 'The Incident' stood in the crossfire. Ron looked at her with his pistol raised. He lowered the gun and looked at the girl, concerned and upset with himself. The detective looked at the girl who flashed her hazel eyes at him. The detective, with his pistol also raised, looked at her with mixed emotions. Overwhelmed with the situation, the detective lowered his weapon, not knowing what else to do. After a long moment of quiet, the detective walked out of the house.

Rain continued to pour out of the depressing sky as detective Sutherland marched toward his parked car. He walked around the front of the vehicle and stopped to look at the street before him. The street was the cul-de-sac, as explained in the Carlisle's story. It was empty, abandoned, dark, and dead. The detective looked at

The Town of Jasper

it and sighed gently as anger began boiling up in him as he looked down at his holstered weapon. He squeezed the handle of the pistol firmly and gaped down the street called Collins Lane. After the anger crashed and twirled inside him like a tornado, he calmly opened the door to his vehicle and got in. Cool and collected, Detective Sutherland slammed the door unexpectedly. He gripped the steering wheel of his undercover Dodge Charger and leaned his forehead against the wheel. He removed the grey ski mask and screamed at the top of his lungs in rage.

The Nail In The Coffin

A Year Before "The Incident"
April 2010

The service had finally ended. Nearly every person from town came to pay their respects. A tall, brawny man with dark brown hair and a handsome face, standing no more than six feet tall, shook the hands of the remaining people and shut the church door. Dressed in a black suit, with his dark hair combed back, the thirty-nine year old, intrepid Irish Catholic, Richard Morrissey, walked up the aisle of the dimly lit church. His knuckles and palms were sore from all of the hand shaking. Father Paul, the beloved man of faith from the town of Jasper and long time best friend of Richard's late father, Ken, stood over the casket saying a prayer silently. He was specially requested by Richard to conduct the service even though it was not his church to do so. Richard's beautiful wife Diane stood in the center aisle of the church, cradling their daughter Victoria in her arms as she slept and held their son Joseph's hand. Richard signaled at her to take the kids home. As she walked out of the church with their children, Richard walked up behind Father Paul, who spoke faintly. Albeit, soft and low toned, Richard could hear him.

"God of power and mercy, you have made death itself the gateway to eternal life. Look with love on our dying brother, and make him one with Your Son in His suffering and death, that, sealed with the blood of Christ, he may come before you free from sin. Amen."

The Town of Jasper

After the prayer, Father Paul's emotions overpowered him, which led him to weep slightly.

"You were a great man who inspired the best out of the ones who knew you. Part me of wishes you never went in that building to save those people. I'll never forget the things you have done for me."

Father Paul wiped tears from his eyelashes with his fingertips.

"Your boy is a special one. He's got a golden heart and a bright soul. Just like his mother and father. We're all going to miss you around here."

Father Paul placed both hands on the wooden casket and looked up at the statue of Jesus.

"Look after this man. He'll fit right in up there, no question."

Father Paul looked back down at the casket again. A tear droplet trickled off his nose and hit the wooden casket.

"Rest in peace. A great man, husband, and father. Rest in peace. My friend."

Father Paul turned around and saw Richard standing behind him. Surprised and startled, Father Paul didn't know what to say to him.

"Richard, I…"

"It's okay. Thank you for saying it."

Father Paul was at a loss of words. It was not common for priests to become emotionally compromised by the deaths of others. However, this was different. It wasn't just a death. It was a loss.

"We should get going," said Father Paul.

Father Paul tried to regain his composure as he walked by Richard, who stood like a statue. Richard looked down as Father Paul walked by him, half ashamed of his behavior.

"Father…" uttered Richard.

Father Paul stopped in the middle of the aisle and turned around to look at Richard. The misery and anguish in the priest's eyes were evident.

"Will you open it?" asked Richard.

Confused and somewhat unaware of what he was referring to, Father Paul looked at Richard curiously.

"What?"

"The casket. Will you open it?"

"Why?"

"Please."

Bewildered at the request, Father Paul became more than reluctant to entertain it due to the pain it would cause Richard.

"Richard. You don't want to…"

"I do," Richard said sternly.

"Richard he, he…he isn't…he's badly mangled."

"I don't care. I need you to open it."

Father Paul was more than concerned. He did not want Richard to see his father the way he was. He didn't deserve that experience. The two stood in silence in front of each other in the aisle of the empty church. Father Paul looked at Richard keenly, hoping he would change his mind. But Richard stood firmly, hoping Father Paul would comply with his request.

"Walk with me, son," Father Paul requested.

Richard walked slowly beside the priest as the two walked in unison up the steps leading to his father's casket. The priest grazed the top of the smooth wood finish with his fingers as he looked down upon it.

23

The Town of Jasper

"Did he ever tell you how he saved my life?"

Richard looked interestingly at the Father Paul, who had grasped his attention.

"No."

Father Paul now placed his palm on the casket and cracked a haphazard smile, reminiscing of the day Ken Morrissey made him who he was today. It took a while for Father Paul to begin the story, as he was still coping with the fact that he was touching his best friend's casket.

"I was sitting on train tracks. I had just been banished from my family. Cast out," Father Paul stated.

Richard looked at his father's casket as he listened to Father Paul's story of his father.

"They didn't see it coming. I just had to let it free and let go…My family didn't understand who I was or what I am. But *he did*," Father Paul said softly and sadly. "And now they're all dead. And I'm here…I'm here…a homosexual priest and a damned son of my father."

Richard glanced at Father Paul and didn't show full eye contact. He looked back at the casket and continued to listen intently.

"I sat on the tracks that day and waited for what I deserved. Putting an end to the misfit that I was declared, and to relinquish my family of their burden of my very existence."

There was an elongated pause as the two of them stood stiff and without a sound.

"Then he arrived. Your father. My friend. Out of the woods and onto the tracks."

Father Paul's eyes watered as he remembered the day as clear as water.

"He saw me sitting, and he knew my intentions from the get go. He was brilliant like that. He could read a person better than a book," Father Paul stated. "I remember him looking at me closely, and asked me my name. When I told him, he took a seat on the tracks with me and he introduced himself. He said he just met a girl, and she was the one. It was your mother, the girl he was talking about. One topic of conversation led to another, and I told him I wanted to become a priest."

Father Paul began to chuckle, as this was his favorite part of the story. He struggled to continue the story as he kept giggling.

"So after I told him that, he wound up going through his confessions."

Father Paul's giggle turned into a moderate laugh, and it made Richard smile. It was good to have a positive tone on such a dark day. After he had his laugh, he got serious and remembered the last thing he said to him that day.

"After we spoke for nearly a half hour, he got up and looked down at me. He said to me. *You're not a gay priest. You're a priest who happens to be gay.* Then he walked away and turned to me and gave that Ken Morrissey smirk. He said, *By the way. The train hasn't come through here in five years.* I remember chuckling as he walked away. That was the first day I met him. A year later, I became a priest. The year after that I had my own church. Years later, I married your mother and father. I have remembered that day every day from the moment our conversation ended until right now. And I'll remember it tomorrow, the next day, and until the end of time. Only I know how grateful I am to have met the man coming out of the woods to confess his sins and save my life."

Father Paul turned to Richard and placed his hand on his right shoulder.

"And now you do too," he said.

The Town of Jasper

Father Paul looked behind him to make sure there were no remaining visitors or drop-ins. He began the process of opening the casket as Richard requested. Levers snapped and clicked as the priest hurried along. Richard stood with his back turned to his father's coffin, looking out into the empty seats of the church. In his hand, he held what he wanted to give to his deceased father. He twirled it around with his fingers as he looked around at the scenic artwork on the windows. Richard couldn't stop thinking of his father and what he had done. He had lost one of the most important people in his life, and the feeling of loss had made his body exhausted. He had never felt such devastation and now empathized with what his father went through when his mother died. He thumbed the tiny object and twirled it around some more.

"Why do bad things happen to good people?" Richard asked as he looked out into the emptiness.

Father Paul looked up at Richard, altering his concentration from getting the casket open.

"Because it makes the good people stronger," the priest stated. "But good things happen to good people too. Always be mindful of that."

Richard didn't acknowledge the statement. His anger made him unmoved by Father Paul's wise words. He continued to fidget with the small object as he waited. A loud clanking sound caused Richard to break from his fidgeting and turn around. Father Paul walked around the other side of the casket.

"You're sure about this?" asked Father Paul.

Richard looked at him and nodded unsurely. Father Paul looked at him, giving him a moment to see if he would change his mind. Richard stood and said nothing. He just held the small object between his thumb and index finger. He finally looked up at Father Paul and gave him a slight nod. The priest sighed.

"Richard, I don't think…"

"Open it," Richard nearly demanded.

Father Paul nodded and lifted up. Richard looked into the casket as Father Paul walked away to give him some space. Inside the casket, Ken Morrissey laid mangled and deteriorated. Richard could barely look at him. His spine cringed at the sight of his father, whose appalling appearance made Richard look away in aversion. After a moment, Richard gathered himself and stood up straight. He took the small object from his hands and placed it on his father's chest. The small object was a nail. The same nail that he hammered into the tree house he and his father built years ago. He slid the nail down his chest and into his hands that cupped together. He held his father's hands, which now cradled the nail, for a couple of minutes. After the moment of silence, Richard let go and took a step away from the casket. He looked at Father Paul.

"You can close it now," Richard stated.

Father Paul walked up to the casket and closed it shut.

Gone

Present Day, 2016
Five Years After "The Incident"

Several years into the investigation and nobody has revealed any information on a one Richard Morrissey. Rumors have spread throughout the station that he is responsible for the safety and direction of the town, but no one will give up any information on him. Some say he is a prophet, others a killer, a liar, a savior, God, protector. Some swear he doesn't even exist. No one knows what he looks like, how old he is, or the area he can be found. Anytime Sutherland asks someone to disclose information on him, they become hostile. The only reason people consent to interrogations and interviews is due to the compensation they receive in the form of food, water, warm clothing, etc.

Detective Sutherland has been on the case for far too long with nothing but stalemate conclusions. Just a name. A name that may not even be real. A name to a person that might not even exist. The detective recorded his observations through his recorder. The next hopeful lead was a former police officer of Jasper, Gary Ford. Reports say that he was unstable and inebriated most of the time.

The detective's front wheel grazed the cement curb. He turned the wheel and turned off the ignition. He gave a panoramic look around the park to see if he could find the officer he was looking for. The detective opened the door to his vehicle and stepped out. The door slammed closed, and the detective began his entrance towards the park. On a sunny Wednesday morning, the "Henry Knox Park" had several children playing on it, along with their parents. 'Before', the park was a very popular place for dog walkers and children after school was out. The park was next to a large farm that was owned by a friendly couple. On occasion, horses and other animals would graze in the field, and the children would feed them.

Detective Sutherland removed his sunglasses and squinted around the playground. At the Far East end of the park, Officer Gary Ford sat on a rusty bench, cradling a small silver object. The detective waited a few moments before starting to walk over to him. He wanted to go over his game plan and mindset before he just presented himself. After all, every other interview had gone horribly. Sutherland's journey across the park consisted of the sound of children giggling and a few dirty looks from their mothers. The officer's dark undercover clothes gave the impression that he was up to no good. Officer Ford sat on the edge of the bench with his blacked out aviators on. He wore army pants and a dirty white t-shirt. His leather jacket smelled of booze and a dumpster. As did Officer Ford. His military style haircut was neat and slicked back. Sutherland placed the grey ski mask over his face and walked over to him.

    The detective sat down on the bench a few feet away from him. Neither of them exchanged eye contact with one another. They both looked straight ahead as if the other wasn't there next to them.

    "Little early to be drinking, Mr. Ford."

    Aside from being a stellar detective, Sutherland had eyes behind, above, in front, and on both sides of his head. His peripheral vision was sharper than most people's regular vision. Officer Ford had a flask tucked in his leather jacket pocket.

The Town of Jasper

Impressed at how the detective caught a glimpse of it, Officer Ford quickly tucked the flask of booze away and adjusted his jacket.

"You have it?" asked Officer Ford curtly.

Sutherland gave the officer a grim look and reached into his jacket pocket. He pulled out an envelope and handed it to the drunken officer, who grabbed it out of his hands. Officer Ford opened up the envelope and started flipping through the bills with his fingers.

"It's all there," informed the detective.

Once the officer was done counting the cash, he folded the envelope and tucked it away in his other jacket pocket.

"Why cash?" asked Sutherland.

"Because you never know. Things might go back," said the officer. "And if they do, I'm buying a one way ticket as far away from this place as the map will let me go."

"Can we begin?" asked the detective.

"On you, detective," he said in a grizzled, monotone voice.

The detective reached into his bag and took out a pen and notepad. He clicked the end of the pen and leaned the notepad up against his right knee.

"My name is Detective Wembley, and I'm going to ask you a series of questions. Some will be tougher to answer than others. I advise you to answer every question as thoroughly as possible, as it is crucial for my research and your compensation".

"Why should I give half a shit about your research?"

"Because I gave half a shit about getting your 'more than generous' compensation. And believe me. It was just *half* a shit," stated Sutherland.

The officer finally looked at the detective and nearly cracked a grin at the emergence of verbal retaliation.

"Go on then, detective. Ask your questions."

He readied his pen by pressing it against the paper of the notepad. Officer Ford took out a cigarette and placed it between his lips.

"How long have you been on the Jasper Police Force?"

"Was going on eighteen years."

"You quit?"

"Retired," he snapped at the detective.

"Does your retirement have anything to do with what happened on the day of 'the incident'?"

Ford did not answer. He looked down, mortified. He felt his hand reach for the flask tucked away in his jacket pocket. Without even realizing it, he restrained his urge to take a healthy guzzle from the silver container. His nonverbal activity answered the question for the detective.

"How long has your hand been shaking like that?"

The officer's hands were shaking considerably. He looked down and insecurely gripped them together to stop the shaking. Sutherland looked up at him and felt sorry for the former officer.

"What happened on the morning of 'The Incident'?"

Officer Ford flicked his lighter and ignited the flame that lit his cigarette. He shot the detective a dirty look. Almost as if he couldn't believe he asked such a question. He exhaled the smoke into the air and began reminiscing. He spoke in an undetermined fashion.

"I had just left the station to do my morning patrol. The weather just started to break, so I drove with the windows down. After my patrol, I would drive over to the elementary school to direct the morning traffic."

The Town of Jasper

Trying to write down key words of what he was explaining, the detective wrote as quickly as he could. The officer took another hit of his cigarette and continued.

"Toward the end of my shift, I would usually roam around the neighboring streets of the school over on the east side of town. Like I did on the day of the incident. On a normal day, kids and their parents would be rushing around outside, and people would be leaving for work. The adjacent streets to the school were always buzzing with activity. Thing was, nobody was outside. I checked the date. I thought, maybe it was a vacation day or holiday and I didn't realize it. I drove around the other streets. Same thing. Silence. There was nobody."

Ford squeezed his flask from the outside of his jacket. Reassuring himself that it was still in there, safe and secure.

"So, you mentioned that the day of the incident was not a 'normal' day," said the detective. "How would you describe it?"

Sutherland asked the question in order to trigger an emotional response to some extent from the officer. He wanted to know more about the morning from his perspective. A fresh start was needed. In order for that to happen, he needed to start asking questions that would create a burning fire in the officer. He looked at Sutherland in a forbidding way through his pitch-black aviator lenses. It seemed like he was trying to look right through the frames.

"An *abnormal* day," Ford said sarcastically and nastily.

The detective had that coming. The officer took another healthy hit from his cigarette and flung it on the floor. He stomped on it with his boot and smeared it in the concrete while he took out another pack and balanced another between his lips. He offered the detective one, who looked at him in a disgusted way. He hated cigarettes. He even hated the sight of them.

"Just quit," Sutherland remarked.

"Me too," said the deranged officer.

Ford placed the pack back into the pocket of his army pants and leaned back with his legs extending out across the ground. A few moments passed by while the detective looked around the park at the children playing. He glanced down at his notepad when he asked the next question.

"What happened after that?" asked Sutherland.

The officer cleared his throat and straightened his posture.

"After that, I kept circling around. To see if I could find *any* sign of activity. I called into one of the other officers, but his signal was down. I continued to try and signal other officers on my COM, but I got no responses. I reached for my cell to call one of my former partners…and that was when I heard the first scream."

Officer Ford had a particular approach to his dialogue now. Almost as if talking in detail about the situation that transpired would rid his soul of the demons inside it. He was not a man of eye contact. When he spoke, it was rarely directly at Sutherland. When it was, it was for a split second.

"The scream came from behind me. I slammed on the brakes and looked around me. I got out of the car quickly and tried to pinpoint where the scream was coming from. I finally saw a woman outside her front door crying hysterically and screaming for help."

The officer seemed at ease now, as if the discussion generated a therapeutic feeling in him.

"I saw the woman from across the street and hurried over to her. I didn't get fifteen feet until I heard more."

"More what?" asked the detective.

Ford ignored the question. It almost seemed like he didn't even hear the detective ask it.

The Town of Jasper

"I turned around and saw a man rush onto his lawn from his doorstep. He was pleading for someone to help his boy. He saw me and ran up to me. He begged. 'Please,' he said. 'My boy isn't breathing.' He said it calmly. I looked at him fearfully. I wasn't prepared for this kind of situation. The Jasper police force was a'"Get Ms. Taylor's house cat out of the tree' kind of department. Not a save the town from the horrors of 'The Incident' kind of department. I fired off a shot to try to sustain some order. It wasn't very effective. Just made people panic more."

"You said 'was' a police force. Isn't there a police force patrolling Jasper now?"

Officer Ford laughed as a defense mechanism against his discomfort. He took a hit from his cigarette.

"Not exactly, detective."

"Can you elaborate?"

"Sure. Before. There was a police force. Now. There isn't."

Sutherland began to get frustrated with his vague responses. He had gotten nowhere with interviews before, but this time he actually had some cooperation. He didn't want to lose it.

"Why not?" asked Sutherland.

"Why not? What do you mean why not? Why do you think why *not*?"

There was a brief pause. The detective was about to follow-up with another question to break the silence, but Ford spoke again. He waved his right hand around the air.

"After it all went down. There was no need for us. Law and order?"

He chuckled nervously, fiddling the cigarette between his fingers.

"Try keeping the peace in a town that's been deemed 'restricted', 'quarantined', whatever the hell they're calling it now. Try directing traffic in a town where only half the people are alive or conscious. Try writing a ticket to a man whose six year old son *has yet to wake up!*"

The detective jerked up at his instinctive outburst. People around the park looked up at them. Some picked up their children and left. Unsettled, Sutherland sat up straight, looking around uncomfortably and somewhat embarrassed. He did not want to create unwanted attention.

"Okay. Just…"

Ford's hands were shaking considerably now. He reached into his leather jacket pocket and took out the bottle. He undid the cap and guzzled it down. The bottle shaking against his lips, the former officer slugged it like it was lemonade on a hot July afternoon. His eyes watered from the booze after he took a healthy slug.

"I never saw him," said the officer, disturbed.

Sutherland looked at the officer curiously. He had an idea of what he was referring to but he did not want to bring it up. He had no intention of bringing it up. The officer began to rock his body back and forth.

"I never," the officer said as he cleared his throat loudly and jolted his neck sideways. "I never saw him. I swear it," he repeated.

The sorrow the detective felt for the officer grew stronger now. He knew what he was talking about from reviewing the officer's file. The boy in the middle of the road. The boy who had haunted the officer every day since 'The Incident'. The boy was in his head, his heart, his mind, his soul, and even in the three bottles of cheap booze he guzzles each day to get him to sleep.

"Officer. You don't have…"

"No. No, ya see. I do," Ford assured him with a smirk of sadness and anger.

He chuckled nervously again and took a toke from his Marlboro.

"He could have lived. If I were more aware, he'd be here. I could see him now over on that swing there. You see it?" asked Ford as he pointed to the swing across the park.

"It was a freak thing. It could have happened to anyone," said Sutherland.

Officer Ford let out a giggle as he grinned. He breathed a heavy breath out of his nostrils.

"That's just the thing. It *could* have happened to anyone. But it happened to *me,*" he said. "Are you a religious person, detective?"

Officer Ford looked up at the sky with his arms extended to the sides.

"Are you a worshipper of God the *ALMIGHTY*?"

He spoke in a tone of hysteria now. As if he had nothing else to lose. The detective found it hard to counter the conversation.

"Sometimes," the detective said in a feeble tone.

The officer's attitude had now completely transformed from a stern hard ass to a fanatical, defeated soul.

"So you believe that God has a plan for everyone? What was his plan for me? That boy?"

Ford laughed harder, almost choking on his own tongue. It became very uncomfortable to watch the officer crumble emotionally like the way he was.

"I know your pain. Something happened to me too," said Sutherland.

Ford looked at him after a slug with droplets of the booze dripping off his wet lips.

"Drunk driver. Hit me dead on. My daughter was in the front seat. It happens quickly, and we can't do anything to stop it," said Sutherland, trying to calm the officer down.

Ford nodded his head in disgust as he sipped again. The bitterness of the alcohol made his lips quiver. He turned to the detective sympathetically.

"Your daughter…is she…"

"Not really," said Sutherland bitterly.

Ford offered the bottle to Sutherland. The liquid swish-swashed and crashed against the inside as the inebriated officer tried to make the exchange. Sutherland resisted the temptation. Ford took the bottle away from the detective and placed it down. He let out a drunken sigh as he looked around.

"I'm not a sinner," said Officer Ford. "I was a good man, doing good by others. I was *out there* that day, *helping*. And then..."

The officer clapped his hands together, causing a resonating echo throughout the park along with a brief ringing in the detective's ear.

"Just like that. Gone…*GONE*," he said.

The detective was speechless. He couldn't say anything to ease this man's suffering. Nothing could.

"They said he was looking at a fox across the road. He just wandered out into the street. It was all in slow motion. I slammed both feet on the brake pedal, and I hit Patrick McBane dead on. His body flung eighteen feet in the air, and he was dead on impact. I remember smelling the rubber from the tires, and the windshield. It was covered in red and shattered. Looked like a massive spider's web. I kept telling myself he was alive and it didn't happen. I kept telling myself that. I still tell myself that."

The Town of Jasper

Sutherland had no response. The conversation had triggered a disturbing and familiar tale of atrocity. He looked over at Officer Ford's bottle of booze and was itching for a swig of it. There was a long silence this time. A couple of tears trickled down Officer Ford's cheek while he uncapped the top and brought the bottle halfway to his lips. He hesitated. He looked at the devil in the form of cheap, distilled brown whiskey under his nose. He clenched his teeth and his lips quivered. He got up and hurled the bottle on the ground, breaking it into tiny shatters of glass. He tried crying but held himself together.

This was one of the tougher interviews Detective Sutherland had conducted. However, Ford knew things. He had information that Sutherland needed. Ford was broken now, and Sutherland needed to strike because he wouldn't get another shot. Ford stood beside the detective with his back facing him. His head was down, and he stared at the broken shatters of glass on the ground. Sutherland clenched his eyes shut and took a breath. But then Ford spoke.

"He might have me killed if he finds out," Officer Ford said as he turned around and looked at Sutherland with tear soaked eyes. "You know that?"

Sutherland tried acting oblivious. However, he knew exactly what he was talking about.

"I can protect you," he claimed.

"No. You can't. After what happened, if he knows I spoke to you, I'm done. He's changed. He doesn't take chances. He'll tie up any loose end if it ensures safety. But he probably already knows you're here. He knows everyone who's ever lived, died, and stepped foot in here."

The detective looked at the man to try to hold back fear. He feared for this man's life. He applied the tip of the pen to the page of his notepad and pressed against it.

"Where is he?"

"I don't know."

The detective had his pen ready to jot down information, like a trigger-happy cowboy.

"What does he look like?"

The officer felt the explanation of Richard Morrissey at the tip of his tongue. The detective leaned in as he thought he finally had a bite on the rod. The officer stopped himself and quivered his lips.

"I don't know."

"Who does know? Someone must know something."

"We're probably being watched," Ford said. "I need to leave."

Officer Ford started walking toward his vehicle. Sutherland got up quickly and followed him.

"Officer, wait!"

"You shouldn't have come here, detective. You should not have come to Jasper. No one will talk. He's more than just a man here."

"I *have* to find him. I'm not leaving."

The officer reached his vehicle and turned to him.

"If you continue with your investigation, your life will be in danger."

"Who will talk to me? Someone knows something. I just need a starting point."

"How many people have you interviewed, Detective?"

Ashamed, Sutherland looked down and away from officer Ford's face.

The Town of Jasper

"Eleven."

"And how many gave you concrete information on him?"

There was a brief pause. The detective became embarrassed and ashamed to admit it. Officer Ford nodded his head in affirmation.

"You're wasting your time here, Detective. Go home. Before you get hurt. Jasper has fallen. Nothing anyone can do now."

Ford turned around and went to open the door to his vehicle. Sutherland reached and grabbed his arm tightly. The officer turned around and looked at him firmly.

"Please," the detective nearly whispered. "I'm desperate. Give. Me. *Something.*"

Officer Ford never took his eyes off him. He exhaled and nodded his head. He put his face inches away from Sutherland's and whispered.

"The woman. Nancy Ringwell. She's your starting point."

"Where is she?"

"I don't know."

"Officer…"

Ford sighed and looked both ways, checking to make sure no one was around. As if he would be able to tell with the quick glance.

"Meet her at the library this time next week. Exactly seven days from today. Make sure no one sees you," said Ford.

"Who is she?" asked Sutherland.

"She used to be someone. You'll see in her what Jasper is now."

The detective released the officer from his tight grip. The two broke away like a boat leaving a dock. The officer opened his driver's side door and sat in his car. He slammed the door shut and ignited the engine. Officer Ford rolled the driver's side window down.

"Detective. You and I, we will never see one another again. I wish you luck."

Officer Ford looked ahead and gently pressed his foot on the gas. The detective looked down at his notes. In large writing was the name…

Nancy Ringwell

Would You Like To Talk About It?
A Year Before "The Incident"
April, 2010

The room had a slight draft, which made it just chilly enough for the hairs to rise on Detective Sutherland's forearms. The couch was itchy, and there were a few pillows lodged in between his ass and back. He threw them aside to not be bothered with them. His defense mechanisms and discomfort ticks clicked in as he kept adjusting his posture and clearing his throat. Nervously, he sipped the glass of water in front of him.

His therapist, Dr. Bergman, a middle aged woman with blonde hair and glasses that fit her face perfectly, remained perfectly relaxed and still as she let him go through his fiddling routine. She smirked somewhat as the discomfort reverberated off of him like the stench from someone who got sprayed by a skunk.

"Would you like to begin?" asked Dr. Bergman.

"Sure. Yes, sure," said Sutherland uncomfortably.

"Okay then," said Dr. Bergman. "How do you feel about being here?'

"I feel okay," said Sutherland.

"Okay?"

"Good…" said Sutherland, using a different adjective to avoid the repetitive question.

"How long have you been a police detective?"

"Twelve years. Maybe thirteen. I don't know."

"You don't know? Or don't remember?"

"I just don't know. What's that matter?" asked Sutherland angrily.

"I'm just trying to get some feedback and some information," said Dr. Bergman. "Do you enjoy your work?"

"I wouldn't do something I hate for twelve years."

"So you do remember."

Sutherland looked at the doctor somewhat angrily. She smiled back at him. He was in no mood for the therapy session, which was mandated by the police force. He remained mum and waited for Dr. Bergman to continue.

"You have a partner, is that correct?"

"It is."

"Do you two get along?"

"Yes. We get along."

"So you and your partner have a close relationship?"

"You assume a lot, doc," said Sutherland.

Dr. Bergman had a particular, slow burn approach on her patients who didn't like to or felt uncomfortable speaking. It'd worked out well for her for as long as her career had lasted.

"Do you want to talk about him?" she asked.

"What do you want to know?" replied Sutherland.

"Says you two have been working together for several years. Do you like having a partner?"

"I do. It's different. It gives me someone to talk to other than myself."

"What else makes it different?"

"He doesn't take as long to answer back," said Sutherland with a sarcastic grin.

"What's his name?"

The Town of Jasper

Sutherland chuckled and leaned back slightly enough for his back to graze the pillows behind him. He crossed his hands together and shrugged his shoulders.

"No idea," he said.

"You don't know?" asked Dr. Bergman, surprised.

"I don't. He never told me it. Probably never will."

"But you get along?" asked the Dr. Bergman inquisitively.

"Yes. We are close," repeated Sutherland.

"Usually the criteria for being close friends with someone is knowing their name," stated Dr. Bergman.

"He doesn't want anyone to know his identity. Probably given the line of work we're in. He uses an alias with all of our cases. I just call him Smith or asshole."

"Okay then," said Dr. Bergman, utterly surprised and slightly annoyed with the progress of the session. She switched tactics and got right into the heart of the issue surrounding the detective.

"How long have you and your wife had problems?"

The question made Sutherland squirm and struggle in his seat. He clenched his lateral muscles together and cleared his throat.

"Couple of years. Maybe more. *I don't remember*," he said rudely.

"Describe the relationship between you two," requested Dr. Bergman.

"It's not much of a relationship anymore."

Sutherland became uncomfortable. He didn't like talking about his wife. He squeezed the couch cushion with both his hands and sat up straight.

"Would you agree that you are, in fact, having problems?"

"We," stated Sutherland

"Excuse me?"

"I would agree that *we* are having problems. She and I."

"So why do you think that is?" asked Dr. Bergman

Sutherland said nothing. He looked at a picture hanging on the drywall to his right. It was a painting. It was of an empty road on a sunny day. The sun was smiling with sunglasses on. There were a few poorly colored clouds and scribble marks that were supposed to be birds. It wasn't professionally done. Looked more like a child drew it. The painting deeply upset him, and it reminded him of the reason why he was the way he was. He closed his eyes and looked away from it.

"Mr. Sutherland?" asked the Doctor.

"What was the question?" asked Sutherland.

"Why do you think you and your wife are having problems?"

Unable to get the haunting images out of his head, he felt the urge to eradicate them. He needed his fix. He'd do just about anything for a dosage of the good stuff or even a bottle of the cheap stuff. His forehead and temple began to sweat as he swallowed continuously.

"Detective…" interjected Dr. Bergman.

Sutherland looked at her with his enlarged pupils. He tried to remember the question for a moment and attempted to block out the dark thoughts.

"Yes," he said softly.

"Yes?"

"No, I mean. What was the question again?"

The detective was confounded and loopy. For a split second, he had forgotten where he was.

"Why are you and your wife having problems?" asked Dr. Bergman once again.

The Town of Jasper

"Because we don't talk," said the detective.

"So it's a communication issue?" assumed Dr. Bergman.

"I suppose."

"Why do you have communication issues? Because of your job?"

"That's part of it."

"What's the other part?" asked Dr. Bergman.

"Because of what happened," he stated firmly.

Dr. Bergman finally trapped him into the corner she worked so hard to get him into. Alas, there was something she could work with to contrive some degree of emotional discussion from him.

"Would you like to talk about it?" she asked.

The unspeakable and terrible memories and images flashed into his head. He clenched his jaw and blinked heavily. Once again, he felt the urge to polish a bottle of liquor and transform into his as of late-intoxicated self.

"No," he said.

"Why do you take narcotics, Mr. Sutherland? Why do you drink heavily?"

Sutherland sat up straight and looked down with his hands clasped together. He didn't open his mouth as he sat coldly.

"Is it for the same reason you don't want to talk about?" asked Dr. Bergman.

Sutherland remained quiet. The room was calm, but an uncomfortable tension lingered like an unpleasant odor.

"Mr. Sutherland."

"Yes," he said softly.

"Do you feel urges to take narcotics and drink when you think about it?" asked Dr. Bergman.

"Yes," he replied.

"Do you want to take narcotics and drink right now?"

"Yes," he repeated truthfully.

"Do you want to talk about your daughter?"

Again. Quiet on his side of the room. Dr. Bergman waited for a response, knowing sure enough she probably would not get one. Several moments passed.

"Mr. Sutherland this is not an interrogation. I'm not looking to get an angle on you. If you don't discuss your issues, I'd be happy to not sign this form that deems you fit for duty, and you can take a leave. Do you understand?" asked Dr. Bergman.

"I understand."

"What do you understand?"

"I understand if I don't cooperate, I'll have to take a leave."

"Why don't you and your wife speak anymore? Because of what happened?"

"Yes."

"Was it because of the way things happened?"

"Yes."

"Do you blame yourself?"

Sutherland jerked his head up quickly and responded.

"For what?" asked Sutherland in a hostile fashion.

Dr. Bergman looked at him intently and folded her legs. She dropped her pen on her notepad and bit her lower lip while she examined him.

"Why don't you tell me…"

Sutherland was cornered. He knew he'd have to talk about it. He wanted her to sign the form. He needed to work to keep his mind busy and off of what had happened. He found it difficult to make eye contact with Dr. Bergman. He felt her gaze shine upon him like a high beam light while he looked at his fidgeting fingers twirling over one another.

"It was quiet," he barely uttered. "We were in my car driving home. Driving down this long street. It was sunny. It was just us on the road."

"What were you talking about?" asked Dr. Bergman.

"We were…it was…I don't remember…" he said unsurely.

"Detective…" interrupted the Doctor, reading his bluff.

"We were talking about ice cream," said Sutherland in a raised tone. He began to shake his head. "It was about ice cream. She shouldn't have been in the front seat."

Sutherland became emotional as he continued. His palms began to moisten and he trembled. His voiced became weak and remorseful. There was a great deal of guilt in his tone.

"She shouldn't have been up there," he repeated. "We were talking about ice cream."

Detective Sutherland began to weep as he discussed the single memory that has haunted his mind since the day of the accident. The doctor felt a deep sadness for him. Something that she rarely felt for her clients.

"What happened after that?" asked Dr. Bergman.

Sutherland stopped talking. He remained still. He looked at the ground. The rug was vacuumed neatly. He remembered the day clearly now. He thought he had most of the memories out of his head. He had tried to purge them out of his head through of deplorable and undesirable means.

"Do you know? Do you remember?" asked Dr. Bergman delicately.

"I remember," said Sutherland remorsefully. "There was the car."

"The one that hit you?" asked Dr. Bergman.

Sutherland nodded as he began to weep. He tried to continue the story before his feelings could overcome him, but his emotions won the race. He placed his right hand over his mouth as he cried. Dr. Bergman gave him time to let it out. After some time, the detective sniffled once and looked up with bloodshot eyes.

"I remember looking over at her at the last second. The last thing I remember was the car coming towards her door at full speed. It was as close as you and I."

Sutherland took a swig of water from the glass as his hands shook. He needed something stronger. Badly. He had never talked about the atrocity until now. It felt foreign to talk about it out loud. It was satisfying, in a way, to get it out of his head.

"He was drunk. The driver. Then she changed after that," he said as he sobbed.

"She has brain damage?" asked Dr. Bergman

Sutherland nodded as he cupped his hands over his face and filled them with tears. He leaned forward on the couch.

"She wanted to be a big girl, and she told me big girls get to ride in the front…And I said *okay*."

"Is that why you drink? Is that why you take narcotics?"

Sutherland nodded his head shamefully.

"Because you feel responsible?"

Sutherland nodded his head again.

"Why else do you think you take them?"

Sutherland stopped crying and pulled himself together. He sniffled again and looked up at the doctor.

"Because I don't want to remember," he stated.

Dr. Bergman looked at the detective and saw how broken and vulnerable he had become. She felt the pain in him and a deep level of grief.

"If I sign this form and you get back to work, do you believe you will stop taking narcotics and drinking alcohol?"

"I believe."

"You believe what?"

"I believe I will stop taking narcotics and drinking alcohol if I get back to work."

Sutherland killed the rest of the water glass, pretending it was booze in his head. The smoothness of the water disappointed the detective. He swallowed hard and looked back at the red painting. Dr. Bergman spoke confidently and collectively amidst the explicit emotional feelings of Sutherland.

"My late father had a tremendous infatuation with Mark Twain and his work. There was a quote he always told me and my sisters to live by whenever we got into trouble or if we ever violated our integrity," said Dr. Bergman. "He would say, *If you tell the truth, you don't have to remember anything.*"

Dr. Bergman looked at Sutherland engagingly for a few moments, hoping the wise words of the great American author and her beloved father would saturate and engrave into his untamed mind. Her notepad rested nicely on her lap as she leaned on it with her forearms.

Sutherland looked down at the floor as he remembered a quote his father used to tell him. He mumbled it to himself, which made Dr. Bergman lean closer to catch a listen.

"Excuse me?" she inquired.

"When shit hits a fan spinning at full speed in front of you, there's two types of people in this world," said Sutherland. "There are people who cover their faces to not get hit with it as they rush past you, and there's people who shove their hand into the cracks to try and stop it."

Dr. Bergman disregarded the appalling quotation and awaited an explanation behind the crudeness.

"That's what my daddy used to tell me," said Sutherland.

"Which one are you?" asked Dr. Bergman.

"I'm the fan," said Sutherland.

Dr. Bergman looked down at the form and considered her next move. She clicked her pen and scribbled her signature next to the "X".

Later that day, Dr. Bergman called a man into an office. The tall, brawny man with dark brown hair and a handsome face, standing no more than six feet tall and no more than a day over thirty-nine sat down in front of Dr. Bergman. She smiled moderately even after a long day. He was calm and at ease with his hands cupped together on the table. Dr. Bergman examined him before proceeding with her questions.

"I had the chance to speak with your partner today," said Dr. Bergman.

The man acknowledged the question nonverbally with a slight downward nod of his head.

"In your professional opinion, do you feel that detective Jack Sutherland is capable of making rational decisions and professional moral judgment in the field?"

"Yes. Yes, I do," stated the man.

"Do you feel that if granted the right to act as an officer of the law he will become a liability for those around him. Including yourself?"

"No. On both counts," stated the man.

"In your professional opinion, do you feel that detective Jack Sutherland will continue to use narcotics and consume alcohol in excess of the legal limit while on duty?"

"No."

"And outside of duty?"

The man looked at Dr. Bergman, unsure and concerned.

"I'm not sure," said the man.

"How's his relationship with his wife?"

"We don't talk about it. I've never really met her," stated the man.

"He stated the two of you are close. Is that correct?"

"That is."

"And you've never met his family?"

"That's right," said the man uncomfortably.

"You've been partners for several years. Is that also correct?"

"That is."

"In your professional opinion, do you believe your long time partner, Detective Jack Sutherland is in dire need of rehabilitation?"

"No. He is not in dire need of anything," stated the man.

"Why haven't you revealed your true identity to him?"

Richard Morrissey sat back in his chair and made the two front legs rise slightly. He clenched his teeth as he uncrossed his hands and placed them onto his lap as he sat back.

"That's none of your professional business," he stated.

James D. Gianetti

The Council

Five Years After "The Incident"
Present Day, 2016

Winter in Jasper had settled in. The air was so painfully chilling that it clenched your skin and froze your joints. From mid November into late March, citizens of Jasper were unable to feel the tips of their toes. In fact, last year's snowfall was so great that kids were almost forced to be homeschooled until it cleared up.

The inside of the church was just as dark and cold as outside. Saint Anthony's, the local Catholic Church for the town of Jasper, was always filled with residents Sunday mornings. Father Paul, the priest of the church, would host the masses that had attracted many before 'The Incident'. Now, the church was vacant, with no one filling the rows of seats, except for dust and spirits. What was once a joyful and glad atmosphere, filled with harmonious prayer and family gatherings, was now a murky, dark cave reduced to a symbol of disbelief and doubt.

The door creaked open. The cold weather made the massive entrance hinges rust. The sound of two Stoneman winter boots echoed throughout the lonesome church. The shadowy figure moved slowly inside. Dressed in a long, black leather jacket that extended past his kneecaps and worn out grey jeans, Richard Morrissey walked leisurely over to the holy water. He dipped his index and middle finger into the water and touched his forehead with it. After, he gave a nice, long panoramic look around the church and almost managed a smile. He took off his pea coat and placed it along one of the benches. He gradually walked down the aisle of the house of God and looked across at the empty seats.

The Town of Jasper

Once he reached the front, he stopped walking to look up at the statue of Jesus overlooking the Church. Richard looked at it with harmony, but his glare slowly turned into a look of rage. His lip quivered as he fixed his gaze on the savior of mankind. His breaths became deeper and heavier. The hell inside him boiled like a teapot. Richard closed his eyes as he felt his face contorting with anger.

"The Father, the Son, and the Holy Spirit," pledged Richard with all his inner strength as he gestured his hand around his forehead.

In the corner from where he stood was a confessional. He stared at it, almost reluctant to proceed to it. Richard blinked constantly out of nervousness and unwillingness. He looked behind him and heard the sound of silence. The quiet was so loud it caused him to look down and accept the situation. The inhale of the frigid church air was depressing and bottomless as he began to move his feet toward the confessional. Richard sat himself down and waited inside the tight and chilly confessional. Nearly a minute passed by before he looked through the peephole next to him. He looked down, upset about something. Richard clenched his teeth and made a face as if he was holding his breath from a repulsive odor.

"Bless me, Father. For I have sinned. It has been ten days since my last confession."

His right leg jumped up and down as a cold sweat emerged on his forehead. He sat there and waited like a schoolboy in the principal's office, feeling the guilt overcome him like a fever. His held his clammy hands together firmly as his knees quavered. Occasionally, a squeak of the wooden bench Richard sat on provided the only form of sound in the place. He put his head down and closed his eyes as he prayed for something beyond forgiveness. He wished and prayed for just a response. Minutes of silence passed as the pause in action started to deeply disturb Richard. Knowing full well there would be no response, Richard spoke. His voice cracked. Each word became harder and harder to produce. On the verge of a complete breakdown of emotions, Richard explained.

"I fear I will sin. I fear I will kill."

Richard swallowed hard and exhaled as if being relieved of severe physical pain.

"I just want to protect everyone. I have to keep everyone safe."

Richard began to whisper to no one in particular.

"I have to keep everyone safe. I have to keep everyone safe," he reassured himself. "These people look to me for the answers, and I don't know if I can provide them."

Silence interrupted the whispers as Richard felt surges of mixed emotions run wildly through his mind.

"You have to help me, Father. Rid me of the sins I will commit. I don't know if I can do it without your blessing. Rid me of my inevitable guilt. Please, I beg you."

Richard placed his face against the peephole of the confessional and felt tears tickle his cheeks. He thought of his children and of his wife. He thought back to family dinners and how they would always eat pizza on Thursdays. He saw his children laughing and smiling. And in that single thought, he snapped out of his weak state of mind. His tears stopped streaming down his eyes, and his voice regained its powerful and deep, dark tone. His entire face transformed from sympathetic and sorrowful to grim and harsh.

"I'm afraid," he whispered. "I'm afraid of the 'what happens next' part. I'm afraid something horrible is going to happen again. I can feel it."

The Town of Jasper

Stillness and quiet came from the opposite side of the confessional. Richard felt his rage take control. His inner demon sitting on his soul's throne. The silence enraged him. It wasn't the silence of the priest that infuriated him, it was the silence of the priest that represented the silence of the town. The current status of the community that had him fired up. He clenched his fist and punched the peephole and shouted at the priest.

"What's it going to take?" he shouted. "They have to wake up! They have to, God dammit!"

Blood trickled through the gaps between his knuckles. Oblivious to it, he cupped his hands together and started hysterically crying. In the room next to him, inside the confessional, sat Father Paul. The priest sat upright with his head against the wall. A victim of the incident and once proud priest, who was beloved by the Catholic community of Jasper, remained in the confessional where Richard had placed him some time ago. The Father's white and gray hair blended nicely with his black attire. He was an older gentleman in his mid to late seventies. Richard kicked open the door and barged out of the confessional. He entered the room where the priest sat and grabbed the priest's hands tightly. He kissed them and whispered to the man.

"Bless me, father, not for my sins. But for the man I will become."

Inside the Town Hall of Jasper, side conversations and quiet banter echoed throughout the main room. The group of men and women ranged from ages thirty to seventy-five and were each selected appropriately by Richard to represent the logical decision-making and direction of the new Jasper. Each member had something in common. They were all unique people with distinctive leadership attributes, and they all would give their life to preserve their loved ones and their town. The Council was the only remaining form of stable authority and government within the quarantined town. The bench included Henry Melrose, Gabrielle Sanchez, Matilda Duffy, Laurie Nigel, Kendrick Peterson, Gale Benson, Benjamin Frye, Susan Baker, Ron Carlisle, and William Van Dam. Upon the formation of The Council, Richard wanted to make it abundantly clear to the members and to the public that the decisions made by them would be final. However, if the townspeople felt the majority decision was too unjust, Richard would make things work. So far, the townsfolk had not vetoed one decision made by them.

    The banter continued on as they awaited the eleventh member. Conversations among groups of two or three were on the topics to be addressed and what decisions would have to be made. No one saw Richard arrive due to his stealthy entrance. Once everyone noticed his attendance, they immediately stopped their conversations and retreated back to their respective seats. Richard paid no attention to anyone on his way in and took a seat at the head of the table. Inside the Town Hall of Jasper, where topics of land zone restrictions were once discussed and petty court cases used to be held, sat The Council. All ten pairs of eyes looked directly at Richard, awaiting his opening statement. Richard looked up in front of him and remembered the first night in the room. Townspeople going absolutely mad, threats made and punches thrown. Absolute anarchy. Richard didn't acknowledge how far they'd come with a smirk or a smile. He simply looked to his right and left at the members of The Council with a grim look on his face.

    "We have a lot to discuss tonight."

The Town of Jasper

There was an awkward pause after an hour of devising solutions for small town matters like people's homes, auto repair, work shifts, event plans, town meetings, and gasoline rationing. Benjamin Frye, an upbeat, optimistic fellow in his late thirties and one of Richard's most valued representatives, looked around and absorbed the unwillingness from the council. Benjamin was responsible for much of the town's event planning and resource strategies, while also acting as the interim pastor, even though he had no formal training. Even though he wasn't even an official pastor, he had an in depth knowledge of the old and new testaments and exceptional public speaking skills. Richard recruited him to be on the council due to his work ethic and firm attitude when need be. In a brave attempt, Benjamin spoke out confidently.

"Richard. If I may…"

With that, Richard looked up intensely at Benjamin. Richard always gave Benjamin the benefit of the doubt when he interjected in Council meetings due to Benjamin's impeccable efficiency and unmatched competence. He trusted Benjamin more so than the others.

"With respect, Richard. Before we get started on other issues, I think we need to address the supply issue. Our resources are dangerously scarce, and the winter has come faster than expected."

The government had cut off the supply of food, water, and medicine to Jasper. The town was running on fumes in regard to resources, and things were getting more and more meager each day. Richard put his hand up, gesturing for Benjamin to stop further commentary.

"Resources and supplies will be handled."

Richard gathered some files in front of him and readied himself to make an opening statement. Before he could do so, Benjamin interrupted.

"When...?"

The nine members of the group all looked down, knowing the remark was bold and stupid rather than brave. Richard looked at Benjamin with a haggard expression. He inhaled the cold, dead air of the room and exhaled it out heavily. Benjamin looked at Richard, hoping to obtain some sort of answer.

"*Soon*," Richard said in a groggy tone.

"What about what we talked about last time, Richard?" asked Matilda, the eldest member of the council, who wore the same clothing to every council meeting. "About the victim's illnesses and progression?"

"We'll worry about that when we have no more doctors to worry about that," Richard said, annoyed.

Richard sampled the room and awaited any further interruption. Every other member of the council knew their place. Benjamin was always trigger-happy when it came to voicing his opinion.

"The cold has knocked on our doors sooner than expected, and our resources are low. I know that. We've survived this far, and after tonight, we'll implement a plan that will not only allow us to survive, but *live*. To start, we need to consider alternatives and more options for obtaining food and valuable resources vital to our town's survival."

"What do you suggest?" Ron Carlisle asked with his arms folded and back leaned against his chair.

"Trade," Richard said strictly.

"Trade?" Matilda asked.

The Town of Jasper

"With whom?" asked Henry Melrose. A middle-aged man with a scruffy beard, beat-up, brown baseball cap, and worn clothes. Henry was one of the few 'townies' of Jasper left.

"The Fillmore Whites," said Richard.

The Council was taken back by the suggestion.

"The Albinos?" shouted William Van Dam, the director of the Jasper Nature Center, who had a habit of always biting his nails to the nub.

"They hate us!" shouted Susan Baker, the infamous superintendent of the Jasper school systems.

"That won't work, boss," said Kendrick, a bulky African-American male in his late thirties. Chatter and side conversations ensued from the suggestion. Richard grew angry from the lack of obedience and faith in the strategy. The back and forth babbling was so loud and quick that Richard could only make out a few words amongst the conversations.

"Fillmore Whites?"

"Trade with them?"

"It'll never work."

"They'll kill us."

"No way."

"We can't."

"Bad idea."

"Definitely not."

"No."

"I'm not going near them."

"They're freaks."

"I agree."

"I do not approve."

Richard slammed his right hand on the table hard enough to stop the bickering and hear the echo of the noise linger throughout the room. The Council regained their composure and looked up at Richard like misbehaved children waiting to be disciplined by their parent. Richard had knocked over some papers as a result of his hand forcefully slamming against the wooden table. Richard bent down and reached for them. He placed them back on the table and looked around the room. He smiled sarcastically at the members, whose eyes remained stuck on him.

"They're people. They breathe, sleep, eat, sweat, shit, piss, and speak. They have a code that they have lived by for decades. They do not like us. Why would they? We've exiled them from our community since they migrated here. You call them 'freaks'. How many of you have seen one?"

Not one member of The Council raised a hand.

"You are so quick to reject them. So quick to say it won't work. How it can't. Who have we become where we discriminate and categorize the different? Five years ago, the opposite sides of town were at each other's throats, now they're coming to each other's aid. It's almost as if everything we've worked for up to this point has taught you nothing."

The members of The Council looked down, feeling remorseful and ashamed.

"Now I'm not saying it's going to be easy. Hell, nothing we've worked for up to this point has been. Truth is, it's going be hard as hell. Now we haven't lost anyone yet. That could change now. I know we're all tired because we haven't stopped working since it happened. We've got people counting on us, loved ones, family, friends. We've got a surreal problem on our hands, and we've dealt with it. The town is grateful. They may not show it. But they are. We all have our reasons for moving forward. Some of us won't survive if we don't do this. This is a way to make things easier while we wait for a cure. We need their resources. They have acres upon acres of land with crops and fresh water. I don't know if it'll work. But we're going to try. Because that's what we do. We try. Because if we don't…"

Richard did not finish the sentence. He let the silence speak for the rest of it. He looked around at the people who suddenly became receptive of the plan after they digested Richard's reminder of the bigger picture.

"What makes you think they'll agree to trade with us?" asked Benjamin.

"Because we're going to ask nicely," said Richard with a sarcastic grin.

There was a brief pause in dialogue as the group transitioned to the next topic of conversation.

"What of this new uprising group? They're some kind of Kool-Aid drinking religious cult. Am I right?" asked Ron Carlisle to the rest of the group.

The members nodded their heads in agreement, all knowing the issue should be addressed and a solution be implemented to deal with them.

"Are they dangerous?" asked Susan Baker.

"They're radicals!" screamed Henry.

"There's something about them," said Laurie Nigel. "No one has ever seen them. That's what rubs me the wrong way."

"If no one's seen them, how do you know they actually exist?" asked Kendrick.

"People say they see them out at night occasionally. Dressed up in dark clothing and black face paint."

"Until they do harm, they are free to protest and rally in whatever way they want. We do not discriminate or display violence against Public Displays of Religion. We all have our ways of coping with the situation," Richard stated. "We'll double down on midnight shifts to be safe."

"I don't think that's necessary," asserted Benjamin. "Like you said, until they do harm. Why cause a panic in town when, we're at our weakest state since the outbreak?"

Richard gave Benjamin an uncompromising look. Benjamin had now become comfortable not only speaking his mind without consent, but resisting demands made by Richard himself. Richard turned his gaze away from Benjamin and surveyed the rest of the crowd.

"Everyone try to find out more about this radical group of people and report any suspicious acts to me *personally*."

The Council acknowledged Richard's request with head nods.

"We have work to do. Starting tomorrow I want an exact supply count. What we have, what we don't, how much of what we need, how much of what we don't, weapons, ammo, clothes, tools, anything of value. By noon tomorrow we'll head into the 'keep out' zone…see what our new friends can do for us."

The members of The Council all rose to their feet, except for Benjamin. Benjamin remained seated and looked at Richard, troubled. As people walked toward the exit, Richard stood up and started his retreat back to his quarters. Before everyone had a chance to vacate, Benjamin spoke out loudly.

"What if they say no?"

Everyone stopped, half annoyed, and looked at Benjamin. Exhausted and uninterested in the question, the members of The Council awaited Richard's answer. Richard stopped at the front exit with his back turned to everyone. Angry at the question, he turned around quickly and looked through Benjamin with his pupils as dark and heavy as coal.

"Let's hope it doesn't go down that way," Richard said in a low, grave tone.

"For whose sake?" asked Benjamin curiously.

Richard turned away and walked toward the exit, leaving his council behind him.

Monster

A Year Before "The Incident"
October 2010

Later that month, brown and yellow leaves littered the suburban streets of the town of Woodland. The brisk air called for an early winter. Pumpkins carved with wacky faces and all sorts of Halloween decorations spread across the yards of the residential block of Buckingham Road. It was the day before Halloween. Most people referred to the eve of Halloween as 'mischief night', where kids would roam the suburban streets and cause mayhem and vandalize people's personal property.

Richard and Detective Sutherland drove around slowly in their vehicle, surveying each street. The sun was setting but offered enough light to provide the dying day with luminosity. Sutherland was eating a piece of candy, and the crunching sounds coming from his mouth annoyed Richard.

"How'd it go with the shrink the other day?" asked Richard.

"It went," said Sutherland bluntly. "These streets are usually the worst. Punks will be out soon."

"This is bullshit," said Richard "Why the hell are we doing suburban cop duty?"

"I don't freakin' know," said Sutherland. "Cap says he needs his two sharpest out tonight. Take it as a compliment."

"This is not detective work," said Richard.

"No argument here," said Sutherland. "Want to hear a joke to cheer you up?"

Richard did not respond, due to his frustrated state. Sutherland glanced at him as he drove the car slowly.

The Town of Jasper

Sutherland got no response from his partner but proceeded with the antics anyway.

"What happens after a king or queen uses the toilet?" asked Sutherland.

Richard played along, knowing he'd have no choice.

"What?"

"A royal flush," said Sutherland with a smile.

There was no emotion of any kind for several seconds. After they both processed the stupidity of the joke itself, the two burst out laughing. Finally, they both simmered down and looked around the neighborhood for any 'criminal activity'.

"I'm sorry I couldn't make the wake the other day. I heard great things about your father."

Richard absorbed the compliment and didn't know how to respond to it. He tried looking busy by looking intently out of the window.

"He would have liked you," said Richard.

"What was his name?"

"Ken."

"Ken what?"

Richard looked at Sutherland and rolled his eyes.

"Nice try."

Sutherland smirked and looked at the road closely as he drove casually.

"You know you didn't have to come so soon," said Sutherland.

"Yes, I did. I need to keep my mind off of everything. It's not that I want to. I have to."

"I understand," said Sutherland.

"I know you do," said Richard, referring to Sutherland's drug addiction.

"We both have our reasons," said Sutherland.

"We both have our reasons," stated Richard.

"If you want to talk about it…" said Sutherland. "You can."

"We should check this block," said Richard, evading the question.

Sutherland accepted and understood the social deflection and made a smooth right turn. The neighborhood was quiet and calm. Dark was favoring the day as the sun descended into the horizon. Sutherland made a left turn up Blueberry Hill. The incline was significant, and the drive up made their backs press up against their seats. At the summit of the hill, there was a stop sign, which Sutherland obeyed as a yield sign instead. There was a street in front of them with a vast, dark patch of woods at the end of it. Sutherland eased the breaks, which squeaked loudly. He flashed the high beams into the woods for any potential punks and wrongdoers.

"Sometimes they hide or meet in here before they make their runs," said Sutherland.

Richard did not acknowledge the question articulately, but rather with a mumbling sound of agreement. Sutherland let the high beams ride for a moment before flashing them off. The street became dark as the engine remained in idle. Finally, Sutherland turned off the car and decided to set up shop. The two men sat and enjoyed each other's company for a time. Their silences were never awkward or uncomfortable.

"Aren't these the same woods that expands all the way to Jasper?" asked Sutherland

"It should be," replied Richard.

The Town of Jasper

"Is it true about what those crazy people say?" asked Sutherland. His tone was sarcastic and tried to induce playful fear on the topic. "About the Fillmore Whites roaming around somewhere in deepest parts of the forest?"

Richard looked at his long time friend and provided a grin due to Sutherland's good-humored nature, which he often enjoyed. Sutherland looked at Richard bashfully as he popped another piece of candy into his mouth.

"I wonder if they're really there?" asked Sutherland with a mouthful of chocolate.

"They're there," said Richard confidently.

Sutherland looked at Richard. He wanted his friend to prove his statement.

"Are they?" Sutherland asked.

"They're there," Richard repeated. "When I was a boy, my father took me to the Ducanan Trail, deep in the heart of the woods. We walked for about an hour and just kept getting *deeper* and *deeper* in. We finally stopped to get a drink of fresh water, and as I filled my canteen, I saw a body on the opposite side of the stream. I called to my father, and when he saw the body, he swam across as quickly as he could."

Sutherland listened closely as Richard recollected the story he remembered so clearly. It gave him peace to talk about it.

"The body was laying on the bank. It was white as paper and had some rag-like clothing on. It was a man. He was one of them. He twisted his ankle trying to catch a fish and fell into the water. My father pumped his stomach and pumped air into his lungs repeatedly. I remember looking across the stream, watching my father try to save his life."

Richard switched gears in the story, thinking about an aspect of life he had pondered over the years.

"What motivates and makes people want to jump in and try to save a complete stranger's life? What makes them want to get involved in their problem? Psychologists say that a day or two after birth, infants show signs of empathy. They call it altruism or something like that," stated Richard. "My father just kept on pumping and breathing more oxygen into him until he got light-headed. He was never one to show defeat. But he showed it in that moment. After he nearly fainted from exhaustion, he said a silent prayer to himself. Shortly after the prayer concluded, the man woke and coughed out a half-gallon of water. My father led the man up to the main trail, and he just looked at us. He was a towering being. Well over six-foot. While we all stood there, a woman and a young man arrived from the trees to greet him. They both had the same white skin and red eyes. The young man looked at the two of us like he has just discovered a new treasure. Then we heard their screams. They headed towards our area quickly. The man looked at us and signaled for us to leave quickly, so we hurried away. I had seen a dead man and a redeemed man on the same day. But it didn't feel like a miracle. We had done a great thing, but deep inside of me, it felt like the beginning of something else."

Sutherland looked at Richard, engaged and intrigued by the tale. He looked back at the dark woods with a bit more interest.

"They're there," Richard said again.

Looking to avoid the enduring, ominous tension, Sutherland thought about something in the back of his mind.

"Have you ever watched a sitcom with no sound?"

Richard shook his head at the dumb question.

"No. I have not."

"I did it the other day. I have to say. It's pretty damn funny without the volume. You just watch the facial expressions and hand gestures, and you just get the idea of what they're saying.," said Sutherland with a slight giggle the entire time.

Richard looked at his partner sternly. Sutherland rolled his eyes at Richard's lack of interest.

"Look, I know this kind of shit doesn't thrill you. But can you at least act like you want to be here? Or act amused to save myself the humiliation of my life outside the badge."

"I was never much of an actor. That's why I got into law enforcement," said Richard wittily.

"Asshole," whispered Sutherland with a smile as he threw another piece of chocolate into his mouth. Another long, comfortable silence progressed among the two of them. Suddenly, Sutherland began to chuckle, and it made Richard look over at him.

"What?" Richard asked.

"Do you remember that first case you and I tackled? With that fortune-teller renting out her business's basement to illegal immigrants?" Sutherland asked comically. "What was her name?"

"Ruth," said Richard, nearly cracking a smile.

"Ruth! Yes that's right. She was…she was out there," said Sutherland.

"She was a man," said Richard.

"Well. 'She was', meaning she used to be. What are those people called? Tran something."

"Transvestite," stated Richard.

"Yes. That's it. She was a transvestite," said Sutherland.

Sutherland began to crack up. Richard found humor in both the story and Sutherland's obnoxious laughter. Sutherland's laughter and hilarity became louder as he reminisced.

"Remember how she ran downstairs when we walked in and that stupid pink wig flew off her head?" asked Sutherland, barely managing to complete his sentence.

"I remember she twisted her ankle running down the stairs," said Richard. "And we saw all the people she was renting the basement out to."

"And that's still my best line," said Sutherland as he looked over at Richard.

The two of them said it together.

"I'm no fortune-teller, but I see myself arresting you in the not so distant future."

Sutherland laughed harder than Richard as the memory created a feeling of comical nostalgia between them.

"She threw her goddamn crystal ball at me," said Sutherland.

"I remember shoving you out of the way of it. One of the many times I saved your ass," said Richard.

"What are you talking about?" asked Sutherland.

"I've saved your neck a handful of times," said Richard. "More than I can count."

"What about me?" Sutherland asked.

"What about you?"

"Remember the raccoon?"

"Please don't tell me you consider that saving my skin."

"It had rabies!" shouted Sutherland.

"Get out of here."

"One day. I'll save your neck, and you'll thank me for it," said Sutherland.

"Yeah. One day," uttered Richard. "But don't expect me to thank you."

The Town of Jasper

The two cooled down from the comical debate and conversation. Bored out of their minds, they both investigated the area for any potential wrongdoers. They found nothing, as expected.

"You ever find it strange?" asked Sutherland.

"What's that?" Richard asked.

"Eight years I've known you. Five of them as your partner," said Sutherland. "And you've never told me your name. You never want to talk about the things you need to talk about. You shelter them."

"I have my reasoning," stated Richard. "I've known you the same amount of time. And I don't know what your wife and daughter look like."

Richard and Sutherland were superior detectives and did their job to the highest degree together. They both understood each other's idiosyncrasies and peculiarities, no matter how irrational. That was why they always got the job done and why they'd remained such close friends.

"We both have our reasons," Sutherland said with a sigh.

"We both have our reasons," concurred Richard.

Sutherland turned the car around and drove down a nearby street. As they drove slowly, Richard saw a group of five young teens across the street, dressed in black hoodies. They all had their hands in their pockets. They removed the eggs from their pockets and launched them at nearby houses. Eggs splattered against the middle class houses, and some windows shattered. They did not see Sutherland and Richard until after they threw the eggs.

"Oh, shit," shouted one of the kids as he saw the police car.

"Run!" screamed one of the others.

The group of troublemakers gathered themselves and scurried away into the darkness.

"Showtime," said Sutherland as Richard bolted out of the vehicle, chasing after the group of hooligans.

Richard chased them as fast he could down the street. They split up into two different directions, far too quick for Richard to catch up to them. One group headed into a nearby patch of woods. Reluctantly, Richard chased after them into the darkness while Sutherland drove after the other group.

Desperately needing to relieve himself, Richard walked over to a nearby tree. At this point the punks and hooligan kids were well beyond finding. Richard unzipped his pants and let out a stream of urine. Closing his eyes in relaxation, he let out a sigh of relief. He had held it in for nearly three hours. The flow of urine lasted nearly thirty seconds, and the sound of liquid waste hitting leaves and dirt made him oblivious to the sound of a screeching animal in the distance. Richard shook out the last few droplets and zipped up his pants. That was when he heard the sound of an animal howling. The sound was fairly clear and echoed loudly throughout the woods. The sound was a canine of sorts barking angrily. However, as Richard listened closer, he heard not just one dog. He heard two. He rushed along the border of the woods to pinpoint where the canines were howling. Richard darted swiftly through branches and avoided trees, the noises got louder and louder. He could now hear people screaming. Richard heard vicious growling, so he started to sprint deeper into the woods until he saw something in the distance. It was the group of hooligans. Richard managed to catch up to them, but they sprinted away.

"Stop!" shouted Richard.

The group was not running from him, but from something far more dangerous. One of the teenagers fell on his stomach. The boy got himself up in a panic and dashed ahead. Richard trailed him and spotted an object on the ground where the teenager fell.

The Town of Jasper

Richard tried to catch his breath as he looked down at the small plastic bag. He knelt down and picked it up. He examined the substance inside and knew it was heroin instantly. Before he examined it further, he heard them. Then, he saw them. Their grayish black hair raised and foam oozing through the gaps of their sharp teeth made Richard stand still. He looked into the pitch black eyes of the alpha. Death became a very real possibility. So real, it allowed Richard's survival instincts, adrenaline, and shock to stir around his soul like a stew. Richard looked deep into the alpha's eyes. The beast's intimidating and horrifying snarling and growling did not have any sort of effect on Richard. He stood his ground and never stopped looking back into the wild animal's pupils. Both beasts and Richard remained perfectly still, looking at each other and trying to instill fear to gain the advantage. Richard knew if he caved, he would die. Richard knew they would strike if he did not make a move. In a heroic act of valor, Richard allowed his demons to control him. Once Richard had accepted that, he moved his left foot toward the fierce creatures. The alpha growled heavier and angrier at Richard's progression. Richard did not move his right foot. Not because he was afraid, but because he knew the next step meant confrontation. Richard's facial expression became sinister as he gaped at the animals. His breathing became heavier as he tried to bestow fear into the eyes of the alpha. He began cracking his knuckles individually as the volcano brewed inside him. He slowly placed his fingers around the handle of his holstered pistol while his left eye began to twitch as he clenched hard on his grinders. Never taking his eyes off of the monsters before him, Richard whispered to himself.

"Receive, Lord, your servants into the place of salvation, which they hope to obtain through your mercy. Amen."

Richard drew his weapon as quick as he could as the alpha let out a savage roar and pounced towards Richard.

Sutherland drove around cautiously looking for the other group of hooligans. To no avail, he tried signaling Richard on his COM.

"No luck over here, they must have fled down Quarry. I put the patrol down there on alert. Anything on your end?"

The other end of the COM was silent, which caused concern on Sutherland's end. He waited another minute and tried signaling him again.

"Check back when ready," requested Sutherland.

Something was wrong. He could feel it. He swung the vehicle around and sped down the road to look for his friend.

The feral alpha wolf lunged at Richard with full force. Richard drew his gun and managed to fire off a shot, missing the wolf by inches. The wolf lunged onto his chest, causing Richard to lose control of his gun. The pistol flung out of his hands and landed several feet away. Richard let out a cry of adrenaline mixed with panic as the beast pierced his chest with his front claws. Richard fell to the ground with the wolf on top of him, snapping its jaw at Richard's face. The foam spewed out of its mouth across Richard's body. Some of the foamy substance made its way into Richard's mouth, causing Richard to gag. Unable to find his weapon, Richard held the wolf's throat with both hands as he vomited on the ground. The severe feeling of disgust galvanized him and gave him extra strength. Richard screamed as he clenched the animal's throat and managed to wrestle it to the side.

The wolf, now furious with Richard, began barking madly. Richard tried to reach for a stone behind him with his right hand. He groped for the rock or any sharp object, but couldn't get a grip on something. Not strong enough to hold the beast off with a single arm, it opened its jaw and took a healthy bite out of Richard's rib cage.

"Ahhh!" Richard screamed in agony.

The other wolf now jumped into the tussle. The second one, the female, bit down hard on his thigh, piercing his skin and taking a chunk out of his pants.

"Son of a bitch," screamed Richard.

Taking advantage of Richard's vulnerability, the alpha went for his jugular. Luckily, Richard saw the beast pounce at him at the last second and ducked his head down just in time before the beast could deliver the deadly blow. The wolf's head slammed into Richard's eye. Dazed, the animal found it hard to see from the blow to its head. Richard, also fuzzy from the collision to his eye, kicked the female off of his leg by delivering his boot to its snout. The female let out a bark of pain and backed off. Richard then reached and picked up a large stone to his right and drove it forcefully into the alpha's jaw next to him. The alpha drew back from the forceful impact of the stone. Richard got up and lunged at the wolf. Richard jumped onto it like a mad man and got his arms around its neck. The wolf squirmed and shook its body to get free. Richard's grip on the wolf grew weaker as it bit at the air in an effort to penetrate flesh. Fortunately for the wolf, Richard's left arm was dangerously close to its mouth. The wolf took a colossal bite at his left forearm arm and bit down. Sinking its razor teeth into his forearm, Richard let out a screech of pain. Releasing his grip from the wolf's throat, the animal tugged at the sleeve of his jacket and ripped it off.

With his left arm completely exposed, Richard noticed a trail of blood running down his forearm to his wrist. Richard, not feeling any pain from the sudden shock of blood loss or fatigue from wrestling two savage wolves, looked down at the murderous animal with killer instinct. The alpha looked at Richard the same way. Both wounded, the fight to the death that would ensue could go either way. The female, still recovering from the brutal blow to her snout, looked on. Richard grew impatient and did not think about anything. Not his loved ones, his past, or his future. He thought only about surviving. Richard telegraphed his aggressive dart toward the wolf that easily jumped on top of him, knocking him to the ground. Its claws dug into his chest, causing severe scrapes across his torso. The wolf slipped and fell on top of him, trying to get a grip on top of his chest. Richard put his hands up in front of his face to block it. The wolf took a bite into his left hand causing Richard to yell in agony.

"ShhhhhhUHHHHH!"

The wolf clenched down harder on his hand. A wave of fury overcame Richard, causing him to clench is right fist and deliver a harsh blow to the beast's eye socket. The wolf barked in pain as Richard freed his left hand from its mouth. Richard delivered another hard punch to the wolf's jaw. All of the sudden, Richard had the advantage. Feeling nothing but pure rage and vehemence, Richard kept delivering wicked blows to the animal's face with his right hand. Feeling the bones in its face crack, Richard kept drilling the wolf with his fist. The animal's gums started gushing blood, and a few of its teeth got knocked out. His knuckles bled significantly, and his hand began to swell up. Richard flung the wolf off him. Richard lifted himself up as the wolf lay, half dead, on the ground, groaning in pain. The female ran for its life in the other direction. Covered in the alpha's blood and his own, Richard picked up the stone off of the ground and walked slowly toward the wounded wolf.

The Town of Jasper

As he walked up to the animal, he stepped on something under a patch of leaves. It was his pistol. He placed the heavy stone in his left hand and picked up the gun with his right.

Choking on its own blood, Richard stood over the wolf with anger, ready to deliver the final blow. The monster looked up at him with its right eye, awaiting its death. He gripped the stone tightly as he looked into its eyes.

"Don't. You don't have to."

"Yes. You do."

"You've already won, Richard. Put it down."

"If you let it live, it will try and kill you again."

"Let it go, Richard. Killing it won't do anything."

"Why are you still thinking about it? Kill it!"

"Richard. It is an animal of God. Let it learn from its mistakes."

"This thing just tried to take your life. Repay it by taking his."

"Redeem this animal. Make it become something different."

"Redeem yourself. Set a precedent to the evil in this world."

"You know it's not the right action."

"You know it's the only action."

"This is murder!"

"This is life and death!"

"Don't give in!"

"DO IT, GOD DAMNIT!"

"Richard. You have to trust me."

"YOU'VE COME THIS FAR. FINISH IT!"

"You are a righteous man! Don't let your emotions blind you!"

"You are a man of authority! Kill this descendant of Satan!"

Richard looked down at the fallen animal. He listened to its agony and its pain. Deep in his soul, he began to feel remorse. His grip on the rock weakened.

"There's so much good in you, Richard."

"It makes you weak, boy. The fire in you gives you strength."

Richard began to question his actions. His shock and adrenaline simmered down as he gaped down at the blood on his clothing and flesh.

"What have I done?" Richard asked himself.

He began hyperventilating and felt a panic attack coming on. Richard dropped the stone on the ground and holstered his gun. His shaking hands were stained with blood. The sight of them almost caused him to faint. He fell to his knees and edged his way to the fallen animal.

"What have I done? I'm so sorry. Jesus Christ, I am."

Richard felt a rush of tears flow down his bloody cheeks as the voices in his head emerged.

"There's more good than evil in this boy."

His dark thoughts of evil vanished in the cold, lonely night.

"Remember, Richard, that the power of good has more might than evil. You are a disciple of God. Not Satan."

Richard put his head down against the wolf's belly and let out a deep weep.

"Say it with me, my son."

Richard stopped his bellowing and began to whisper to himself.

"Gracious Heavenly Father, in Jesus Christ's name, I approach Your throne of grace and ask for your help in my time of need. *Before your eyes I have sinned. This fallen animal that you have rightfully created bares wounds and injury from the doing of*

The Town of Jasper

my evil fists. Protect me and deliver me, Lord, from every evil spirit and evil influence afflicting my life. I humbly ask and seek your presence, and pray for the wisdom and power of your Holy Spirit, and the presence of your holy angels to help in this matter. Illuminate my mind with the truth of my situation, and teach me to war against this evil intrusion, Lord, and lead me into the victory of your precious Son, Christ Jesus, Whose blood was shed for me, over two thousand years ago, to deliver and set me free from the power of sin, Satan, and his kingdom of darkness."

In the single act of prayer, Richard felt at ease. He felt all of his guilt and sin exit his body. He looked back down at the fallen animal and at the stone of death in front of him. Richard closed his eyes and exhaled deeply. Thoughts ran through his wild mind intensely as he took another deep breath to try to calm himself down. He looked at his torn clothes and mangled body spattered with stains of blood and torn flesh. He felt the blood painted across his belly. With his right side badly bruised and left rib cage with a healthy flesh wound, Richard felt as light as the air itself. In the center of his mind, the loud sound of a finger snapping echoed in his head like a drum beating in the middle of the Grand Canyon. The snapping sound resonated deep into the back of his mind, down into his spirit. Richard got himself up off the ground, in pain and badly mangled. The COM attached to his belt signaled in.

"No luck over here, they must have fled down Quarry. I put the patrol down there on alert. Anything on your end?"

Menacingly and without hesitation, Richard drew his pistol from his holster and fired off a round into the wolf's skull.

As Richard made his way out of the woods, something caught his attention. On the yard, across the street from where he walked, stood an object. Standing about the same height as him, the object seemed to be looking right back at him. Richard stopped walking to look at it when it fixed its gaze on him. The object, standing freakishly still, mesmerized Richard into a hypnotic state. He felt his feet move toward the object without looking both ways to cross the street. Looking at it curiously at all angles, he took his hands out of his pockets and crossed his arms. The object, which was situated on the edge of the yard in front of the sidewalk, was nothing more than a yard decoration of a monster. Standing just a few inches taller than Richard, the figure was an evil-looking creature. Its fangs and claws were in attack formation, and its blood-red eyes could raise your arm hairs by glancing into them. Blood dripping down its mouth and blood stains across its clothing, the creature resembled pure evil. Richard stood as still as stone, looking right into its eyes. The object that has spooked children around the neighborhoods for weeks had completely taken over Richard's imagination.

Deep in Richard's mind, he wanted the monster to be real. He wanted it to run after and stop the bands of hooligans wandering the streets of town causing trouble. He wanted the monster to come to life. Just for the night. Just for a moment. He wanted the monster to grab him and rid him of his guilt and pain. Looking at it became therapeutic for him. Anyone else would be appalled and repulsed at the site of it, but Richard embraced its brutality, horror, and malevolence. Richard took a step back but continued his stare. His expression became more and more strict until he almost looked angry at the figure. He breathed heavily and gaped at it with fire in his eyes. He began cracking his knuckled individually as a volcano brewed inside him. His left eye began to twitch as he clenched his teeth. Never taking his eyes off of the monster before him, Richard's entire body began to tremble. Both Richard and the figure stood in front of one another, looking deeply into each other's souls.

Before anything else transpired, a car drove up behind him in a hurry. Sutherland got out of the car to check on his friend.

"Jesus Christ, where the hell have you been?" asked Sutherland.

Richard turned his bloody and beaten body around. Sutherland looked at him in awe, wondering what in the hell happened to him.

"What the hell happened to you? Are you hurt?" asked Sutherland nervously.

"No," stated Richard grimly. "I'm driving."

The two got into the vehicle and closed the doors. Sutherland looked at Richard from the passenger seat, concerned for his health and mental state. Richard leaned back as the car idled and exhaled. He closed his eyes as he tried to relax and find his inner peace.

"I lied," said Richard.

"About what?" Sutherland asked.

"I have watched a sitcom with the sound off."

Men Of Science

Five Years After "The Incident"
Present Day, 2016

And it came to pass, that the beggar died, and was carried by the angels into Abraham's bosom. And the rich man also died: and he was buried in hell" Luke 16:22

A couple of days after his somewhat productive fieldwork and interviewing, Detective Sutherland reported back to headquarters to discuss his findings. He poured himself some hot coffee outside the Captain's office and knew it would not be a pleasant meeting of the minds. He placed the mug on his wooden desk and opened up the top drawer. He reached for the small airplane bottle of whiskey and poured some into his coffee before he made his way in.

"Please tell me you have something more than a fucking name."

Police Captain Rory Larson sat down, examining Detective Sutherland's data, recordings, and findings. The captain slammed the file down angrily. The captain was a particularly angry fellow, who often lost his temper. He was a tall man with a receding hairline. His hairy arms were spread across the wooden table in front of Sutherland, who never got intimidated by his superior's renowned, grizzly demeanor.

"What in fuck's name are we going to do with that?"

"It's more than a name. It's a lead."

"A lead? Really? And this cop told you to go forth with this?"

The Town of Jasper

"The officer informed me it would be a good idea. A step in the right direction."

"We don't need a 'step' in the right direction. We need a kick in the God damn door!"

"I truly believe that Ms. Ringwell will…"

The Captain got up angrily. He had run out of patience with the detective and the case as a whole. In fact, the detective had been getting under his skin since he started the investigation.

"Oh, cut the fluff shit out!"

Captain Larson was a 'no bullshit' kind of guy. Not in particularly good shape, the Irish Boston native was as straight as an arrow and not a man to trifle with. The Captain walked around the room with his arms folded. Sleeves rolled up, the fifty-eight year old Captain's voice was raspy and haggard.

"This cop. Officer Ford. What makes you think he's not leading you into a maze? The guy hasn't been sober in three years."

"We paid him."

"Yeah, and you paid the last dozen also! We are running out of time *and* money. You've been on this case for far too long and haven't gotten anywhere! And don't think I don't know about you fuckin' around with the booze and other bullshit! You better clean up your act. And do so quickly."

The detective scratched his eyebrow and clenched his jaw. He became frustrated at what the Captain was throwing at him. But he was right. He was becoming unstable and heavily reliant on booze and pills as a way of ridding the frustration of the continuous stalemate of an investigation along with his personal matters.

"Now, this 'lead' of yours. If she's alive," said the captain. "She could just be some broad he screwed and sent to the curb. You really want to take a chance on this?"

"Absolutely," said Sutherland.

Captain Larson sighed.

"You're on thin ice on this one. I told you this case was fucked from the start."

"People are afraid. He's using *fear* to control them."

"How do you know? What makes you think they're not working with him? Feeding you bullshit?"

"Look, I just need more time," shouted Sutherland.

The captain looked down at the detective angrily and shook his head. He then leaned back in his chair and looked up at the ceiling. A tidal wave of stress crashed into him as he closed his eyes.

"What you're doing beyond that wall detective. Whatever it is you're asking…your approach…It's not working," said Captain Larson, who now opened his eyes and looked directly at Sutherland. "D.C. has hired you to get the job done last week. You've been on this for what feels like forever, and every time I pick up the phone, I plead to the director of the FBI to provide you more time. Richard Morrissey has been deemed a terrorist to the town and country based on rumors and possible hearsay, so you need to get your ass in there and give us something that will give us an opportunity to take the son of a bitch out and get things back to normal. Typically, they'd send in a team and get it done overnight, but they don't want to move multiple people beyond the wall because they don't know what he is capable of doing. For all we know, he has knowledge on how this all happened and perhaps knowledge on how to spread it."

The statement sat in the room like bad joke. The detective grew tired of being berated by his superior so he pushed his seat backwards. The friction of the floor and the seat legs caused a screeching sound that gave the Captain goosebumps.

"We finished?" asked Sutherland.

The Town of Jasper

"There's something else," said Captain Larson.

The detective didn't bother to ask what. He had no interest in talking about the matter anymore. He was exhausted and needed a decent night's rest.

"The President is in the process of discussing a potential 'cleansing process' of the town. Nothing has been approved yet, but they're talking."

The detective's expression became disgusted and horrified. He felt himself wake up from exhaustion as chills rushed down his spine.

"Wait. Captain, there are children in there! The people aren't *dead*!"

"Doesn't matter. The White House doesn't like to gamble with national safety. Whatever this thing is. This 'disease'. They're afraid it'll go airborne, and with one of the most highly populated cities in the country less than thirty miles out, they don't want to take any chances."

"It's been five years. If it was airborne, it would have affected other parts of the area already. What about the CDC? Have they found anything yet?"

"Ask them yourself. Your meeting with them is in five minutes," said Captain Larson. "And hey…"

Sutherland looked at the Captain.

"Take some time off. Clear your head."

The detective disregarded the suggestion and walked out of the room.

In the conference room down the hall, the detective checked his watch. He sat in the leather chair and felt anxiety rush through him. Feeling like an anchor at the bottom of the ocean, Sutherland began to think about everything. In his head, he heard the screams of hundreds of people. He fixed his gaze in front of him, looking at nothing in particular. He watched the paint dry on the wall as he felt the weight of an entire town of innocent people sit on his shoulders. Blocking out everything around him, all he could hear was the noise coming from the central air, which sounded like waves rippling on the shoreline. His eardrums rang in his head, as he no longer heard anything else. In fact, he could no longer see anything. His eyes were wide open but his mind elsewhere.

    He reached into his pocket and squeezed the orange vial. He remained perfectly still, but his mind and thoughts were ricocheting throughout his body. He slowly began to lift the bottle of pills from his pocket when the knock on the door broke his thoughts as well as his dangerous urge to take the edge off. The detective's joints jolted to life and his eyes jerked up. Like waking up from a nightmare, the detective's facial expression was that of a petrified boy. He cleared his throat and looked over at the door.

    "Come in," he said in a low tone. Realizing nobody could have heard him say it, he gathered himself. "Come in!"

    The door creaked open. A man in a long white lab coat walked in the room. Standing about six-foot, the middle-aged representative of the CDC wore glasses that looked like magnifying glasses.

    "Detective Sutherland?"

    Still a little dazed, the detective remained seated and titled his head upward to look at the man.

    "Yes. Yes. Nice to meet you."

    The two men shook hands.

    "Please sit down."

    The CDC representative took a seat across from the detective. The representative seemed on edge. Anxious, even. The

The Town of Jasper

detective gathered his notes together and took out his pen. He looked up at the representative and clicked his pen.

"Please state your name and occupation for the record."

Finding it hard to produce words, the representative leaned forward and pushed his glasses up the brim of his nose. He was an atypical science type, with the thick glasses and high-pitched voice.

"Kenneth. Dr. Kenneth Armstrong…Head of the Health Science of Informatics at the Center for Disease Control."

The detective jotted the information down sluggishly.

"In your own words. What is happening to the people of Jasper?"

Very uncomfortable, Dr. Armstrong fidgeted his hands and began to feel hot flashes pulse down his face to his spine.

"Well. It's really hard to say. The specifics of it are very complex, and even the most finite of data, which is tough to attain, could *possibly*…

Reading his bullshit as easily as a children's book, the detective was no longer in the 'playing games' business.

"Dr. Armstrong," he practically screamed.

Dr. Armstrong exhaled noisily. He calmed himself down.

"At this time, we don't know."

The detective nearly dropped his pen at the hopelessness behind the man's words. How could they not know?

"This 'thing' or whatever you want to call it…we haven't pinpointed how it happened. There's nothing."

"Nothing?"

Dr. Armstrong adjusted his glasses and shook his head.

"It's unlike anything we've ever seen. Other things we've controlled and kept from the public, like Ebola, Small Pox, Malaria," said Dr. Armstrong. "Those we could prevent and fight.

We had something to work with. And it's not just people, Detective. It happened to the animals and crops too. This…It's almost unimaginable. Divine, even."

"*Divine*…?"

The tension grew like a fungus in the room as Dr. Armstrong became more and more apprehensive.

"Are you trying to tell me, along with the people of the town, *and* the White House, that this is untreatable because it's *unscientific*?"

"I'm telling you we've been doing everything we can since the day of the incident, and we've found *nothing.*"

"How can that be? I mean. What about the people you've been working on?"

Concerned and deeply upset, Dr. Armstrong could empathize with the detective's frustration and apprehension.

"They've been in an elongated hibernated state. Each of the subjects who are 'unconscious' is undergoing an anomaly in their sleep patterns. For example, REM, rapid eye movement sleep, has four to five cycles in a single night's rest. While in REM sleep, most of the muscles become paralyzed, and the activity of the brain's neurons becomes quite intense. Similar to the activity during wakefulness. However, these subjects are undergoing only *one* cycle. A very long, paradoxical cycle of slumber where the subject's brains are triggering dreams.

"So. They are having dreams?"

"Yes. Quite a few actually," claimed the doctor. "In fact, most of them may only be dreaming. Completely oblivious that they have been living a fantasy for the last five years."

"Jesus."

"Incredible, if you think about it. Having a five-year long dream."

"Or nightmare," said the detective.

The doctor's fascinated expression turned dismal as he looked down at the table.

"Right. Or that."

"What about their health?"

"The test subjects we've been getting reports on have shown no irregularities in regard to their vitals. Their tissue growth and repair is occurring naturally. Blood pressure is at reasonable levels. Blood supply to muscles and energy restoration are all normal. As odd as it sounds, they don't need to consume the necessary nutrients and balanced diet for their vitals to remain stable. It's as if they're immortal."

"Immortal…" said Sutherland, half convinced. "So what you're saying is these people can be in this state forever. Unless they wake up?"

"Perhaps," said Dr Armstrong.

"What about the other people. The ones who are up and walking?"

"We supplied medicine to them for a period of time. But I'm afraid we have been ordered to stop supplying resources to the town."

"You're cutting them off?"

"If it were up to me, Detective, I would…"

Detective Sutherland interjected and deprived Dr. Armstrong of finishing his statement.

"Where did you take the medicine you give them?"

"Well. We didn't take it anywhere. We are restricted from going beyond the wall. We drop it inside the wall, and the townspeople take it."

Dr. Armstrong smiled anxiously at Detective Sutherland, who simply returned a dark and grim gaze back at him. The doctor felt his gaze like a punch in the mouth.

"I don't believe you," said the detective.

"Excuse me?"

"I said I don't believe you."

Dr. Armstrong was confused and oblivious to the comment. Sutherland pushed his chair back and leaned forward.

"There has to be a way to cure it. There has to be a way to wake those people up."

"There's not, detective. Not at this time."

"Well, when?"

The detective, who had become exhausted with bad news and redundant data, became frustrated with Dr. Armstrong and his conclusions.

"When will you and your people have *something* to fix this?"

"Me and the other *doctors* have been working around the clock to do something about it. With a hundred some odd victims, all with different brain activity, it's been difficult to identify a feasible solution. If there were something to be done, we would have done it by now. We're not *holding* anything back from anyone."

"These people haven't seen their loved ones up and walking in five years. Tell me doctor, from your 'divine' area of medical expertise, when will these people wake?"

Dr. Armstrong could understand the detective's frustration. He knew he wasn't angry with him. Sutherland was a good man who truly cared about the cases he worked on, along with the victims in it. He has recorded no sound data, no clues, and no breadcrumbs leading to anything.

The Town of Jasper

"Detective, you have to come to the realization that these people may never wake up. Your case to find answers could take years. And for what? You've been hired to find out what the problem is and conduct informational interviews. Well, you've done it. You weren't hired to cure this thing. Your job is done, Detective. You've done everything you can."

"Not everything."

Dr. Armstrong looked at the detective through his thick lenses, wondering about the 'not everything' he was referring to.

"There's a terrorist running the town. The people are afraid. I need answers," said Sutherland.

"What will that accomplish?"

The detective looked up, completely baffled at Dr. Armstrong's question.

"I don't know. But I need to save *lives*."

"If you kill him or arrest him or whatever you have planned, someone else will just take his place. The town isn't civilized anymore. The people we supply the medicine to have told us what's been going on beyond the wall. Each time we go back, they say it's getting worse."

Trying to come to grips with what the doctor was saying, the detective shook his head.

"Let it go. Whatever plans Washington has for the town…just let them do it."

"I can't," whispered the detective.

"What?"

"I CAN'T," he shouted.

Taken aback by his scream, Dr. Armstrong jolted back.

"I can't because I don't believe in any of your bull crap about how this is a fucking *spiritual accident* or whatever the hell you want to call it. I can't let Washington get beyond that wall because I'm a fucking *HUMAN BEING!*"

The detective panted quietly after his outburst. Dr. Armstrong did not flinch. He looked at the detective and nodded his head with understanding. He got up from his chair and tugged on the bottom of his shirt, straightening it. In his briefcase was a file ,which he reluctantly pried out. Dr. Armstrong adjusted his glasses by pushing them up the brim of his nose with his fingers and looked intently at the file, seemingly petrified of what was inside. As if opening it up would release a thousand demons. Dr. Armstrong did not look at the detective, but rather continued his distracted gaze at the file.

"Two-hundred-eighty-three."

The sound of Sutherland's voice woke Dr. Armstrong from his look of intent, and he fixed his eyes on Sutherland.

"Come again?" asked Dr. Armstrong.

"Two hundred eighty-three," Sutherland repeated. "That's how many victims. One hundred eighty-one men, fifty-six women, forty-four children."

The two men exchanged no verbal interaction. It was as if there was a moment of silence for the piece of data.

"You're a scientific man, I understand," said the Doctor Armstrong. "You don't believe in fantasy or *fictional* occurrences. But there's one thing that's been eating at me as a scientific man myself, Detective."

The two men now exchanged direct eye contact.

"These people. These two hundred eighty-three. Over the last five years, me and a handful of researchers crosschecked every possible medical record and file for each of the victims. Each of them has some degree of illness or condition, both severe and mild. Whether it is asthma or cancer. They all have something."

The Town of Jasper

"So what? Is that supposed to mean something?" asked Sutherland.

"Normally it wouldn't," stated Dr. Armstrong. "But we also crosschecked all the conscience victims' files in Jasper."

Dr. Armstrong shook his head delicately at Sutherland.

"Most of which do not have any true medical or physical irregularity," stated Dr. Armstrong firmly.

Sutherland didn't know if he wanted to believe the coincidence or find ways to consider it irrational.

"What are you saying?"

Not even knowing whether to believe it himself, Dr. Armstrong continued on with the hypothesis.

"Some of our sources on the inside have relayed information as best they can to us. They're saying the victims haven't shown any signs or symptoms of their conditions."

"How is that possible?" asked Sutherland.

"It isn't," stated Dr. Armstrong. "Left untreated, those with the more severe illnesses would have died years ago."

Sutherland did his best to comprehend all the intangible facts. The situation had gone from unexplainable to unimaginable. Sutherland had no response.

That's not the only thing," said Dr. Armstrong. "Five years have passed."

The doctor slid the file across the table, stopping perfectly in front of the detective. Curious of what was inside, the detective flung the file open and saw pictures.

"These are pictures of some of the victims during the first week of the incident. Behind them are pictures that were taken three years ago, and behind those are ones from a few days ago."

The pictures were of people's upper body and faces. All of whom were asleep in beds. The detective studied several of them.

"We noticed it after the second year. These files have been kept under wraps from the public for good reason," stated Dr. Armstrong.

The detective flipped through more pictures of the victims, quickly glancing at each one. He saw men, women, teenagers, senior citizens, etc. The detective then came across the picture of a baby girl. The detective froze. He picked up the pictures of the infant and held the photos in his hands. Horrified, the true pain and realism of the atrocity suddenly hit the detective like a locomotive train. His scar began to tingle. The detective looked at the second picture of the baby. The pictures were identical.

"There is something wrong, Detective."

Deeply confused, the detective looked at both of them. Pupils going back and forth, Detective Sutherland was at a loss of words.

"Detective. These people…they're not aging."

Heroes

Four Months Before "The Incident"
May 2011

Inside the interrogation room, Richard sat in front of a thirty-three year old Caucasian man, who folded his lanky arms as he looked around the room. The thuggish man had buzzed blonde hair, a poor complexion, and smelled of Ax body spray and marijuana. Richard looked at him with an austere expression.

"Where'd you get the drugs?"

The man mumbled and avoided eye contact with Richard. The black tattoo on his right forearm became visible as he brushed his hair back.

"Where'd you get them, Ryan?"

"I don't know," said the man feebly.

"Seven months ago, I found a bag of heroin on the ground. It fell out of Trevor Kinkade's pocket. He's sixteen. I gave him twenty-four in a municipal cell and community service. I'd like to offer a similar deal to you. Just tell me who sold you the drugs."

"I just told you, I don't know."

"You do understand the severity of the situation don't you, Ryan? This is a possession charge and intent to distribute."

"I don't sell the shit!" shouted Ryan.

"Then tell me who does."

"I want to talk to my lawyer," stated Ryan.

Richard leaned back, displeased and deeply frustrated. Behind him, the door opened and Sutherland marched in. He stood beside Richard and looked over the file. He clenched his teeth.

"So, Mr. Pectin, where do we stand with your declaration of guilt?"

The degenerate of a man ignored Sutherland with his arms crossed.

"Uncross your arms," said Sutherland.

"Eat shit," said Ryan.

Sutherland slammed the file on the table, making a snapping sound. He looked at the man with anger boiling inside of him.

"There's been fourteen possession charges in the last six months. Nine have been kids ages eighteen and lower. We know you're one of many distributors. We just want the supplier. This way, you can go back to your every day life with a slap on the wrist, and we can put the bad guys away. Everybody wins. Who's the supplier?"

Ryan started to chuckle, showing his disgusting yellow teeth. Sutherland looked at him in wonder.

"What in the holy shit can you possibly be laughing at?"

"I want to speak to my lawyer," said Ryan.

Sutherland reached for his sidearm and took it out of his holster. The sight of the gun caused Ryan to look up. Sutherland placed the pistol on the table. He walked up to the suspect and grabbed the back of his neck and head. He slammed the man's head down against the steel table. Ryan let out a shriek of pain and shock as Sutherland pressed his cheek against the table.

"Who is selling you this horse shit?"

"Fuck you!"

Sutherland grabbed Ryan's collar and hurled him to the ground. Ryan's chair fell on its side as Sutherland got on top of the kid.

"Who the fuck is the supplier?"

"Jack..." said Richard.

"Who the fuck is it?"

"I don't know!"

Sutherland raised his fist and before he could deliver a blow, Richard rushed up behind him and pulled him off the man.

"Let me go!" Sutherland shouted. "Let me the fuck go!"

A few days later, in the town of Woodland, Memorial Day was in full swing at the Morrissey's. The barbeque was fired up, and the beers were on ice. The kids played in the backyard, and a few friends and family gathered on the patio. Father Paul was among the attendees, chatting with a look of benevolence. Richard cooked on the deck for everyone as he always did. The meat and food sizzled on the grill as Diane came up behind Richard, carrying a large bowl of sliced watermelon and kissed him on the cheek.

"What are you doing with the mustard?" she asked.

"Putting it on my burger."

"Mustard? Really?" Diane asked.

"Yeah," said Richard.

Diane looked at him awkwardly.

"No?" asked Richard.

Diane shook her head and smiled at him.

"Where are the ribs?" she asked.

"They're inside. I got the Brewman kind."

Diane sighed with slight annoyance and disapproval.

"Why'd you get those? I thought you were going to get the other kind?"

"C'mon. Brewman is best bank for your buck."

"Best what?" asked Diane.

"Bank for your buck..." repeated Richard unsurely.

Diane looked at him awkwardly again, holding the large bowl of watermelon.

"No?" asked Richard.

Diane shook her head again and smiled cheerfully.

"Bang for your buck, Einstein," she replied.

"Really?"

"Really."

"That's why I married you. You're not like most girls. You know those kinds of things," said Richard.

"And you're not like most guys either," said Diane.

"Oh yeah? How's that?" asked Richard.

"You're the kind of guy who puts mustard on a hamburger," she said playfully.

Diane kissed Richard on the cheek again and took a quick glimpse of the grill.

"You're going to burn the burgers," she said playfully.

Richard glanced at her and smirked as Diane walked down the deck stairs, carrying the large bowl of watermelon in her hands. From the deck, Richard looked around his backyard at the people enjoying the day and each other's company. Father Paul got up from the table and reached for the big bowl Diane carried. Richard found himself caught in a daze, somewhere between joy and confusion, as he gazed upon the people he cherished most in his life. A pop from the barbeque made him look down quickly and flip one of the patties. The flipped burger was somewhat burnt, and it made Richard laugh. He gathered the food onto a plate and accidentally dropped a bun on the ground.

"Damn," Richard whispered as he bent down to pick up the piece of bread.

On the deck's wood floor, an army of black ants clustered around a piece of fallen watermelon. Richard looked at the dozens of ants briefly before he stood up. A knock on the door caused Richard to rush. He turned the grill off and sat things down. He wiped his hands on a towel and turned off the gas. The knocking continued as Richard rushed towards the door. Richard swung the door open and was greeted by Detective Sutherland. A bottle of whiskey hung by Sutherland's right hand.

"Hey," said Sutherland, seemingly out of breath.

"Where's the wife and kid?" asked Richard.

"They're not going to make it," said Sutherland uncomfortably.

Richard looked at Sutherland sharply for a quick moment, knowing something was wrong. He was looking forward to meeting Sutherland's family, but didn't feel the need to ask or question the statement any further. He welcomed his friend inside the house after a brief pause of awkwardness.

"Ok. Yeah, come on in. Everyone is out back," said Richard.

"Ok, then," said Sutherland. "I brought some of the good stuff."

"Perfect, I'll take that from you," said Richard, taking the bottle from Sutherland. "You're just in time. Food is pretty much ready."

Richard led Sutherland outside and down the stairs of the deck. The two walked toward the patio table, where Diane, Father Paul, and the Morrissey's neighbors, Owen and Joanne, greeted him. Sutherland greeted each of them with a welcoming and warming smile and gave a kiss to Diane.

"Please, sit," requested Diane courteously. "Richard and I are going to go grab the food."

"Thank you," said Sutherland.

"Let me give you a hand, dear," said Father Paul.

"Please. Relax, Father. Sit," said Diane.

Reluctantly, knowing full well Diane would order him away, Father Paul sat down on his chair. Sutherland looked around, trying to come up with something to start a conversation. He was never really too fond of being in social situations with people he didn't know well.

"Couldn't ask for a better day," said Sutherland with a cheap smile.

"Absolutely," said Father Paul with excitement.

"Were you at the parade today?" asked Joanne.

"No, actually. I was off duty today."

"You're a police officer?" asked Owen.

"Detective. I'm his partner," said Sutherland, referring to Richard.

"Oh, wow," said Joanne.

Owen and Joanne looked around in a good-humored fashion and looked at Sutherland.

"So. You must know, then," said Owen.

"Know what?" asked Sutherland.

"His name. Well, his real one," said Joanne.

Sutherland looked at the couple, confused.

"No, actually, I don't. He's never told me. I thought I was the only one."

Owen and Joanne sat back, somewhat disappointed. No one knew the true identity of Richard Morrissey. Not even his neighbors.

"Father Paul over here knows," said Joanne.

"Yeah, and he's an uncrackable vault," stated Owen.

"I'll never tell," said Father Paul with a smile.

The Town of Jasper

Richard and Diane arrived at the scene with food trays in their hands. Everyone cleared the table for them as they landed the large trays of barbecued food. Everybody looked at the spread of delicious food with desire and big appetites.

"Can I get anybody anything?" asked Diane.

"No, please sit. You've done enough," said Owen.

Diane sat down at the table as Father Paul positioned himself in his seat to say a group prayer.

"Excuse me, one minute," said Richard.

Richard ran up the deck's stairs and walked up to the piece of watermelon. More ants cluttered on and around it, fascinating Richard. In one giant stomp, Richard crashed his right foot down on the watermelon, crushing the ants and piece of fruit.

"If everyone is comfortable, I'd like to say a quick prayer."

No one at the table opposed or declined the offer. Richard rushed back and sat down at the table. Father Paul closed his eyes and began.

"Lord, we thank you for bestowing upon us health and happiness along with great people and success. Your meal before us makes us inordinately grateful for your creations, and may those creations serve the better men and the faithful women. We thank you, Christ our Lord, for providing us on this day of remembrance the feeling of love and admiration beyond the ones we call our own. And as a side note, thank you for creating Diane who, in addition to her beauty and elegance, has been granted the talent to prepare such appetizing meals as the one before us."

Richard cleared his throat sarcastically. Everyone at the table shared a chuckle.

"And, of course. Thank you for creating the not-so-good-looking man she calls a husband, whom in addition to his clumsiness and ignorance claims to assist his wife in preparing the previously stated delicious meal."

The table shared another laugh, including Richard who always enjoyed Father Paul's humor and wit. Father Paul continued.

"Also, on this day of remembrance and praise of heroes, may we remember and praise a man whom we miss so dearly. On September ninth last year, a building went up in flames. As the people inside became trapped and helpless, Ken Morrissey ran inside to their rescue. We do not know the reasons for his heroic actions, but from knowing him well, we know that's just who he was. Ken Morrissey ran inside the inferno before the fire department could arrive with nothing more to protect him than his courage and valor. At the end of the day, even those powerful traits of his could not protect the man I call a savior. In his acts of the purest form of heroism, Ken Morrissey saved nine lives. We know the Lord Christ our savior works in mysterious ways, and we show anger towards him for allowing Ken's destiny to be short lived. But I beg you to not look at it that way moving forward. Look at it from the other side of the fence. Look at it as Ken's purpose and due diligence for the Almighty. Ken's purpose for God was to save those nine people. And those nine people will create and live pros…

"Amen," interject Richard.

Father Paul looked at Richard, concerned. He understood his discomfort, but felt it was necessary to commemorate his father. The table went quiet. No one knew how to appropriately break the tension. Finally, Richard spoke out.

"Shall we eat?" he asked in a joyful tone.

Everyone began reaching and passing food, napkins, and utensils. Richard and Diane made sure everyone had enough food before they helped themselves.

"Let me ask you all a question," said Richard. "Is it bank or BANG for your buck? You know that old saying…"

"Here we go," uttered Diane.

Everyone looked at Richard and at each other for confirmation. In unison, they all shouted.

"*BANG.*"

Diane laughed as Richard put his head down.

"It is?" he asked.

"It is," said Owen as he giggled.

"So I hear you guys are thinking about moving?" asked Joanne.

Richard and Diane looked at one another hoping one of them would answer the question for each other. Richard wiped his mouth with a napkin.

"We're considering it," he said.

"We've just been talking," said Diane.

"Anywhere in particular?" asked Father Paul.

"We have a few towns in mind," said Diane. "We looked at a few pretty houses."

"I suggested we move into a townhouse community. There are some very nice ones at reasonable prices in the area. They're how you folks say, 'BANG for your buck'."

Everyone lifted a glass to Richard's comment and shared a laugh. Diane looked at Richard with a grin and interjected.

"*But* I told him. I don't want to move into a condo. I want to live in a house with a personality. Somewhere unique. I don't want to be just another number," said Diane.

Everyone at the table nodded in approval and agreement.

"Well, whatever you both decide, I'm sure it will be the best choice for you and the children," said Father Paul.

"Speaking of which, where are the kids?" Diane asked.

"I saw them playing behind the tree before," said Richard.

Diane called for Joseph and Victoria. Both of them came running from behind the tree onto the patio to greet the table. Victoria ran up to Diane out of breath and Joseph trailed her.

"Hey, sweetheart. Did you say hello to everyone?"

Victoria looked at everyone, short of breath, and waved. Everyone smiled and waved back.

"Did you take your medication?" Diane asked.

Victoria shook her head and grabbed onto the inhaler around her neck. She pressed onto the device and sucked in the medicine from the inhaler.

"Victoria, look who came to visit you," said Richard, pointing to Sutherland.

Victoria looked at Sutherland timidly. Sutherland looked at her and smiled comfortingly.

"Go give him a hug," said Richard.

Victoria walked up to Sutherland and wrapped her tiny arms around his neck. Sutherland hugged the little girl and felt a deep level of affection.

"How you doin', kiddo?" asked Sutherland.

"Good," said Victoria.

"You listening to mom and dad?"

Victoria nodded her head, which made Sutherland smile. It also reminded him of his little girl, Shannon, and who she used to be. He saw her in Victoria, and it made his heart shatter. He smiled at the gorgeous little girl through the pain and cleared his throat.

"Okay, kid," he said softly. "Be good now, and have some fun."

Victoria ran off. Richard looked at Sutherland, whose discomfort was clear, with concern,. Joseph stood beside Diane with his head down.

"Joseph, say hello. Father Paul wants to see your eyes."

"Hey, Joey," said Father Paul cheerfully.

Joseph did not lift his head. He became socially inept around large crowds. Awaiting any form of greeting, Father Paul smiled at the boy from across the table.

"Joseph," said Richard. "Eyes."

Joseph looked up at the table of friendly people. He looked at Father Paul with a blank expression.

"Hello, Father," he said grimly.

"Good to see you, son. You're getting big like your dad," said Father Paul.

"Thank you," said Joseph.

"Okay, honey, go and find your sister. Tell me when you're hungry, okay?"

"I will," Joseph told his mother before he rushed off.

"Beautiful children," said Owen.

"Yes," said Joanne. "I wish our Jessica was that age again."

Diane smiled at the compliments, but everyone saw her struggle underneath it. Diane loved her children more than life itself and wished their mental and physical health would turn around.

"It'll all work out, my dear," said Father Paul reassuringly.

Diane smiled at the comforting words of their long time friend, Father Paul. Suddenly, the attention shifted to Sutherland without him knowing. Sutherland could not stop thinking about the bottle of whiskey in the kitchen. He lost his focus as he daydreamed about it.

"I'm sorry, Detective. I never got your name," said Owen.

Sutherland did not hear the man ask the question. He just saw the man's mouth move from his peripheral vision as he looked at the sliding screen door separating him from his reliever of pain.

"Detective..." said Owen politely.

Sutherland looked back at the able and realized everyone shifted their gaze upon him. He looked around in a state of confusion.

"I'm sorry?" he asked.

"Your name," said Owen. "I don't think I ever asked."

"Oh. It's Jack," said Sutherland. "That's my fault for not properly introducing myself."

"No worries," said Owen. "Do you - uh. Do you have children?"

"Um. Yes," said Sutherland as he cleared his throat and sat up uncomfortably. "A daughter."

"Oh wow. How old?" asked Joanne, interested.

"She's uh. She's seven," said Sutherland.

"Aren't they the best at that age?" Joanne inquired.

Sutherland became very uncomfortable. Richard eyed him from across the table, knowing he was uneasy. Sutherland put on a cheerful smile.

"She's an angel," he said lightly.

"It won't last," said Owen. "Teenage years will make you pull your hair out."

The table shared a slight giggle as Sutherland nodded his head with a mild grin. He swallowed hard and looked back at the screen door. Richard interrupted the conversation to take some of the tension off of Sutherland.

The Town of Jasper

"Let me clear some of those plates for you guys," he suggested.

"No, please," said Father Paul. "Allow us to do it. You must."

"No, no, no," said Diane.

The group bickered back and forth about the chores until everyone wound up taking things into the house. Finally, all the plates and food were neatly put away, and the day turned into the early evening. The group indulged in a variety of desserts, from red velvet cake to sprinkled cupcakes. Victoria was asleep on the couch while Joseph watched television.

"Coffee anyone?" asked Diane.

"Hold on, honey," said Richard as he held something behind his back. "How about a little surprise first?"

Richard revealed an assortment of small fireworks from behind his back. Everyone laughed and clapped, insinuating a nonverbal agreement.

"What do you guys say?" Richard asked.

"Let's do it," said Owen

"I'm going to go put Victoria to bed, first," said Diane.

"Leave her," said Richard.

"I'm going to use the bathroom for a minute," said Sutherland. "Don't wait up."

In the bathroom, Sutherland splashed cold water onto his face and looked at himself in the mirror. He felt a deep anxiety and restlessness. He pondered over the decision and kept questioning his inner strength.

"Don't do it," he whispered to himself. "Don't."

He felt his hands shake, so he clutched onto the counter firmly. His breathing became heavier and intensified. Once more, he looked into the mirror and remembered a time where he enjoyed holidays like this. He remembered having fun with his daughter and loving his wife. A different time. But not so long ago. He stormed out of the bathroom and rushed to the kitchen. He looked around to make sure no one saw him and snagged the bottle of Jim Beam off the counter. He rushed back into the bathroom, where he guzzled a quarter of the bottle. Caught up in the obsession of emptying the bottle, Sutherland forgot to close the bathroom door. Once he was finally done slugging, he slammed the bottle on the counter and reached for the vial inside his pocket. His hands shook madly as he uncapped the top. The tiny white pills spilled into his hands, and he tried placing three into his mouth. Two landed on his tongue while the third hit the floor.

"Dammit," he said as he looked around for it.

As he searched the bathroom floor for the pill, Victoria stood from the hallway with a stuffed monkey in her arms. Sutherland looked up at her with distraught eyes from the inside of the bathroom.

"Hey, sweetheart," he said softly. "Everything okay?"

"I can't sleep, Uncle Jack," she said tenderly. "Can you tuck me in?"

Sutherland looked at the little girl on his knees and saw the innocence and virtue of the child. His heart sank as he found it hard to produce the words.

"Of. Yeah. Of course," he said. "I'll be there in one minute."

Victoria rushed back into her room as Sutherland looked down at the floor in shame and disgust with himself. His focus altered, and he felt sober. He swallowed hard and felt like a disgrace. At the corner of his eye, he saw the little white pill. He plucked it off the ground with two fingers and flushed it down the toilet.

Inside her room, Victoria laid on her bed with the blanket half on. Sutherland walked inside the room quietly and gradually. He knelt beside her bed and reached for her blanket. He placed it neatly over Victoria, who never stopped looking up at him. Booze on his breath and narcotics in his system, the devil on the inside did not win the battle with Sutherland as he smiled at Victoria.

"Uncle Jack," she whispered.

"Yes?"

"How did my grandpa die?"

Taken aback by the question, Sutherland had no idea how to properly word the answer. He fought the booze and drugs in his system to stay as focused as possible. He looked down at Victoria.

"He died because he was very brave. He saved a lot of people, but he got really sick while he was saving them," said Sutherland. "He was a hero."

"Was there a fire?" asked Victoria.

Sutherland nodded his head.

"Is that how my daddy's going to die?"

Sutherland looked at the innocent girl and felt sorrow. Her obliviousness was heartbreaking yet adorable. He held her arm and squeezed gently.

"No, darling. Your daddy is going to live for a long time."

"And you too?" she asked softly.

Sutherland smiled and felt tears accumulate in his eyes. His grip around the girl's arm got slightly tighter.

"And me too," he said. "Now go to bed."

Sutherland bent over and kissed Victoria on the forehead. He lifted himself up and began to walk over to the door.

"Good night, Uncle Jack," said Victoria sweetly. "I love you."

Sutherland stopped walking and closed his eyes tightly. He now wished the booze and narcotics would hit him like a freight train. He swallowed hard again and looked over in Victoria's direction.

"I love you too, Shannon," he whispered weakly.

The Town of Jasper

To The Place Where No One Goes

Five Years After "The Incident"
Present Day 2016

Richard poured himself some hot tea. The steam arising from the liquid zigzagged off the brim of the tiny pink mug. Richard lifted the plastic cup up to his nose and whiffed it. The steamy aroma of the piping hot tea produced a sensational expression on Richard's face. Richard carefully placed the cup on top of the plastic cup coaster as he averted his attention across the small table.

"Mr. Rabbit. Would you like some more?"

In a private room, Richard set up a small plastic table along with four plastic chairs. One of the four plastic chairs was for himself, which his behind barely fit on, one for two stuffed animals, a rabbit and a monkey, and one chair for his four-year old daughter, Victoria, one of the many victims of the day that everyone remembered but wanted to forget. The seat where his daughter would sit was empty, and the lonesome seat made Richard want to split in two. He gazed at the stuffed animal rabbit beside him, looking for an answer. Richard went ahead and poured some tea into the cup in front of it.

"I'll take that as a *yes*."

Since she was two, Richard always played 'tea time' with Victoria every Sunday. He would sit at the same table with her in the living room, where they would talk about everything from magic castles, to unicorns, favorite candies, and magic genies and three wishes. They were the topics of conversation Richard looked forward to the most during the week.

"Mr. Monkey, it looks like you could use a 'wake me up'." Richard reached for a different pot and poured some coffee into the monkey's cup. "There's some coffee."

Richard tried to lift the mood by exhaling deeply and breathing out with a smile. He looked around the table and smiled at the stuffed animals. He did his best to not look up at the empty seat. In fact, it took everything. He knew what he was doing was extreme, but he was just trying get back what he once had. He took a sip from the cup and closed his eyes, trying not to reminisce of the tea parties before everything went to hell. However, the memories and recollections became an inevitable occurrence in his twisted mind.

Richard felt himself back in his old living room with his conscious daughter. He remembered the way she smiled with most of her top molars missing. He remembered seeing Diane every time he looked into her eyes. He remembered how he was going to give her the world. He remembered Sunday mornings that smelled of freshly made pancakes. He remembered how she would jump into his arms when he came down the stairs to start the day. He remembered how alive and excited she'd get and how'd she hold his hand and drag him to her own little Sunday breakfast. He remembered how she would have everything set up for her father at her plastic table. Everything was so neat and well placed, from the silverware to the handkerchiefs. He remembered how Victoria would hold hands with her table of stuffed animals and lead a prayer. He remembered everything. Every detail of the life that had been put on pause while he moved forward.   Richard swallowed and opened his eyes painfully. Trying to hold in tears for the last several minutes, they finally escaped out of his tear ducts and dropped beside the plastic cup in front of him. He looked up at the empty seat again. The vacant spot at the table horrified him and broke his heart into a shattered glass. Richard let out a choking weep but stopped it by chugging the rest of his tea. He placed the cup back down and began to aggressively smack himself in the face.

"Come on. Wake up! Wake up, Rich."

After he nearly beat the hell out of his face, he stopped. He looked up at the empty seat again and slammed his fist on the table, nearly causing it to collapse. Plastic cups clinked, and his cup fell onto the floor.

"God dammit!" He pounded his fists on the table again. "GOD. DAMMIT!"

Knowing his daughter would not like to see him like this, he reclaimed his serenity. He adjusted his shoulders and sat up straight. He calmly picked up the fallen cup and placed it back onto the plastic coaster.

"Sorry, honey. Forgive me."

The silence that transpired was haunting. Richard could hear his eardrums whistling. Trying to stay calm, he put both hands on the table. He looked at the back of each hand and stared at the gold wedding ring on his left ring finger. Never taking his eyes off of the ring, he whispered to himself.

"What do I do, honey? I don't think I can keep going like this. Please. Tell me."

The gold ring glimmered elegantly off the florescent light. His wife, Diane, always knew the right thing to say to him when he was in a time of struggle. She was great like that. Now, Richard had no one but himself to turn to. The acknowledged leader of Jasper found himself in a dark corner.

"What would you do?" He continued to whisper to himself as he looked at his wedding ring. "What would you do?"

Feeling the spirit of Diane ease his soul, he knew what she would do. She was the strongest woman in the world. He had to be strong too. He had to be. He got up off of the chair and walked into an adjacent room. A few moments later, he walked out with a cake lit with candles. He placed the cake in front of where his daughter normally sat. He knelt next to the seat and looked at the tiny, burning flames.

"Make a wish, darling."

The wax from the candles dripped onto the pink and white icing. There were nine candles on the cake, along with a big number nine in the center. Richard looked at the candles burn and ventured into a brief thought. After several seconds, he blew the candles out and returned back to his seat. He sat down on the tiny chair and reached his right hand toward the stuffed animal rabbit next to him. He grabbed the stuffed animal's hand and placed it up against the table. He then did the same with his left, lightly reaching across the table and clenching the hand of the stuffed monkey. He placed their hands on the table and looked up ahead and smiled like everything was normal. With all of his inner strength, Richard remained composed and held the hands of the stuffed animals. He looked at the blank space and showed his white teeth with a cheerful smile.

"Happy birthday, sweetheart."

There was an abrupt knock on the door. The sound of it woke Richard up in a panic. Having fallen asleep on the floor, he got himself up in a hurry. There was another knock on the door.

"Wuh...one minute," Richard shouted.

Richard looked at the table, concerned and worried that someone would see it. Richard hurried over to the door and cracked it enough so only his upper body and face showed. At the door stood the town's constable, Ron Carlisle. His bulky body stood up straight and true, offering an intimidating posture.

"They're ready," he said in a neutral tone.

Haggard, with a distraught look on his face, Richard mumbled and nodded his head.

"Okay," he whispered. "Give me a moment".

"Everything okay?"

"Yuh…yeah. Everything is fine. Just buy me a couple minutes, would you?" Richard asked as he rushed to put on his black long jacket.

"You got it," Ron said as he stroked his Mohawk haircut and walked away.

Richard closed the door and locked it. He exhaled and leaned his back up against the door.

Things ran like clockwork outside the town hall. It was just before noon, and the sun glared through the partly cloudy sky. The chilling November breeze didn't affect the countless citizens rushing in every direction and shouting orders to one another. Benjamin read a gospel from the Bible to a group of people who prayed for their safety. Everyone was anxious and unsure of the decision, but they executed their tasks as requested. It was a controlled mayhem as Richard spoke to a couple of men, one of which was former officer Gary Ford. Each of them listened intently as their nerves started to get the better of them. Richard was solid as a rock, without a doubt in his mind as he continued to prepare the two men for the plan.

"Now listen up," said Richard. "We don't want to create any initial tension with these people. We're going in armed. But keep the guns out of sight. If they see us with them, they will kill us."

The men nodded their heads nervously as they agreed with Richard's tactic. The looming plan coming to fruition began to take a toll on their nerves.

"How many are we going in with?" asked the other man named Dallas. Dallas was a forty-year-old gym teacher and varsity girl's soccer coach at Jasper High School. His nerves always got the best of him in situations like this.

"We have three trucks. Three men each vehicle," said Richard. "Two men will hang back and stand as lookout. I don't want to go in there with too many men. They'll get the wrong idea if we do. So this is the only way we get this done."

Richard regained the men's loyalty and confidence. They were ready to go through with the plan, no matter what the outcome may be.

"Okay, boss. Let's do it," said Officer Ford.

"Good," said Richard. "Now get something in your stomachs. We're wheels up in five."

Richard walked away from the two men and proceeded toward his old friend, who was working under the hood of one of the vehicles. His cut sleeve shirt showed his numerous tattoos and brawny, dirty arms. The vehicle was an old, beat up pickup truck, which had plenty of supplies. Ron saw him approaching and began wiping his hands with a cloth.

"You sure about this?" asked Ron.

"Sure as I can be," said Richard.

"If things go south over there, I need you in charge," Richard stated.

Ron looked at Richard sympathetically. Richard had put a significant amount of trust into Ron since the atrocity, making him his second in command and constable. Ron was honored by his comment.

"You'll be back," Ron said.

Richard patted his friend on the shoulder as a gesture of a long time friendship and trust. Richard admired his confidence and benevolence, even in the midst of a near suicide mission. The plan was a go and everything was set up. Richard broke away from Ron and stood up in the bed of the truck. He looked across at the scene and crowd of people in front of him.

Benjamin walked up to him slowly with a notebook in his hands. His expression looked busy and full of activity. Richard glanced down at his notebook as Benjamin crosschecked and jotted things down quickly.

"I inspected each cargo. Everything is remedied and systematized effectively. Shouldn't cause too much tension on the back tires. Weapons are loaded with safeties off. Hopefully, they stay that way. There's flares in each bed should any of you..."

"Thank you..." said Richard, cutting him off. "Good work."

Benjamin nodded his head and closed his notebook. He was worried about the situation and did not believe the Fillmore Whites would trade willingly. He was a sucker to the tales and legends of their hostility and did not think a confrontation was the most appropriate step, given their dire situation.

"Please reconsider," Benjamin asked pleadingly. "If what they say about them is true..."

Richard was not changing his mind about the plan. Too much time and effort had gone into it. There was too much momentum to turn back now. If successful, it would be a turning point for Jasper in the wake of the incident. The citizens of Jasper needed a win, and this was a chance at that. Richard whispered to Benjamin.

"We have no choice. Don't burn the house down while I'm gone," he requested jokingly.

"I will hold a sermon, and we will pray for you and the others. I'll keep everyone's minds at ease, you have my word."

"Thank you, Benjamin," said Richard.

A group of six men, who all stood in a pack, checking their ammo and smoking cigarettes, didn't bother to acknowledge Richard's command. Zoned in on the task, they all got into their respective vehicles and didn't say a word. The townspeople looked on as the man entered the trucks, most of the townspeople afraid of the plan going wrong. The people thought it could lead to something worse if negotiations fail. The citizens of Jasper resented the Fillmore Whites while things were civilized in their town, let alone during a crisis. Officer Ford and Dallas strolled toward the truck as Richard reached into his pocket. He jingled and jangled the keys to the pickup and threw them to Dallas. The keys made a sling-like sound as the man caught them. Richard jumped down from the truck and smiled at Dallas.

"Feel like driving?"

"Yeah, why not," Dallas said somewhat excitedly.

Richard opened the passenger door and motioned for Officer Ford to go in first.

"After you officer," said Richard.

"Beauty before age," joked Officer Ford.

Richard cracked a smirk and put his hand on Officer Ford's suede Jacket.

"In that case, allow me," Richard said with a smile.

Officer Ford chuckled and climbed into the truck. Once officer Ford sat, Richard climbed into the truck and slammed the door. With the window open, he looked to his left at the remaining townspeople. With trepidation and concern in their eyes, Richard

The Town of Jasper

knew this plan had to work. As Dallas twisted the keys in the ignition, the engine resonated a roaring sound. The townspeople all stood and watched as Richard stared back at them with as much benevolence as he could show. But deep down, he was just as concerned as they were.

"We ready to roll?" Dallas shouted.

Richard broke his gaze and looked at the men in the truck. He patted the side of the truck and whirled his right hand in the air, signaling to the other vehicles.

"Showtime," Richard said firmly.

The trucks drove away, heading in the direction of the place where no one went. While the nature of the plan was perilous and deadly, a plot far worse and heinous was developing right under everyone's nose. Both plans would be executed in short time.

Hole

Three Months Before "The Incident"
June 2011

It was a moderately paced morning, with the sun shafting through the windows. The glow through the glass made the second story of the suburban home shine like a beacon. Inside the living room, a small plastic table was set up with stuffed animals occupying each small, plastic seat. Inside the kitchen, adjacent to the living room, Diane Morrissey shuffled constantly from the stove, fridge, and to the toaster systematically as she prepared breakfast. The smell of cinnamon and bacon resonated throughout the house, fabricating a superlative Saturday morning. Richard walked downstairs in no hurry. As he bypassed Victoria in the living room setting up her tea party, he was pleasantly taken aback by the aroma coming from the kitchen.

"Who are you, and what have you done with my wife?" Richard asked sarcastically, cheerfully.

Diane chuckled and showed off her pearly white teeth. Richard wrapped his arms around her and kissed her. He held her in his burly arms for several seconds as he hummed a melody and twirled his hips around. Diane began to giggle as Richard looked over her shoulders at the stove.

"Hun," he said calmly.

Diane looked up into his eyes as he continued to hold her in his arms. Richard looked down at her and whispered.

"The kitchen's on fire," he said.

Smoke emitted from the frying pan as Diane flung herself free from Richard's arms in a panic and began to wave the smoke away with an oven mitt. Richard opened up the kitchen window and grabbed a small towel. The two of them waved off the smoke together, praying the smoke alarm wouldn't go off. As the two of them waved away, they broke out into laughter. After a minute or so, the two of them stopped from exhaustion and fatigue. Richard panted and leaned up against the counter. Diane smiled and cupped her hands over her head.

"I like my bacon crispy anyway," Richard said comically.

Diane burst out laughing as she threw her oven mitt at him. Richard tried dodging it as he laughed and threw his towel at her. Diane laughed more as Richard hugged her.

"You tried," he said as he kissed her forehead. "Now if you'll excuse me, I have an early tea time."

Richard kissed Diane again and walked into the living room where Victoria was waiting.

"Hello, my love," he said as he examined the table which was surrounded by stuffed animals in plastic seats. On the table, small plastic teacups were situated perfectly and elegantly.

"Hello, Daddy," said the four-year-old tenderly. "Sit down, its time. Mr. Monkey is getting thirsty."

"Oh, well, in that case…" Richard said as he sat down on the small plastic chair.

Victoria, so tiny at only three feet, began pouring tea into each cup. Her weak wrists shook as she poured the liquid in. Richard watched her intently and smiled with pride. She tip toed to the end of the table next to Richard and poured with her inhaler dangling from the piece of string around her neck. Like her mother, she had asthma.

"Did you huff and puff and blow the house down yet?" asked Richard, referring to her using the inhaler.

"Yes, I did. Me and Mommy did it together."

"Good girl," said Richard.

The plastic teapot trembled from her shaking wrist as she poured.

"I got it, sweetie," Richard said as he tried to grab the teapot.

"I gooot it," Victoria said as she flung the pot away from his grasp. Richard smiled.

"Okay, then," he said as he crossed his arms.

Victoria poured tea into his cup, filling it to the brim. Once she was finished, she retreated back to her seat. Richard lifted his glass to his lips as his daughter cried out.

"No, daddy! We have to say grace!"

Richard put the cup down immediately and smacked himself in the head.

"Of course," he shouted.

Victoria held the hands of the two stuffed animals adjacent to her and closed her eyes. Richard, confused, grabbed the stuffed animal's other hand and closed his eyes. A few moments passed as Richard opened his left eye to look at Victoria. Before Richard could begin a prayer to break the silence, Victoria had started without him.

"Thank you, God, for the tea on the table. Thank you for being such a good God and helping us out all the time. Also, I hope you have a really good day. Amen."

"Amen," said Richard.

Richard sipped from his cup and looked at his beloved daughter.

"MMMMMM, that's real tasty, sweetheart. Just the way I like it."

The Town of Jasper

She smiled, showing off her snow-white teeth. She had two teeth missing, making the gaps very visible. Richard and Victoria did this every Saturday morning. He loved it as much as she did. Diane walked into the living room.

"Babe," she said.

Richard turned around and looked at her.

"Would you mind running to the store? We need a few things for dinner tonight. Is he still coming later?" asked Diane.

"Uh yeah, I think so," he said as he got up.

Richard walked over to Victoria, who played with her stuffed monkey, and kissed her on the head. He walked over to Diane and took the list from her hand. As he examined it, she looked at him with a neutral expression.

"Is he coming tonight?" Diane asked.

"That's what he said," said Richard as he glanced at the list.

"What about…?"

"I don't know," Richard said weakly.

"Are they still fighting?"

Richard looked up at Diane and gave an unsure expression.

"I was really hoping to finally meet her. He never brings her around."

"I know you were," said Richard. "I'll talk to him."

"Go run out, and we'll talk about it when you get back," she said.

Diane kissed Richard on the forehead.

"Don't burn the house down while I'm gone," asked Richard teasingly.

Diane broke down in hysterical laughter as Richard walked out of the front door.

124

Richard walked up to the convenient store called 'The Corner Store' just before noon. The store was owned by a Greek man named Nick. Richard knew his last name but he just couldn't pronounce it correctly. As he walked up to the entrance, a man approached almost at the same time. Richard held the door for the man, who sported a backwards Yankee hat, a dungaree vest over a ragged Grateful Dead T-shirt, and blue jeans with white paint stains scattered across them. The man looked haggard and flushed, almost like he was ill. Richard walked in behind him as the bell on the door jingled. The owner, Nick, saw Richard and his face lit up.

"Hello, my friend!" shouted Nick.

"We're friends?" Richard asked comically.

Nick laughed out loud. Nick was an easy man to make laugh, who became more jovial when Richard visited his store.

"You know there are plenty other convenience stores," Nick said humorously.

Richard walked down the aisle towards refrigerators. Richard shouted out as he smiled.

"I know, but unfortunately yours is the only one within three miles of my house."

Richard took out his phone as he glanced at the selection of name brand beers, from Miller Lite to Amstel. He sent out a quick text and grabbed some beer and a bottle of white wine from the refrigerator. He looked at the bottle of wine and shouted out to Nick.

"Hey when are you going to start ordering the expensive stuff?"

Nick did not say anything. Next to Richard, there was a man in about his mid forties. The man opened the refrigerator door adjacent to Richard and looked at the different gallons of milk. He looked up at Richard and nodded with a smirk. Richard did the same and walked toward the register.

"Hey, Nick your boy still playing litt…"

At the front of the store, at the counter, the man in the cutoff dungaree vest and backwards Yankee hat held a Beretta M9 to Nick. The man had a Mohawk, sloppy beard that connected to his hair, and tattoos up and down his forearm. Nick had his hands held slightly above his head as he looked directly at the muzzle of the pistol. Pale-faced and petrified, Nick began to panic.

"Please," Nick whispered quietly.

"Don't," said the gunman assertively.

Richard remained still, with a six-pack of Budweiser in one hand and a bottle of wine in the other. After a few moments, Richard gently placed the items on the floor. He tiptoed to get an angle on the gunman. Nick glanced at Richard frighteningly. The gunman, with his weapon still pointed directly at Nick, looked at Richard. He pointed his index finger at him.

"Don't you try it, Superman," he shouted.

Richard halted and held his hands outward.

"It's okay," Richard said gently. "It's okay…"

The gunman shook his head.

"No, it isn't," said the gunman, firmly and assuredly.

Richard was at a crossroads in the conflict. He didn't have a true play to get out of the situation. Even given the circumstance, Richard did not feel afraid of dying. He wasn't convinced the man had it in him to kill.

"I can help you…just put…"

"You're gonna help me? How you gonna do that? How you gonna help me?" shouted the gunman with a crackling, nervous tone.

The gunman's heart raced. He wasn't thinking clearly. His emotions nearly made him faint. The gunman's gun remained raised at Nick, whose eyes were now closed with his hands in the air. The gunman wiped his face with his left hand and began to clear his throat. Richard observed and felt sorry for him. The man was clearly troubled. He wasn't doing this as a criminal. He was doing this for someone else. More time elapsed as everyone stood still, not making any sudden movements. The man with the milk walked down the center aisle and immediately halted when he saw the scene. He looked at Richard who looked back at him, half convinced that the situation would turn out fine. Nick opened his eyes and glanced down at his .38 pistol beneath the register. Richard knew he was looking at the gun because he was the one who signed the permit for him to have it in his store. Nick glanced up at Richard who shook his head, indicating he did not want Nick to make a move towards the gun.

"Give me the money," the gunman demanded quietly. "Just give me it."

Nick slowly shifted towards the register and clicked it open. He began shuffling through the bills.

"Slowly," demanded the man.

Nick began allocating the money slowly.

"Put it all on the counter," requested the gunman.

Nick placed all the bills on the counter neatly. The man walked up to the counter.

"Hands on the counter right now," he stated.

Nick did as he requested. He placed both hands on the counter and began to sweat heavily. The gunman started counting the money and shook his head and sighed with concern.

"This isn't…no. This isn't enough. It's not…" said the gunman, nearly on the verge of hysteria.

The Town of Jasper

"It's all I have," said Nick delicately.

The gunman did quick math as he shuffled through the bills sloppily with his one hand.

"It's not enough," he kept repeating under his breath.

Richard looked at the man and felt remorse. Even Nick, who was being held hostage, felt sorrow for the man.

"What are their names?" asked Richard.

The gunman shot a glance at Richard and said nothing. He kept looking at the pile of money that wasn't enough. The whole situation was heartbreaking to see.

"I have two of my own…Nick has two as well. I know it's not easy. But this isn't the way."

The gunman felt his arm weaken as the gun descended down from Nick. The gunman experienced hot flashes and dizziness as his finger pressed weakly against the trigger. Ashamed, the only reason why the man had the gun still raised was out of principal and pride. He stared at the cash laid across the counter.

"I need more. Where is the rest?" The gunman asked aggressively.

Nick just shook his head as he looked at the crumbling man. The gunman sighed and clenched his eyes. He banged his hand on the table.

"This isn't enough!" he shouted, causing Nick to jolt.

"It's all I have," Nick said, frightened.

The gunman nearly started to weep as he bent his knees slightly and constantly adjusted his hat. He always had the gun pointed in the direction of Nick, who was now more afraid of the man aimlessly pulling the trigger from his distraught state. The man let out a deep sigh and pressed his cap against his head. He looked at Richard.

"Alyssa and Zachary…They're twins," said the gunman.

Richard looked at the man with optimism, seeing an opening for an outcome where no one got killed. However, the situation presented a confusing circumstance with a still irresolute conclusion.

"How old?" asked Richard.

"They're turning ten next week," he said peacefully.

The gunman began to tremble and come out of his crazed state. He began to breathe heavily and blink rapidly.

"I, I, I was - uh laid off. Bills are coming in, I can't find work. My daughter has a condition and we don't have the insurance to keep covering it. I don't know what…I don't…"

The man shook his head pointing the gun away from Nick.

"I'm behind three months on the rent; we're going to get evicted soon. My wife doesn't know…God dammit," said the gunman, disgusted.

He clenched his eyes and he wiped his sweaty face with his left hand again.

"*I'm in too deep,* and if I screw up, I'm going to lose them," he said. "I will."

"No, you won't," said Richard unwaveringly. "You *won't*."

The gunman looked at Richard, half convinced with a look of pure desperation.

"What am I doing? What is this?" he asked as he looked at his gun and at the cash on the counter. "What have I done?"

"You've done nothing," said Richard.

The gunman looked at Richard with mixed expressions of mild amazement, grief, and gratitude. He crammed the gun into his pants behind his back and tucked his plaid shirt over it. He looked at Richard and than at Nick. He did not say anything, but he was apologizing for his actions.

The Town of Jasper

"My name is Richard Morrissey."

The gunman looked at him as if he was an authoritative figure and he was a subordinate.

"Ron Carlisle," said the gunman weakly.

"Ron, I want you to stop by my house tomorrow at 14 Alpine Lane at eight A.M.," Richard said.

Ron, perplexed, fumbled and murmured some words no one could hear or understand.

"Just be there. And your wife," Richard requested.

"Yes, sir," said Ron lightly.

After a brief, awkward moment, the gunman glanced at Nick and the other customer, fairly humiliated. He gave Richard a final glance as he walked out of the store. The bell jingled as the door swung open.

Richard swung the door open to his house and closed it tenderly. He walked in with the bottle of wine and beer and placed them on the counter. Diane walked into the kitchen as Richard removed the bottles, one by one, out of the cardboard.

"How'd things go at the store?"

Richard tilted his head and flared his eyebrows.

"Dangerously," he said.

Diane looked at him curiously as she sipped her early afternoon coffee.

"Anything from him yet?"

Richard reached into his pocket and yanked out his cell phone. He clicked the button that lit up his home screen, which showed his two children with their arms around one another at the beach. There were no unread messages. He placed the phone on the counter and opened the refrigerator.

"Nothing yet," he said unsurprisingly. "Where are the kids?"

"Victoria is downstairs watching her TV show, and Joseph is outside," said Diane. "Tell him to stomp his feet when he comes in. He tracks mud from the yard every time."

"Problem could have been avoided if we just bought a beautiful condo," said Richard teasingly.

"Don't start with that," she said.

Richard looked out the window to try to find his son. He could not see him from the quick glance over his wife's shoulder. The day was vivid and bright. Richard walked outside into the backyard to find out what his son was up to. He surveyed the yard for a few moments until he saw his son behind the gigantic Northern Red Oak. He could only see a portion of his son's body, whose back was turned to him. Curious, Richard walked leisurely towards his son. As he got closer to his seven-year-old boy, he noticed he was looking at something. He was kneeling and silent as he looked at the figure. Somewhat concerned, Richard picked up his pace and circled around his son to see what he was staring at.

"Joseph..." said Richard in a low tone, so as not to startle the boy.

Joseph did not turn around to greet his father, instead his eyes remained fixed on what was lying before him. Joseph was diagnosed with a form of Asperger's syndrome and showed signs of autism. There were times where he'd keep to himself and not want to communicate with others. He rarely made eye contact with people.

Richard was taken by surprise when he saw what he was looking at so intently. Positioned directly behind him, Richard joined his son in an ogle of the scene. Under the gigantic Northern Red Oak, lay a dead fox. On its side, the gorgeous animal was not breathing. His orange fur coat remained still, and his elegant tail with a white tip grazed the grass horizontally.

"I felt its heart," said Joseph in a saddened tenor. "It's not thumping."

It took a few moments for Richard to break his gaze and focus on his son's safety.

"Don't get too close to it. It can hurt you, Joseph," he said.

"How can it hurt me? It's gone," said Joseph.

"How long have you been out here?" Richard asked.

"I don't know…A while, I guess."

Richard looked at the fallen animal again, unsure of what to do.

"Are we going to leave it?" Joseph asked.

"I don't know," Richard said unsurely.

"If we leave it, other animals are going to hurt it."

"It's already dead. It won't feel the pain," said Richard.

"Yeah, but its family and friends don't know it's dead. Can't we bring it to them?" asked Joseph.

"I don't know where its family is. They're animals, Joseph, they separate all of the time."

The boy continued to only look at the fox with his father. He was very curious and concerned for the animal and giving it a proper burial.

"You think it has a sister like me?"

"Maybe," said Richard.

"Will you bury it since it's dead?"

"I suppose I can."

"Are you going to bury me when I'm dead?"

Richard looked at his overly inquisitive son in a troubling way.

"No, Joseph," he said.

"Why?" the boy asked.

"Because you're going to bury me," said Richard.

Joseph did not say anything else as he and his father stood at a distance from the fallen animal lying dead beneath the gigantic Northern Red Oak tree.

Richard opened the door for Joseph, who scurried inside under his arm. He walked into the kitchen and saw Diane placing the beer bottles into the refrigerator. He snatched the empty cardboard holder and began ripping it up as he looked outside at the dead fox. From the kitchen window, all he could see was the end of the fox's legs. He ripped the cardboard more as he walked into the living room. He walked up to the massive living room window that expanded one hundred thirty-five feet by two hundred feet. Now he could see the fox's full body. Ripping the box sporadically with less focus, he shifted all his attention to the animal. He leaned as close as he could to the window.

"What are you looking at, babe?" asked Diane.

Richard did not answer. He took another haphazard rip at the box, which was now in many small pieces. He squinted and thought something to himself. He thought about what to do with the body. He thought about what his son had said. He broke his stare and walked through the kitchen. Victoria was twirling around with her Barbie doll. He dodged her and hurried down the stairs leading to the garage. He twisted the squeaky knob and swung the door open. The cold ventilation from the garage made his neck hair rise. He grabbed the shovel that was next to a big container labeled…

Halloween

The Town of Jasper

    He lifted the shovel and marched outside like a Trojan warrior ready for battle. Outside, the day was in its prime with no clouds in the sky. Richard pressed on towards the tree through the patio and onto the lawn. He saw the enormous Northern Red Oak and walked up beside it. He checked out the deceased body of the fox once again and looked down at the ground. He looked around at the grass surrounding him like a dog searching for the most proper spot to urinate. He found an appropriate area next to the fox so he could properly bury it, per his son's request. He patted the ground with his feet. The ground was soft since the weather was warm, but in the cold, it was like trying to dig through concrete. He stabbed the ground, which made his forearms flex. He flung the first piece of dirt layered with green grass aside next to the tree. He spiked the shard end of the shovel into the ground again and again until he started to sweat. He kept at it for a full sixty seconds and found himself panting for air. He wiped his forehead with his forearm and leaned on the shovel. He looked over at the lifeless animal again and wondered if it knew even in death, how hard he was working to bury it. He gave it another minute before he started heaving more dirt.

    It took nearly half an hour for Richard to dig a big enough hole for the animal to fit in. Once he finished digging, he threw the shovel and wiped his forehead. He walked slowly over to the fox, who remained perfectly still on the ground. Richard awkwardly gauged how he would drag the animal to into the hole. He figured it would be most efficient to drag it by its feet. He looked at it once more and then bent over to grab its bony legs. Richard reached gradually, as if touching it would transmit some kind of disease. Richard reached for its ankles, and as soon as he touched the animal, it jolted up. Richard lost his balance and back-pedaled in shock. He fell on his buttocks and rolled into the hole. The fox ran as fast as it could through his neighbor's yard and out of sight. Richard panted heavily as his pulse skyrocketed. At a loss for words, Richard remained in the hole, finding it impossible to catch his breath. His hands shook, and his mind raced as he tried to gather the logic of it all. As he was trying to process the situation that transpired, he laid in the hole on his back. The clouds above passed by leisurely. Richard closed his eyes and began to catch his breath as he got comfortable inside the dirt-filled crevice. He felt his phone buzz in his pocket. He reached for it and checked the message. The message was from Sutherland. The message read.

Not coming tonigt. Problems. Pectin being releasd erly with parole.

The following morning, at eight o'clock, the doorbell rang. Richard was in the living room with his daughter playing 'tea time', and Diane walked towards the door in her white apron. She patted her hand on the apron and opened the door. Outside, stood Ron Carlisle, dressed nicely in a collared shirt, brown leather jacket, and jeans with his wife, Kathy.

"Hello…" Diane said. "Can I help you?"

Ron stood like a chicken with its head cut off at the door. Fumbling with his words and acting as polite as possible, he nervously fiddled his hands together.

"Is uh. Is Richard Morrissey here?" he asked nervously.

"Yes…" Diane said as she looked at Ron oddly. "Honey…someone is here to see you…" she shouted.

Richard got up from the small plastic table and presented himself at the front door. He locked eyes with Ron, who was standing like a kid who was forced to apologize to his neighbor for hitting a baseball through their window.

"Come in," he said.

Ron looked at Diane and nodded before he and his wife walked inside the house. Kathy introduced herself and shook Diane's hand.

"Can I get you something?" Diane asked

"Oh, no thank you, ma'am," said Ron.

Ron awkwardly walked farther into the house alongside Kathy. Ron peeked into the living room and saw Victoria performing her weekend morning ritual with her breakfast club.

"Victoria, say hello," requested Richard.

Victoria stopped her routine and looked up at Ron with her striking and elegant hazel eyes. Ron looked at her innocently and smiled.

"Hello," she said shyly as she put her head down.

Ron chuckled lightly and looked at Richard.

"Beautiful girl," he said.

"We have a girl too. Her name is Alyssa."

"Oh that's wonderful," said Diane civilly

"Yeah, she's okay, that one," Richard said with a sigh. "She's a handful, though. Don't let her fool you."

Diane smiled at the couple and gestured for them to walk into the kitchen.

"Please join us in the kitchen, breakfast is nearly ready," said Diane.

"Oh no, we don't want to impose," said Kathy.

"Please! Don't be silly," said Diane.

Diane was oblivious of the planned arrival of the guests, but she was always good at adapting to spontaneous situations and creating a friendly atmosphere. That was one of the reasons she and Richard worked so well together. That was one of the reasons why Richard married her. Richard walked Ron into the kitchen as Kathy trailed Diane to help prepare her traditional Sunday morning breakfast of blueberry pancakes and fresh fruit. Diane had a secret recipe that she would never tell Richard, or anyone else for that matter. While the women prepared the morning meal, Richard directed Ron to the kitchen table. It was a large white, round table that was always perfectly clean. Richard would always joke that the table was always so clean that 'you could eat off it'. Richard and Ron took a seat, and Diane brought over two fresh cups of coffee.

"Thank you very much. You are very kind," said Ron gratefully.

"Please, it's my pleasure," said Diane kindly.

Diane walked away from the table and called for the kids to come to the kitchen.

"So where do you guys live?" asked Diane.

Diane lifted a tray of food and talked as she brought it over to the table.

"We live in Jasper," said Kathy.

"Oh, wow. Have you lived there long?"

"Oh, only about three years now. Maybe less."

"Wonderful. How do you guys like it there?"

Kathy looked at Ron and smirked. She looked at Diane and smiled again.

"It's a wonderful town."

The kids came stampeding into the kitchen with their bellies empty. They sat up on their high chairs at the island table across the big, clean white one. Diane strolled over and got them settled in with their plates, knives, and orange juice. She looked across at Kathy, who was still standing.

"Kathy, please sit. Relax."

"Thank you," Kathy said as she took a seat.

"How about you guys?" Asked Kathy. "What made you choose Woodland?"

"We almost didn't," said Richard. "Joseph was two, and Diane was pregnant with Victoria. We were looking at some condos a couple of towns over, just to start small."

"Makes sense," said Kathy.

Diane chimed in as she brought things over to the table.

"But we didn't want to be…"

"Another number," said Richard, finishing his wife's sentence with a smile. She smiled back at him and gave him a delicate punch on the arm. "We are actually thinking about moving."

"Oh, really? Any particular towns in mind?" asked Kathy.

Diane looked at her husband and smiled.

"We're just fishing around at the moment. Looking for the best fit for us."

"Well, I wish you luck with your search. I'm sure you will find what you're looking for."

"Thank you," said Diane. "So how long you two been married?"

"Fifteen years, now. Right, hun?" asked Ron.

"Fifteen and three months, but who's counting?" said Kathy.

Everyone shared a laugh at the humorous remark.

"How about you two?"

Richard looked at Diane as he leaned back in his chair. He smiled at her, as she did to him.

"We got married young," said Richard.

"A couple across the street from us just got engaged. Their wedding is next summer," said Kathy. "They're in their early twenties. They're just kids."

"That's not marriage," said Richard. "They're 'together', and they love each other. But marriage truly starts when you have children."

Richard looked at Ron after he said it. Ron looked down at the table, avoiding eye contact with Richard.

"Couldn't agree more," said Kathy with a smile.

"So how did you two wind up getting to know one another?" asked Diane.

Ron looked nervously at Richard, not knowing what to say or how to say it. Richard sipped his coffee from the brim slowly and placed it down. Diane came walking over to the table and placed the plate with a stack full of pancakes in the center. He swallowed and looked at Kathy. Diane sat and placed a napkin on her lap.

"Yeah, I was wondering the same thing," said Kathy.

"It's actually a funny story. A couple of days ago, I was at a traffic light and the cars were going and stopping and going and stopping. I must have taken my eyes off the road for a quick second, and I wound up bumping him from behind. Luckily, no one was hurt and there was no damage to our cars," Richard said.

"I wish there was, you would have done me a favor," Ron said jokingly, going along with the lie.

Everyone at the table chuckled.

"Yeah, but you had to see the look on his face when he got out. He was pissed! I thought he was going to shoot me!" Richard said as the women laughed.

The Town of Jasper

"Anyway, we wound up exchanging information. He said he was relatively new in town and had young kids like us, so I figured I'd invite him and his lovely wife over and welcome them to the neighborhood…and here we are," Richard said with a smile.

The women smiled and nodded. The four of them ate and drank until Diane broke the silence.

"So, what do you guys do?"

Kathy patted her mouth with her napkin and cleared her throat.

"I work at the bank in town here."

"Oh, wow, great," Diane said. "And what about you Ron?"

Nervously, Ron tried to put together a haphazard response to cover his current dire situation.

"I do some…"

"Ron is actually going to be working with Al over at the hardware store," interjected Richard. "He's got a foot out the door towards retirement and he needs someone to take over after he's gone."

"Oh, wow, that's great. Al's been looking for someone for a while now," said Diane. "It's a shame he never had any children to pass it down to."

"Yeah, I spoke to him about it today and told him I found the right guy for him," Richard stated.

Surprised, Kathy looked at Ron.

"I didn't know you quit your other job, honey?"

Ron looked at Richard quickly and then at wife. It was a lot for him to process because he wasn't even aware of the current situation.

"Well, I mean, it all happened so quickly. I was going to wait for the right time to tell you, sweetie. I just wanted to wait for everything to be final," Ron said as best he could with a straight face.

There was a brief pause in the conversation. Diane looked at Richard, who sipped his coffee from the brim. Diane raised her glass.

"I think that's great news. So, to new opportunities and new friends."

"Absolutely," Richard said as he lifted his glass.

The Carlisle's smiled in approval, and the four clinked glasses together at the very clean round white table. Ron looked at Richard and gave him a nod. Richard gave no expression as he sipped his coffee from the brim and focused his attention outside the window.

"Hey, Dad," his son Joseph shouted from across the room. Richard looked up at him.

"Did you bury it yet?" he asked.

Richard looked at Joseph and bit his lower lip.

"Almost."

US, WHO THEY WILL THANK

Present Day 2016
Five Years After "The Incident"

Pilate said to them, "What then shall I do with Jesus who is called Christ?"

They all said to him, "Let Him be crucified!"

Then the governor said, "Why, what evil has He done?"

But they cried out all the more, saying, "Let Him be crucified!"

As the acoustics of the engine and undercarriage echoed, Richard, Dallas, and Ford remained relatively mum inside the car. Richard looked outside the left window with his arm hanging out. He ran thoughts through his head that made him do some critical thinking. He tried to remember his last encounter with the feared tribe with his father. He tried to recollect the setting and environment and how it may have changed over the years. Maybe they changed. Maybe they would welcome them. Maybe they wouldn't. Richard honed in on his thoughts and didn't hear Dallas speak out.

"What are we thinking?" Dallas asked nervously.

"About what?" asked Ford.

"You know. About things. About this," said Dallas.

Richard remained silent as he thought about his wife and children. The whole plan had him thinking about the life he once had. He thought about them back at the hospital, praying that this plan worked out.

"I'm thinking we get in. Get out. And go home in one piece with what we need," said Gary.

"But do we really need to do this? I mean. What about the government giving us supplies and food?" asked Dallas.

"The government ain't helping anymore," said Ford. "They don't want to bother with us. Stay straight, you're veering off a little."

Richard adjusted the side mirror and looked into the reflection at the two vehicles behind them that were keeping at reasonable speeds as requested. They weren't far from their destination. Just over a mile or so until they were feet on the ground. Richard wasn't fearful or panicked. He had a feeling of calmness and stability. The whole plan and its potential consequences provided him an unwavering feeling. It kept his nerves on their toes but also at ease. He wasn't afraid of what bad things could happen, but prepared himself to do what was necessary if need be. His emotions stirred and brewed in him, which caused him to zone out again. They passed a big sign on the left side of the main road that read,

Help Keep Jasper Safe
Don't Text And Drive

"How you think this is going to go down?" Dallas asked Richard.

Richard ignored him. In fact, he didn't even hear him ask the question.

"Whatever happens, happens," chimed Gary. "We didn't get this far not to find out."

The Town of Jasper

Fear and panic began to show in Dallas' voice as he drove nervously. Two hands on the steering wheel, he kept looking back and forth at the road and the men sitting next to him.

"Are the rumors true? Ya know, about these Albino people?"

"I don't know. I've never seen one," said Gary.

"I heard they kill trespassers on site. And that they hang their heads on spikes as trophies," Dallas said with a trembling tone.

"Don't wrap your head around the bullshit you heard from the townsfolk who ain't got nothing better to talk about," Gary asserted.

A few moments of silence passed by as the car coasted forward. On the dashboard, there was a picture of a family of four. A husband, wife, and two small girls. Dallas focused on it for a few moments and felt a feeling of remorse overcome him for an instant. The truck once belonged to a man named Reed, who worked as an electrician before he fell victim, along with the rest of his family. No one in town knew him too well, since he moved to Jasper only a few months before everything went wrong. Dallas looked at the photo of the smiling family again for a quick second and then set his eyes back on the road.

"You think they're there?" Dallas asked.

"I don't know," said Gary softly. "Guess we'll know soon enough."

Dallas nodded his head and clenched his jaw. The destination was just a half a mile away. The car fell deathly quiet as the three men sat as still as statues. Looking for something to keep their minds off the task, the men diverted their attention on the area that surrounded them.

"They're there," Richard said gravely while looking out the window.

The two men glanced to their right almost simultaneously. They both acknowledged the fact and no one said another word the rest of the ride.

Several religious sects and groups had formed after 'The Incident'. Most groups were not hostile or antagonistic, and there hadn't been occurrences of brutality or force from any group. Most groups were ragtag bands of no more than several people, who prayed together for the unconscious. Others got together to drink and play poker, while others served as neighborhood watches for specific parts of town. Each with a different purpose on how to deal with the situation, and each willing to give it their all to foster what they once had. Each of these groups, along with the rest of Jasper, were oblivious to a certain assemblage of fundamentalist, known as The Redeemers. The Redeemers, which started out as four men, now eighteen people, were a collection of extremists who had brainwashed one another with the frame of mind of eradicating the unconscious for the greater good. They felt their sole purpose was to carry out the orders from The Almighty and wipe out the condemned. Their leader had ingrained a belief that 'The Incident' was a test for them and that the nature of what happened went against the grain of God's natural plans for humanity. The Redeemers feel the victims of 'The Incident' were playing God. Covertly hand selected by their leader, the group of radicals each wielded an uncanny belief in the Catholic faith. Their logical ways of thinking and processing had dissolved in their heads over the past five years of living within a wall. Their strong belief in the Almighty rivaled that of their feeling of disgust and odium of living within a wall. Their leader targeted the more religious citizens of

The Town of Jasper

Jasper. He drafted individuals with nothing to lose, who wanted more than just to live the rest of their days without purpose. A master of persuasion, their leader was very intelligent and knew how to get what he wanted.

An hour after the convoy left to meet the Fillmore Whites, eighteen people gathered around a in a circle in the deep woods. Fourteen men and four women stood in the dark, hollow forest, waiting further instruction. The mood was dull and dreary. No one uttered a word. A man stood in the corner and sharpened a Browning Black Label hunting knife against a tall tree while another sat on a milk crate and read the Bible silently to himself. The others waited anxiously, fidgeting with their fingers and tip-toed around the area. Alas, a shadowy figure emerged and approached the group of people. Everyone broke their routine and looked up. The six-foot two man with sloppy black hair looked around. Dressed in ragged brown pants with a navy blue shirt, everyone made a path for him as he walked towards the center of the circle. Eighteen people gathered around him and held hands. In front of him stood a wooden stool with a large bowl on top of it. In the bowl, there was nearly three pounds of ash. The man in charge closed his eyes, with everyone eventually doing the same. Their leader spoke out.

"Jesus, tender and loving Lamb of God, Utmost Sacrifice of all sacrifices, Your glory is reverberated in the highest. Being preoccupied with my well-being, You chose to self-sacrifice Yourself, Setting aside all Your personal glories. I thank You, Lord Jesus, for Your act of love! Your action has drawn me closer to You. Teach me to model in smaller things, To sacrifice in order to help others, Guiding my soul to endure abstinence. Lamb of God, I thank you endlessly!"

The man opened his eyes and looked up. The eighteen surrounding people, whose eyes were still closed, remained in the same positions, holding each other's hands. The leader began to speak with his eyes open.

"Don't be fearful of the things we must do. Don't be reluctant of the things we have planned. We are servants of our savior, the Almighty. We will eradicate the damned and liberate the fallen. We will prevail in our continuing journey to bring balance back to our community. We are Redeemers. Disciples of God. Sent not to punish the non-believers, but to enlighten the unmindful. In the end, when it is finished, it will be us who they will thank."

The man did not continue his speech. The ongoing silence was the queue for everyone to lift their heads and open their eyes. They all looked up at the man before them in the center of the circle. Each person let go of the hand next to them and listened closely. The leader, with a look of determination and drive, scoured the area and spoke out.

"Is everyone armed?"

Everyone nodded their heads.

"No guns. We do this quietly. We've planned for this, and we're ready. Remember. No hesitation. No uncertainty."

More nods from the surrounding individuals. The plan was in motion, and the people were eager to execute it. No one seemed nervous or afraid. They each expressed a casual look with a clear conscience.

"We'll split up in groups of four. One group North, the others South, East, and West. We'll hit the hospital from all sides once it's dark enough."

The leader dabbed his fingers into the bowl of ash. He soaked his dirty fingers in the bowl like he was searching for a lost treasure beneath it. He removed his hands from the ash and started to rub his cheeks. Black ash spread across the man's lean face as he closed his eyes. The leader lifted his eyelids and spoke tenderly.

"Let's begin," he said.

The members of the group began to plunge their hands into the bowl one by one. They applied it like a moisturizer to their faces. Across the area, a man placed his hand against a tree and began hyperventilating. A panic attack had overcome him and was taking its course. The leader noticed this and began his stroll across the grass up to the man. The group looked on at the scene without saying a thing. The man in his mid forties began breathing heavily, putting his weight against the tree with his hand pressed against it. His back hunched horizontally as he inhaled and exhaled. Before the leader could place his hand against the man's back, the hyperventilating man vomited against the tree. The leader showed no sign of emotion; he let the man get it out before he approached him further. Spewing out chunks of canned beans and old bread, the man began to cry. Crying and spitting out fluids from his mouth, the leader placed his hand gently against the man's back. The hysterical man looked down at the floor and spoke out frantically.

"What are we doing? Is this really the right thing?"

The leader patted the man gently and rubbed his spine softly. He placed his right hand against the man's shoulder.

"Bradley...This is," the leader said softly. "Sit, sit."

Bradley wiped his eyes with his filthy sleeve and sat down on the ground with his back against the tree. The leader knelt down in front of him as the rest of the group watched. Bradley looked at the leader, embarrassed. The man in charge cupped his hands together on his lap and looked up at Bradley.

"I know it isn't easy. But it is what's necessary. These are sick people. We have been tasked by the mightiest power in this universe to guide their journey to him. They don't *deserve* this anymore. It's been five years. *Five years* and they haven't woken. Their spirits have floated in limbo long enough."

"But God will choose their path. He hasn't made his decision for them yet," Bradley said with a whimper.

"Don't you see it, Bradley? God has chosen *us* to make the decision for him. He can't do this alone. And with them gone, there won't be a need for the wall anymore. *We* can end this and get things back to the way they were."

The leader clutched Bradley's hands.

"He needs *us*," said the leader assertively. "We are helping these people achieve salvation and immortality."

Bradley began to nod his head and stopped his sobbing. His superior was restoring his faith.

"When I knocked on your door and asked you to be a part of this, I knew. I always knew you were strong. At first, you called me a madman, and now you are walking this road of righteousness with me," stated the leader.

Bradley looked deep into his leader's eyes, hypnotized by his words. Completely still and stern, Bradley nodded his head again.

"Say it with me," asked the leader.

Bradley closed his eyes and remained still with his chest out and shoulders held high. The leader and Bradley both recited the words together.

"We are Redeemers. Disciples of God. Sent not to punish the non-believers, but to enlighten the unmindful. In the end, when it is finished. It will be us who they will thank."

The Town of Jasper

The leader got up off his knees while Bradley's eyes remained closed. The leader walked beside him and unsheathed his M-9 Bayonet Knife. He clutched Bradley's scalp aggressively and in one swift stroke, the leader opened up the man's throat, spilling out blood and other fluids across the soil. There was no reaction by any of the other members, who all watched as the man slowly died in front of them like it was something they had seen before. The leader sheathed his knife and looked up at his group of devoted individuals.

"Remember. No hesitation. No uncertainty."

James D. Gianetti

BEHIND THE BIG BROWN DOOR
Two Months Before "The Incident"
July 2011

The bright, sun-filled morning complimented the passive suburban street called Hewitt. A few small children rode their bikes down the street, and there was even a small lemonade stand being set up by a few little girls with their mother. The traditional weekend morning on the suburban street consisted of a few joggers, small children playing, and a few Labrador retrievers being walked by their owners. At the end of the block stood a house to the right. It was a mid-sized home painted pearl white, with a white fence and a big brown door. Standing on no more than a half-acre, the house resembled a middle class worker's dream home. On the bright, sun-filled morning on the passive suburban street of Hewitt, in the pearl white house with the big brown door, chaos ensued.

  Detective Sutherland raised his voice loudly. He and his wife Olivia were going through the morning motions with their daily screaming match about their problems. Their marriage was on the brink of collapse, and it had decayed over the last three years. In the bedroom, his wife Olivia pointed her finger at him and flailed her arms like a lunatic.

  "You are a son of a bitch! You're never here! You're never here!" screamed Olivia.

  "Oh, bullshit! Don't throw that in my face again! I'm here now!" shouted Sutherland.

  "Your daughter doesn't even know you anymore. You leave in the morning before she gets up and come home at night all messed up when she's asleep! So don't tell me *you're here*!" hollered Olivia.

"I won't do this shit today! I won't!" barked Sutherland.

"You won't? You won't what? Tell me, Jack, when will you *do* something? Tell me that "*detective*", she said mockingly.

Detective Sutherland picked up a lamp on the night stand and yanked the chord. He threw it against the wall in her direction, and it smashed into pieces.

"I said I'm not doing this today! I won't let you! I will *NOT!*" he shouted.

As Olivia began to slightly cry, she shook her head at her husband.

"I'm gonna take her from you," she said. Look at yourself."

Detective Sutherland popped an orange vial with shaking hands. He dropped four pills into his hand and placed two back into the vial. He placed two on his tongue and swallowed.

"You're a disaster," said Olivia. "And one day you're going to come home, and there will be no one."

Detective Sutherland ran his fingers through his dirty blonde hair and began to pant angrily. He clenched the wooden bedroom counter which he leaned on. He bit the inside of his cheeks as he tried controlling himself.

"You think you're going to take her from me?" Sutherland asked sinisterly.

Olivia looked at him, somewhat intimidated, but held her ground like the strong woman she was.

"I know I am," she confirmed in a whispering tone. "You've done enough to her. I won't let you cause more harm."

Detective Sutherland walked up to Olivia with heavy footsteps. Olivia cowered back with fear as Sutherland got close to her with an uncompromising look in his eye.

"What the fuck does that mean?" asked Sutherland, enraged.

"Try it, you son of a bitch. Be a *man* and just do it," she said, egging him on. "Because I'm going to make sure you never see us again."

Detective Sutherland rose his hand ready to strike Olivia as hard as he could. The rage had mixed with his adrenaline, creating an unyielding frame of judgment. He raised his hand, and Olivia reached for a pair of scissors on her dresser. She raised the scissors towards Sutherland's face ready to defend herself as she panted. The two of them looked at one another with fury as Olivia found herself leaving the room with the scissors still in her hand.

Downstairs, in the kitchen, their seven-year-old daughter Shannon was sitting at the kitchen table with her golden blonde hair brushed against her shoulders. She looked concerned, but not afraid. Her brain damage had caused her to become oblivious and mostly unaware of her surroundings. She was often mute and unable to speak fluently or comprehensively. She colored sloppily in a coloring book. Olivia walked up behind her and brushed her hair with her hand.

"Hello, my love. Everything's okay, don't worry," she said comfortingly.

Upstairs, nearly collapsing from his emotions, Sutherland began swallowing and blinking profusely. Slightly hyperventilating now, the detective walked over to the orange vial on the counter. Frantically, he pondered over swallowing a couple more, but decided against it. He reached into his pocket and took out another vial of medication. He popped the top and placed a couple of tablets into his palm, threw them back, and leaned against the wooden furniture. He looked at himself in the mirror and saw a pale face and flushed eyes. He looked like a living corpse. Wondering where it all went to hell, he retreated from the mirror and found his way stampeding out of the house in an angry stir. The wheels spun wildly and kicked up some smoke as he sped down the quiet residential street.

The tires came to a squeaking halt as the detective turned the car off. His body became numb, as he couldn't remember how he even got to the supermarket. His surroundings spun, and the next thing Sutherland knew, he was in the liquor section of the grocery store, clutching a bottle of Red Label. As he grasped the glass bottle of booze, a flustered woman appeared and seemed to be troubled about something. He looked over at her as she began to slightly cry. She looked up at him and looked away quickly. He thought about saying something, but remembered he had an appointment with the backseat of his car and the warm bottle of hard stuff in five minutes. He snagged the bottle off the shelf and walked past the woman who covered her face as she wept.

"I'm sorry," she yelled out to him.

Her comment made the detective stop walking. Amidst his inebriated state, he felt a degree of due diligence to turn around and ask what in the hell she was sorry for.

"Excuse me?" he asked. "Do I know you?"

The woman put her head down and walked away, trying to avoid confrontation. Sutherland followed her down the aisle.

"Excuse me," he said. "Stop."

He caught up to the mysterious woman halfway down the narrow aisle with paper towels and toilet paper surrounding them. She looked up with her sorrowful face.

"Do I know you?" he asked.

The woman didn't acknowledge the detective's question. She just became more upset.

"I'm so sorry," she said.

"About what?"

"I can feel your pain. Your suffering. It's echoing off of you, Jack."

"My pain? How do you know my…"

"Whatever you do, you have to always believe things will turn and never lose it. Or they won't. Things won't turn if you lose it. Because after it happens, you're going to need to find a way to get inside."

"Who the hell are you? *Get inside* where?" asked Sutherland as he looked around. "What's going to happen?"

The woman looked at Sutherland's firearm, which was in plain view. She looked at him apprehensively.

"You shouldn't have that out in the open. Might rub people the wrong way," she said.

Sutherland looked down at his sidearm and tucked it away. His body leaned to the left, and he nearly stumbled over trying to cover the gun with his shirt. He regained his balance and he wiped his eyes with his fingers.

After he regained his balance and composure, he looked up at the deranged woman in front of him who had vanished into thin air. Wondering where she went, Sutherland looked up and down the aisle frantically. He rushed towards the neighboring sections of the store and saw no trace of her. He looked back at the bottle in his hands and remembered he had more important plans.

Several hours later, Sutherland woke up in the backseat of his car. The bottle of booze was half-filled in his left hand, and his sidearm was held gently in his right. He had no recollection of getting to where he was. In fact, he had no idea of where he was. After a couple minutes, the reasoning behind why he was there became clearer. He grasped the grip of his sidearm and lifted himself up off the back seat. It was about an hour past dusk, with the streetlights providing the only form of light. Sutherland tried to clear his head and sober up. He looked outside from backseat of his car at a run-down apartment building. The neighborhood was seedy and derelict. Sutherland leaned his head against the back seat's headrest and took a deep breath. Before he could doze off again, a ruckus of someone walking outside woke him up. It was Ryan Pectin. Sutherland had finally remembered why he parked outside the residence. The scoundrel of a man got into a dark green sedan. The model was unidentifiable. Ryan Pectin got into the front seat, and the vehicle sped away. Sutherland mustered up his sobriety and climbed into the driver's seat.

  The engine fired up, and Sutherland drove cautiously down the road. He kept his distance from the dark green car and had his front lights turned off. Up ahead, the green car veered off to the right and parked on the side of a dark street. Sutherland parked about fifty yards away and waited for Pectin to make a move.

  After a few minutes passed, a teenage boy walked up to the dark green car. The kid was no more than seventeen. Sutherland looked closely at the exchange of drugs and money. The teenage kid was handed a few bags of drugs and walked away slyly.

Sutherland waited for the boy to leave the area and grabbed two latex gloves and a small rectangular piece of plywood out of his glove compartment. He put the gloves on and opened the driver's side door gently. He walked along the sidewalk with soundless footsteps. Once he was within ten yards of the dark green car, Sutherland drew his firearm and made his move to the driver's side window. He pointed the gun at the driver, who happened to be Ryan Pectin. Pectin jolted in shock at the detective's sudden arrival.

"Unlock the car and put your hands on the wheel," demanded Sutherland.

Pectin acted unafraid and cocky. There was a red-haired girl in the passenger seat who wasn't as fearless.

"Haven't you heard, Detective? I've been released on good behavior," said Pectin sarcastically.

"Unlock the car. Put your hands on the wheel."

Pectin smirked and did as Sutherland commanded. Sutherland opened the back seat door and sat inside. He pointed his gun at Pectin whose hands remained firmly gripped on the wheel. The red-haired girl began to panic.

"Please, don't shoot us," she said, afraid.

"Shut the fuck up," said Sutherland.

The girl shut her mouth and looked ahead. Sutherland looked over at the back of Pectin's head. He began to attach a silencer to his pistol, which made the red-haired girl nearly cry.

"*You don't sell this shit*," said Sutherland, mimicking Pectin.

"It was the first time…"

"Wrong answer," said Sutherland, pointing his pistol at the back of Pectin's head. The silencer attached was about six inches long. "*Drive.*"

The Town of Jasper

Sutherland directed Pectin to a secluded area with nothing but a grass field surrounding them. The thousand-acre land was vacated, with patch of woods in the distance providing the only form of environmental variety.

"Kill the lights," said Sutherland.

Pectin turned the light off, creating a pitch black surrounding. Sutherland's pistol remained pointed at Ryan Pectin.

"Where'd you get the drugs?"

"I'm telling you, I don't know…"

Sutherland shot two rounds through the windshield causing Pectin and the girl to jump in fear.

"Jesus, fuck!" shouted Pectin. "It's some guy I don't know his name. I met him once through a friend. Something with an E, maybe."

"What does he look like?"

"I don't remember. I was messed up when I saw him."

Sutherland opened the backseat door and slammed it shut. He opened the driver's side door and pulled Pectin out of it. He threw him to the ground and pointed the gun at his head. Ryan Pectin began to tremble and held his hands up to his face.

"Please, I don't know what he looks like. I fucking swear!"

Sutherland looked at the girl in the front seat, who started to hysterically cry.

"Get into the driver's seat."

Hesitantly and petrified, the red-haired girl climbed into the driver's seat. Sutherland pointed the gun at Pectin's face with malice. He threw the piece of plywood beside him.

"Wedge this between the tire and the ground and put your hand over it," said Sutherland.

Ryan Pectin began to cry and weep as he wedged the piece of plywood between the ground and the tire. He placed his trembling hand over the beige piece of wood and began to weep.

"What does he look like?"

Pectin cried out loud and uttered something unclear through his hysterical state. Sutherland lifted his head and pointed his gun at the frantic girl.

"Reverse it," he said grimly.

The girl began to cry more hysterically as she reluctantly put the car in reverse.

"Wait! Please!" shouted Pectin.

"Who is he?"

"Don't do it! My fucking hand! Please, no!"

Sutherland looked at the girl and waited for her to comply with his bidding. The girl closed her eyes and pressed her foot on the gas. The tire rolled over Pectin's knuckles slowly, causing him to shriek.

"AHHHHH. Holy shit! My hand! My hand!"

Tears streamed down the girls' face as Ryan Pectin bellowed in pain. She quickly put the car in drive and released the pressure off Pectin's hand. Pectin held his wrist and rolled around on the ground like a fish out of water.

"His name is Elvin! Holy fuhhhhhaahhhhh!"

"Elvin what?" shouted Sutherland.

"I don't know his last name. No one ever told me! He's not in the drug scene anymore. He's big on fucking guns now. Black market or some shit. Fuck!"

Sutherland looked at the girl in the front seat.

"Step out of the car."

The girl got out of the car slowly with her hands raised.

"On your stomach," said Sutherland.

The Town of Jasper

    The girl got on her stomach beside Pectin. Sutherland sat in the driver's seat of the dark green car. He put the car in gear and drove away, leaving them in the dark, vacated land.

James D. Gianetti

The Things They're Going To Do

Present Day 2016
Five Years After "The Incident"

The room was dark and gloomy. Nearly the entire building was empty and abandoned. The power and electricity had been shut down for weeks. What was once the Jasper Library was now home to rats, mold, and darkness. Detective Sutherland walked through the dark hallway, stepping over unidentified liquid substances and rat droppings. He could smell the foul stench of a cigarette burning from the end of the room. He reached for his notepad and read what he had written on it. He sauntered a little further and weaved past dust-filled bookshelves. Detective Sutherland looked inside and caught a glimpse of a shadowy figure smoking a cigarette on a table in the corner. The person was sitting down, puffing smoke out of her mouth through her lips. Her demeanor resembled a prostitute in an inner city. Sutherland took out his grey ski mask. His thumb grazed his scar as he pulled the mask over his face. He walked up to her holding a plastic bag in his hands. The woman did not acknowledge the detective as he stood in front of her.

"Ms. Ringwell?"

Ms. Ringwell exhaled some smoke and fixed her eyes on what the detective had in his hands. Sutherland noticed her eyes honed on the cigarettes he brought with him. He reached into his jacket pocket and flipped the box of Marlboro cigarettes on the table. The woman looked at the box attentively, in an almost spellbound way. She began blinking rapidly and mumbled to

161

The Town of Jasper

herself. The detective looked at her, wondering why she was acting the way she was. She stared at the box of cigarettes and mumbled faster. The detective reached his hand slowly into the plastic bag and rolled a can across the table. Like a lizard snatching a fly in midair with its tongue, Ms. Ringwell snatched the rolling can and gripped it tightly. The detective took a seat in front of her and placed his notepad on the table. The woman rubbed the top of the can against the ground, creating a disturbing sound that made the detective's skin jump. She popped the top open, and before she could put her hand in to eat the food, the detective slid a fork across the table. The woman, Nancy Ringwell, the once head nurse at the Jasper Hospital, looked at Sutherland and slowly picked up the fork with shame.

"Gary Ford sent me," said the detective. "Said you might be able to help me."

Ms. Ringwell didn't acknowledge him as she stuffed the food down her mouth quickly.

"Possibly," she replied rudely, with food in her mouth.

"Richard Morrissey? You know him?"

"I know *of* him," she said.

"Any idea what he might look like?"

"Handsome fella. Only saw him a few times. Tall. Dark hair. Nothing out of the ordinary about his look."

Concerned, the detective straightened his shirt and posture. He glanced at his series of notes and questions.

"Ms. Ringwell, I'm going to ask you a series of…"

"Yeah, yeah, yeah. A series of questions. And let me guess. I need to answer them to the best of my ability, so you can get on with your never-ending case, and I can earn my food and cigarettes, which you'll have to pry out of my dead hands to get back," she said in a bleary tone.

The detective nodded his head, not having the energy or patience to verbally retaliate.

"Let's get started, then."

Looking down at his notes, the detective felt a tedious routine play out in his head. He'd been asking the same questions to dozens upon dozens of people. He'd made little progress up to this point. He looked down at his paper, where the first question read:

Describe the events of 'The Incident' in your own words. He asked himself why the hell did it matter? Why does their point of view of that day help his case to stop Richard Morrissey and help beat the 'disease'? These types of tedious, dreary questions wouldn't solve the case. Detective Sutherland disregarded his own question and looked straight into Ms. Ringwell's eyes.

"Why the hell did this place go to shit?" he asked aggressively.

Surprised by his tone and the wording of the question, Ms. Ringwell looked at him, somewhat intimidated. She flicked her cigarette on the ground and placed her hands together against the table. She began mumbling again. It sounded like a prayer. She stopped herself and snapped out of it. The woman shifted in and out of hysteria, which caused concern for the detective.

"The first week was hell. Absolute horror," she said. "Hundreds of people outside the ER, screaming and shouting. We were short-staffed that morning, so the first thing we did was get on the line as quick as we could to call in the other staff members. Every doctor, nurse, assistant, EMT, anyone with half a degree in medicine was on duty. Still wasn't even close to enough."

The Town of Jasper

Sutherland didn't bother writing anything down. He was past that. He leaned in and listened closely to the crazed individual.

"People held their children and loved ones in their arms. *Screaming* in terror. We didn't know where to put them all. First one on a bed was a young kid. Teenager from what I can recall. Name was Zach. His mother and father kept crying out 'HE WAS DEAD. BUT HE CAME BACK.' That was the case for all of them. Nothing we've ever seen before, Detective. No vital signs and then…"

Ms. Ringwell snapped her fingers. The sound reverberated throughout the room. She smiled and blinked madly.

"Back to life. After that, things got messy. More people barged in, hysterical, and the police were nowhere to be found. However, I do remember an officer running in with a small boy over his shoulder. He said he was hit by a car."

The detective put his head down, knowing what she was referring to. With all the people he'd interviewed, some stories intersected and crossed paths. Each unforgettably horrifying in its own way.

"We did the best we could with the staff we had. After the first hour, there were so many outside. We had to seal the door shut."

Ms. Ringwell felt herself choke up from her emotions while telling the story. Recollecting the horrors and terror of the day made her smug attitude vulnerable to emotion.

"We had to seal them outside. *People,*" she said as she blinked heavily a few times. "We didn't have the room or the resources. We didn't know what to do."

There was a pause in the story. Ms. Ringwell drank some water from the glass next to her. She cleared her throat and took a breath.

"Shortly after, they broke the door down. Someone drove their car right into the sealed door. They stormed in like madmen and attacked us like we were animals. One man pushed me against a wall and damn near choked me to death. If it weren't for the officer firing his gun to break up the violence, I don't know what would have happened."

Ms. Ringwell took another gulp from the glass. Sutherland absorbed the story she told thus far with a grain of salt due to her unstable psychological state. His impatience began to boil.

"Where are the victims being held?"

"We stacked people in every inch and corner of the hospital. We even had to double up siblings on some beds. We..."

Straying off topic, the detective became more and more impatient. He felt a surge of anger build up in his chest.

"Where are the victims?" he asked in a raised voice.

Perplexed and slightly delirious, Ms. Ringwell shook her head with confusion and exhaustion.

"I don't know. I don't remember," she said pathetically.

"Ms. Ringwell. Where are the victims?" asked Sutherland.

"I don't know!" screamed Ms. Ringwell.

Ms. Ringwell began to weep. Detective Sutherland nearly banged his hand against the table in anger. He gently pushed his fist down on the table and looked at the crying woman.

"Were there deaths? Did you lose people after 'The Incident'?"

Ms. Ringwell's crying slowed down. She looked up at the detective and nodded her head in fear and guilt. She sniffled and cleared her throat.

"There will be," she said softly.

"What does that mean?" he inquired.

The Town of Jasper

"There's not going to be deaths," she stated. "There's going to be murders."

Grasping his full attention, Sutherland leaned over and whispered to the hysterical woman.

"Is it him? Richard Morrissey? Where is he?"

The woman shed more tears and sniffed through her nostrils.
She looked up at him with bloodshot eyes.

"It's not him," she whispered.

Confused, the detective looked at her curiously.

"*Them.* Those *goddamn* monsters," she said softly.

"Monsters? Who? Who are you talking about? How many did they kill?"

"They threatened my life. I saw them one night. They only come out at night. They said they'd do things to me if I spoke about the things they're going to do," she said in horror.

Repulsed and disturbed, the detective was at a loss for words.

"What is it? What are they going to do? You can tell me," he asked calmly.

"They promise redemption and rebirth of the fallen. They say things are going to go back. Things are going to turn," she said.

"Ms. Ringwell, I don't understand. Who are these people?" Sutherland asked again.

Ms. Ringwell sat up straight and leaned across the table. She seemed weak, barely able to lean across it. The detective inched closer to her. She whispered to him from a few feet away.

"They are coming, Detective. It's going to happen. And soon."

Sutherland looked at her, eager for the reveal of what she was talking about. His hands were on the table as he leaned in, putting balance on his forearms and elbows.

"Who is coming?"

Ms. Ringwell's hands trembled as she remembered the atrocity and barbarity. The trembling from her hands soon made their way to her face as she shook as if she was being mildly electrocuted. She blinked constantly and struggled to find the words.

"The ones with the faces like coal."

The Town of Jasper

Pseudonyms & Conundrums

Two Months Before "The Incident"
July 2011

There was a long, white fence along the side of the road that caught Richard's eye as he and Sutherland drove leisurely down the streets of suburbia. It was a quiet and soothing ride as usual.

"My kid is turning seven on Thursday," said Sutherland. "Any ideas of what I should get her?"

Richard did not acknowledge the question, as his attention was still fixed on the fence and the scenery outside the moving vehicle.

"Hey…" Sutherland said, waking Richard from his stare.

Richard looked at him as if he just woke from a long nap. Sutherland glanced at him, but also managed to keep his eyes on the road.

"What's that?" Richard asked.

Sutherland glimpsed at him for a few seconds, suggesting he was an idiot for not listening to his question.

"My seven-year old. Birthday. What should I get her?"

"I don't know. What does she like?"

Sutherland shrugged his shoulders, one hand on the wheel.

"Maybe I'll get her one of those doll sets or something. I don't know."

"That could work."

"Well, you have a little girl. What does she like?"

Richard leaned forward and stretched out his back. He ran his fingers through his hair and removed his sunglasses.

"I usually get her what she asks for," said Richard.

Sutherland looked at him as if he cracked the code to a scientific formula. His long time partner looked back at him and put his sunglasses back on.

"Just ask her," Richard repeated.

"I can't," said Sutherland.

"Why?"

"She's mentally disabled. Remember."

"Yes, I'm sorry. It was my fault for asking."

"No. Trust me, it was *my fault* for asking," said Sutherland.

"You and Olivia going to do something for her? Maybe a birthday party so I can finally meet your adoring future ex wife and loving daughter. Or has no progress been made in that area yet?"

"Not really. We're still going through some *changes* right now. We're not very pleasant to be around."

"You've been going through *changes* since I've known you. If you don't want me to come over, if that's the reason, just tell me," said Richard jokingly.

"Shut up," said Sutherland

He adjusted his seat's position with his left hand and kept his right hand on the wheel. The two of them sat quietly as Richard began to think to himself.

"We should talk," Richard said.

"About what?"

"About you. About what you did."

Sutherland became annoyed and let out a sigh. Richard glanced at him quickly, hoping he would talk.

"There's nothing to talk about. The guy was a criminal who was selling drugs to kids who don't know any better. I don't give a fuck about the politically correct bullshit when sixteen year olds are shooting up instead of getting a proper education."

Richard did not disagree with Sutherland's statement. However, he had become fearful of Sutherland's mental stability as of late.

"You've been different since the accident. Reckless. Dangerous. You have your reasons, and I'm not saying you're wrong."

"What are you saying?" asked Sutherland.

Richard averted his gaze to the surrounding suburban area instead of at Sutherland. After a few seconds, Richard looked over at Sutherland.

"Just make sure those reasons don't end with a gun pointed at your face."

They drove further down the road with the radio playing at a low volume. It was jazz music. Richard liked listening to it because he found it soothing.

"How do you make it work?" asked Sutherland.

"What?"

"You and your wife. How do you make it work?"

"It just does," said Richard.

"My therapist tells me I should be able to be myself around her. And if I'm not, then I might have made a mistake," said Sutherland. "But it was no mistake. I am who I am around her, and that's why we have problems."

Richard did not respond to the remark as he looked outside the window. He thought about Diane and what it was that made them so perfect for one another. The pause in the conversation went on for a moment.

"The reason why it works for us...it's not because I can be *myself* around her. It's because I can be the person I *want* to be around her," said Richard.

Sutherland shot a glance over at Richard and did not reply. He understood the difference.

"I swear sometimes I can just see the light, and it makes me feel something. Like a change is coming. I don't know if it's a good or bad one, but a change. Like life is going to get different," said Sutherland. "But what scares the hell out of me is what happens when I get there. The 'what happens next' part."

"Things always turn," said Richard assuredly. "Guys like us, we're always fighting like hell for the good when the shit hits. And then when times get better, we prepare for the shit to hit. It's who we are. What we've become."

Sutherland looked over at Richard, who spoke fluently and confidently like he always did. Sutherland looked back at the road as he drove with one hand and scratched his right knee with the other.

"That light at the end of that dark passage. There's always another dark passage after it," said Richard. "Thing's always turn."

Looking to change the subject, Sutherland thought of something quick.

"So what do you think of this?" he asked in regard to the case.

Richard disregarded the question as he fixed his gaze ahead through the windshield. They were coming up on a farm that spanned nearly twenty acres. Something in the distance caused Richard's concern.

"What?" Sutherland asked.

The farmhouse was a cliché, with its massive land and a big red barn. The house was old and beautiful, standing two stories high and painted a yellowish beige that reminded them of a sunset. Sutherland pulled onto the land and drove up the path to the house, kicking up a dust storm behind them. As they drove, Richard continued to admire the land curiously.

"You have something on your mind," said Sutherland. "What do you see?"

"It's not what I see...it's what I *don't*," said Richard calmly.

Sutherland looked at his friend for a moment and found himself equally curious about the peculiar surrounding. He drove slowly as he scanned the land.

"Where are all the farm animals?" asked Richard. "And why are the crops all dead?"

Detective Sutherland drove slowly up the path to the yellowish beige house. He looked at Richard again, who was looking out the side window.

"So what do you think of this?" he asked again.

Richard looked at him with no real sign of concern or emotion.

"I think we got a farm with no animals and no crops. And a farm with no animals and no crops is no farm at all," he said.

The car came to a stop in front of the house. The two detectives stepped out of the vehicle and approached the house with more reluctance than caution. Detective Sutherland knocked on the door. The two of them looked around from the front porch. The property was inert and lonely. They looked inside the window next to the door to see if anyone was home. The two began to tiptoe around the porch as they waited.

"Hey, let me ask you something," said Sutherland.

Richard stopped his wandering and looked up at him.

"What's that?"

"Don't you get tired of using fake names for each case? Why do you always use a different pseudonym?"

"It would take the fun out of it," said Richard playfully.

"Asshole," said Sutherland as he paced around.

"If you really want to know, check my file…"

"No. I told myself I would make it my duty to get it out of you…"

"You won't," said Richard confidently. "I think it's best no one knows my identity, given our job description. We've gone over this how many times? The last thing I need is some lunatic tracing their way to my family."

Detective Sutherland looked at Richard with his arms crossed in an annoyed, yet understanding fashion.

"Besides, you're a detective. You'll find it out one way or another."

"So you're referring to me as a lunatic?" asked Sutherland, reverting back to the previous statement.

"No, you're harmless," Richard said jokingly.

Sutherland smiled and raised his eyebrows as he leaned forward towards his partner and friend.

"Harmless? My hairy, pale ass! You want to see harmless, I'll…"

The door opened, and an older woman answered. They both gathered themselves by standing up straight and brushing their suits with their hands.

"Hello, ma'am. My name is Detective Sutherland, and this is my partner…"

Sutherland gestured to Richard to say his name. However, Richard looked at Sutherland cool and collectively and then fixed his eyes on the old woman.

"Detective Wembley," he said.

The Town of Jasper

"Nice to meet you both. I'm Mary. I'm glad you're here. Can I get you gentleman anything?" asked the old woman.

"No, thank you, miss," said Sutherland.

"Please, follow me," requested Mary.

The two of them followed Mary off the front porch and around the house. Sutherland looked at his partner with a baffled and playful expression.

"Wembley? Where'd you pull that from?"

"Your hairy, pale ass," said Richard jokingly.

Sutherland shook his head as they followed Mary to the crime scene. The sun spread over the land like butter on toast, creating a dazzlingly vivid atmosphere. In the back of the house was a large cornfield. The crops were all dead and mysteriously dried out. The two of them began to sweat as they followed the old woman into the cornfield. Sutherland touched his sidearm and signaled to Richard to do the same. Both men entered with extreme caution.

"Excuse me, miss. If you don't mind me asking, why are all of your crops not growing?" asked Sutherland.

"Oh, well, I don't even know how to explain it. It's a freak thing. I planted everything properly, and there was just no harvest. Nothing," she said.

"And what about the animals? Where are they?" asked Richard.

"Oh, well, they're inside the barns today. Too hot for them to come out. I had to sell some of them this year to keep afloat."

Richard was perplexed to say the least. However, he didn't think much into it, as it was not his place or assigned task to look into.

"It's just up ahead now," Mary said as they got deeper into the heart of the field.

Their footsteps caused a ruckus of crackling and snapping sounds. Up ahead, someone was lying on the ground. The person was on their stomach with their face planted in the ground. As they both got closer, Mary stood back, as she couldn't stomach the site. The victim sported a denim jacket and brown pants. The deceased person was a male. Detective Sutherland knelt down to examine the corpse. There were stab wounds speckled across the man's back.

"How long's he been here?"

"Had to be last night. I do a full sweep of the property every morning with my dogs," Mary said. "They would have detected this if it happened before then."

Sutherland examined the stab wounds closer and looked around at the body while Richard examined the area around him trying to pinpoint the path in which he came from. Sutherland turned the body over and was taken aback. More stab wounds were scattered across the man's chest. Richard looked back at the man now turned on his back and didn't flinch at the gruesome scene. Sutherland looked up at him from his knees.

"Multiple stab wounds, almost definitely a homicide. Probably on the run from someone and tried to lose him in here. Probably bled out before he could escape."

"Could have been hiding in here," chimed Richard.

"*Possibly*," said Sutherland with a glance at him.

"Do you recognize this man?" Richard asked Mary.

Mary glanced at the corpse long enough to know if she recognized the man's face. She cringed back after the brief glance.

"No, I don't. I've never seen him before," she said.

"You're sure?" asked Sutherland.

"Yes," she repeated. "I'm sure."

The Town of Jasper

Richard began to walk down a straight line. He followed the man's fresh footprints that were still relatively fresh. The humidity made him wipe his forehead as he paced as slowly and gracefully as he could. The man's tracks led all the way out of the dead cornfield and into the nearby woods. Richard stopped and looked into the deep woods, trying to pinpoint a conclusion as to what direction he came from and what or whom he was running from. It was probably a straightforward flee from danger case, where the man probably owed someone money. Most likely a loan shark or mobster. There weren't many cases like this in the small town of Woodland. Richard walked back to the crime scene and found Sutherland laying out the man's belongings.

"We got a wallet, a Swiss knife, a cell phone, some change, and a little bag of a familiar face," said Sutherland, holding up a small plastic bag of heroin. "I don't think our pal here is from around these neck of the woods, hence the Nebraska license…you find anything?"

"He came from the woods. Had to have been late last night. Possibly the early morning. His trail is still fresh. I'm gonna do another pass."

"Fair enough. Ma'am we are going to call in some forensic investigators and analysts to block off the area here, and we're going to do what we can to get to the bottom of everything, so you can go back to living your life," said Sutherland.

"Okay. Whatever you need to do is fine," said Mary.

Sutherland got on his COM and called in the necessary units. He remained knelt down as he signaled headquarters. After he released the button on the COM, he saw something at the corner of his eye through the blinding rays of the sun. On the tight trail inside the cornfield, Sutherland saw his daughter Shannon. Her soft, long hair wafted delicately in the breeze. He squinted while his pupils doubled in size. She was waving to him the way she used in their living room window when he'd leave for work. The way she used to wave at him before the crash. The sun's rays beat down on Sutherland's eyes as he found himself waving back to the side effect of the previous night's booze and the morning's narcotics. Sutherland never heard Richard talking to him as he fell stunned at the apparition of his beloved daughter.

"Hey…" interjected Richard. "Jack!"

Sutherland snapped out of it and looked up at Richard, who looked down at him, awaiting an answer.

"What?" asked Sutherland.

"I found this in the center of the cornfield."

Sutherland looked back at the trail and saw that his daughter was gone. Grief and angst conquered his mind and heart as he got up off the ground and saw Richard holding a gun case. Richard placed it on the ground and revealed the weapons inside it.

"Sawed-off, fifteen inch barrel, Bushmaster Carbon 15, SCAR, Thompson T1B," said Richard.

"These aren't legal," said Sutherland.

The two overlooked the firearms for a few moments and said nothing. Finally, Sutherland spoke out.

"What about an E-Z Bake oven?"

"E-Z Bake oven," confirmed Richard.

"Yeah. Right," said Sutherland.

"You don't want to buy her one of those."

"Why not?"

"Do you like to bake?"

"No."

"Than don't buy it for her."

"What do you mean?"

"I mean, every night all you're going to hear is 'Daddy help me bake', and I know you have a soft spot, and you can never say no. So unless you plan on becoming an amateur, part-time muffin man, don't buy it."

Sutherland stood up and put his hands on his hips. He was in a pickle and had no idea what to do about it.

"So what should I do?"

Richard looked at Sutherland and smiled slightly.

"Just ask her," he said as he patted him on the shoulder and walked by him.

THE RICH AND THE RAGS

Present Day, 2016
Five Years After "The Incident"

The convoy came to a halt. The adrenaline pumped in their veins as each man waited for Richard to make the first move. Richard examined the steep hill before them and pulled on the lever that opened his door. The rest of the men exited their vehicles and looked around at the environment. Each man looked at one another, confused, without much to say. The whole scene led some of the men to have doubtful thoughts.

"I bet they're watching us right now," said Dallas.

A man named Jim reached for his hunter's rifle in the bed of his truck.

"No," Richard said firmly.

Jim, in his usual camouflaged hunting attire and brown cap looked at Richard somewhat confused.

"Put it back," Richard demanded.

Jim placed the weapon back down gently and became annoyed at the fact that they were going in somewhat defenseless. Richard stared at Jim after he placed the gun back with the look of a father looking down at his undisciplined child. He looked at the rest of the group, determined. Richard walked in front of the group of men, with his long black overcoat blowing gracefully in the frigid airstream.

"If you're wondering if they're here, if they're watching us, or if they're dangerous, the answer is yes. Stay focused, stay close, and don't show fear. Weapons tucked away. Gary, Kendrick, and Liam, stay here. If we're not back in two hours, stick to the plan.

The Town of Jasper

Full clips, safety off, and a round in the chamber. They'll see you before you see them, so be ready. The rest of us, let's move."

The group of men proceeded up the path into the wilderness. The forest was dark and gloomy, with a damp feeling to it. Wet leaves littered the ground as the men walked softly over them. Trying to keep quiet as best as possible, the men tried not to be the last in line. Richard led the group full steam ahead. Remembering the area from hiking with his father, he knew he had a ways to go before he reached their community. The surrounding trees, leaves, and rocks gave the men a chilling sensation up and down their spines. Some men exhaled heavily, trying to rid their nerves. The air was nippy, and the sky was grey. The group of men walked closely together, almost like they were magnetized to one another. Dallas, feeling jumpy since he left the car, walked slowly and tried his best not to look around. Jim walked behind Dallas and clumsily stepped on a branch, which made a loud cracking noise. The sound of the snapping twig made Dallas jump with fear.

"Ah!" yelped Dallas.

The group turned around quickly and looked at the two of them. Jim put his hands up.

"It's okay. Just a branch. No one panic," he said.

The rest of the group shook their heads, while Richard did not bother to acknowledge the situation. He stopped and looked up at the landscape. He gave a slow, panoramic stare at the wooded area. The men looked at him, awaiting his motion forward. Richard gave another keen look at the adjacent areas from their position.

Finally, Richard started moving forward with his band of frightened men following closely behind.

"What the hell are we doin' here?" asked a man named Simpson. "We're sitting ducks for these freaks."

"Quiet your voice," snapped Gary with a whisper.

"Screw you, Ford. We shouldn't even be here! This is a suicide mission," said Simpson, unconvinced.

"Shut the hell up," whispered Dallas, who became petrified.

The group continued to walk quietly ahead into the darkness. As he walked, Richard gave a look in a different direction every ten steps. While everyone else was oblivious, Richard knew.

"How much further, boss?" asked a young kid named Jason. He sported a grey sweatshirt with his hood up.

Richard did not look back at the boy. He walked slower, as he heard the faint sound of the Jasper River up ahead.

"Don't worry about the distance. Just worry about getting your right hand out of your pocket. If they see that, they'll think you have something that can harm them in it. And if they think that, they'll make sure they kill you before you kill them," Richard said.

Richard had eyes in the back and sides of his head. He saw everything. Something his father taught him about always being aware of your surroundings. The Jasper River was now on their right as they got closer. Richard remembered the path from years back. Images from that day popped in and out of his head as the Jasper River flowed gracefully. The men looked at the fresh water like a teenager seeing a woman's breasts for the first time. A few men spoke out from behind Richard.

"That looks fresh."

"Probably cold too."

"Should we…"

"Don't dare break formation," demanded Richard.

The men all puckered up at Richard's command, like soldiers addressing a high-ranking officer. The men were thirsty. With supplies running thin, some of them hadn't tasted cold water in weeks.

The Town of Jasper

"If all goes according to plan, you'll be drinking it soon," Richard claimed. "Let's keep moving. And don't look at the damn river."

Richard marched ahead with the men tailing close behind. Each of them dreaming of fresh water and a full meal in their stomachs. The path ahead contained trees for miles to their right and left. The narrow path had fresh tracks on it. Richard knelt down and observed them. A couple of men looked over Richard to catch a glimpse.

"Are those fresh?" asked Jim.

Richard pointed his finger at the prints to try to make sense of it. Richard looked up ahead at the distance. He extended is legs upward and stood tall as he gaped with an interested expression. Richard knew. The rest were oblivious. But Richard knew. He walked slowly up ahead. The thought of fresh tracks made most of the men behind him uneasy. Keeping at a less than moderate pace, Richard surveyed the area more extensively. He tried his best to look through the dark woods beside them. He didn't look to see if they were there; he knew they were. Richard felt a degree of relief that he hadn't been killed yet. Keeping at the same pace, they coasted forward, one foot in front of the other. Their steps were soft and quiet. They walked the same way a teenager would when they would sneak out of the house late at night and hope to not wake their parents. The men behind Richard began looking to their sides, trembling with fear. Some even stepped on each other's feet, not paying attention enough to watch their footing. Out of the corner of his eye, Richard saw a shadowy figure speed through the trees. Richard nearly came to a stop but decided to keep moving forward and disregard it. Fortunately, the men behind him didn't see it. They were all as silent as church mice as they got closer to the end of the path. They were all oblivious. But Richard knew. As they continued their trek for another fifty yards, the shadowy figure sped through the dark wilderness again. Richard caught the sudden movement from his peripherals and reached for his knife that he usually kept at his side. After remembering his own 'no weapons in sight' policy, he resisted. The tracks on the path had vanished, which grasped Richard's attention immediately. However, before he could process another thought, the shadowy figure burst out of the wilderness with a full head of steam. Richard halted as the men behind him did the same. Nearly giving all of them a heart attack, the group of men locked eyes on the figure that now stood directly ahead. In front of them stood a massive buck. Weighing nearly two hundred pounds, Richard counted ten pointers on its rack. The animal stopped dead in its track as soon as it noticed them. It stared at them with its pitch-black marble eyes. The group's hearts pumped out of their chests as they froze still, staring at the buck. They were oblivious. But Richard knew. The buck, equally as petrified, stood awkwardly and stared at them, not knowing what to do. Richard could see the fear in its eyes. They were oblivious. But Richard knew. Richard knew the animal wasn't staring at them with fear. It was staring at what was behind them.

"Nobody move," Richard said. "They're right behind us."

Each member of the group, including Richard, did not move a single muscle in their body. The sheer feeling of trepidation made each person incapable of moving.

"Holy shit, holy shit," whispered Dallas.

"What the hell do we do?" asked Jim quietly.

The sound of something stretching could be heard behind them. It sounded like someone pulling back on the knocking point of a bow and arrow. Richard swallowed hard as the other men tried their best to keep still. Richard's eyes remained on the buck in front of them, who was also doing its best to remain stationary. The pulling sound stopped, which made Richard's heart feel as light as a feather. A few moments passed.

"FEEEEYEEEEWF!"

The three-foot arrow struck the buck directly between the lung and the shoulder blade. The arrow came from their right. The scene made the men jump with shock.

"Holy shit!" screamed Jason.

The buck let out a quick cry of pain and tried galloping away.

"FEEEEYEEEEWF!"

The second arrow came from their left and pierced right through its jugular. The buck fell hard to the ground and died instantly. Richard looked at the dead animal laying on the ground, knowing damn well he and his group would suffer a similar fate if they tried to run.

"Everyone put your hands up. Now," Richard commanded.

"Richard," said Dallas, nearly pissing his pants. "They're going to kill us if we do."

His men looked at him with tears of fear nearly tricking down their cheeks. Finally, they reluctantly raised their hands in the air. Richard did the same.

"Slowly turn around," Richard asked.

The men shifted their bodies as slow as possible one hundred and eighty degrees. Richard did the same. The men, who had never seen one of them before, were about to witness a century-old local legend. They only knew them through bullshit stories from drunken idiots at bars, or crazy people from town who hated the fact they lived so close to them. As the men turned, they braced their eyes, as everything that was told to them was about to go out the window. As each man turned, they laid their eyes on them. The horror painted across the men's faces with their hands in the air. They did not dare to think about making a sound. The men looked upon a group of twenty Fillmore Whites. Their ragged clothing and pale skin made the men's skin creep. Their deformities made their legs tremble. Too petrified to process rational thought, the group nearly pissed themselves at the sight of their sharp weapons. The group of Fillmore Whites stood in attack formation, ready to gut all of them with a few strokes of their blades. Richard was the last to turn around with his hands up. The two groups stood looking at one another for what seemed like hours. About three minutes passed before Richard made the decision to make the first move. He slowly moved forward between his men, grazing their elbows and shoulders. Each of them looked at Richard like he was absolutely mad as he made his way into the line of fire. Richard looked at the albino people, unafraid, with his hands just above his ears. The Fillmores, ready to attack at the first sudden movement, watched him closely. No more than twenty yards apart, Richard saw a vision playing out in his head. He saw his wife Diane sleeping beside him in their bedroom. His son who was only four years old rushed in the room and tugged on his sheets to wake him up. He looked at his son who whispered at the floor in the softest, most fragile voice.

"I can't sleep. The monsters are making noises in the closet."

Richard looked at his son and remembered that this vision was of a day that had happened before. Richard remembered what he told him.

"What do you want me to do? Do you want to sleep with me and mommy?"

The Town of Jasper

"No. I want you to open the closet and kill them. Before they get Victoria."

Richard stood before the large pack of Fillmore Whites. He didn't have anything to lose at this point. He felt like he was levitating as he opened his mouth.

"My name is Richard Morrissey. We are not here to cause harm. These are some of my people. We need your help."

Richard stood in between both groups with his hands raised. The Fillmore Whites, looked at him intently, showing no signs of peace or welcome. Richard examined the several standing in the front lines.

"Our town has sick people. We are in desperate need of food and water," Richard said calmly.

The Fillmore Whites remained in attack formation, unimpressed by Richard's request to barter. They were ready to strike. Each of them wanted nothing more than to see what Richard's insides looked like. Groaning and clenching their rotten teeth, they gripped their spears, axes, and machetes, ready to fight.

"May I speak to the one in charge?" asked Richard somewhat politely.

One Fillmore stepped up and pointed his razor-sharp edged wooden spear at Richard. His physique resembled that of a Trojan warrior. The right side of his jaw was indented significantly. His left eye was black, while his right was bright red. Richard exchanged a glance of serenity, which proved his bravery given the dire situation he was in. The brawny Fillmore White took another healthy step toward Richard with his spear pointed directly at him.

"YEW. SHOULD NOT BE HERE," he said loudly. His tone was brute like and heavy.

Richard did not flinch at the man's aggressive, high-pitched voice.

"I know we're trespassing on your land," he said. "But…"

"YOU HAVE COME TO HARM US?" shouted the albino man.

"No," Richard said softly. "We did not come to fight. We came to help."

The Fillmore White, whose temper began to rise, handed his spear to the Fillmore White next to him. The man marched towards Richard who placed his hands down. The Fillmore White picked up steam as he inhaled and exhaled loudly. His expression became grim and uncompromising while he walked with heavy feet up to Richard. The giant of a man tightly gripped his right hand around Richard's neck. The men behind Richard drew their guns and took aim at the members of the tribe with trembling hands. The Fillmore Whites behind their alleged leader readied their spears and pulled back on their bows, ready for a fight. Richard choked and gagged as the Fillmore White grasped his six fingers perfectly around Richard's jugular. Losing oxygen, Richard continued to stay calm and fearless. The Fillmore, nearly lifting Richard off the ground, breathed out a toxic vapor of breath that would have made Richard vomit if not for the man's hand blocking his throat's passageway. It wasn't until Richard was inches away from the man's face that he noticed his third eye. Located just above his nose, his third pupil was half the size of the other two.

"NO HELP," said the man in a cavernous tone.

The Fillmore reached for his hand blade and began to unsheathe it from his side. Richard's men stood behind, ready to fire. Fearing this was the end, Richard could hear the metal blade grazing against the man's holster as he pulled it out. Richard looked directly into the Fillmore White's eyes with a look of emptiness.

Richard didn't see the end in his last moments, he just saw his son beside his bed. He heard him whisper.

"Will you make the monsters go away?"

The Fillmore White, gripping a nearly unconscious Richard, groaned angrily at him and kneed him in the stomach forcefully. Richard let out a moan and fell to his knees. The brute of a man brought down his right forearm hard against Richard's back, which caused him to hit the ground. The albino man grabbed the back of Richard's shirt and whispered to him.

"No help," the Fillmore White said.

The albino leader raised his blade up in the air with his right hand, ready to sever Richard's head with one swing. Richard's men gripped the handles of their guns tightly, ready to take every last savage out. Before the enormous Fillmore White could bring the sharp-edged machete down against Richard's neck, a man appeared from the woods.

"HOHNWYA!" hollered the mysterious man.

The Fillmore with the machete looked up at the man walking out of the woods and let go of Richard. He placed the machete back in his holster and watched the man approach him slowly. The mysterious man was a Fillmore White. He walked gradually up to the machete wielding Fillmore and shot him a disappointed look. The albino man looked down at Richard, who tried to catch his breath and composure. The mysterious man, about six feet tall, with pale skin, dark black hair, and a boyish face, reached his scrawny arm out for Richard. The man's unbecoming attire extended to his kneecaps, showing off his scrawny, pasty legs. Richard looked at the man, who exchanged a friendly smile. He ignored his friendly gesture and got himself up off the ground. Richard looked at the man who showed an expression of friendliness firmly. Richard's men remained in a ready to fire stance.

"I remember you," the Fillmore White said in near perfect English.

Richard looked surprised at his smooth translation. Richard became curious about how the man remembered him. Dressed in shredded, stained clothing, the man's expression of friendliness turned somewhat strict.

"Your father saved my father years back. I remember the day every day," the albino man said.

Richard looked at the man, more intrigued than puzzled.

"When I saw you walk onto our land. I wasn't certain. But when you said your name just now. I knew it had to be you…Richard. Son of my father's savior."

Richard didn't say anything to the man. He stood in front of him and slightly nodded his head. The albino man reached out his hand. Richard looked down his frosty white forearm at the man's hand. He counted five fingers. The man was offering a handshake. Richard looked at the man's face, which grinned at him. His eyes were a shade of pink, or maybe red.

"My name is Edmund. Nice to meet you, Richard."

Richard processed Edmund's gesture for a moment. He focused in on the man's colorless fingers long enough to make it awkward. After a few moments, Richard looked up at the leader of the Fillmore Whites and shook his hand firmly. Edmund smiled at him as they gripped each other's hands and shook. Once they released, Richard took a relatively deep breath as he looked behind Edmund at his group of blood hungry natives.

"My community is in danger. Something's happened. It's difficult to explain…"

"I know," said Edmund.

The Town of Jasper

Richard looked at him inquisitively.

"Just because there is a boundary between us doesn't mean we don't know things that are happening," Edmund stated.

"Then you know that we need your help," said Richard.

"Our kinds have never seen eye to eye. Especially not in the flesh like this. Why would we help a community that does not welcome my people?"

Richard was not anticipating a verbal debate such as this with a Fillmore White. He found it quite comforting to have a coherent, intellectual discussion with one of them.

"I didn't come here expecting it to be easy. But we can help you as much as you can help us," Richard assured.

Edmund smiled and gave a small chuckle. He glanced over Richard's shoulder at the men who looked on unsure if they were in danger or not anymore.

"You are a lot like your father. A natural leader. I'll never forget what you and he did. In a way, I owe you a favor. But I'm afraid I can't help you. I'm sorry, son of my father's savior."

"How many of your people are there?" asked Richard.

Edmund looked at him closely.

"Are you threatening me?"

Richard looked at him with sweat accumulating on his face. His expression was daring and bold, but Edmund's expression rivaled that of Richards.

"I think it's time you leave," suggested Edmund.

Edmund turned his back and walked away. Richard called out to him.

"We can barter," Richard shouted.

Edmund turned around and looked at him.

"We can trade," Richard repeated.

Edmund took a step forward and looked at Richard, skeptical of his offer.

"And what would you have to offer us?" Edmund asked.

"We have money," Richard said.

Edmund chuckled out loud as he became incredibly amused at such an outlandish offer of exchange.

"And do what with it? Stroll through your little town, shop in your nice little stores, donate to the needy in your big town church?"

Richard looked away from him as he became frustrated with the stalemate. Edmund turned his body around and started to walk away.

"We have three trucks of supplies. There's warm clothes, weapons, ammunition, and medicine," Richard stated firmly.

Edmund turned around and looked at Richard, intrigued. These were things he and his people could use. Richard knew that. They needed the warmer clothes for the harsh winters and the guns and ammunition would allow them to hunt their prey with ease. They were also desperate for even the most basic supplies.

"There's more than enough in the trucks for the group of you."

Edmund looked at Richard, intrigued with the potential exchange of goods. The two men stood in front of their men as Richard awaited a response. Edmund looked over his shoulder at his group of men. He looked down at the ground with his right hand around his hip with a look of remorse mixed with exhaustion.

"Why did your father save mine that day? Why didn't he just leave him for dead?" Edmund asked while he stared at the soil.

Richard let the question stand in between them for a several moments. Richard let the question saturate in his head for a few moments and walked quickly in long, heavy strides up to

Edmund. He got up close to Edmund and looked him straight in the eyes from no more than a foot away. He whispered to him as Edmund looked at him relatively astounded by his advance.

"Because he was a human *being*. Just like me. Just like you," Richard said in a hollow tone.

Edmund looked into Richard's eyes, impressed.

"What makes you believe we are alike?" asked Edmund.

Richard backed away a foot or two and gazed upon Edmund.

"Why did you stop your men from killing us?" Richard asked.

Edmund looked at him and gave a cheerful smirk. He nodded his head in approval and extended his hand. Richard looked at his fingers for a moment and gripped tightly onto his new friend's hand. The two released their hands from one another's grip and Edmund looked over Richard's left shoulder. He let out a loud whistle that echoed throughout the vicinity. In unison, nearly a hundred Fillmore Whites appeared from the woods in all directions. Richard looked around, astonished. Richard's men looked on in amazement and became overwhelmed at the sight of how many there were. Edmund looked at Richard and gave him a pat on the shoulder.

"Let's go take a look at your trucks," he said in a friendly tone.

By the time the trucks were unloaded, the sun began to set. It would be a little over an hour until it was dark. As the men unloaded the last of the supplies from the beds, Edmund inspected the cargo carefully. As he did this, Richard spoke to him.

"We load up on what you can give us today, and I'll return first thing tomorrow," Richard stated.

Edmund inspected the cargo and approved. He gestured to a few bulky men to carry it away. Two tall, brawny men picked up some supplies and carried them away. Edmund walked up to Richard slowly.

"Before you leave, my friend. Walk with me. My people will help load your trucks with fresh water and some food," said Edmund.

Curious, Richard looked at his men and nodded.

"Fire up the engines. We're leaving in ten," Richard stated firmly.

Richard walked with Edmund past groups of his men carrying fresh water, vegetables, fruits, and other resources towards the trucks. Richard looked around and saw something up ahead.

"Your people. I'm sorry for what's happening to them," said Edmund sympathetically. "The Almighty sometimes has an *unexplainable* way of testing us."

"You think this is all a 'test'?" asked Richard.

"I certainly hope so. If not, it's a punishment," said Edmund.

"Punishment from what?" asked Richard.

"I'm not sure. I wish I had the answers to most things. But I'm just a man in charge of a community of outcasts. And you. You are just a man in charge of a community of outcasts."

Richard stopped and looked at Edmund. Edmund looked at Richard with a neutral look.

"Like you said. We are alike," Edmund reassured him.

Richard ignored the statement and walked onward with Edmund. The path was leading to something as more Fillmore Whites walked by them, looking at Richard questionably.

"What happened to your father?" asked Richard.

The Town of Jasper

Edmund let the question digest as he walked slowly along the path.

"He died. It's been several years since he passed. The winter was hard on his lungs. He wasn't strong enough. We didn't have enough to keep him alive."

Richard nearly stopped to offer condolences. However, he just walked slower.

"I'm sorry," Richard said.

Edmund nodded his head remorsefully. He looked at Richard with a look of sadness mixed with defeat.

"And yours?" Edmund asked inquisitively.

Richard did not answer. He looked down at the ground, trying to allow his silence to answer the question for him.

Edmund nodded his head and looked down as well.

"If it weren't for him, my father would have died at that ravine. And you and I wouldn't be talking right now," said Edmund.

There was a brief pause in the conversation as Edmund walked forward and looked around until he fixed his eyes back on Richard.

"Part of me just wishes you came a little earlier."

Richard looked down as he felt a deep sorrow overcome him. There was another pause in the conversation as they walked another twenty feet.

"I'm here *now.*" Richard said in a low, yet deep tone.

Edmund looked at him and smiled.

"Yes. You are here, now," said Edmund.

They had reached the end of the trail, which provided one of the most incredible views Richard has ever laid eyes on. Edmund smiled as he looked at the awe on Richard's face. In front of them were hundreds of acres of land, with animals of all kinds and small wooden huts in a row. In the center were about a dozen greenhouses, spanning five hundred feet long and two hundred feet wide.

"You built this?" Richard asked shockingly.

"Not just me. My people." Edmund said.

"How?" Richard asked.

"After your father saved my mine, I took it upon myself to learn everything about your kind. Your language, your styles, and your way of life. It was the only way our people could have survived. And now we can do more than just survive," Edmund said proudly.

Richard felt honored that his father was such a significant part of the formation of their community. Richard began to feel a sense of hope, as he saw more than enough resources to help save his own community. Richard continued to look around at everything. He studied every corner of the place as best he could.

"This is incredible," Richard stated.

"It is. After the horrible day, none of our plants or seeds would grow or blossom. They were all dead. Then a few days later, they grew again. Much faster and much bigger. It was a miracle," said Edmund. "But there is still much work to be done. While we have food, water, and shelter, my people still suffer. We may be flourishing, but we are not at our strongest state. Not yet." Edmund claimed.

"We can help you achieve that," Richard assured.

Edmund nodded proudly, knowing it to be true.

"You offered us money." Edmund said.

Richard did not say anything. Edmund looked at him sternly.

"You must know that money isn't the key to the door. Even when your people were awake, it was insignificant to the things you and your kind take for granted every day."

The Town of Jasper

Richard listened, intrigued by the topic of conversation.

"*My People.* Some of them weren't fortunate enough to have been born with all of their limbs. Some of them even have more than the common man. Some can't walk, some are blind, others can't taste, most can't feel, and none can smell. And those are the lucky ones."

Richard became empathetic as he listened on.

"Your people, the ones who are still awake. They're all the wealthiest people in the world," Edmund declared.

Richard was at a loss for words. Edmund walked up closely to him.

"Close your eyes, friend," he asked politely.

Richard shut his eyes and saw complete darkness as Edmund watched.

"Would you trade any dollar amount to not have the eyes you have shut? To not be able to open them and see your children grow?"

Richard kept his eyes shut, but pictured an image of his family at a birthday party in his head. He saw his son riding without training wheels for the first time. He saw his daughter jumping up and down with a five-dollar bill she got from the tooth fairy after she lost her first tooth. Richard felt his emotions stir in his stomach. Edmund walked up to Richard and gently gripped his hand. Edmund began to speak, emotionally poignant.

"How much is it worth to you to be able to feel the softness of a flower bud or the roughness of tree bark? To hear the sounds of birds in the morning?"

Richard could hear the crackle and sorrow in Edmund's voice.

"To smell an oven with a holiday turkey…to taste the flavor of a Georgia peach?"

Richard opened his eyes and saw tears trickling down Edmund's face. Richard didn't know what to say or do. Edmund let go and wiped away his tears with his forearms. He looked at Richard with tear soaked eyes.

"There is no price big enough to buy those things. Your people have them at no cost," Edmund said as he wiped his cheeks quickly.

Richard stood there, helpless. Wishing he could do or say something to ease things over with his new friend, Richard reached under his shirt for the pistol wedged in between his pants. He handed it to Edmund who looked at the weapon.

"Keep it," said Edmund.

"Take it," Richard nearly demanded.

Edmund reached for the weapon hesitantly and held the firearm in his hand. He gripped the handle and inspected the gun like a foreign object.

"When this is all over. When things go back. We will remove the barrier that splits us apart," Richard said with poise.

Edmund showed his somewhat white teeth as he grinned.

"Or we'll die trying," Edmund replied with a grin.

Richard nodded at Edmund and grabbed onto his right shoulder, which nonverbally gestured everything was going to work out for the best. Edmund nodded as Richard released and walked away towards the trucks.

The Town of Jasper

Two Cops Walk Into A Biker Bar

Two Months Before "The Incident"
July 2011

Richard and Sutherland drove down a long, one-lane road quietly. Richard looked over a file as Sutherland looked over at him curiously every so often as he drove. The two said nothing for a while, staying occupied on the road and the paperwork. Richard gave the file a final glance and closed it up.

"So I asked her what she wanted."

"What?" asked Richard.

"My daughter. I asked her what she wanted."

"For what?"

"Her birthday…"

"What'd she say?"

"She wanted a horse. We settled on a dog."

Richard shook his head and gave Sutherland a look of disapproval, who smirked playfully.

"What?"

"Lot of work."

"You have one?"

"No. But my neighbor does. Thing barks all night. I want to shoot the damn thing."

Sutherland looked at Richard with worry. He looked back at the road and thought to himself and about what he agreed to get himself into.

"Mine won't bark like that," he said.

"Oh, yes. It will," said Richard with a laugh. "And it'll bite the hell out of you for a while."

"What do you mean?"

"It'll be teething. That's what dogs do when they're pups. They bite."

"So you're trying to tell me I agreed to get something that's going to keep me up all night and bite me in the ass every time I walk into the house?"

"Oh, and it'll ruin all your furniture and belongings," Richard said with a smile and laugh.

Sutherland looked worried as he drove. He felt that he had made a big mistake and started to wonder how he could get out of it.

"What about a cat?"

"You don't want to do that," Richard said.

"Why? Your neighbor has one of those too?"

"He did…"

"What happened to it?"

"I shot the damn thing…"

Sutherland looked at Richard, surprised, not knowing if he was serious or not. Richard looked at him with a stern look on his face.

"Seriously?"

Richard continued to look at Sutherland seriously until he couldn't hold it in anymore. Richard burst out laughing, causing Sutherland to breathe a sigh of relief.

"You're an asshole," he said.

Richard laughed harder and did so for another minute or so. He checked the file once more to refresh. He looked at Sutherland, who remained focused on the road.

"A cat…" Richard said as he chuckled.

The Town of Jasper

The two of them pulled up outside a run-down pub. Outside, there were an array of motorcycles and muscle cars with people in bandanas and tattoos smoking cigarettes or drinking unidentified liquor. The seedy bar attracted the ill-famed and morbid lower class, from hit men to pill popping proletarians. Sutherland got on his COM.

"We are outside the location now," said Sutherland into his COM.

His COM buzzed in as a voice came in loudly with minor static.

"Copy. Confirmation on safe word 'checkmate'. Again. Safe word, 'checkmate'."

In case of a hostage situation or any sudden danger, the two were assigned code words to say in a near death situation. If their cover was ever blown or if they had a definite confirmation of the killer, they would strategically implement the 'safe word' into their dialogue and reinforcements would arrive to the scene. Once the code words were confirmed, the rest of the force would surround the area to break in and make the necessary arrests.

Undercover, Sutherland and Richard got out of the car wearing denim jeans and t-shirts. The clientele of hooligans looked at them awkwardly as they walked into the bar. The two were tasked with finding the murderer of the victim at the farm. Their evidence and findings led them to Finn's Bar and Darts, home to drug dealers, criminals, and loan sharks. The dimly lit bar was home to the lowest of the low in the area, and nobody ever went in just for a drink. Sutherland and Richard walked up to the bar after receiving stares and glances from mostly everyone in the bar. Richard addressed the bartender with a tap on the wood table.

"Two Buds…" asked Richard.

Though they dressed the part, their charisma and allure was far from modified to the conventional patrons of the hole in the wall bar. A few brawny men in cutoff denim jackets played pool, while a few other men and questionable women played darts. Each person offered a foul and rotten vocabulary and incoherent drawls that almost seemed like a special language for the regulars of the place. The waitress with a black tattoo and nose ring placed two bottles of beer on the table.

"Two Buds," she said.

Richard flipped the woman a ten-dollar bill.

"Keep it," he said as he grabbed his beer.

The two sipped and said nothing, appearing relaxed and on a break from hard labor.

"We should go undercover more often," Richard whispered jokingly.

"You see our guy yet?" asked Sutherland as he sipped the bottle.

Richard scanned the room quickly, making it seem like he wasn't evidently looking for the suspected murderer. They were searching for a man named Elvin Bosh, a known drug smuggler, gun dealer, and loan shark. A heavy set, but built man, Caucasian, brown beard, and tattoos decorating his flesh like a Macy's Christmas tree. Richard took a small sip from the cold bottle as he found the target out of the corner of his eye.

"Two o'clock. Against the wall, under the Rocky Mountain picture," said Richard.

Sutherland took another sip and waited ten seconds to look. After the time passed, he glanced over to the right and saw the man they were looking for. Fitting the description, they believed they found the suspected murderer.

"That's not right," said Sutherland.

"What?"

"Those are the Appalachian Mountains."

Richard looked at Sutherland and rolled his eyes. Sutherland looked at him and sipped his beer.

"I'm just gonna go…"

"Yeah," said Richard.

Sutherland put his beer down and walked toward the man. Two other thugs accompanied the man named Elvin. One thug was an African-American man, who was about five foot seven, and another, was a tall Caucasian man, with a very thin stature also decorated in tattoos. The two looked at Sutherland, unreceptive as he approached them. Appearing frantic and nervous, Sutherland addressed Elvin.

"You Elvin?" Sutherland asked nervously.

Elvin looked at him through his knock-off Oakley sunglasses. His face was smug, and his double chin resembled a jellyroll.

"Who the fuck are you?" he asked rudely.

"I'm a friend of Max," said Sutherland.

"How do you know him?"

"Met him through a friend," said Sutherland confidently and collectively.

"You sure have a lot of friends," said Elvin.

"You got some left?"

Elvin looked at the man next to him. He gave him a nod, suspicious of Sutherland.

"Check this asshole," demanded Elvin.

His right hand man walked up to Sutherland, who acted apprehensive and edgy. The man patted Sutherland down from his shoulders to his ankles. The man looked at Elvin.

"He's clean."

Elvin stared at Sutherland through his pitch-black lenses, not totally convinced. He reached behind his back and took out a pistol. He presented it to Sutherland, showcasing his willingness to kill him if he was a turncoat of any kind.

"Let's take a walk outside," suggested Elvin.

Without much of a choice, Sutherland nodded his head timidly as Elvin and his cronies escorted him towards the back exit. Richard remained at the bar. He eyed Sutherland exiting the bar while he sipped his beer. He looked back at the picture of the mountain closely. He squinted at it while he drank from his beer bottle.

Outside, Elvin and his partners in crime led Sutherland towards a run-down sedan. The two men walked with their weapons in their hands, ready to shoot Sutherland if need be. Elvin stopped near the trunk of the car and looked at Sutherland.

"What did you say your name was again?" asked Elvin.

"Phil Duncan," said Sutherland.

"Okay then, Phil Duncan. Friend of Max. What's your fancy?"

"Well I'm a hunter, and I'm looking for a reliable side arm should I come across something unexpected. What I'm looking for isn't exactly game warden approved," said Sutherland. "Do you do any hunting?" Sutherland inquired.

"No. My daddy did a whole lot. He hunted elk. Those big, bucked bastard ones. He'd come home and drag the damn thing by the horns into the garage," said Elvin.

"You sure it wasn't my mother in law?" asked Sutherland.

There were a few chuckles among the crowd. Elvin remained focused, as he didn't let himself become emotionally compromised by humor.

The Town of Jasper

"Funny thing is how my daddy died. Driving home late one night and one of those big-bucked son of a bitches dashed out in the middle of the road. Pops hit it dead on and he skidded off the highway into a telephone pole. Killed him instantly."

There was a concise moment of silence, as Sutherland felt somewhat tense given the nature of the story. Elvin lifted his hand and pointed his finger at Sutherland.

"That's called *irony*," Elvin said as he pointed.

Another short moment of silence arose as Sutherland stood awkwardly.

"So Mr. Duncan. The hunter. Let's take a look inside and see if we can't find you some protection," said Elvin.

Elvin clicked the lever to the trunk and lifted the hood. It made a walloping, squeaking sound as it lifted upwards. Inside the trunk, there was a cache of illegal weapons. Sutherland observed it from behind Elvin, knowing he had evidence to put him in jail for illegal possession. He also saw bags of drugs and paraphernalia in plain site. He thought he would be able to convict him for the guns and drugs and get him on a technicality for the murder of the man at the farm. Sutherland said nothing as he walked up beside Elvin.

"Gorgeous. Aren't they?" Elvin asked boastfully.

"Yes, they are," Sutherland said in a low tone.

Sutherland skimmed the weapons in the trunk, looking for the one he was in search of. Finally, he saw a gun that caught his attention. A Glock 40 Generation 4. It was beside an AK 47. The gun was in pristine condition, and Sutherland believed it was the weapon used to kill the man at the farm.

"One catch your eye? asked Elvin

Sutherland looked around aimlessly, acting as oblivious as possible. He pointed to another gun on the left side of the trunk.

"What are you asking for that one?" asked Sutherland

Elvin peeked over Sutherland's shoulder at the gun he was referring to. He gave it a good look.

"Two," he said. "Non-negotiable."

Elvin stepped away from Sutherland to give him some space.

"Go head. You can pet her," he said.

Sutherland looked at Elvin unsurely. The other two men looked at him carefully, on guard for any sudden moves on behalf of the detective. Sutherland looked at the gun again and slowly reached his hand for it. He wrapped his fingers around the handle and felt the smooth steel against his fingertips. He gripped the gun and removed it from the trunk. By the time he was holding it in his hands and inspecting it, the two men had their guns drawn on him. He looked at the men oddly and then at Elvin.

"Just a precaution, friend of Max," said Elvin.

Sutherland looked back at the two cronies somewhat angrily, and he examined the weapon in his hands. He aimed down his sights and checked the clip. He placed the gun on top of the towel and glanced over at the GLOCK.

"What about the GLOCK?" asked Sutherland.

Elvin made a grumbling sound as he thought about it.

"One of my personal favorites. I'd hate to see it go, so I'd have to say six. Not much of a hunter's weapon, Duncan..."

"Someone's birthday's coming up. I forgot to get him something," said Sutherland insinuating the gun was for his alleged friend. "I can't do six. Can you do better?"

Elvin smiled at Sutherland and crossed his big, brawny arms, which showed his multiple tattoos through his shirtsleeve shirt.

The Town of Jasper

"I can do five-fifty…since you're a friend," said Elvin with a squalid tone.

Sutherland said nothing, as the two men remained ready to fire with their guns pointed up at him. Each of their weapons had silencers attached, to avoid any noisy confrontations. He looked back in to the trunk and reached for the gun slowly. He gripped the handle and raised it up gradually.

"I like the weight," Sutherland said.

He ejected the magazine and checked the bullets inside. The magazine was fully loaded with shiny gold bullets. The bullets matched the same kind that forensics found inside the murdered man's head.

"She likes you," said Elvin.

Inside the bar, Richard finished his beer and slammed it down on the bar. He signaled to the bartender with his right hand.

"Can I get another one?" he asked somewhat rudely.

He was now sitting on a high chair, glancing at the entire scene in the bar. He looked down the bar, hoping to catch the bartender's attention. To no avail, he turned himself around to find two people walking towards him. One of the approaching men was of Latino descent and the other was a Caucasian with a tattoo on his shaved head. They walked up to Richard with guns pointed at him. Richard looked at both of them, acting confused.

"Walk with us. *Detective…*" said the Latino man.

Outside, Sutherland inserted the magazine back and cocked the lever. He aimed down his sights with both hands on the gun. Satisfied with the weapon and its condition, he nodded his head.

"Five-fifty?" asked Sutherland, confirming the price.

Elvin looked at him and smiled, showing his brown and yellow teeth. He started clapping his hands together slowly and loudly.

"Well done. Jolly good show!" Elvin said with a laugh and a bad English accent.

His men held their guns up at Sutherland, with a look of intent now. Sutherland felt the situation had made a dire turn.

"The hunter. You've managed to track your mark by following the trail. You've gone 'unnoticed' by your target all the way until the very end. And here you are. The hunter who is going to be killed by the thing he has been *hunting*."

Elvin smiled and clapped his hands together and pointed them at Sutherland.

"Irony," he said.

Sutherland knew the men would pick up any 'safe word' and kill him instantly. He gripped the GLOCK tightly in his sweaty palms as he tried to remain calm. He looked for an angle, but the proximity of the two gunslingers pointing their guns at his head made it difficult for any plan of defense.

Richard walked in front of the two men planning his next move. Up ahead, some men were playing a game of pool and a man sipped a bottle of Coors Light. After the man sipped it, he placed it down on the pool table and angled his next shot. Richard walked up straight and reached for the bottle. All in an instant, Richard grabbed the bottle and swung it behind him, breaking it against the side of the Caucasian man's head. The man fell to the ground instantly. Shocked by the blow, the Latino man hesitated and panicked. Richard gave him a harsh kick to the stomach, sending him against the wall. Richard grabbed the Latino man's wrists and pounded them against the wall creating cracks and holes in the cheap drywall. The man dropped the gun to the floor, allowing Richard to kick it out of reach. He threw the man up against the table and grabbed one of the pool sticks off the wall. He got up behind the Latino man and wrapped the stick around his jugular, choking him. The man gurgled and gagged as Richard pulled as hard as he could. Some of the men in the area stepped back in shock as the strangling man broke free by rocking his head back forcefully, crashing into Richard's nose. Richard lost his balance and back peddled. The Latino man grabbed a pool stick and swung it at Richard, who deflected it with his left arm. Richard delivered a blow to the right side of the man's face, which sent the man crashing against the pool table. Richard managed to get behind the man and slammed his head against the table three times, each blow more forceful than the last. The man fell to the ground as Richard walked over to the gun he kicked on the floor. Enraged and wounded, everyone in the bar watched Richard as he picked up the gun and walked over both men, headed toward the exit of the bar.

"Why don't you go ahead and empty that magazine again, Detective?" requested Elvin.

Sutherland reluctantly emptied the clip and held it in his hands. He looked at the top bullet again and dropped it on the floor.

"Now get on your COM and let them know that we will kill you if they advance."

Sutherland looked at Elvin angrily, figuring out that he was a lot smarter than he looked. Sutherland signaled his COM.

"No need to engage. Situation under control."

Elvin uncrossed his arms and reached behind his back. He yanked out his gun and took one step towards Sutherland. He pointed the gun at Sutherland but then fell to the ground. Sutherland did not hear the shot go off that pierced right through

Elvin's temple. Distraught and befuddled, Sutherland looked around. Another shot went off that hit one of the gunman's chest. Richard had entered the scene just in time. The other gunman aimed his gun at Richard quickly. Richard did not have the quicker hand as Sutherland jolted upwards and tackled the man to the ground before he would shoot Richard. Sutherland got on top of the man and gave him a lethal blow to the head with his elbow, knocking him unconscious. Panting heavily, Sutherland began to feel around his body to make sure he wasn't hit. In awe and trembling, Sutherland looked at Richard, who hovered over him. Sutherland smiled with relief as he fell onto the ground.

"They knew who we were," he said as he caught his breath.

"Cat's outa the bag," said Richard jokingly.

"One day it's going to be me who saves *your* ass, you know," said Sutherland.

"Yeah. That'll be the same day you find out my 'true identity'," said Richard.

"Asshole," said Sutherland.

Richard laughed as he helped his partner up. The two strolled back into the bar and found the rest of the police force inside. The police chief walked up to them to check on their safety and condition.

"Checkmate," said Richard sarcastically to the chief.

The two walked up to the bar and Richard signaled the petrified bartender with his right hand.

"Two Buds.

… The Town of Jasper

AND DELIVER US FROM EVIL

Present Day 2016
Five Years After "The Incident"

He will wipe every tear from their eyes. There will be no more death or mourning or crying or pain, for the old order of things has passed away.

The drive back to town was another silent one. The sun was descending into the horizon as the trucks drove in unison at a moderate pace. The men's nerves were all vanquished at this point. Dallas drove quietly, with one hand on the wheel as he leaned back. Ford sat in the middle with his arms crossed. He did not need to ask the men how things went. He knew by the amount of supplies in the bed of the truck that the negotiations went well. Richard's right arm dangled out of the window as the wind blew against his face. Calm and collected, Richard could only think of how much a victory the day was. He kept thinking about Edmund, his people, and what he said to him. Edmund put a lot of things into perspective in a time where the only perspective was survival. The more they drove, the more Richard felt a compelling feeling of responsibility. He began to feel responsible for the safety of both sides of the divide. Both Jasper and the Fillmore Whites. He prayed that a relationship would spark between the two. If he could make it so, Jasper would have a good chance of beating the crisis. He thought about everything, as his arms swayed out of the window. Richard pondered the thought of taking a quick nap, but before he could do so, he saw something peculiar in the distant darkness. There appeared to be a pile of rubble of sorts in the road. Hard to make out what it was, Richard did not remember it being there on the way up. He figured was fallen debris from one of the tall trees. Dallas was driving at a relatively high-speed when Richard requested he turn on the high beams.

"Put on the high beams for a second," requested Richard as they got closer to it.

Dallas flicked he truck's bright lights and the debris-like object was right in front of them.

"Stop the truck!" Richard demanded.

The breaks screeched and hissed as Dallas stomped on the pedal with both feet. The truck hit the spike strip roadblock at just over thirty miles an hour. The vehicle skidded sideways as smoke engulfed from the left side tires. The car nearly flipped over, as the vehicle balanced itself for a split second on two wheels. Finally, the truck came to a halt on the grass-patched shoulder, inches away from a tree. The two trucks behind them stopped short, missing the roadblock. The men got out of their vehicles to see if anyone was hurt in the accident.

The group of men stood on the side of the road, staring at the truck that wouldn't be able to make it back to town. Not even half of the way, Richard began to think about how to resolve the issue.

"You think they did it?" asked Jason.

Richard continued to contemplate as he looked at the roadblock that was placed in the road no more than an hour ago. He retraced their steps that led directly into the woods. He counted two pairs of tracks.

"Is it drivable?" asked Dallas.

"Probably not," Gary confirmed.

Richard, annoyed and angry, inhaled deeply at the sight of the damaged vehicle. For the first time since before the incident, things were actually starting to go his way. He remembered something his wife would always say when he had a bad day.

"Life will always have bumps in the road. Sometimes there's no avoiding them."

Richard's knees began to weaken as he knew who created the interference. The whispers and banter behind him continued.

"I think we made a mistake making a deal with those people."

"Gentleman, we are exposed out here. We're sitting ducks…"

"We need to move…"

"They're probably watching us right now…"

"It wasn't them!" Richard screamed as he rose up. "It was someone else."

The men stopped their banter and looked at him, interested in his hypothesis. Richard looked at the broken-down car with his left hand on his hip and right arm dangling. Dressed in a dirty brown leather jacket and black denim jeans, Richard fixed his eyes on the precious cargo.

"*Someone* did this. Someone who didn't want this plan to work."

Richard turned to his men with a sinister gander. The men were taken back by his expression, feeling like accused, frightened schoolboys. After what felt like hours, Gary spoke out.

"Who would do this?" asked Gary Ford.

Richard looked at him attentively. Richard had a pretty concrete idea of who caused it. Both hands on his hips now, Richard thought of a two-minute offense in his head. He quickly turned around and pointed at the other trucks.

"Let's get this cargo on the other beds," Richard said almost desperately.

"We can always go back for it," interjected Jim.

"No! Whoever did this could intercept the supplies we leave behind," said Richard as he looked around the area. "We're taking it all back."

The group of men stood still, looking at one another, skeptical of the plan. Richard darted glances in all directions and turned around again. He looked at the men like a football coach ready to run drills. Richard clapped his hands.

"Let's move!"

The men snapped out of it and walked around like headless chickens bumping into one another.

It took nearly an hour and a half to get the cargo from the broken down truck into the other two. By this time, the moon took over for the sun and it became dark. The men, exhausted, looked at each other and the two trucks filled to the brim with supplies. Richard pointed to Dallas and Gary.

"You two ride in the bed with Kendrick. I'll ride in the back of Jim's."

The two men climbed up into the bed of the trucks and rested against supplies. Richard placed his foot on the back wheel of Jim's truck and situated himself between two large bags of vegetables. The car's engines rumbled as fumes emitted from the exhausts. The trucks peeled off the side of the road as Richard watched the broken down vehicle get smaller and smaller as he sat in the cargo bed.

The Town of Jasper

The sun had set. The night was dark. Their guard was down. The group of Redeemers waited in the woods, looking for the signal. The leader looked up at the night sky, waiting for the right moment.

"It's time," he said frigidly.

In unison, the group of ash faced lunatics walked towards a couple of big brown cardboard boxes, which contained black robes and cloak-like clothing. Each member of the group grabbed a black cloak and put it on. It took nearly two minutes for the group of radicals to get dressed. The leader swung his black cloak over his shoulders and put his arms through the sleeves. He didn't say anything to anyone as he walked forwards. The men and women both acknowledged his progression by throwing up their hoods over their heads. The area was a congested mess of black-faced individuals all picking up different things from nearby milk crates, equipped with knives and small machetes. Some of the women picked up containers with gallons of oil inside them. A select few men attached silencers to their pistols and shoved them into their pants. After a few moments, every member of the Redeemers was equipped with a weapon to kill. The leader addressed them for the last time before they headed out. The leader, whose face was unrecognizable from the black tar, gave a look of intent and purpose.

"Remember, they have limited guns. It *has* to be quiet. We need to get this done before they come back. We don't have long. But we have prepared for this, and we are ready. We will send these suffering souls to the kingdom of the Lord himself. They have suffered long enough. And so have we. We will deliver them from evil and in the end…"

In unity, the group finished his sentence.

"*IT WILL BE US WHO THEY WILL THANK*".

The town of Jasper was without light and silent. There was no more than a wanderer or two in the streets passing the time or inspecting the area for any dangers. The moon glimmered, providing the main source of light on the feeble, desolate town.

They cut through the woods to get to the hospital. It was just a ten-minute walk or so on foot. Once they were outside, the leader looked ahead through the trees as did the rest of group in their black gowns and ash faces. The leader, looked into the void of darkness at the hospital standing tall and proud. Practically unguarded, Jasper Hospital shined like a beacon of hope in the darkness. The leader remembered the void of darkness that once was. He recalled Jasper before the incident. He remembered the center of town always being alive and animate. Cars would drive through, people would walk their dogs, kids would run along with their friends, people would laugh and exchange pointless conversation of weekend plans, dinner recipes, and ball game scores. All of that became a distant memory. All of that nearly an old tale of what once was. The leader, along with the rest of the Redeemers, had come to believe that what they were about to do would free the community of its darkness and that the old order of things would make a comeback. They felt necessary sacrifices had to be made to achieve bona fide salvation. Over the last five years of suffering and struggle, they have become sociopaths and fundamentalists of the Catholic faith and had linked it to human sacrifice. Deep in their perverse and lost minds, they felt they had to eliminate every last victim. The leader looked to his left and nodded, and they made their progression towards the hospital. They split into three groups.

The Town of Jasper

Their footsteps were mute and steady in the darkness. Three of them walked slowly towards the main entrance of the hospital, where no more than a few guards overlooked the area. They would be able to slip in without a problem. The two cloaked individuals followed the leader with two milk gallons filled with gasoline in each hand. On the other sides of the hospital, the other groups made their way to their assigned entrances. They were right on schedule.

As the three shadowy figures went unseen by the oblivious lookouts, they took cover behind a parked car. They were no more than fifty yards from the main door. In front of the main entrance, three guards, two men and a woman, stood within fifteen feet of each other. They were having a conversation about sitcoms they used to watch. They were carrying weapons. The men each bared hunting rifles with long distance scopes and the woman carried an AK-47.

The leader devised a plan in his head that would allow them to get by without incident or unwanted attention.

"We need to lure them away," whispered one of the followers, a man named Paul.

The leader continued to investigate the hospital guards as well as the building.

"There's only three. We can take care of them if we're quick about it," said the other Redeemer named Jade.

The leader, maintaining composure and a level head, continued to fix his gaze on every part of the area.

"We need to move," said Jade. "The others are going to be inside soon."

The leader ducked his head back under the cover of the car and looked at his two followers. He gave them a nod, and they both rushed in opposite directions of the car.

To the vehicle's right and left were two other broken down vehicles. One was an old minivan and the other a U-Haul truck. The leader closed his eyes as the other two took their positions behind the cars. The leader lightly tapped the back of his head against the outside of the broken down, rusted sedan and removed a harmonica from his pocket. The leader's harmonica was a gift from his mother on his birthday when he was just a boy. The leader ran his thumb over the worn out instrument. He closed his eyes and recollected on the days he would sit under the tall peach tree on his parent's fifteen-acre property in Senoia, Georgia. He remembered how he would blow beautiful melodies from the very same harmonica for hours under the tree. He'd rest his head against the bark and watch the sunset in the distance. Everything was bright and simple then. Some days he'd sit under that peach tree for so long, he'd fall asleep, and when he woke, it would be dark.

The leader's head rested against the rusted vehicle as he reminisced about old times. Times he wanted back. He lifted his eyelids and saw the darkness. He placed the harmonica against his lips and cringed like an adolescent child eating a piece of broccoli. He blew into the instrument and the gorgeous, resonating sound from the tiny musical tool could be heard from a long distance. He played like he used to under the tall peach tree. The nostalgic memories of his lips against the iron device, along with the familiar reverberation and tempo of his long-lost passion, had reduced him to a few trickling tears down his jaw line. The music caught the guard's attention. Like lost dogs, the three of them looked around, confused and oblivious.

"What is that?" asked the female guard named Ashley. She was a beautiful girl, with her dirty blonde hair tied back. She wasn't much of a guard, but she was sharp when she wanted to be.

The Town of Jasper

"Where's that coming from?" asked Neil Hackett, one of the accompanying guards.

The three of them looked around while Jade and Paul peeked over the vehicle at the guards walking and looking around aimlessly. The leader continued to play, louder and with more enthusiasm.

"I think it's coming from that way," said the Spanish man, Rafael Hidalgo, the third guard on duty. He pointed in the direction of the vehicle they were hiding behind.

"Stay sharp," said Neil as they drew their weapons and tiptoed toward the vehicle. The three of them reluctantly pressed onward in the direction of where the sound of the harmonica was playing.

"Light?" asked Neil as he took lead toward the broken down sedan. They were no more than twenty yards from the broken down car.

Ashley fumbled with the flashlight and clicked the button. The light emitted and she pointed it at the car. She shined the light in the area of the vehicle as the elegant music continued to play loudly. The guards aimed down their sights on the vehicle, ready to put down any potential threat.

The leader continued to play the jingle at a moderate tempo and rhythm, as Jade and Paul prepped for the right moment to execute the plan. The group of three guards, feeling more trepidation than adrenaline, crept closer to the car. Now just fifteen yards away, the sound of the harmonica became much louder and fast-paced. Curious and bewildered, Neil pointed a Remington Model 798 rifle with his right eye honed in on the scope at the car. The man with rifle shouted out.

"Hands! Let me see your hands!" shouted Neil.

The loud and upbeat tune of the harmonica came to an eerie stop. The silence was a horrifying ingredient in the dusky night. Neil, along with Ashley and Rafael, stopped with their guns pointed. The leader, sat behind the vehicle, looking at the darkness before him. His tears dried up, he placed the harmonica back into his pocket, and he reached for something else.

Pulse skyrocketing, Neil held the rifle while his shoulders began to tremble. His adrenaline kept him focused at what was behind the car. He knew whatever was behind the car was a threat at this point. He knew it was him, or whatever it was behind the car. He knew if he let his guard down for just a second, it'd be him. One in the chamber, Neil took a step forward.

Their footsteps were soft, quiet, and quick. As if they were running on air, the two Redeemers, Paul and Jade, made their way behind the guards. Knives in their hands, they both got within ten yards of Ashley and Rafael, who stood behind Neil. Unaware of the ambush, the two gun-wielding guards kept their focus on the vehicle.

Now within five yards of them, the Redeemer's steady pace turned into a full on sprint. The sound of loud footsteps along the ground caught Ashley's attention. Before she could process it, Jade plunged her knife into Ashley's throat. Gargling on her own blood, Ashley fell to the ground. In an instant, Rafael turned around in a panic. Paul ran up to him and tackled him to the ground, causing Rafael's gun to fly out of his hands. The ruckus caught the attention of Neil, whose rifle remained pointed at the vehicle. Now on the ground, Rafael looked up at the ash face of the cloaked Redeemer and nearly had a heart attack from the shock and fear. Paul raised his blade in the air and brought it down hard against the man's chest. Neil swung his body and rifle around in terror and aimed his weapon wildly. Before he could squeeze the trigger, there was a sound of a bullet initiating through a silencer. The bullet struck the center of the Neil's forehead. A clean shot right through. Neil's eyes lolled before he tumbled awkwardly to the ground. The leader lowered his right arm with his pistol in hand. He didn't say a word as he looked at Jade and Paul. He walked forward and knelt down next to the corpse for which he was responsible. He looked at the hole in the back of the man's head and looked away, somewhat appalled at his doing.

"In company with Christ, Who died and now lives, may they rejoice in Your kingdom, where all our tears are wiped away. Unite us together again in one family, to sing Your praise forever and ever. Amen."

After another moment of brief silence, the three Redeemers collected the guards' weapons and walked toward the hospital with gallons of gasoline in their hands.

The three of them walked moderately down the hall without checking their surroundings. They knew every in and out of the plan and layout of the building. They veered to the right, down the hall where the other group of Redeemers walked towards them at the same moderate pace. A distraught and confused woman, no more than thirty, walked aimlessly out of a room and into the line of fire. She looked to her left at the oncoming group and nearly fainted from shock. She gasped so loud that she let out a faint shriek. Without wanting to cause a mess or commotion, a single round ignited from the silencer from one of the Redeemers. Right between the eyes, the woman fell dead to the floor instantly. Without breaking stride, the two groups rendezvoused at the middle of the hall and both turned down the main passageway. The Redeemers walked with more authority, approaching another canal of hallways just several yards away. The plan was unraveling itself and was on the track to fruition. Before they got within five feet of the new branch of hallways, four Redeemers appeared in surprise formation with their blades and guns raised. The leader and his followers all stopped emotionless. With the barrel of the silencer close enough to smell the gunpowder, the leader waited sternly for the man to point it away from his face. As the man ascended the weapon away from the leader's head, the entire group stopped for a few seconds. The leader looked at his side at his two companions, who immediately started pouring the oil along the ground.

The leader walked ahead at the first door on the right. He opened it softly. A man and a woman, presumably a husband and wife or brother and sister, stood watching over a dozen victims laid across the floor on air mattresses and blankets. The two of them, looked up at the leader, with a sense of fright that froze them. The woman, Mary Jo Pettinson, had a children's book in her hands that she was reading to the young ones. The man was dressed in a black and white plaid shirt. The leader recognized him. His name was Robert, and he owned the local jewelry store.

"Who are you?" asked Mary Jo, softly and frightened.

The leader's blackened face was harsh, yet empathetic. He looked at the dozen victims on the ground. There were children, adults, and a few seniors scattered across the floor. The leader looked at the woman, remembering his plan.

"We are the bridge between darkness and heaven."

One of the leader's companions entered the room and fired off two rounds, penetrating each of their foreheads killing them instantly. The leader looked at the two innocent lives fall. Now there were fourteen people laid across the ground. Somewhat distraught, the leader looked around at the helpless victims of the horrible incident. He walked around and over their delicate bodies.

The Town of Jasper

He looked up at the Redeemer at the door, who carried a gallon of oil in his hand.

"Let us end their agony."

The Redeemer began pouring oil over each of the bodies. Once each victim was soaked with oil, the leader took out a match and rubbed it against the rugged sand paper on the small pack. The flame ignited and he flicked it on the ground. He took out another one and ignited the tip. The small flame nearly grazed his fingertips as it lit. He flung it on the other side of the room. Lastly, he lit the third one and flung it in the center of the room. The flame was hot enough to create precipitation on their faces as they watched until the leader spoke out. "Let this flame be the beacon and the bridge of eternal light for these souls that have been plunged into the darkness for too long. Let this flame act as the beginning for these innocents. Let this flame deliver them into the hands of the creator of all things. Soon He will invite them into his kingdom, and they will dine with the saints at the table of the Lord. And in the end…"

"*It will be us, who they will thank,*" they all said together.

It took less than five minutes for the room to engulf in flames, burning each victim to their death.

The car coasted down the road at a moderate speed. Only a half-mile from the hospital, Richard relaxed his back in the cargo bed, looking up at the stars. The thought of his father relaxed him. The feeling of ease was one he had not felt in a long time. Another thing Richard felt for the first time in a long time was hope. He felt that he might have finally broken a barrier that would change Jasper, even after everything went back to the way it was. The feeling of achievement made him oblivious to the faint smell of smoke down the road. Just a quarter mile from the hospital, no one in the truck noticed the stench. The truck progressed a little further when Dallas noticed something through the trees.

"What is that?" he asked as he leaned his head past the wheel and squinted.

"What is what?" asked Gary Ford.

"Up ahead, look. I see something. Looks like…"

The men in the truck stopped talking. The truck in front of them slowed down and reared off to the side. Dumbstruck and slightly afraid, Dallas looked at the scene from less than a quarter mile away. Dallas pulled up next to the other truck and no one exchanged a word to one another. They looked at the hospital in an indescribable fashion of shock and awe. Richard, in the cargo bed, sat up and wondered why they had stopped. He looked at Dallas in the driver's seat and noticed he was looking at something with the other men in the other truck. He looked up and saw what they were staring at with such amazement. Richard felt an ice wave of fear crash against his chest and wish-wash down his spine. The hospital was engulfed in flames and Richard nearly fainted at the scene. Lightly shaking his head, with his mouth half-open, Richard whispered his wife and children's names, fearing he lost them the same way he did his father.

Why

One Month Before "The Incident"
August 2011

Richard sat inside the confessional inside Father Paul's church. He was slightly nervous even though he'd confessed his sins numerous times before. Father Paul waited patiently for his friend to begin.

"Bless me, Father, for I have sinned. It has been a week since my last confession. The other day, my partner and I got involved in a situation that prohibited me from not using violence. I killed. And it makes me afraid. I knew I'd have to do those kinds of things when I joined the force but...I am afraid that this won't be the last of the killing. A demon inside of me flickers, and it tells me that it's just the beginning of something."

Father Paul let the confession saturate. It pained him to hear it from a man he considered family, and one whom he loved so dearly. Typically, Father Paul offered advice on how to combat the feelings of guilt and culpability. He would normally request Richard say an Act of Contrition and rid him of his sins. This time, he used a difference approach.

"Why?" asked Father Paul.

"Why what?" Richard asked, confused.

"Why did you kill?"

"He was going to kill someone close to me."

"Someone you care deeply for?"

"Yes."

"So, in fact, you acted as a protector."

"Maybe," said Richard. "But why?"

"Why what, my son?"

"Why does it feel like something darker?"

"I always feared this conversation would happen when you decided to take this path. I knew the dangers and how it could hurt you," said Father Paul.

A long pause occurred thereafter. Richard had nothing to say about his friend's opinion.

"I think you need to step away from it all," said Father Paul.

"Is that what he would want from me?" asked Richard, referring to his father.

"That's what he would want *for* you," said Father Paul. "So do I."

Outside, on a brisk summer evening, the rain was somewhat heavy. Richard walked without an umbrella and chose not to drive to the church. During his stroll, he began to think about what Father Paul had told him. He had a lot to think about and crammed his head with pros, cons, 'ifs' and 'thans'. About halfway down the road, a car pulled up beside him and rolled the window down. Richard turned to his left and saw Sutherland.

"Hey, asshole, did you forget it was raining?" asked Sutherland.

"What, do you drive around town looking for people to talk to? Go get some friends," said Richard.

"I have a few. They're all inside like normal people."

Richard laughed.

"Get in," said Sutherland.

Richard opened up the passenger side door and got in.

"Where you coming from?"

"The church," said Richard.

"Where's your car?"

"Just felt like walking today. Have a lot on my mind."

"Ok..." said Sutherland curiously.

"It's nothing," said Richard.

Sutherland cranked the heat to full so Richard could dry off.

"By the way. This doesn't qualify as you saving my ass," said Richard.

"No, of course not," said Sutherland. "But it does qualify as *warming* your ass."

Richard looked at Sutherland sternly.

"The seat warmers. Get it?"

Richard shook his head at the bad joke and looked outside the window. He became very quiet as he dwelled. Sutherland put his hand by the vent to make sure hot air was blowing out.

"When I was six years old, my father and I built this tree house. It wasn't much, but it was perfect. It took us all day to build. My father was so good with his hands. He taught me all the basics. When it was finished, we would spend countless summer nights in it. We'd eat dinner, listen to the radio, read comics," said Richard with delight in his tone and a slight grin across his face.

Sutherland looked at his friend and drove slowly. He didn't butt in because he was surprised that Richard was revealing something that he'd been holding in for quite some time.

"One day a nail came loose, and I yanked it out. I showed it to him and told him it was broken. He said, *Richard, nothing lasts forever. But you can fix it. You can put it back. It's not easy fixing things, but sometimes it's worth trying to put the pieces back.*"

Sutherland smiled. The description of the drawl and lingo of Ken Morrissey reminded Sutherland of his own father. Richard continued to speak.

"At nine fifty-five on September ninth, my father called me and told me there was an accident. That a building caught fire. I hadn't turned on the news yet to know what he was talking about. I could barely hear him on the other line through the static and screaming. He was inside the building because he was saving people. I could just tell in the way he spoke that he wasn't getting out. That something was wrong. He saved nine people. He told me he hadn't much time to speak and he needed to try and save more. He said he just wanted to talk to me. When I asked him why he went in, he simply stated *because no one else would.* He saved nine people."

Sutherland said nothing as he felt sorrow and remorse. He never knew the specifics of the death of Ken Morrissey. He just knew he was gone.

"He asked me to put the kids on the phone quickly and that he wanted to say hello. But it was just me at home," said Richard sadly.

Sutherland shook his head slightly and looked outside the window in discomfort and grief.

"Then I just heard static. And it was over," said Richard.

Sutherland pulled up outside Richard's house and parked it along the side of the road. Richard did not get out. He put his head down as the heat continued to dry him off. Sutherland let his friend have a moment.

"My mother died giving birth to me. I've had this hauntingly innate feeling of guilt since I can remember. My father always spoke of her, and every time he did, I'd think about how I was the reason why she was gone and how that was one of the things that couldn't be fixed. It wasn't worth trying to put back because she was gone."

The Town of Jasper

"You don't have to…" said Sutherland, trying to comfort his friend.

"I don't tell you my real name because it never mattered. It's what keeps us going. There's so much we don't know about one another. Our line of work, we're always trying to piece together some kind of puzzle. Our missing pieces are what drive our friendship forward. If we find everything out, then there's nothing. There's just you and me and nothing."

"Why are you telling me all this?" asked Sutherland.

"After what happened at the bar. I didn't know if I'd get another chance to," said Richard.

Richard opened the door and stepped outside into the rain.

"I'll see ya around," said Richard.

"Yeah," said Sutherland, still perplexed. "I'll see ya."

Faces Like Coal

Present Day 2016
Five Years After "The Incident"

Richard kicked the door off its hinges. The inferno was still fresh as the entire hospital burned. The cavalry of men followed Richard inside to help in any way possible. The intense heat of the building made them cover their faces. Richard pushed forward in a panic, moving as fast as he possibly could to save his family. Some debris from the ceiling came crashing down on the ground.

"Get as many out as you can!" Richard shouted.

Everyone scattered throughout the hospital, busting down doors and trying to extinguish flames in certain areas. The hospital was complete, utter mayhem. The extreme heat waves made it hard for Richard to breathe, let alone see in front of him as he sprinted toward the room where his family was. Up ahead was the hallway leading to the room where they were. However, he saw something in the distance. A blackish figure ran by. Without having any time to process a thought, he ran ahead. The door to the private room where his wife and two children were was only fifty-feet away. As he got closer, the heat and temperature peaked. Nearly suffering from first-degree burns, he got within twenty-five feet of the door. Praying they were alive, Richard felt his heart and thoughts vanish. He was completely unsure of his family's fate. The bitter feeling of nostalgia hit him as he remembered the day he had to say goodbye to his father. As he got within ten feet of the door, something blindsided him, knocking him on the ground.

The Town of Jasper

Dazed from the heat, Richard looked up with blurred vision. Something was on top of him. He could not make out what or who it was because a chunk of the ceiling came crashing down beside him. The fragments spewed out, causing Richard to cover his face with his hands. The person on top of him put their hands around his neck and choked him. Richard grabbed the person's wrists tightly and gasped for air. Eyesight blurred and fuzzy, Richard experienced a panic attack of sorts as he struggled to breathe. The Redeemer gripped down tightly on Richard's jugular and pressed forcefully. Gagging, Richard grabbed the Redeemer by the collar area and managed to get his fingernails around his neck. Doing whatever had to be done to escape the grasp, Richard dug his dirty nails into the Redeemer's neck. Nearly piercing flesh, the Redeemer released his grip and grabbed his neck out of instinct.

Richard coughed and held his own throat as the inferno ensued around him. He picked himself up and threw himself at the black-cloaked man. Richard got on top of the man and took a few wild swings at his head. The man deflected his blows with his forearms. Richard grabbed the man's cloak and gave him a harsh blow to the head with his elbow. A chunk of the ceiling came crashing down and struck Richard on the head, causing Richard to fall off of the Redeemer. The cloaked man was dazed as well as the two of them crawled on the floor aimlessly, hoping to come to before the other got the upper hand. Richard shifted his distorted focus on the door to his left where his family was behind. His vision cleared as he looked at it on his back. A feeling of lifelessness overcame him as the cloaked individual came out of his daze and reached for a sharp metal object lying on the ground beside him. The Redeemer clutched it and rose to his feet. He looked down at Richard, who kept his eyes on the door, not knowing the reaper was knocking on his own. All of Richard's optimism was sinking like a ship at the bottom of the deep blue sea. He had lost everything, and he couldn't feel pain. The hollowness in his soul was all that remained within him. A conflagration surrounded the two men. The Redeemer walked up to Richard and towered over him. Richard tilted his head to look at the provider of his fate. He saw the ash on the person's face, along with the sharp object in his hand. He wondered what possessed the person to commit such acts. He asked himself what the town had come to in the wake of the indescribable incident. Richard saw in the cloaked man a true representation of what people could become once something had been ravaged and left for dead. There was little hesitation on behalf of the Redeemer as he kneeled on Richard's stomach and grabbed his collar with his left hand. His clutch was strong and firm as he raised the long, sharp-edged piece of metal above his head. Richard looked at the crazed extremist the man had become with no expression of fear or anger. He just shifted his attention on the door to his left as the cloaked man descended the sharp edge towards Richard's throat. In a flash, Richard saw his family. He saw his father, his wife, his two children, and Father Paul. He saw all of them smiling at him. They were all together and happy. Happily welcoming him into the door of eternal life. Richard did not feel the jagged edge of the sharp object pierce his flesh. Something had happened. He looked up at the cloaked man and noticed that he had a bullet hole between his eyes. Than he heard a deafening bang as the second bullet pierced the man's right cheek, sending him flying backwards.

  Behind Richard stood Jim, holding someone over his shoulder with a gun in his right hand.

  "We have to move, Rich!"

  Richard looked up at him, touching his chest and throat, wondering if he was still alive. He looked at Jim, unsure of what to say. He patted himself down again and began to think as straight as he could.

"Get the trucks! Bring them around to every exit!" Richard shouted.

Jim darted the other way with the person still in his arms. Richard looked at the door again and hesitated a moment. Unsure of what he would find, he was ready for it. He ran as fast as he could towards it and threw himself at it with his left shoulder. The door flew off as Richard stumbled into the room. He looked around in a panic and felt his hollow soul fill up to the brim with radiance again.

There they were, his family alive and well. He ran for his two children and threw them both over his shoulders. Outside the room, there were loud crackling sounds as the hospital began to fall apart. He sprinted outside the room towards the nearest exit, balancing both his children in his arms. He kicked the exit door open and rushed outside into the night. As he rushed outside, Ron pulled a truck up to the exit. Richard placed his children into the cargo of the truck carefully and ran back inside to retrieve his wife. The other members of the group pulled what trucks were available up to each exit and entrance to gather as many victims as possible.

"Keep pushing! Everyone armed! Kill anything in a black coat! Take *ONE* alive!" ordered Richard.

"They're the ones who did this?" asked one of the men.

Richard ignored the question as he bolted back inside the hospital. Ducking and squirming through and over debris, he hurried to the private room to get his wife out of danger. He drew his pistol and checked all corners for any sign of an imminent threat. Fully coherent, Richard checked the corners amidst the flames and the havoc. He bent down and made a full on dash for the private room. With the door already kicked down, he entered the room, drawing his weapon for any threats in the room. He looked at the bed in which his wife was laying on and his heart dropped. His wife was missing.

As Richard and his group rushed into the hospital to get everyone out to safety, the Redeemers and their leader slipped out of the exits where no one could see them. The leader led the charge as he shouted demands to his fellow psychopaths.

"Get back to the rendezvous points; you know what to do!"

As black figures ran across the property like ants marching around a piece of fallen picnic food, the leader saw a man carrying someone. The man carrying the person was a tall, brawny man who carried the human being with ease over his shoulder. The leader rushed up to him with eagerness.

"Is it her?" the leader asked.

The big brawny man nodded as the chaos ensued around them. The leader began to run away from the scene, ordering the man to follow.

"Let's move, quickly!" ordered the leader.

Richard began to search the room frantically, calling his wife's name as if she would answer him back. He kicked things over and searched every nook and cranny like a mad man. He looked at the entrance of the door in a panic and jolted out. With his gun held tightly in his hand, he aimed down his sights as he hurried down the inflamed hallway. All he saw was fire and people dragging or carrying victims out of the devastation. He began searching rooms and asking people if they took her away. He ran up to a man who carried out a little boy.

"Have you seen Diane? Have you seen my wife?"

The Town of Jasper

The man shook his head and continued his rescue. Richard asked everyone in the vicinity, but no one knew. Richard picked up a woman and carried her outside to safety. As he placed her down, he ran up to Ron Carlisle.

"Where's Diane? Is she here? Is she safe? Did someone take her?" he asked frantically.

"I don't know," said Ron apprehensively. "I didn't see anyone carry her out."

Richard nearly vomited as his head felt as light as a balloon. He looked around the corners of the area and began to think to himself as he held in his bodily fluids.

"Do we have anyone at the south exit?" he asked

"I'm not sure. Maybe Dallas pulled a truck around…" Ron said as Richard bolted for the south exit.

"Richard!" shouted Ron. "Shit."

Bystanders stood around him, awaiting some form of direction.

"Keep on with the rescue!" Ron shouted. "Two of you guard the trucks!"

As more people dashed inside, Ron ran after Richard. Richard galloped for the south exit, which was no more than a hundred yards away. He already ran fifty. With his wife's safety and all he had done to protect her to this point on his mind, his worry turned into rage. A fiery rage that awoke his inner evil. Richard reached the south exit with Ron closely behind. Upon arrival, Richard looked to his left and saw a few black figures scampering away. He stopped and planted his feet. He fired off a few rounds in their direction. Ron stopped as he saw Richard open fire. He took out his gun and aimed down his sight at the targets. With no clear shot he lowered the gun and looked at Richard, awaiting some sort of move or direction. Richard bolted after them.

Richard turned around as he ran and shouted to Ron. There was an explosion from inside the hospital that broke a window and sent Ron stumbling to the ground.

"Man this exit!" Richard shouted.

A mad dash ensued as Richard gained on the cloaked men's trail. His chest ached as he hustled after them. He had a visual of two of them as he progressed. He raised his weapon and fired off two more shots in their direction. They were heading toward the wooded area leading into the Jasper nature center, which spanned about fifty acres of tranquil woodland, several small cabins for the local troupe, and a trout filled pond in the center.

Richard's knees weakened and his joints ached as he picked up speed. The two trailing Redeemers were no more than a few hundred feet from the woods. Richard raised his gun as he sprinted. He fired off two rounds. The first bullet hit the tree to their left causing one of them to duck down as they rushed into the woods. The second bullet whizzed passed the others head, causing him to bow his head as he hurried to safety. Richard fired off the remaining four rounds at the last black-cloaked men, missing them by just inches. The group of Redeemers vanished into the darkness. Richard watched them disappear into the dark woods in front of him as the hospital lit up in flames behind him.

The rest of the Redeemers scattered, flocking to the checkpoint as planned. The checkpoint was at an arbitrary location in the deep woods, right by a small pond where they were scheduled to reconvene after the destruction of the hospital. Once all of them were together, the leader came forward in the center. He looked around quickly and counted.

"Let's begin," he said.

The Town of Jasper

All of the Redeemers began undressing by removing their black robes and washed the ash off their faces with the pond water. All of them did this except the leader and two other men. After the rest of them looked like normal human beings, they threw their robes in a pile. One of them poured oil over the pile of cloaks and lit a match. He threw the burning match onto the pile, causing the black clothing to go up in flames instantly. The leader looked at four of them and nodded. With his signal, three men and one woman bent down and placed their faces inches away from the burning fire. They groaned and grunted as their faces burned and smoldered. The rest of them watched them as they cleaned themselves more. After a few minutes, their faces were charred and burnt. They would be able to blend right in with the other rescuers at the hospital.

"That'll be enough," the leader said. "You know the plan. Get to the hospital as fast as possible. Come from different directions."

The three men and woman nodded. Soon after, they vanished into the woods.

"The rest of you get back into town," the leader said.

"And what of her?" asked the brawny man, gesturing to Diane who was laid on the ground. The leader looked at her.

"She's coming with us."

The group vanished like smoke in an airstream.

The Table With The Note

One Month Before "The Incident"
August 2011

Sutherland drove slowly down the one lane highway. The dog in the front seat stared at him with his tongue out and a wagging tail. The yellow lab was a pup and no more than six months old. Sutherland was going to surprise Shannon with the dog for her birthday. He made a sharp turn off the main drag and was no more than a couple of minutes from his house. He kept looking over to his left at the dog that danced around the passenger seat and tried climbing up to the window.

"Don't do that," said Sutherland to the dog. "You're going to…"

The pup tried to climb up to the window and fell backwards on the seat. He got himself up in an excited hurry and began to spin around with a jolt of energy. Sutherland grabbed the dog's back and tried to hold him in place. The retriever gnawed on his hand, thinking he was trying to play.

"No, don't do that."

Almost missing the turn to his street by wrestling with the dog, he made the right turn with one hand while keeping the dog still with the other. He drove down the road slowly until he reached his house. He pulled the car into the driveway and saw that Olivia's car was not in the driveway. He figured she might have parked in the garage or stepped out with Shannon for a quick moment. He put the car in park and snatched the dog off the seat.

The Town of Jasper

He walked up the walkway to the front door, cradling the puppy in his arms. Sutherland seemed happy for the first time in a while. He knew Shannon was going to love the surprise and thought he might have a chance at fixing things with Olivia. And for the first time in a long time, he did not feel the urge to use. He jiggled the key into the slot and opened the door with the dog in his hands. The door pushed open and Sutherland walked inside.

The house was quiet and stagnant. The detective walked into his house as if it were haunted, or like he'd never seen it before. Things were missing. Most of the furniture was gone. The couch, TV, kitchen, chairs, and dining room table. All gone. Bewildered to say the very least, Sutherland walked into each room and found nothing. The pattern of vanished belongings continued as he searched the house frantically. On the kitchen table, there was a note. Sutherland placed the dog down on the floor and snatched the note off the counter. His hands and fingers trembled as he read the note nervously. On the torn off piece of lined paper, the note read,

Jack,

When you read this, we are already long gone. I am taking Shannon with me to start over. She does not deserve a life with a father like you in it. You don't deserve a life with a daughter like her in it. We gave you too many second chances. Please do not follow us.

Detective Sutherland read the note and felt the shock clench him, causing him to freeze. He stared at the writing on the note for so long his eyes crossed. His body leaned backwards and it crashed into the refrigerator behind him. His back slid down it slowly until he fell to the floor. Clutching the note in his palm, Sutherland fell on his side and began to cry. The small yellow lab trotted up to him and began to lick his face.

After spending nearly thirty minutes on the floor, the puppy began to sob in the corner, knowing that something was wrong with his new owner. The detective felt an oncoming craving. A strong recommendation from his inner demons insisting he relinquish his pain with the help of an old and familiar friend. He threw himself up like a jack rabbit on speed and ran up to his bedroom.

He opened the top drawer and quickly sorted through his socks and underwear until he reached the small orange tube on the bottom of the pile. He pulled it out and unscrewed the top with the twist of his palm. He emptied out several pills into his hand and looked at them like a crazed attic. He popped them all in his mouth and swallowed. He marched down the stairs and opened up the freezer where he found Johnny Walker. He twisted the cap off and flung it across the room. He chugged from the bottle and crashed the bottle on the table with a scouring gasp. The puppy barked and cried, detecting something wasn't right. Sutherland took another gulp and crashed it down on the table, almost cracking the marble granite. Realizing he gave into his addiction again, he looked at the bottle and heard his wife's voice in his head. He heard her call him a loser and a sorry excuse for a father. He took the bottle and threw it against the wall, causing it to shatter into pieces. The small dog began to back off and sob as it became afraid of its master's drastic transformation. Sutherland screamed at the top of his lungs and began to punch the drywall repeatedly with both hands. He punched the walls so hard that his forearms went through each time. After his knuckles were bloodied and fingers slightly fractured, he grabbed his car keys and stampeded out of the door in an intoxicated rage.

    Nearly rolling his ankle by tripping down the front porch steps, he dropped his keys on the ground. He gathered himself in an angry hurry and swung the door open to his car. The door slammed shut, nearly shattering the window into shards of glass. Well under the influence and overly drunk, the detective pulled the transmission lever to reverse and he sped out of the driveway like a madman. He clipped the side of his mailbox as he reversed. He put the car in drive and sped down the road like a Formula One driver. Hitting a speed limit of sixty down residential streets, Sutherland became a lethal weapon on the road. The path in front of him becoming more and more hazy and blurred; the drunken detective started to weave left and right. By some miracle, he managed to get to the main drag without injuring anyone or causing any damage to his vehicle. However, at this point, his judgment was nonexistent and he became half conscience. Fuzzy-eyed and drooling, he slammed onto the gas with his foot and began to cut drivers off one by one, nearly clipping their rear ends with each pass. As the vehicle picked up the pace at a dangerous rate, the drugs mixed with the alcohol had kicked in, causing him to pass out behind the wheel. Sutherland's head rested against the headrest as his foot remained on the gas pedal. The vehicle stayed straight for a brief time before the sound of a tractor-trailer barely woke him up from his intoxicated state. His heavy eyelids lifted up at the sound of the truck's deafening horn. Sutherland sobered up, as he saw death ringing his doorbell repeatedly. Sutherland swung the wheel to the right with both hands, and the car skidded out of control, heading towards the side of the road where a patch of woods stood. The massive truck swerved at the same time, almost sending it topping over on itself, if not for the quick reflexes and smart maneuvering of the driver. Sutherland's vehicle, unable to stay on all fours, flipped over from the wild turn at the excessive rate in which its driver was traveling. Like a slinky down a flight of stairs, Sutherland's vehicle rolled and rolled until it finally crashed into a tree, stopping it's momentum. The airbag deployed instantly, knocking Sutherland unconscious as he and his vehicle remained upside down. The tires still spun slowly, and the hazard lights flashed. The driver of the tractor-trailer rushed to the scene. Once he saw the vehicle and its condition pinned up against the tree, he knew there was no way the driver survived.

A month later, inside a quiet, lonely hospital room, Jack Sutherland's heavy eyelids opened halfway. He had been in a coma since the crash and had finally woken. Unable to comprehend who, what, when, where, or why, he opened his eyes all the way. It took him about thirty seconds to realize he was in a hospital room being cared for. The room was empty. There were no nurses or doctors around. The sound of quiet and the numerous plugs and machines provided the only form of company for the man who had escaped death by the helpful hand of God. He tried to think and remember how he wound up in the hospital. The last thing he remembered was reading something, but he couldn't remember what or whom it was from. Slowly and surely, things started to come back to him. He read a note, and it was from his wife. He couldn't remember what she wrote, but he remembered feeling pain after reading it. Than he saw the front of the truck coming at him and then the impactful feel of the airbag against his face. He looked outside, not knowing what season it was. September had that deceptive look to it. Could be fall or the dead of summer, he thought. He asked himself how long he was in the hospital. Questions filled his head

The Town of Jasper

and flashes of the accident spontaneously popped in and out. The two like a tornado spinning and spinning in a cycle around his mind. On the table next to him, there was a note. On the neat, lined paper, the note read,

Jack,

When you read this, that means my prayers have been answered. My family and I have been visiting you, saying our prayers twice a week. Knowing you best, I know why you resorted to the addiction. The blame you put on yourself. I always understood. You had your reasons. Black or white, you had your reasons. When you read this, call me. I have retired, and my family and I have moved to Jasper. When you're ready, please come find me. Address is 19 Vervalen Street.

Your asshole partner

A young nurse walked into the room and saw him reading the note. She was very surprised to see him up; in fact, she did a double take when she saw him. She rushed into the room to check up on him as he placed the note down.

"Mr. Sutherland, how are you feeling? Do you know where you are?" asked the young nurse.

He looked up at her, distracted by all that has happened along with the note he just read. He looked at her, flummoxed and bemused as he looked outside the room's window. He looked back into her green eyes. She was close enough for him to see the freckles on her cheeks. She looked at him, puzzled.

"What month is it?"

"It's September," she replied.

"September…" he whispered in a bewildered tone.

He looked at the note again and placed it back on the table where he picked it up. He tried sitting up, and the nurse jumped in to help him. She put her hand on his back and held his arm.

"I got it, I'm up. Thank you," he said.

Sutherland exhaled, as sitting himself up straight was a difficult task. The nurse conducted some more routine checkups on him. He touched the large bandage across his left cheek.

"We stitched it up. There will be permanent scar tissue. I'm going to go get the doctor, just hang tight," she said as she scurried out of the room.

"Wait…" asked Richard. "Can you turn the TV on?"

The nurse walked over to the TV and clicked it on. The news channel appeared as a news anchor covered the current story.

"News okay?"

"Fine. Thank you."

The nurse raised the volume on the television and walked out of the room. Sutherland adjusted his seated posture and listened to the current event. The male news anchor was covering the story. The news headline read:

UNIMAGINABLE INCIDENT IN SMALL TOWN

Sutherland listened closely as the reporter continued the story. He heard the words 'disease' and 'quarantine'. Finally, he heard the name 'Jasper', and it made him quiver his eyebrows. He grabbed the note off the table beside him again and read through the note quickly. Then he became worried and fearful as he saw it.

moved to Jasper

The Town of Jasper

A couple of nurses joined a doctor in the room. Sutherland paid no attention to their smiles and benevolent words celebrating his awakening. He tried to listen to the news anchor amidst the background voices. He heard the news anchor say, "*a large portion of the town's population has been pronounced dead.*"

Sutherland panicked as the doctor and nurses surrounded him. He looked at them in a panic and tried to get out of the bed. To their surprise, the nurses held him down as the doctor tried to reason with him.

"Mr. Sutherland, please relax. You are not ready to move around yet!" shouted the doctor.

"My friend!" he shouted. "My friend's in that town! I need to find him!"

The nurses had a difficult time holding him down, and more attendants came rushing in from the commotion he was causing. He kept looking at the television. After a few nurses were able to pin him back down on the table, the doctor turned the television off.

"I need to find my friend," he said as he was being held down. "I need to find my friend."

James D. Gianetti

Men With No Shadow

Present Day 2016
Five Years After "The Incident"

The only thing they could see was the evaporation of their panting breaths. They held their knives, sharpened and ready to strike, as they tiptoed into the 'Keep Out Zone'. The three Redeemers zigzagged between trees without a sound, so as not to alert their prey. Moving quickly, they touched each tree they passed while they glided inaudibly through the lurid thicket. The pitch-black individuals stood beside one another as they looked into the darkness of the place where no one went.

"We need to be efficient. We cannot hesitate," whispered the leader.

"We will be efficient," stated one of the Redeemers. "This is the way we get the blood off our hands."

The leader looked at the man as the evaporation emitted from his mouth.

"We have something more than blood on our hands," said the leader.

The forest went silent. Their breathing was the loudest acoustic of the dark and lonely surrounding. Something in the distance was getting closer as they progressed. It was tall and big. The leader made a fist in the air, signaling the other two members two halt. The members came to a stop and took cover behind a tree.

In the distance, the Fillmore White sat alone around a small self-made fire. He was cooking something, presumably an animal of some kind. He did not hear the silent footsteps getting within arms reach of him.

245

The Town of Jasper

The three dark figures gripped their knives tightly with moist palms. They gaped ahead at the Fillmore White and circled around him in a triangular formation. They crept and crept, silent as a church mouse.

A resonating, snapping sound to the left altered the deformed man's attention. He grabbed a sharp stick beside him and stood up. He surveyed the pitch-black area on high alert for potential danger.

One of the Redeemers bolted away from their respective tree and leaped onto the albino man, shoving his knife into his massive back. The Fillmore White let out a howl. The Redeemer covered the Fillmore White's mouth with his hand, preventing him from making further noise. The man panted heavily as the knife plunged deeper into his back. The leader appeared with the other cloaked man, walking towards the shocked Fillmore White. His huge, pinkish eyes looked at them in fear as he felt a sudden chill throughout his body. With his right lower body numb, he fell backward onto the Redeemer's chest. The Redeemer who murdered him held the gigantic being tightly with one hand around his mouth and the other clutching the knife lodged in his back. The Fillmore White kept staring at the leader with fear in his eyes. It took him three minutes to die.

"Let's get him up. We're losing time," said the leader.

As the two men lifted the man off the ground, another Fillmore White appeared with a pile of twigs in his hand. He looked at the three of them, along with his fallen brethren. Enraged, the man let out a loud scream to signal the rest of the tribe. The leader took out his knife and threw it at the man. The blade struck the man in the shoulder, sending him to the ground.

"Run!" shouted the leader.

The three Redeemers ran, with one of them carrying the dead Fillmore White over his shoulder. They moved as quickly as they could as the howls and groans of more Fillmore Whites closing in on them became louder. They followed the path they came in from and made decent time towards their car. Arrows began whizzing by their heads as they ducked down to avoid getting struck with one. The chase continued through the blackness as the Fillmore Whites gained significant ground on the three Redeemers. The leader took the lead as the man carrying the Fillmore White trailed. Running with adrenaline and tunnel vision, the Redeemer trailing the leader did not see one of them to his right side. The Fillmore White pulled back on his bow and fired it towards him. The arrow struck the man in the leg, making him scream in pain. The leader turned around as he ran to see what had happened.

"Keep moving! The car is up ahead!" the leader yelled.

The car was in eyesight from where they sprinted. The Redeemer with the arrow in his leg trailed behind, allowing the man holding the Fillmore White to pass him. More arrows and rocks hissed by them, with some grazing their flesh and clothing. The Fillmore White who hit the trailing Redeemer pulled back on his bow again and let off another arrow. The arrow hit the man holding the dead Fillmore White in the back. The dead albino man flew out of his arms and rolled down the path. The leader turned around and made a break for the deceased man. The leader let out a cry as he struggled to lift the gigantic man over his shoulder. The leader managed to barely reach the exit unscathed as the other two men lay wounded behind him.

The injured men gripped the arrows stuck in their bodies and rolled around on the ground like drunken fools. Several Fillmore Whites appeared out of the darkness, surrounding the fallen men in a circle. They carried torches and spears in their hands. They looked at them churlishly, hoping to get a chance to embellish their land with their bowels and intestines. A few droplets of sweat dripped off the Redeemers' noses as they clenched their teeth in pain and fear. Their light brown flesh became visible, due to the ash fading off from the inordinate amount of sweat coming from both their glands. At last, Edmund appeared and walked into the circle, looking down at the men in wonder.

"They are one of them! I told you no trust!" hollered one of the Fillmore Whites.

Edmund walked slowly towards the Fillmore White who shouted. Edmund got in his face, causing the shouting man to look away disobediently. Edmund looked down at his fellow tribesman with a disgusted look on his face. He regressed his eyes back on the fallen Redeemers and knelt beside one of them. A believer of the local tales and horror stories, the Redeemer cowered back in fear of Edmund, praying them not to be true. The Fillmore White, whom the leader of the Redeemers threw the knife at, walked beside Edmund and handed him the blade that he removed from his shoulder. There was fresh blood on the blade.

Edmund yanked the arrow out of the Redeemer's leg, causing him to shriek in pain. Some blood seeped out of the Redeemer's thigh as he panted in agony. Edmund examined the blood on the tip of the arrow and knife.

"You see? We bleed the same blood as you," said Edmund.

Edmund got up and nodded to his men. Two brawny Fillmore Whites picked the wounded Redeemer up by the arms and dragged him back to their community while two other Fillmore Whites dragged the other. The two men covered in black begged for mercy as the Fillmore Whites dragged them ruthlessly towards their village.

Dusk evaporated into dawn as Richard and the others gathered every survivor out of the hospital. Richard ordered everyone to vacate to their housing quarters until further notice. It took nearly ten hours for them to put the fire out. Fortunately, a few people within the town were volunteer firefighters who knew how to work the nearby hydrants. Everyone worked their muscles and bodies to the brink of collapse as some of them dropped down to their knees and backs outside the hospital. Ron walked over to Richard who stood and looked at the charred and debilitated building. His long, black leather long-jacket became decorated with large burn marks and ash. The two stood there without exchanging a word.

At the corner of their eyes, Benjamin appeared to the scene. Horrified and fatigued, he looked at the wreckage in shock and distress. He looked at Richard with grief and sorrow on his face. Richard looked at him with no expression.

"Did everyone make it out?" asked Benjamin with fear in his tone. "Is everyone…"

Benjamin vomited from the emotions of worry and trepidation. He held his knees and spit the rest of the fluids out. Benjamin's purge went almost unnoticed by Richard. Once Benjamin finished, he wiped his mouth with his sleeve.

"There was a fire in the woods," said Benjamin, exhausted. "They got a jump on me. There were too many. Their faces were blacked out. I couldn't…Richard, I'm sorry."

"Did you see Diane?" asked Ron.

Benjamin panted from his exhaustive state and his recent vomit. He looked at Richard and shook his head with disbelief.

"They have her?" he asked.

The Town of Jasper

Richard did not look at Benjamin or Ron. He continued to look at the destruction of everything he built. Still wondering when the nightmare would end and if he'd wake, Richard shut his eyes and wondered if his wife was still alive.

"Make sure everyone gets plenty of water and food," said Richard.

His voice caught Ron and Benjamin's attention quickly.

"Ration as best you can. I'm going to see them," stated Richard.

Ron and Benjamin acknowledged Richard with a nod. Before they knew it, Richard was already walking away.

Richard walked up the path of the 'Keep Out Zone' and noticed fresh tracks along the path. The tracks caught both his concern and attention. The walk was hard on his knees after all the physical work and lifting of the last dozen hours. The day was partly cloudy, with a goose-bumpy chill in the air. Richard was curious why he hadn't seen one of them yet. Usually, a few roamed around the borders when someone passed through. Finally, Richard reached the entry point to their community, waiting to be greeted by Edmund or one of his men. Richard waited patiently, placing his hands in his jacket to keep warm. As he stood around, two gigantic Fillmore Whites stood behind him, completely undetected by Richard. Their heavy breathing made Richard aware of their presence as he slid his hands out of his pocket. Something was wrong. He could feel it. He turned around slowly. The two men held sharp spears pointed at him in attack formation. Richard looked them, wondering why they were acting so hostile.

"Go," said one of them in a deep tone, signaling him to walk straight into the village.

Richard did as they commanded and trotted down the path into the heart of their village with the two albino men trailing behind him.

The village, surrounded by greenhouses and huts of all sizes, was relatively quiet. Some clothing hung by stringed clothing lines. There were fire pits beside each hut and each greenhouse was filled with fresh vegetables and gorgeous plant life. Richard continued forward as he heard commotion around the corner. As he turned around the bend past one of the massive greenhouses, there was a crowd of people surrounding something.

"Move!" shouted one of the men behind him.

As Richard got within feet of the crowd, some of them turned to look at him. Their red and pink eyes and pale white faces locked on Richard. The two albino men grabbed him by the back shoulders, dragging him into the middle of the scene. They threw him to his knees as Richard looked at the two black-faced prisoners in the center. The Redeemers were petrified and stunned as they sat, tied to a wooden beam.

"You send these men to kill!" cried one of them as he grabbed Richard.

"No!" Edmund yelled, situated front and center. "This man is not our enemy!" He said, referring to Richard. "Lift him up, now."

The two men lifted Richard up onto his feet. Edmund walked up to him with his people surrounding them. His pinkish eyes had a look of deep concern in them.

"How are you, friend?" asked Edmund.

Richard panted and looked around.

"What's happening here?"

"Last night, one of my people was murdered. Three men in black came in at night. One got away. But these two, we caught."

Richard looked at the men tied to the beam.

"They attacked us too. You have to know I did not send them."

"I know you didn't," he said kindly. "These men, they have no shadow. The darkness surrounds them always. I know you did not send them here. But my people need to be convinced otherwise"

"So what now?" asked Richard.

"One of these men has to die. And I can't be the one. It has to be you."

"Me?" asked Richard.

"If you want my people's trust, you will do what's necessary. I am not an advocate of killing, friend, but this is what has to happen if we are to continue our agreement. And our friendship."

Richard understood the reality of the situation and looked at the two prisoners with anger.

"I need one of them. Alive," stated Richard.

"I only need one of them dead," said Edmund sadly.

Edmund handed Richard the same pistol Richard gave to him during their first encounter. Richard shook his head in disapproval.

"No," said Richard sinisterly.

Richard walked towards the prisoners with Edmund by his side. Edmund signaled to some of his men to release one of them. Two Fillmore Whites untied a Redeemer from the beam and tied a rope around his hands and feet.

"Bring that one to his truck," ordered Edmund.

Richard knelt in front of the prisoner as the Fillmore Whites began banging drums and chanting in uproar. They wanted blood. They chanted in symphony, causing the captive Redeemer to look around him with trepidation. Richard looked at him gravely.

"Who are you?" Richard asked sinisterly. "Where did you take her?"

The radical man remained silent on the matter. He closed his eyes and began to breathe in and out slowly while he shook his head. Richard grabbed the man's throat as the chanting in the back intensified. The man's eyes popped open as he looked at Richard.

"You'll never find us. And you'll never see us coming," he whispered assuredly.

Richard became infuriated as the drums beat louder. Edmund, not wanting to witness the scene, walked away back to his quarters.

"I just see you," Richard said severely as he stood up.

Richard looked around him at the crowd of Fillmore's chanting for vengeance. Richard bit the inside of his cheeks as he looked at the savage race with evil and intensity. He began to let the iniquity of the scene and fierceness of the people fuel his rage. Richard walked up to the gigantic albino man who nearly severed his head. He unsheathed the machete out of the enormous man's holster. He plucked a burning torch out of the ground with his other hand and marched up to the prisoner. He planted the torch and machete into the soil and began to untie the Redeemer. With the same rope, Richard tied the man's hands tightly behind the wooden beam and shoved a piece of cloth into his mouth. The dirty rag made the Redeemer choke and gag. Richard then tied the man's feet to the bottom of the wood post and pulled the man's hood down, showing his face of ash.

Richard couldn't hear himself think as the chants echoed throughout the village. The prisoner in the black cloak looked at Richard with fear of imminent death in his eyes. He shook his head and begged for salvation as Richard yanked the torch out of the earth and walked slowly up to him. The man's begging words were inarticulate and incomprehensible through the gag as Richard touched the torch against the man's black cloak. The fabric caught fire quickly and began to spread around his body. The immense heat made the man yelp and scream. The chanting mantra ensued louder than ever as the prisoner went up in flames. His legs and knees jerked and wobbled as the he hollered in the purest of agony. Richard looked at the man burn with a wicked delight while the band of albinos screamed and cheered behind him. The Redeemer's shrieks and yelps of agony were mute in the acoustics of the cries and hollers of the Fillmore Whites' vengeance.

As the man slowly burned to death, Richard yanked the machete out of the dirt and got close enough to the burning Redeemer to feel the burning flames against his face. Richard lifted the machete with his right hand above his head and brought it down hard against the Redeemer's chest. He swung the machete repeatedly against the Redeemer's already dead body as blood spewed onto Richard's face and clothing. The chants of the surrounding Fillmore Whites died down as they looked on in surprise and a degree of terror. Finally, in one swift swing, Richard devoured the Redeemer's head, sending it rolling around on the ground. Suddenly, the yells and screams of the Fillmore Whites came to a complete stop. The tribe of mutilated albinos looked at Richard, whose face was covered in blood and sweat, with a sense of subordination. Richard panted as he looked around at the group of villagers. He had gained back their trust and allegiance.

Tomorrow

The Night Before "The Incident"
September 2011

Settling into their new home in Jasper, Richard dried his hair with his towel while Diane sat on their bed reading a book. Their kids were getting ready for bed, as it was getting late at night. Diane looked at Richard over the top rim of her book.

"Anything new on him yet?" she asked.

The question put Richard out of his optimistic and bright attitude.

"Not yet," he said.

Diane knew the question bothered Richard. She also knew how much the situation was hurting him.

"We'll make sure the kids keep him in mind when they say their prayers tonight. You going to see him soon?"

"Tomorrow," he said.

Richard looked at Diane as she went back to her reading. Feeling his powerful gaze upon her, she reverted her eyes up at him as he watched her. She smiled at him and put the book down.

"What?" Diane asked, giggling.

"Just looking at something beautiful," Richard said.

Diane was flattered as she grinned at Richard. Richard squinted at the wall behind her and walked up to it.

"The color they painted the wall, so beautiful," Richard said jokingly.

Diane grabbed her pillow and hit him in the back with it with her one free hand. Richard clutched the pillow, and Diane pulled him on top of her. Richard began to kiss her and stole the book out of her hands. He flung it off to the side of the bed as the

The Town of Jasper

two began to fool around. He caressed her breasts as she began to reach down his leg. Their tongues battled one another aggressively. Richard felt his erection getting stiffer as he kissed her forehead. Before anything could progress, Victoria entered the room.

"Mommy," said their little girl.

Victoria stood at the door with her stuffed monkey gripped tightly near her face. The two of them looked at her, feeling the emotions and sexual drive deteriorate. Diane looked up at Richard.

"It's story time," Diane said with a smile.

"And what timing it is," said Richard.

"Be right there, sweetheart," said Diane.

Victoria scurried away back to her room.

"I didn't want to be another number," said Diane.

"What?" asked Richard.

"The townhouses. I didn't want it because they were all the same. One after the other. I wanted to live in a place that was different. I didn't want to be just another number."

Richard kissed Diane on the forehead.

"I'm really glad we live here," he said with a smile.

Diane kissed him back and slipped away from the bed as Richard fell on his side. He got himself out and walked with Diane toward Victoria's room. Her new room was painted pink with unicorns and stuffed animals scattered throughout the floor, shelves, and walls. Victoria sat on her bed as Diane lay beside her. She pulled the blanket over her and stroked her hair. Richard sat at the end of the bed.

"Which one do you want me to read tonight?"

"I changed my mind. No story tonight," she said.

"No story?" Richard asked surprisingly.

"No. We can do a story tomorrow," she said kindly.

"Than what do you want to do tonight, sweetie?" asked Diane delicately.

Victoria shrugged her shoulders as she began to get more tired. The comfort of her parents close to her made her feel safe. She began to doze off. Richard grabbed Diane's ankle gently. She looked at him as she stroked her daughter's hair. Richard got up as quietly as possible after Victoria dozed off. He walked out of the room to check up on his Joseph in the neighboring room. Inside his room, Joseph settled himself into his bed. Richard poked his head in to make sure he was okay and ready to check in for the night. He walked into the room and stood over his eight-year-old boy.

"Everything all set?" asked Richard.

"Yup," said Joseph, looking directly at the ceiling.

"Okay," said Richard.

"Did you see it?" asked Joseph.

Richard looked at him, confused. He had not idea to what his son was referring to.

"See what?"

"My art project," said Joseph.

"Eyes," said Richard.

Joseph looked at Richard.

"What art project?" asked Richard.

"The one I made. It's on the fridge," said Joseph, looking at his father.

"Oh, I didn't get a chance to see it yet. I'll go check it out right away," said Richard as he walked towards the door. He shut the bedroom light.

"Love you, dad," said Joseph.

"Love you, kiddo."

Richard walked down the stairs into the kitchen. He flicked the light on and took a look at the front of the refrigerator. There were coupons, post-it notes, pictures, and other papers decorating the outside of the fridge door. Richard moved his eyes in all directions, trying to locate his son's art project. It only took him a few seconds to find it centered in the middle. The project was a finished drawing of something. He removed the magnet that held the drawing on the door and held it up towards his eyes. The picture was of a man. The man had dark brown hair and had a jacket on that Richard recognized. It was a brown leather jacket that Richard would always wear on the weekends while raking leaves or shoveling snow. On top it read…

My Dad

My Hero

The words punctured Richard's heart as he stared at the photo. It is always a father's duty to be an influential figure in his son's life. To be a son's hero or daughter's protector was commonplace for any good father. But when it is said, written, or reminded of the fact, it created an indescribable feeling that went well beyond pride. Richard could not stop staring at the photo as his body went numb. Unable to find the words or feelings to feel, Richard just stood and stared. After some time passed, Richard placed the drawing back onto the fridge. His hands shook as he placed the magnet over it, which held it in place. He looked at it again and began to walk away from it. He flicked the lights off in the kitchen and walked up the stairs into the dark hallway. He walked up to the front of his son's room and poked his head inside. Before he was able to thank him, Joseph had slipped into a deep sleep.

In the other room, Diane was humming a soothing melody to Victoria, who had also fallen into a deep sleep. Diane looked up at Richard as she continued to hum. Richard leaned his shoulder on the wall and observed everything that was important to him in his

life. In that moment, Richard felt one of those feelings that reminded him that he had what so many people would die for. Richard left the two of them in peace and walked into the master bedroom. He sat on the edge of the bed without a worry, knowing his family was safe and
sound. He did not know that would be the last time he would ever feel that way. The next morning, everything would change.

The Town of Jasper

The Pink House On Gansevoort Street

Present Day 2016
Five Years After "The Incident"

Detective Sutherland looked both ways before crossing the road of Gansevoort Street. Trying to be as incognito as possible, he walked quickly towards the house. The old, brick house stood on an acre of land. The detective constantly checked his surroundings to make sure no one would spot him. At this point, everyone in Jasper knew everyone, and if they saw him, at worst, his cover would be blown. He took a few strides up the steps and knocked on the door. He quickly placed the grey ski mask over his face. He looked behind him again to make sure no one was tailing him. If they were, he wouldn't know anyway. Walter Cavill, a late fifty something, dark-skinned man with salt and pepper, hair cracked open the door and poked his head through.

"Who are you?" he asked. "What's with the mask?"

Walter seemed uneasy about something. The isolation over the years had taken a significant toll on him, and it showed in his face.

"I'm looking for Walter Cavill. I was told I could find him here."

Sutherland knew the man was Cavill, but wanted things to be under the radar. Walter used to be the head of organization and management at Jasper Hospital. He had access and information on patient and staff. Information Sutherland wanted. He didn't want him knowing he was a detective. Walter looked at him curiously, trying to figure him out in any way possible.

"Who are you?" he asked again. "You better come up with something good."

"My name is Tom Wembley."

"I don't know you, Tom Wembley. If no one knows you in Jasper now, you're a dead man walking."

"I represent the Red Cross," Sutherland said. "Nancy Ringwell said I could find you here.

"Red Cross gave up on us some time ago," said Walter. "Are you here to provide resources, food, or medicine?"

"No," said Sutherland. "I'm here to ask you a few questions."

Walter kicked open the door and pointed his shotgun at Sutherland's head. The detective put his hands up.

"I don't know your face. Who are you? Tell me the truth, or I will blow a hole between your ears."

"My name is Detective Foster. I am here to find out what's going on in this town. That, and I'm looking for someone."

Walter gripped the shotgun firmly and was ready to fire.

"Who?"

"Can we talk inside? I'm unarmed. Feel free to check for yourself. I have a trunk load of canned food and bottled water," said Sutherland.

"I want to see identification. Reach for your badge and ID *slowly*."

Sutherland slowly reached into his pocket and took out his wallet. He opened it slowly and slid out his ID. Walter squinted at the ID and saw he was telling the truth.

"My badge is in the glove compartment of my car. I can go get it if you want."

The Town of Jasper

Walter looked at his car parked across the street. He looked back at Sutherland with the gun still in his face. He nodded at him to go to his car.

Sutherland rushed off the porch and ran towards his car. He looked both ways before he crossed the road again. He reached his car and fumbled for the keys in his pocket. He opened the passenger door and bent his back down to open the glove. He reached inside and pulled out his badge. He showed it to Walter from across the road. He thumbed the trunk button and it popped open. He lifted up the hatch and took out a case of water with canned food on top of it. Walter looked at him and said nothing. Sutherland closed the trunk and walked into the house with the water and canned food.

"Consider this a down payment," said Sutherland as he placed it on the table.

"Take a seat," said Walter as he reached for one of the cans and water bottles. On the television, there was a football game on. The Jets were playing the Falcons. Sutherland looked at the television, confused, knowing that there was no cable in Jasper anymore. The game was a repeat, because the detective remembered the game. He remembered it clearly because he bet big on the Falcons and came up short. The house was filled with a faint odor that made Sutherland's nostrils wince. It wasn't like anything he had smelled before. It smelled of burnt hair mixed with fresh paint.

On the shelves and countertops, were multiple photos of Walter when he looked healthier. Some photos were of him and a woman. Others were of him and a golden retriever. He looked happy in the photos. Walter popped open one of the caps and slugged the water in seconds. Sutherland watched somewhat uncomfortably, but understandably. Walter reached for a can and began opening it with his pocketknife. The detective looked outside the sliding door window into the backyard. There was a small shed and a jungle gym at opposite sides of the half-acre of crab grass. There was also a fire pit towards the end of he property. In the center, there were small objects aligned to form a symbol of some sort. The detective squinted and leaned his forearm against the cold glass. Old, torn clothing decorated the center of the yard and spelled,

Save Us

"Don't tell me what happens," asked Walter.

The detective turned around and looked at the starving man eating. He looked at Sutherland innocently.

"What?" asked Sutherland.

"The game. Don't tell me what happens. It's the game of the week. Been looking forward to it," he said. "Now, please sit. Sit," he said, trying to get him away from the window.

Sutherland looked at the man in a perturbed fashion and looked outside the window again. He looked at the massive shed painted a dark beige color. The windows were blocked by something, making it seem impossible to see what was inside.

"That's a cute dog," said Sutherland as he gazed outside. "I have one just like it."

Walter stopped eating from the can and looked up at him. Sutherland felt the man's stare upon the back of his head. The man chewed slowly and looked down, saddened.

"It was my wife's," Walter said.

The Town of Jasper

Sutherland looked at a picture of Walter and his wife next to it. The frame's glass was cracked and shattered. Walter looked at the detective examining it.

"I was coming home from a business trip late that night. It was past midnight by maybe an hour or two," said Walter. "I opened the door and heard my wife upstairs. She wasn't alone."

Sutherland's attention locked on Walter's story as he leaned up against the window's glass. Every moment or so, he'd look back at the broken photo. Walter continued.

"*The screams,*" said Walter. "She was cheating. Twenty years of marriage down some dirty sewer. So, I made myself a cup of coffee, and I sat at my dining room table as they went at it. And while I sat there, I pondered about the ways I was going to kill them."

Sutherland became distressed, sympathetic, and understanding in one mixed emotion. Walter told the story with an eerie confidence.

"I didn't know if I wanted to make it slow or do it quickly. So I sat down at my dining room table, and I pondered like I never fucking pondered before" h,e said angrily. "Then after hours passed and the screams stopped, I made my way up the stairs. I was going to kill the man she was with first. Strangle him with my bare hands. Then her. So I opened the door, and I saw the two of them under my sheets. Naked. They didn't hear me come in. I got on top of the man and when I placed my hands around his neck I didn't feel a pulse. Same thing with my wife."

Sutherland looked back outside, knowing the rest of the story. He'd heard versions of it before.

"It was my wife's dog," he said.

The thought of what transpired after that made the man very uncomfortable and sickened. He coughed, swallowed, and managed to regain his poise. Sutherland slipped away from the window.

"So, Detective. What would you like to know?" Walter asked, looking to change the subject as quickly as possible.

Sutherland got situated and took out his notepad and pen. He leaned it against his right leg, as he knew each question had to be asked appropriately. He needed to take a slow burn approach to get what he needed.

"Well, I just want some information on the hospital. Patient and staff details for the most part. If you have any information on symptoms post-incident or things of that nature, it would be greatly appreciated on our end."

Walter looked at him funny as he ate some of the canned ravioli. He chewed and swallowed as he wiped his mouth with the back of his hand.

"I'm not sure if anything was salvaged..." Walter stated.

"Salvaged?" asked Sutherland.

"The hospital was burned down," said Walter.

Walter looked down into the can of food and ate some more. He thought about something as he chewed and grinded the food in his mouth slowly. Sutherland was bewildered.

"Burned down? How?"

Walter finished the can of food and reached for another one. He began opening it with his pocketknife as he tried to remember.

"The Redeemers," said Walter. "Crazy sons of bitches."

Confused, Sutherland didn't know to whom Walter was referring to.

"Redeemers? I don't understand. Are those the people who Ms. Ringwell was talking about? The faces like coal?"

The Town of Jasper

"That's right," said Walter brusquely. "Crazy bitch that Nancy is now, but she's still sharp as a tack."

"Did anyone inside survive? Are they safe?" asked Sutherland hectically.

"Not everyone. But most of them are fine, now. I hear they're thinking about forming a safe zone. Don't know where yet."

"Where are they now? Are they being treated?"

"They're fine," said Walter, not totally convinced the detective was trustworthy.

"Where are they, Mr. Cavill? That's a lot of food and water for *they're fine*," Sutherland reminded him. "I'm here to help."

"Strangers don't help anymore. They kill. They try to get a read on you. Find your weak spot. And if they do, you're history," said Walter.

Sutherland dropped his pen and looked at him. The detective knew already, but he wanted to hear it.

"What happened to this place?"

"Segregation," said Walter. "Before everything, the town was separated between the West and East side of the tracks. The rich and lower middle class had bad blood. But people came together as a unity after the incident. But when things started to get bad and they cut off the food and water supply, people separated from the herd one after the other. It wasn't supposed to be this way," he said with a quirk. "Different groups and bands of crazies formed when things got worse and people got hungrier. Most of them formed their own codes and beliefs. Some small, quiet book club sort of things. Women resorted to prostitution."

Sutherland looked at Walter, bothered by the statement. Walter looked at him, knowing it troubled the detective. He shrugged his shoulders.

"People would do anything to keep moving. To survive," said Walter.

"You ever tickle your fancy there?" asked Sutherland.

"Occasionally…" said Walter. "I'm a man with needs, Detective. Since my wife died…"

"Where can I find them?"

"Looking for love, Detective?" asked Walter with a creepy look.

Sutherland provided a look of sternness and austerity. It made Walter's strange grin turn strict in a hurry.

"I'm not entirely sure. I'm a little loopy, Detective, I haven't eaten. Memory is mush to say the least," Walter said nervously.

"What about the other groups?" interjected Sutherland.

"Others became hostile, who resorted to more violent approaches, like the Redeemers. There's the albino group of Navajos up in the hills. Savage son of a guns with the red eyes and deformities. But they always kept to themselves until after we got cut off. A few people think the albinos are the one who burned the hospital and that they're the coal-faced lunatics."

"What of the survivors? The victims. Where are they now since the hospital?" asked Sutherland.

Walter smirked and chuckled as he polished off the rest of the can and placed it down. Walter showed more signs of reluctance to the detective's question.

"Shit is good," he said.

Sutherland got up off the couch and looked at Walter.

"You'll get sick of them. Or maybe you won't," said Sutherland.

The Town of Jasper

Sutherland walked towards the door, insinuating he would not provide Walter with the rest of the food and water. Walter got up off the couch quickly.

"Wait," said Walter. "Hold on a sec."

"Where are they?" asked Sutherland.

"I can't tell you that."

"Why not?"

"Because we don't take chances anymore," said Walter.

"Neither do I," said Sutherland. "I hope you enjoyed that one."

Sutherland paced away from him again, hoping Walter would fold on his bluff.

"They're spread out," he shouted, causing Sutherland to stop in front of the door. "He doesn't want them all in one place in case of another attack."

The detective retreated back to his car and carried in the rest of the food and water. He placed it down on the floor and wherever there was room on the table. There was enough food to last a single person a week.

"Don't go through it in one shot," said Sutherland.

Sutherland walked for the door for the last time and stopped when he reached it. He looked behind him at Walter with his notepad in his hand.

"You wouldn't happen to know where I could find Richard Morrissey, would you?

Walter looked at the detective like a deer in the headlights. He began to wonder why the detective wanted to know, and if that was the main reason he stopped by. Covering up his whereabouts and not showing any sign of knowing him, Walter shook off the question and the fact that it took him by surprise.

268

"There is no one here by that name, Detective. You must be mistaken," said Walter.

Sutherland cracked a slight smile. He didn't know why he did, but it just formed from the side of his jaw. He looked at Walter and nodded.

"Must be..." said the detective.

Sutherland walked out of the front door and off the porch. Behind him, Walter closed the door and reached for the shotgun. Sutherland retreated back to his car and fired up the engine. He looked over at Walter's house again and waited. The engine warmed up as Sutherland counted down in his head. After about a minute passed by, Sutherland turned the car off and swung the door open. He marched with heavy footsteps towards Walter's house as the anger and adrenaline spun like a tornado inside him. He reached for his side arm and removed it from his holster. He knocked on the door again with his pistol.

"What the hell?" Walter screamed from the inside. "Who the hell is this now?"

Walter opened the door a crack. Sutherland kicked it open, sending the door crashing against Walter's nose. Walter hit the ground hard as blood spewed from his nostrils. Sutherland reached down, grabbed him by the collar, and pointed his gun inches away from his face.

"Where is he?" shouted Sutherland "Where is Morrissey?"

"I don't know!" shrieked Walter in pain.

Sutherland pressed the pistol against Walter's forehead. Walter began to panic and shake.

"Where is the house? Where are the women?"

"I don't know," repeated Walter, fearful for his life.

Sutherland cocked the lever back on the pistol and pressed it against Walter's forehead again.

The Town of Jasper

"Where is it?" hollered Sutherland.

"It wasn't supposed to be this way!" Walter yelled frantically. "It wasn't supposed to be this way!"

"Shut up," said Sutherland.

"It wasn't supposed to be…it was my wife's dog," Walter said as he became hysterical.

"Shut the fuck up!" shouted Sutherland. "Where is the fucking house?"

Feeling the anger like an unstable force in him, Sutherland pistol whipped Walter on the side of the head and picked him up by his shirt.

"Where is it? Where is the house?" demanded Sutherland loudly.

"I don't know! I don't…It wasn't supposed to be this way! Please, I don't know…"

Sutherland shot Walter in the leg, causing a flesh wound. Walter screamed and bellowed deafeningly as he fell to the floor. Sutherland pointed the gun at Walter's head as Walter clutched his leg in agony.

"It's at the end of the street!" shouted Walter. "It's the pink house!"

The anger and adrenaline simmered throughout the detective's body as he walked out of Walter's house and back into his vehicle.

A lofty house painted a reddish pink color, with decorative lights hanging from the windows and gutters, stood at the end of Gansevoort Street. Detective Sutherland walked up the driveway and towards the walkway leading up to the front porch of the tall pink house. A minute or two went by after he knocked on the door, when a woman with long, brown frizzy hair with a shade of purple, opened it. She was on the heavy side, with a sluggish face. She had a stench of cheap cigarettes, and it looked like she had just been handled a few times already. She looked at the detective strangely.

"Can I help you?" asked the woman calmly.

"Hi, I'm a friend of Walter Cavill. Can I come in?"

"What's your name, friend of Walter Cavill? Haven't ever seen you around…"

"I'm Michael Allen. I keep to myself, mostly."

"What street do you live on?" asked the woman.

"On Arnold Street. I'm the house at the end of the block."

"Stop lying to me," said the woman.

"Okay. Truth is…" said Sutherland as he reached behind his shirt. "Truth is, I'm a detective from the outside."

Sutherland held his gun in front of him, showing it off to the woman who looked at it without much fear. Sutherland looked at the woman through his black lenses. The woman looked back at him, unafraid.

"You gonna shoot me cowboy? You think that's the first time someone drew a gun in here? What else you got?"

"I've got a very short temper and a dwindling sense of patience. You can let me in now or the FBI in tomorrow," said Sutherland in a controlling manner.

The woman smirked at Sutherland.

"Take the mask off," she asked. "Prove that you're an outsider."

Reluctantly, Sutherland removed the mask, showing his face to the woman. She examined his face closely. After a few seconds, she consented.

"What happened to the other guy?" she asked, referring to his scar.

"What makes you think it was a guy?"

Barely impressed at his attempt at intimidation, Martha looked him up and down again.

"Five minutes," she stated. "Take your shoes off."

Inside the brothel, women of all ages, shapes, and sizes walked around and slept. Sutherland inspected the bottom level of the house as he followed the woman who he suspected to be the madam. There were dark stains on the walls, and the house smelled of cat litter that hadn't been changed in a long time. The place made the detective sick. A few women walked by half naked and checked out the detective. Disregarding their advances, the detective leaned up against the wall in the kitchen, where the woman poured herself some hot coffee.

"Coffee?" she asked.

"No. I'm fine," said Sutherland.

"So. Detective. What would you like to know?"

"What's your name?" he asked.

"Martha…"

"Your daddy have a last name?" asked Sutherland sarcastically.

"Brown…"she said rudely.

"How long have you been spinning tricks here, Ms. Brown?"

The woman did not feel comfortable cooperating with him, but she had no choice in the matter but to do so. She took a breath and complied.

"After things got bad. I needed to find a way to survive…"

"So you decided to get involved in this business?"

"Didn't have much of a choice," she said.

"There's always a choice, Ms. Brown. What is your compensation for your services here? I assume it isn't cash…"

"Food. Water. Warm clothes, sometimes. Mostly food and things like that," she said.

"Are resources regulated here? How did the people in charge not trace the variance back to you?"

"Please," she said with a laugh. "Our regular clients are the higher-ups here. Plus, we methodize our business. We make sure we see just enough clients a week to slip under the radar."

"What did you do before the incident? Before *all this*?"

"I was a librarian. I did it for fifteen years," she said as she sipped her mug.

"Married?"

"Yes."

"I take it your husband is a victim."

"Yes."

"And he is alive?"

"Yes, he is. I visit him every day. Are you going to report me?"

"I have no interest in your business here. I do, however, have an interest in where I can find the safe zone."

Martha sipped again and looked closely at the detective. She looked down at the table, knowing her back was against a wall. She tapped her fingers on the counter with her fingernails.

"You have somebody here…"

"Excuse me?" said the detective.

"You have someone here. Someone you want to find. I can tell…"

"Ms. Brown, my business is to get to the bottom of law and order here. Clearly, things are getting worse and things have changed. I am collecting quantitative data on the incident and trying to see if I can help the CDC in any way possible."

Martha sipped her coffee and continued to tap her fingers one by one on the table. She placed the cup down and smiled, showing her dimples to the detective.

"Whatever you say, officer," she said eerily. "That wall is never coming down," she mumbled as she sipped.

"Come again?" interjected Sutherland.

"The wall. It's never coming down," she repeated.

"Where is the safe zone?" asked Sutherland again.

"Are you sure you don't want to spend a little time with one of my women here? You seem a little…"

"Where is it?" Sutherland asked with a raised tone.

There was a pause in the conversation that dragged out for a while. The women in the house all stopped and stared at the two of them, hoping there wouldn't be some sort of altercation that would cause unwanted attention. Martha finished her coffee and got up off her chair. She placed the cup into the sink and shuffled some dishes around.

"It's not in motion yet. Rumors going around that it's going to be at the school," she said. "But you won't get close to it. It'll be heavily guarded. He'll have the place running like Santa's factory."

"Since the attack, I know," said Sutherland.

"Right," said Martha.

"Out of curiosity, are you familiar with a woman by the name of Olivia Sutherland?"

"She's not one of mine, if that's what you're asking," said Martha.

"That's not what I'm asking," said Sutherland angrily.

"I haven't heard of her."

"Richard Morrissey ever spend any time here?"

"Richard Morrissey is a decent and good man," she said.

"So you're saying your business here is *indecent*?"

"Don't try to put words in my mouth, detective."

"You've had worse things put in your mouth, I'm sure, now why don't you try to do a *decent* and honest thing and tell me where he can be found."

"Why do you want to find him?" Martha asked.

"I ask. You answer," said Sutherland.

Martha examined Sutherland, trying to get a read on him. Something about the detective's intentions struck her funny.

"You don't even know why you want to find him, do you?"

"I ask. You answer," said Sutherland angrily.

Martha smirked at him.

"Maybe I'll just take you to him and watch him kill you for treason."

Sutherland sniggered. He liked the fact that he got the best of the woman. She cracked and she knew it now. Sutherland had gotten the information he needed.

"And then what? Maybe get your slate wiped clean for what you do here? I bet he doesn't know the business on this side of the street."

"Is there anything else I can do for you today, officer?" Martha asked politely and with a grin.

"No," said Sutherland grimly.

"Then I'll walk you out," she replied calmly.

Martha escorted the detective through the living room, where a few women looked at them walk by. A couple of women smiled at the detective, hoping to woo him with their charm. To no avail, the detective looked at them shamefully. Martha opened the front door.

"I do thank you for your time, detective. Do come back. Men in uniform are always welcome. Maybe next time you'll come without the badge," she said cheerfully.

"It's not too late to get involved in something a little less rated R, Ms. Brown."

"Life is rated R, detective," she replied.

The detective didn't find her comment amusing. He provided a look of disappointment.

"It's never too late," he repeated in an effort to reassure the broken woman.

She smiled. Almost flattered at the comment. She even chuckled slightly. The woman was beyond a normal life and had adapted to a new way of doing business.

"And do what? Go back to shelving books and putting on a fake smile forty hours a week? I don't really think the world wants another librarian," Martha said, somewhat confidently.

"I think you need to stop thinking about what the world wants and start focusing on what you want *from* this world," said the detective as he stepped out of the house. "Because it doesn't need more whores."

Martha Brown watched Sutherland leave the property from the porch of the tall pink house at the end of Gansevoort Street.

The Plea

One Week After "The Incident"
September 2011

A week after the incident, Sutherland was cleared from the hospital and free to go home. Sutherland barged into the front entrance of the police station and marched towards a group of officers huddled around Captain Rory Larson. Anxious and angst-ridden, Detective Sutherland came within feet of the crowd, causing Captain Larson to notice Sutherland's sudden appearance. Slightly aggravated to see him, he dismissed the men prematurely. Detective Sutherland didn't look at any of the bypassing officers directly. His gaze was set on Captain Larson.

"You shouldn't be back so soon," said Captain Larson.

"What is happening?" asked Sutherland.

"Go home," suggested Larson. "It's too soon."

"What is happening?" shouted Sutherland.

A few men stopped what they were doing and looked up at the two of them. Sutherland's scream caught some unwanted attention. Captain Larson sighed deeply as his blood pressure rose.

"They're walling the town off," said Captain Larson with grief.

"Is it true? Is he in there?" asked Sutherland, referring to Richard.

"How'd you find out?" asked the captain.

Sutherland reached into his pocket and took out the folded note Richard wrote to him. He turned it over and showed Captain Larson.

"I need to get inside," said Sutherland.

"What?" asked Captain Larson.

"I need to get inside," Sutherland repeated.

"Why?"

"I need to find him. Get him out."

"We don't have jurisdiction in there," stated Captain Larson.

"Get jurisdiction in there," demanded Sutherland. "Ask for it."

"This isn't something I can have approved overnight. This isn't some town-zoning meeting where a corrupt councilman can look the other way. This thing has become a phenomenon overnight. It's way out of our league."

"Maybe for the band of pansies you call officers here. But I'm getting inside there one way or another," said Sutherland.

"Is that so? Well, let me tell you something, Ranger Rick, the White House…"

"Spare me the bullshit, Captain," said Sutherland in a raised voice.

"Watch yourself, Detective. Don't let personal matters get in the way of your oh-so-prominent reputation," said Captain Larson sarcastically. "Richard was a great man. Best of the best. Damn good detective, too. But there isn't a damn thing we can do. If there were, I'd pry his ass out myself."

"I'm not asking," stated Sutherland.

"Neither am I," stated the captain.

Neither man said anything for a few moments. They both stood as the stalemate became aggravating. Two stubborn men who never backed down from one another were at a crossroads.

"We don't know what the fuck this thing is, Jack," said the captain, calming down. "These people died, and now we're getting reports they're coming back. But they're dormant or asleep or whatever the hell you want to call it. CDC will do what they do, and all we can do is wait."

"I can't just wait. He wouldn't," said Sutherland.

The captain looked at Sutherland, not knowing whether to feel anger, remorse, or both. Stressed out, he stroked his hair a few times and placed his hands on his desk.

"How in the hell do you expect me to convince the goddamn White House?" asked Captain Doyle.

"Let them know that after they quarantine the town, after no one has the balls to go past the wall, and after everyone forgets Jasper exists and runs far away from it, there is somebody among the runaways who is willing to go against the fucking grain."

"I don't know," said the captain. "You're not stable as of late."

"I'm fine," asserted Sutherland.

"Fine? You're a goddamn wrecking ball with a history of drug and alcohol abuse. How's that going to look when I try to pitch you to them?"

"They won't have a choice," Sutherland implied.

"If you get the green light and you fuck up in there, I'm pulling your ass out. *And* I'm taking your badge. The only reason why I'm not putting you on leave is because we are short on officers," informed Captain Larson.

"Everything that I have to lose, I've already lost," declared Sutherland.

The captain looked at Sutherland and felt his passion and urgency to take the case. The captain knew Sutherland was right. No one would dare take the risk of going into a quarantined zone. Sutherland had nothing to lose. He'd soon realize everything he had or ever loved was inside the wall.

The Town of Jasper

"They'll want something in return. You'll need to work with the CDC and gather information on what's happening inside there and what's going on with the victims. They won't give a shit about your plans to rescue him," said Captain Larson.

"I'll do both," stated Sutherland gravely. "Do you have his file, by chance?"

"Why? Want to finally find out what his real name is?" asked the captain

"No, I want to find out what his blood type is," said Sutherland sarcastically.

The captain looked at him with a minor snarl. He reached for a file on his desk and handed it to Sutherland. He opened it and reviewed his old partners basic information. Under his name, it said John Smith.

"He wasn't kidding about using the alias. I heard he changed it back to his real one. But that's anyone's guess," said the captain.

"Has anyone heard from him?"

"No. And all connection is lost at this point. Nothing will go through."

Sutherland said nothing as he reviewed the file of a tangible man with a fictitious identity. He thought about the countless days they worked together and about the good man he was. Before he could think about it any further, he closed the file and placed it on the captain's desk.

"Keep me updated," requested Sutherland.

Sutherland turned his back to the captain and began to walk away. Captain Larson put his head down and called out to him.

"He's not the only one inside," he called out.

Sutherland stopped walking and turned himself around to face the captain. His expression was probing to say the least, as he had no idea what Captain Larson was referring to.

"What?" asked Sutherland.

"Olivia. She's inside," said the captain.

Sutherland froze. He wasn't aware of the alleged fact. He knew his wife moved away. He just didn't know where.

"Who the hell told you that?" asked Sutherland aggressively.

"We were provided a full roster from the CDC. She was on it. And your daughter."

"They're in Jasper?" Sutherland asked fearfully and worriedly.

"They are."

"Are they victims?"

"I don't know," stated the captain.

Sutherland stood in a state of shock for a moment until he found himself walking away. A man with nothing and everything to lose, the detective opened the door and walked out of the building with a new purpose in his life. A motive that would challenge him beyond his imagination and push him past the point of no return.

The Fourth Little Pig Built A Safe Zone
Present Day 2016
Five Years After "The Incident"

The hospital stood in complete ruin. Bent and broken into a mirror image of what Jasper has become, the once safe haven of the incident's victims, now a landmark of deterioration and no hope. The townspeople became vulnerable and defenseless against an enemy they never saw coming and whose identity was shrouded in mystery. Richard demanded all surviving victims be brought to their homes until an alternative refuge be found. Richard orchestrated a council meeting to devise a plan in the aftermath of the Redeemer's attack.

Inside Town Hall, the representatives of The Council sat silently. Richard sat at the helm, overlooking them, eager to get the process started. There was a different brand of solemnity, as it has been less than forty-eight hours since the attack on the hospital. An adequate plan had to be implemented to ensure the safety of the victims. If not, another attack could be looming and take them by surprise again. However, Richard would not allow that to happen.

"How many did we lose?" asked Richard, opening up the conversation.

"Fifty one," said Ron from across the table with his hulking arms crossed.

The room went silent as they mourned the dead victims.

"Were we able to salvage any of the medical supplies?" Richard asked.

"We salvaged about half," said Jim firmly as he straightened his hunting cap. "The supplies are in the music room of the school."

"Ok. We have resources provided by the Fillmore Whites that will make up for our losses. Tomorrow I will conduct a eulogy at the cemetery to honor and bury our dead. In the meantime, we need a plan. And we need one today," he said. "I've thought about it. I want to move the remaining victims into the school. We will create a safe zone where no one will be able to penetrate the defenses."

"A safe zone?" asked Matilda.

"Yes," said Richard. "We are going to double the barriers with more people and board up every vulnerable spot within the school."

"How are we going to get more hands on deck? We are short, as is," said Henry.

"I'm going to enlist some help from our isolated groups," Richard said.

"Such as who?" asked William, unconvinced.

Richard looked at him ominously and threateningly. William looked down at the table in front of him.

"My apologies, Richard," said William as he bit on his pointer finger in discomfort.

Richard's eyes remained on William until he finally broke his gaze away to scan the rest of the council.

"Everyone has a price. Everyone is for sale," he said. "I'm tired of Jasper being a snow globe that our own people shake until it drops. Every able and capable body in this place is going to help."

"These other groups could be involved with the Redeemers," Ron said.

"They're going to be involved with *us* now," Richard said confidently.

The room fell quiet as The Council acknowledged Richard's stubbornly optimistic approach.

"What about these maniacs? What if they strike again?" asked Benjamin worriedly.

"They could be planning the next attack soon," said Jim.

"I think we need to focus on catching these 'Redeemers' and putting them on trial for their crimes," asserted Susan.

"Trial? They deserve to be killed," Benjamin declared.

"This is not a death penalty state!" asserted Susan.

"We are no longer part of a state! Look around you. We are trapped behind a wall. We're goddamn ants marching in a sandbox," William shouted.

"Enough," Richard said with a raised voice. "I am worried about the safety of our victims. That is our top priority right now. The school is our best option. We will have guards stationed at each entrance and exit, same as the hospital. As far as the Redeemers are concerned, they are far more than a group of radicals with free speech. They are dangerous and now a significant threat."

"We don't even know who they are," said Kendrick. "And what about what they found in the woods? They burnt their clothes."

Some side banter and mumbling occurred that annoyed Richard. He slammed his hand on the table and got their attention. Each of them went stone cold as they looked at Richard. He looked at his followers, ready to prep them for what was to come. Like a football coach ready to prep his players for game time.

"As far as we are concerned, the Redeemers have declared a war on Jasper. I can only assume the motive for their actions is to get the wall taken down by killing our innocent victims. Either way, when we find them, we will pry them out of their hole and kill every last one of them...unless somebody here objects and would like to have somebody they love die by their hands again."

Nobody said a word as the fear of killing others made them think. Things were happening fast, and there was little time to process the situation. The law and order had gone from democratic to murderous in a day. Richard awaited any form of response.

"Okay, then. We're done here," he said as he pushed his chair back.

The Council dispersed quietly and gradually. Ron hung around, trying to look busy as the other members passed him by. After the room cleared out, Ron walked up to Richard. Ron knew the situation had Richard apprehensive, to say the least. He also knew he would do whatever it took to get the town back to safety. And that was what worried him.

"Whatever you do, I know you will do it for the better of the community," Ron said. "But I'm worried about you, Richard."

"I'm worried about me too," Richard responded calmly.

Benjamin came rushing back into the room with a frantic expression on his face. Richard and Ron both looked at him with wonder.

"Richard," he said, out of breath. "Come quick!"

Outside the old tavern on West Road, a crowd of people gathered and cheered out wildly. On the curb and into the street, about twenty-five to thirty townspeople looked at someone situated in front of them. A man named Flynn led the assembly of the angry mob by pointing to the person in the center. Flynn was a tall, greasy blonde haired man, with a toned physique and rugged face. His long hair brushed up on his shoulders sloppily. His denim jacket was as dirty as his denim jeans.

The Town of Jasper

"These people are savages! They always have been! I told you they were not to be trusted. I told Richard! It's time we put our foot down!"

The crowd cheered and roared in agreement as Richard took cover behind the tavern building and eavesdropped.

"They burned down the hospital. They killed our loved ones! And yet, we trade with them? We provide them resources? That ends today!" Flynn hollered.

The crowd pumped their fists in rage and consent. Ron Carlisle walked into the middle of the crowd, wondering what the fuss was all about.

"What is going on here?" Ron asked.

"Changing of the guard!" hollered Flynn. "We have exposed those outcasts and fiends for who they really are."

Ron looked at the man in the middle lying dead on the floor. It was a Fillmore White dressed in a dark cloak. It had some ash painted on his face, lending people to believe they were the murderous group known as the Redeemers.

"Where did you find him?" asked Ron.

"He was found in the woods. A couple of men caught him running from the hospital."

"What men?" Ron questioned.

Two men, Burt Ryloth and Earl Pike, stepped forward. Two men with a southern style to them and sometimes incomprehensible drawl.

"We did," said Earl. "Gave us a good fight, but we brought him down." "How many more of us have to fall, constable, until we take a stand?" asked Flynn. "The madness and murder ends today!"

"Richard needs to be told of this," stated Ron.

"Richard is blind. He trusts these monsters. The people have spoken!" shouted Flynn. "No longer will one man lead this town. We, the people, will now lead it."

The mob of people cheered and chanted loudly. Ron looked around, somewhat overwhelmed.

"We will discuss this at the next council meeting. Everyone return back to your quarters," demanded Ron.

"The discussion is now," stated Flynn decisively. "These people have suffered enough. We all have. We cannot delay this any further."

People amongst the crowd nodded and mumbled in agreement. Flynn was winning over their vote of confidence. Ron looked around, feeling like it was one against the group of them.

"We need to gather more evidence," rebutted Ron. "We need Richard and The Council's approval."

"These things aren't reasonable beings. They're killers. I will not stand here and wait for another attack that puts a community that has stood for hundreds of years in harm's way. If Richard and your council don't approve, then…" said Flynn.

"Then what…?" Ron asked angrily.

"Than we fear the worst for them."

"We have plans that will protect us against another attack," said Ron. "We are going to build a safe zone at the school. We need…"

"We will not part take in your efforts to build another wall inside a wall. We need to go on the offensive. Take the fight to them, constable," stated Flynn firmly.

Ron looked at Flynn, concerned and apprehensive. A feeling of intensiveness and uncertainty overpowered him. He looked at the Fillmore White in the middle of the crowd and a great wave of fear crashed into him.

The Town of Jasper

"Let's get the body out of here. I don't want the children to see it," said Ron. "Benjamin and Jim, would you mind helping me with…."

Before Ron could finish his request, Richard pushed people out of the way and stormed into the center of the crowd. He dragged a beaten and mangled man by his legs and situated him in the middle of the mob of disgruntled citizens. Flynn and Ron looked at both Richard and the prisoner, confounded. Richard looked around at everyone on the verge of collapse of exhaustion. He breathed heavily, struggling with each breath.

"It's not them," he said. "It's not the Fillmores."

He looked at Flynn and Ron standing next to one another. The prisoner grunted and whimpered in soreness and pain.

"He was caught in their territory the same night of the attack on the hospital. He and two others killed one of their people," said Richard as the crowd looked down at the dead Fillmore White. "Their leader said three of them snuck in and tried to murder them. One got away."

"Where is the other one they caught?" asked Ron.

Richard looked at everyone adamantly with an unbending expression, suggesting the alleged. Everyone was taken back by the fact.

"I'm a dangerous man," he stated gravely. "Dangerous is what's going to keep us here. Keep all of you *alive*."

Everyone looked at Richard in fear. They never knew him to be a hostile man, certainly not a killer. The brutal truth equipped them with a troubling apprehension and foreboding. Ron felt ashamed to a degree, nearly conforming his belief and loyalties to an alleged fact. Richard provided Flynn a look of malevolence and iniquity. Flynn looked at him, afraid, and paced backwards. Richard was done compromising in a democratic way.

"So I hear you're all unhappy with the leadership here. And that you plan to overthrow it," said Richard. "Overthrow *me*."

The crowd went silent as Richard and Flynn stood in the middle of the crowd of dumbstruck citizens. Ron and Benjamin stood beside each other and watched. Richard flailed his arms out to his sides at the assembly of people.

"Take it. It's yours. It always has been," Richard claimed. "I am not your enemy."

The crowd went silent as they listened to Richard speak.

"I know you're concerned, and I know you're afraid. You all want this to work. I know that, and I respect that about you all. Look around and behold how far we've come. I am not your enemy," said Richard calmly. "Bear with me a little while longer. And I swear to you, we will slaughter every last one of them."

Richard unsheathed a machete from his belt holster and knelt next to the wounded Redeemer. He picked the black-cloaked individual by the neck and sat him upright with the machete held against his throat.

"I will help you slaughter our *true* enemy."

The crowd nodded in agreement as they began to simmer down. Richard regained their confidence in his leadership as well as their allegiance. Richard threw the Redeemer to the ground and stood up. He looked directly at Flynn, who stood baffled and bemused. Richard dangled and rocked the machete delicately in his hand as he gaped into the man's petrified eyes. He walked up to Flynn, slowly, as the entire crowd watched. He got within a few feet of Flynn, who began to tremble.

"Pick one," Richard said faintly.

"Wh-what?" asked Flynn, perplexed.

The Town of Jasper

Richard pointed the machete cradled in his left hand at Flynn's body and limbs.

"Which one do you want to lose?" Richard asked severely.

Flynn looked at Richard, confused and bewildered. Richard straightened his back and puffed his chest out. His facial expression remained grave and unforgiving. Flynn shook his head slightly as he looked at Richard.

"I...I don't under..."

Richard unholstered his pistol with his right hand and pointed it at Flynn's head. Flynn panted and tilted his body backwards as he became restless and turbulent.

"Hold him down," Richard requested from the bystanders.

Two men reluctantly grabbed Flynn, who began to panic.

"Wait, wait, wait," Flynn begged.

Richard lowered the gun and sharpened the sharp edge of the ax by scraping it against the cold, concrete ground. A loud clinging sound echoed that made Flynn's heart sink. Richard crept up to Flynn and placed the blade of the ax on his ankle. Flynn squirmed and panted heavily. Richard slowly grazed the blade up against Flynn's leg past his knee up his thigh. The crowd looked on helplessly.

"Please don't...please no," Flynn begged.

"Pick one," Richard repeated.

Flynn became hysterical as he closed his eyes and begged. The two men clutched him down as he squirmed. Richard grew impatient. Flynn continued to plea without fruition as Richard looked at the two men.

"Hold his arms out," he asked.

"No, no, no, no! Please don't do this! You don't have to!"

The men pulled his arms to the side, extending them horizontally. Flynn shook his head at Richard as tears rushed down his cheeks.

"Pick one," Richard requested again.

Flynn began to cry hysterically.

"I don't know. Please, you don't have to. I don't know," he said pitifully.

Richard walked up to Flynn and pointed the gun at his face. He pressed the muzzle against his temple as Flynn cried.

"I don't know...I don't know..." Flynn repeated as he sobbed.

Richard pressed harder against his temple and shook the gun. Flynn sniveled and sobbed as he whispered something. Richard lessened the force of the gun against his face and listened to the defeated man. Flynn whispered, very softly.

"The arm," he said. "The arm."

Richard took the gun away from his face and stood up straight. Richard felt the emotions play tug of war in his head as he clenched the ax. Flynn's arms were still being tugged at both sides by the two men. The rest of the group got further and further away from Richard as they became petrified at the scene that would transpire.

Deliver it. One swing.

Richard...this isn't you. Show compassion.

He is showing compassion! He should kill him!

Let this man be...

Let this man be...

Let this man be...

The Town of Jasper

Flynn clenched his eyes closed, awaiting the treacherous fate of his arm. Richard clutched the handle of the ax and rested the blade against Flynn's right shoulder.

"Oh Jesus, no," Flynn said as he nearly vomited in shock.

Richard pursed his lips as he felt the rage build up inside him. He pressed the blade harder against his arm with both hands on the handle. Highly focused on making the correct and most effective incision, Richard lost himself in a dangerous frame of mind. In the back of his head, he heard his father, wife, and daughter in unison.

Let this man be!

Let this man be!

Let this man be!

Richard's hands shook as his mind twisted and turned. The helpless bystanders, along with Flynn, all awaited the brutal hack. Richard pressed on the blade as hard as he could, which made Flynn moan in pain and nearly pierce his flesh. Richard's forehead began to sweat as he raised the ax, ready to sever the man's limb with one slash. He raised the ax above his right shoulder with both hands around the handle. He swung the ax downward, letting out a moderate yell. The blade of the ax landed inches away from Flynn's leg. Everyone who had looked away looked up and noticed that Flynn's arm was still in tact. Flynn, who nearly fainted, opened his eyes and saw the ax beside him. His body trembled as he looked up at Richard, hyperventilating. Richard looked at him wickedly along with the rest of the clan.

"Be at the school tomorrow," Richard said bleakly. "All of you."

The entire group of rebels looked at their leader. Richard provided an unbending and radical panoramic stare of categorical authority. Everybody remained still as statues while Flynn remained on the ground, holding onto his right arm. They looked at Richard with their tails between their legs.

"Be there...*or I'll pick for you,*" Richard stated to all of them.

The crowd looked at Richard, deeply afraid and obedient. At a loss of words, no one uttered a single word.

"Ron, put the Fillmore into my truck. He deserves a proper burial by his people," Richard demanded angrily.

"What of this one?" asked one of the bystanders timidly, referring to the wounded Redeemer.

"You all wanted justice and blood when you were so sure and *convinced* it was the *monster*," said Richard. "So, rest assured. You'll have your justice. You'll get your blood."

The Town of Jasper

Straight And True

One Month After "The Incident"
October 2011

A relatively small tent was set up just outside the wall. The day was very still, with little patches of clouds clustering together. The sun was mild, with typical late autumn temperatures hovering in the mid forties. Sutherland's investigation had finally started, after getting the approval from the Federal Government. However, he was not cleared to enter inside the wall until further approvals and agreements were validated.

FBI, local police, EMT, CDC, etc. huddled around the scene. Everyone wore masks to protect themselves against the potential 'contagion' possessed by the victim. The group of them looked like paparazzi trying to get the best angle or shot. Trying to block out the background banter of the scene, Detective Sutherland scoped the perimeter of the area, thinking only to himself. Feeling a chill in his fingertips, he placed his hands in his jacket pockets and swayed his shoulders back and forth. Why did this go down? *Why?* he asked. *Why do it?* Abruptly, the detective heard the faint sound of a shouting voice behind him. A CSI agent barged in front of him, grazing his jacket with his elbow and forearm.

"Make way! Coming through!"

Two men rushed by, rolling a crate filled with medical supplies, headed for the inside of the tent. The detective paid no attention to it and continued to look around. Across the road, no more than a hundred feet, a marine was speaking with a couple of people, which captured the detective's attention. He took his hands out of his jacket pockets and walked past the tent and up to the soldier. Disregarding the current interrogation, the detective took initiative.

"What happened here, soldier?" asked Sutherland.

The two interrogators, a Latino man with a neat beard and a woman with her hair in a ponytail, looked at Detective Sutherland in a 'what the hell asshole?' kind of way. Caught off guard, the soldier, Private O'Brien, shifted his attention to Detective Sutherland.

"Uh, excuse me, sir?"

"What happened here?"

The soldier straightened his shoulders and swallowed. He spoke with a controlled anxiety.

"Uh, well. We had a jumper today."

The detective looked over his shoulder at the tent. He focused on the tent for a couple of seconds and looked back at the soldier.

"A jumper?"

"Yes, sir. There have been three attempts this month alone. This is the only one that made it over."

"*She* was the only one that made it over," said Sutherland.

He reached his hands into his jacket pockets again and squinted at the top of the wall. Wondering.

"How many shots, private?"

"One, sir. She got as far as you see her."

"How'd she get past you?"

"She must have had help. Maybe she found a weak spot within the walls, or I must've taken my eye away for a second. I saw her running outside the barrier. Running straight ahead."

Something wasn't adding up. Something was way off. The detective knelt and felt the stone cold concrete. He shook his head.

If she had help to get out, she had to have had a better escape plan once over the wall. Why run straight? This was always the toughest part of the detective's long career. However, he loved the challenge of exploring the psychology of a victim or murderer's mind.

"Why run straight?" Sutherland whispered to himself. "Where were you trying to go?"

Even if she had gotten past the trained marksman, where would she go?

"What did she have on her?"

"On her?" asked the private.

"Identification? Cash? Weapons? Her favorite hair brush?"

"She had nothing, sir."

Nothing. She had nothing on her. *A woman jumps the wall in the winter with no identification, money, or protection. How far did she expect to get?* the detective thought to himself, intensely. Running circles around his head trying to pinpoint a motive, he took another look up at the wall. *What the hell is going on in there? What would make this woman jump? It was pretty much suicide...* That's when it clicked. This wasn't a way out. She wasn't trying to escape. She wanted to be killed. A straight shot. One bullet. No pain. The detective looked at the tent and started his path towards it.

"Any other questions, Detective?" asked the soldier curiously.

Sutherland ignored the soldier and strolled towards the tent, occupied and littered with cops, EMT, and investigators scavenging and taking photos inside. The detective flung the flaps open and entered the 'crime scene'. The inside of the tent was dark and lifeless. There was a different kind of chill inside it. Pictures flashed every second at every angle. The detective squinted at each flash, trying to get a look at the victim. The area was condensed and tight, with little room to work with. People had side conversations to add to the flashing pictures every other second. Getting irritated, the detective felt it necessary to take a step forward past the 'barricade' consisting of caution tape. Pretentious CSI Unit representative James Foley interjected immediately at Detective Sutherland's progressive movement toward the victim.

"Excuse me, sir! You can't go any further!" shouted Foley.

The detective disregarded Foley's assertion and bent his knees. He knelt down at the victim's side, with his ass nearly grazing the cold ground. Mara Blair. Forty-four years of age, hair color black, five foot seven inches, blood type O positive, eligible kidney donor, nothing on her person at time of death, two children, husband deceased before 'The Incident'. The woman's right eye still lulled half-open, and her black hair was in a frazzled mess. Skin seemed dirty, and there was an accumulation of filth under her nails. The left side of the woman's face laid on the ground with the right exposed. Feet were badly bruised and right eye had a relatively large mark around it. The ground was filled with fresh bloodstains from the penetration of the bullet entering straight and true through the frontal and out the parietal part of the skull. Cerebrospinal fluid leaked across the ground, along with the a few remnants of the woman's parietal lobe. The deceased woman was surrounded by her own brain matter. The detective always had the strong stomach for the job. That was why he was so good at his job. The detective had solved the case before the soldier fired the shot.

"Hey, asshole, get what you came for?" asked Foley rudely.

The detective ignored the man again. Agent Foley became frustrated and deeply angered at the detective's disregard of him.

"Who let Sherlock Holmes in here?" he asked as he looked around angrily. "Hey, detective jerkoff, I have work to do. Let me give you the crash course. Crazy woman jumps wall thinking she can get out. Soldier shoots her. The end."

The detective once again ignored the ignorant and arrogant CSI agent. He continued to stare at the woman's face and the diameter of the gun wound in the back of the woman's head.

"Third one this week," said the detective. The statement wasn't directed towards anyone in particular.

"Excuse me?" Foley asked.

Detective Sutherland lifted himself up, slowly. He looked at the bombastic and uninformed CSI rep with a look of confidence and poise.

"Third one who tried to get over?" he repeated.

"Yeah. And I'm sure there will be others," said Foley arrogantly.

"I'm sure," assured the detective.

"People must really want to live outside the wall," said another CSI agent at the corner of the tent.

The detective glanced at the man who spoke and quickly reverted his attention to the conceited CSI agent.

"No. They just don't want to die *inside it*."

Silent Night

Present Day 2016
Five Years After "The Incident"

The Safe Zone was built in a short time, with the help of every citizen in Jasper and resources attained from the Fillmore Whites. The school resembled a fortress, with guards stationed at every corner and at every window. Men and women were assigned daily patrols surrounding the area for any potential danger. The remaining surviving victims were placed in the main gym, with others scattered in some of the bigger classrooms. Richard was very pleased with how fast things had progressed. However, he still had an unsettled matter with his prisoner to learn more of the location of his abducted wife and the Redeemers next potential attack on them.

However, it was also Christmas season in Jasper. To reward everyone's hard work, Richard had organized and tasked each remaining person in Jasper to decorate and embellish the town to make it look like Christmas. The citizens worked effectively and in just a short week, the town looked magnificent. Every streetlight and house was decorated with lights and a wreath. Most people's lawns had blow-up snowmen and candle bags that extended for miles. Richard gathered a choir to sing Christmas carols in the band shell and encouraged everyone to ice skate on the frozen pond. Richard wanted to deliver the kind of town spirit that once was before 'The Incident'. Jasper needed it. It deserved it. Everyone was in a jolly mood and in the spirit of Christmas. Everyone gathered in the center of town by the band shell. Richard surveyed the scene and felt a sense of satisfaction, due to the fact that he was able to pull off a good Christmas for the town. People wore ugly sweaters, Santa hats, and some even dressed up as Saint Nick himself. Finally, Jasper celebrated a victory.

Inside a chilled, forlorn room, a light flickered as it dangled from the ceiling. Richard stood on a small wooden stool in front of the prisoner, with a pot of water beside him. The completely nude prisoner was black and blue and bruised from head to toe. He was unrecognizable from the wounds and dry blood painted across his face. Richard's hands were stained with blood. The prisoner was unconscious as he remained chained like an animal. The townspeople were unaware of Richard's tactics and brutal interrogative techniques. He sat on the stool and placed his hands on his knees. Ron stood against the wall in the corner with his broad arms crossed against his burly chest. The light made a buzzing sound as it flickered on and off. Richard looked down at the blood stained ground as the room shifted in and out of darkness. The man hadn't given out any information on the Redeemers or his wife. His silence had angered Richard to the point of nearly beating the man to death. His rage was becoming uncontrollable, and he felt that he was running out of time.

    Minutes passed as Richard sat waiting. Uneasy and tense, he waited and then waited some more. He thought about things. He thought about his wife and if they were harming her. He thought about the attack, and the safe zone, and the whole incident since the start of it all. Finally, the sound of the prisoner waking up disrupted his thoughts. The man coughed and choked as Richard looked up at the man and stood up. He lifted the bucket up and swung it in front of the man, splashing him with water. The man jolted awake and blinked out the water in his eyes. The water dripped and dribbled off the man's body as he came to from a short doze. He gasped and struggled to speak.

"Thank you," he whispered to Richard.

"For what?" Richard asked as he put the pot on the stool.

"For not pouring the hot water this time," the man said weakly.

The room, dark and nippy, which once was an old law office that sheltered the most proficient and decorated pupils of justice, now served different purposes for Richard Morrissey. He walked slowly to the window that offered a small crack of light from the golden glow of decorations from outside. Richard gazed outside through the window with his right hand against the glass. Outside, the people of Jasper celebrated the holiday. They laughed, sang, danced, and remembered with one another. Some people ice-skated on the pond down the street and others roasted marshmallows on fire pits they brought from their homes. While all that was happening, the choir sang in the band shell. Their delicate and tender voices created an atmosphere Richard hadn't seen in quite a while. The prisoner grunted behind him with his wrists locked around a chain that hung from the ceiling. On the ground, his feet were tied together with a rope. His head lolled in front of him, and he barely had the strength to lift it up. The carolers, in perfect synchronization, sang together outside.

"Siiilent night. Hoooly night.
All is calm. All is bright.
Round yon virgin, mother, and child.
Holy infant, so tender, and mild"

Richard continued listening to the beauty of their voices. He loved every moment of it. He let it sink in as he closed his eyes and remembered the bright memories in his life. Especially the

The Town of Jasper

memories he used to have during Christmas with his father and his children.

"I love the sound of Christmas carolers. So soft and so powerful. There's nothing quite like it," Richard said out loud.

The prisoner behind him listened but did not lift his head. He just dangled there, with his chest pumping in and out as he breathed. Richard stood at the window for a few more seconds to admire the sight. The room stunk of human waste and body odor. Richard pushed his arm off the window and looked at the prisoner. With the carolers and happy citizens behind him, Richard paced towards the man. He walked within inches of the prisoner's face, who didn't bother to lift his head and look Richard in the eye. Richard smirked and looked at the floor.

"Ya know. Some days. I wake up. I imagine myself walking into my kitchen. I see my wife there making breakfast with her red apron and my two children sitting at the table. I see them turning around and laughing. They turn around and laugh to tell me it was all a joke. Just a big joke. That they were playing all along."

The prisoner's body was damp with his sweat and filth. He dangled his head side to side slowly, as if the wind was brushing it in each direction.

"But then, I realize. That it's just me imagining it. And it's all in my head."

Richard stared at the man sinisterly now, wanting to kill him with a single blow. He had an unprecedented degree of hatred towards the man who was held up by chains in front of him.

"One day, what I imagine is going to come true. Everything is going to go back to the way it used to be. Only you'll be dead, and I'll be here. Your people tried preventing that reality.

That's why I'm doing this to you. That's why I'm going to do what I'm going to do. Everything turns around."

Drool and water trickled down the man's face as he appeared past the point of exhaustion. The man mustered up all of his strength to lift his head up to look at Richard.

"They're not coming for you. You know that now, I hope," said Richard.

"I know," he said weakly. "I know that now."

"Just tell me where they have her. I don't care about them anymore. I just want her back. We can work the rest of it out after," Richard said with a friendly tone.

The prisoner remained silent. Something about him made Richard believe he would break. He felt the ice thawing in him, and he was ready to break it. The prisoner mumbled and groaned barely loud enough for Richard to hear. It sounded like he was trying to tell him something. Richard waited for it to come out. Ron looked up at Richard, wondering if the man was actually going to spill the beans.

"Go on, now" Richard said. "Go on…"

The prisoner cleared his throat and looked up at Richard. His face trembled. Richard waited keenly. Finally, the prisoner exhaled and said nothing. He wasn't going to talk and played Richard for a fool. Richard nodded and grabbed the pot of water and walked toward the sink. He filled up the pot with water until it reached three quarters of the way to the top. The prisoner looked at him, becoming more anxious. Richard looked at him from the sink at the other side of the room with a snarl. Once filled, Richard carried the pot over to the rusted stove and placed it down. The gas made a sparking sound, as Richard turned the knob to high. After several seconds, the fire ignited under the pot of water. The prisoner squirmed at the sight of the boiling water, causing the shackles to rattle. Ron sighed with discomfort as the situation became uncomfortable and inevitably gruesome.

Richard watched as the water trembled and quaked. Finally, the surface quivered and vibrated madly. He turned the gas switch off and carried the bucket over to the prisoner. His face of friendliness turned sour as the prisoner made squeamish sounds and begged. Richard stood in front of him as he awaited an answer. The prisoner looked at Richard as he panicked and hyperventilated.

"They aren't coming for you," Richard repeated, holding the handles of the piping pot of water in his hands.

The prisoner swallowed and tried to say something but the wear and tear of torment and afflict made him unable to produce a sentence. He wobbled his head and opened his mouth. Finally, he spoke out.

"I, I, I, I, I know they aren't coming for me," he said. "I know that now."

He started to breathe with raspy lungs, and it made him sound like a lung cancer victim.

"They aren't coming for me. But they are coming for *you*," said the prisoner. "And you're going to die a monster. The rescuer of Jasper who keeps the wall standing up around us. You're going to die within a barrier you continue to build higher and higher."

Relentlessly, Richard splashed the man with the boiling hot water, and the man shouted in agony. Richard took his hand and covered it against the man's mouth so no one could hear his hollers of pain. He got behind the man with his hand held over his mouth.

"Tell me where she is. Tell me where they are!"

"Richard," said Ron, trying to chime in.

"I don't know. I swear it," said the prisoner through Richard's dirty hand.

Richard let go of the man and reached for the red tool set situated on the ground. He swung the lid open and reached for the pliers. The prisoner's flesh crawled as Richard snuffed around for the tool.

"Noooo. Nooooo," whispered the prisoner.

Richard clutched the pliers and grabbed the man's mouth with his left hand.

"Open it," he said solemnly.

"Richard..." said Ron softly.

The man closed his mouth shut.

"Open it!"

Richard pried the man's mouth open. The prisoner gagged and moaned as Richard took the pliers and clicked them against the man's central incisor.

"UGHHH! AGHHHHH!"

"Shh, shh, shh," Richard whispered.

With a single twist of his wrist, Richard plucked the man's front tooth out like a root stuck in the ground. The prisoner's gums bled profusely down his chin. He gagged in agony and swallowed his own blood. Richard held the man's tooth that was still in the pliers and examined it. After inspecting it, he threw the tooth on the floor. Richard glanced around the man's body, looking for places to inflict more pain. He looked at the man's left hand and grabbed it. Humming a soothing melody, Richard held the prisoner's pointer finger between his thumb and forefinger. He wedged the sharp points of the pliers between his finger and nail and clamped down hard.

"MMMMMMM! MMMMMMM! MMM!" moaned the prisoner.

The Town of Jasper

Richard slowly moved his wrist upward and removed the nail off the prisoner's finger. The snapping noise sounded like someone cracking their knuckles all at once. The prisoner groaned fiercely as the pain shot down his wrist to his shoulder. Richard ripped the bandage off that was the man's middle fingernail causing the prisoner to nearly pass out. The blood bubbled and sizzled off the prisoner's fingers, making Ron look way in disgust. Ron nearly vomited, fighting his body to not to let the fluids stirring inside his stomach rise up through his throat.

Richard, in one wind up, slapped the man across the face. The captive barely came to as he cried. The prisoner did not shed any tears. He had drained all the bodily fluids he had left. Richard looked at Ron and gave him a nonverbal signal. Ron reached for a gallon of oil and poured it on the prisoner. Richard threw the pliers back into the red toolbox and walked up to the man. Richard looked down at the prisoner's feet that were dirtied with filth and grub. Richard bent his knees to become eye level with the prisoner who was pretty much dead already.

"It's a funny thing. If you were thrown into a lake with your feet and hands tied together, you'd have no way to get loose of the rope and get back to the top. But I'd bet that you'd squirm, use all of your strength, and fight like absolute hell to break free. You'd do whatever it took to stay alive," stated Richard sinisterly. "But the funny part is we're all going to die at some point. Either at the bottom of a lake with our hands and feet tied together or on our very own bed. So why are we all not fighting like hell each and every moment to stay alive? To live?"

Richard took out a pack of matches and plucked one out. He flicked his wrist as the friction between the match and stride of sandpaper created a petite flame. He placed it close to the prisoner's face, who looked away and tried evading the flame. The hostage trembled madly as the flame went out. Somewhat annoyed, Richard flung it aside and lit another one.

"THE BARN HOUSE ON DICKINSON!"

The detainee gasped, coughed, and spit out blood as the scream pierced his broken lungs. His face shook as he got the words out to Richard just in time to save his life. Richard retreated to the sink and glanced outside again before he splashed cold water on his face to wash the blood off. The prisoner whispered out loud enough for Richard to hear.

"Thhhrrr isssss. There hisssss a spushul plashe in *hell* fer yew… Hon the devil's therrrone."

Richard splashed some sink water on his face and wiped off the blood and sweat with a dirty towel. He strolled towards the door and placed his hand on the knob. He squeezed it with all his strength and turned to look at the prisoner.

"When I get there. I'll kick you off it," said Richard.

Richard reached for his black, long jacket hanging on the door and reached his arms through the sleeves. He looked down at the stains of blood and unidentifiable human liquid on his shirt and zipped up his jacket to avoid revealing them. He opened the door, and he and Ron made their way to the center of town to join the festivities.

Outside, Benjamin led a harmonious sermon. Richard made his way to the band shell and observed from the outside. The banter, laughter, and cheer came to a halt when they saw Richard standing among them. Richard took his hands out of his jacket pockets and exhaled the cold air. The mist evaporated in front of his face as the people looked at him. He looked around and up at Benjamin, who had halted his sermon. Richard walked slowly through the crowd and took over for Benjamin, who happily stepped down. Richard looked across the sea of citizens and let out another chilled breath.

"It's been five years. Five years and they haven't woken. I'm not going to stand here and ask you to forget what happened. I'm not going to ask you to forget what those monsters did. I'm asking you to enjoy and endure the moments like this. These moments give us that chance to set aside our dark thoughts and remember the good we have."

A brief pause ensued as Richard caught his breath from the brisk air.

"Look at this town."

The crowd looked around them at the gorgeousness they had created. They all nodded their heads to one another and smiled.

"Things like celebrating the holidays are something that came as a formality before. Now it is something we cherish. You've shown each other that you're not willing to give up. Because we won't. Because we will move forward, like we always do. It's not going to be easy. But nothing since that day has been. But this is how we get through it. With each other. We are all ten times as strong now than we were five years past."

A few *yeahs* and *absolutelys* echoed throughout the crowd.

"I promise you, just keep pushing with me, and we will all get through it. We will make it. They will wake…they will wake."

Most of the people in the crowd nodded their heads and smiled. Some cried, thinking about their loved ones who have been dormant for five years and counting. But they all had hope. They all held onto it like a reality.

"The Council and I decided to move everyone into the school. That's the safest place for them now," said Richard. "A group of people who call themselves Redeemers attacked us when our guard was down…we lost people."

Many people in the crowd formed sad and angry expressions. They wanted vengeance and retribution for their murdered loved ones.

"Starting tomorrow, we are going to form a safe haven within and around the school. We need all hands on deck if we are going to keep this town safe, as we have kept it since the start. We have formed a bond with the Fillmore Whites, who have agreed to trade with us until things get back to the way they used to be. And maybe even after that. We have a threat within our walls, and we need to become people we haven't seen yet. You will need to be prepared to do things beyond your element. Things we need to do to survive. I'm getting tired of burying our people. We're all tired."

The townspeople listened, fully comprehensive of the alleged reality of the situation. Their anger galvanized their thoughts as they nodded their heads, while others buried their heads down in deep grief.

"I'm a dangerous man," Richard said. "And you are too. Dangerous is a must now."

The only sound came from the occasional whistle of cold wind and the sniffles among the crowd. The group of all ages huddled together, in much need of direction.

"We will bury our dead and provide them the burials they did not deserve," Richard stated.

More silence occurred with the sounds of throats clearing and sniffling ensuing. Richard was very much concerned and more exhausted than anything. He hadn't gotten any rest in nearly a day.

"I am sorry for what has happened. You know I am. I tried to keep this place safe, but I don't think safe is a reality in this town anymore. At least not right now. And I know that is a scary thing

The Town of Jasper

to understand. If we died right now and went to hell, it would take us a week to find out we weren't in this place."

The townsfolk looked down with pride as they agreed.

"The thing about our victims...our loved ones. They don't know us."

Some of the townsfolk looked up, intrigued at the statement. Richard looked at a man and pointed to him.

"They know Todd Arnold, the contractor. His kids know him as Dad who coaches their little league games and puts three meals on the table every night," Richard said.

Todd Arnold got choked up as he nodded his head. Richard looked at a woman and gestured his hand in her direction.

"They know Joanne, the public school teacher. The one who put herself through college waiting tables seven days a week while also taking care of her sick mother."

Joanne shed tears as the people around her patted her on the back.

"But they don't know us now. They don't know *US*," he repeated. "The thing about our victims and our loved ones, whether you're dead or *asleep*... you don't even know it. It's nothing. It's simple. It's only difficult for the living. For the ones who love you. It's difficult for us, because *we* are the ones who *live with it*."

Richard began to walk around as he focused on his delivery. He finally put an anchor down on himself and swallowed. He stood still and spoke.

"I want to thank all of you for becoming the people you are today. We all wouldn't have made it without your courage and strength. None of you are my blood. But all of you are my family. May our loved ones rest in peace and awake in peace."

"Amen," said a few of the bystanders.

A majority of the crowd nodded their heads in agreement and muttered words of harmony and accord. Richard had restored some of the lost faith, and it was time to move forward with a new approach.

Richard began to walk through the crowd and hugged, kissed, and acknowledged nearly everyone left in Jasper. Christmas carolers ensued with their delicate harmony of sound, and it made Richard stop and listen. He placed his cold, dry hands in his pockets and closed his eyes to try to think of a happier time. As he reminisced of the times that once were, Benjamin walked up beside him.

"Incredible. Aren't they?" he asked.

Richard's eyes opened as he looked beside him at one of his most trusted delegates and friend.

"They are," said Richard.

"I never got a chance to extend my gratitude."

"For what?" asked Richard.

"When it all happened. And shortly after. You saw something in me. Something I didn't even see. One of your many fortes," said Benjamin gratefully.

"You've done things here, Benjamin. Things that don't require gratefulness on your end."

The comment by Richard made Benjamin smile. It made him proud of himself. A feeling he had not had time to appreciate in quite a while. The two stood and watched the carolers sing as the broken town around them was finally immersed in peace and happiness.

"I trust you with this town, Richard. We all do. And for that, I thank you," said Benjamin.

Richard's eyes remained locked on the carolers as he let the compliment linger in the air like a pleasant perfume.

The Town of Jasper

"I trust you too, Ben. With this place."

Benjamin smiled and patted his friend on the shoulder. After a few moments of enjoyment, Benjamin broke away, leaving Richard to resume his peaceful state of mind.

James D. Gianetti

Precedent and Potential

One Month After "The Incident"
October 2011

Jasper Town Hall was electric and filled with residents. Nearly every conscious person in town made it to the hearing. Members of the 'East' and 'West' were all in attendance and each of them was more anxious, confused, and demanding than the next. It sounded like the trading floor of Wall Street, with people elbowing one another to get through. Arguments broke out, even a few short fistfights transpired. Everyone who attended was hoping to receive some answers from the town's mayor, who was yet to be seen since 'The Incident'. It had been a month since the day, and people wanted answers. The town had been quarantined by the federal government, which meant nobody could go in or out until the CDC figured things out. The citizens of Jasper continued their loud banter and demanded the mayor show his face and establish a solution. Police officers tried withholding the peace in the room by attempting to quiet people down and break up the occasional sloppy brawl. Friends, neighbors, and co-workers gathered around and barked at one another, as if they were their worst of enemies. The town of Jasper had been shattered into shards of glass, scattered on the floor and waiting to be stepped on. Things were shouted across the room such as, "You think you're better than us because you're on the East side of the tracks?" Along with, "The West side should be disconnected from Jasper!" It seemed like every single person in Town Hall was yelling at someone. If they weren't, they were just yelling to blend in.

The Town of Jasper

Throughout the entire thirty minutes of disputes, disagreements, and quarrelling, Richard leaned against the back wall, observing it all. He watched, as the town ripped itself apart before him. Richard didn't just look. He observed. He observed almost every person in the room. He listened to their problems, their concerns, their wants, how many children they had, how many people they loved who were lost. He calculated it all in his head.

An officer walked up to the podium to try and calm the crowd down.

"Everyone, please! Quiet down now!"

"Where the hell is the mayor?" shouted a resident

"The mayor… The mayor is…"

The officer couldn't answer the question. He had no idea where the mayor was. No one did. The townspeople disrupted his attempt at peace by throwing objects at him. The officer took cover against the podium as people threw coins, keys, even shoes at the officer.

In the back, Richard continued to observe. A man stood next to him, who could be easily mistaken for a hobo. The man's body was shaking and he was drinking a bottle of something. It was covered in a brown garbage bag. It looked like the man hadn't slept in days. He was more than troubled. He seemed petrified of something.

"Are you okay?" asked Richard.

The haggard man looked at him. He blinked, which in itself seemed hard for him to do.

"Fuh…fine."

"You believe all this?"

The sluggish man ignored the question.

"You look…familiar. Have I met you before?"

Somewhat intrigued at the thought, Richard looked upon the drunken fellow and smirked.

"Must have one of those faces," he said.

The worn out, fatigued man smirked back and guzzled whatever was inside the bottle. His brown overcoat had wet spots from where he spilled the alcohol. The mysterious figure grinned at him and smiled as he drank. He let out his right hand to his new drunken friend.

"Richard Morrissey."

Reeking of the booze, the man looked up at him. He reached out and grasped his hand firmly.

"Neil Miller".

Richard looked at him curiously.

"Principal Neil Miller?"

He took another healthy slug from the bottle. Neil chuckled drunkenly.

"Once upon a time in Jasper," he said with whiskey breath. "I've had parent teacher conferences more hostile than this, believe me."

Richard looked up at the chaos in front of him. He almost basked in it all. As if the pandemonium fueled him. Before another shout, cry, punch, or bottle could be thrown, Richard walked toward the podium. He pushed and shoved through the mob to make his way to center stage. The herd of people was like a riptide pushing him back and forth in zigzags. The podium got closer as Richard gathered more strength to push himself forward. A brusque man with a Mohawk and tattoos bumped into him. He recognized Richard.

"Richard," Ron Carlisle said with a relief. "This is madness."

"I know. Are you and Kathy all right?"

The Town of Jasper

"Yeah," he said. "For now."

"I'm making a push for the front," said Richard.

The screams echoed behind him, as Richard made a final push, shove, and duck towards the podium. He walked onto the stage, up to the officer who looked up at him afraid. He quickly put his hand on his firearm in self-defense. Richard put his hands up in peace.

"No need for that," he said calmly.

The officer, afraid, holstered his weapon and looked at Richard as if he were more than a man.

"What's your name, officer?"

"Ford. Gary Ford."

"Officer Ford. Please step down. I'll take it from here."

His words were calm and collected. He showed no sign of panic or terror. Officer Ford stepped down, looking at Richard while he did it. Richard Morrissey stood in front of the town of Jasper. He waited patiently. Showing a dull facial expression as he looked at the onslaught of chaos pursue. Slowly but surely, people started looking up at him. Each person who looked at him shut their mouths immediately. His posture, with his hands behind his back and back perfectly straight, resembled that of an army cadet. The loud roar of screams and cries simmered down. It took nearly sixty seconds for the banter to stop while Richard stood at the podium waiting to be heard and obeyed. As everyone quieted down, thoughts ran wildly in his head.

"What the hell are you doing? Get down from there now! What are you going to say? These people won't listen to you! You're a nobody!"

Richard disregarded the dark thoughts.

"You think you can lead these people?"

"I know I can," Richard whispered to himself.

By now, the entire room was quiet. All eyes were on him. He erased the thoughts in his mind and looked up nervously. Every pair of eyes in town was hooked on him. Richard began to doubt himself. What the hell was he doing up there? He didn't know what to say. In fact, he didn't even remember getting up to this point. Then, all of a sudden, he heard his wife in his head. She whispered in his ear.

"*You can do this, honey. Tell these people what they want to hear. You are a born leader, Richard. Be yourself, and they will follow you*".

Richard looked up at the people who were all waiting for him to say something. Richard glanced around the room at the pain and sorrow their faces. He saw what the devastation of 'The Incident' had done to the town. What it had done to him.

"For the last half hour, I've stood and watched a town tear itself apart. I watched neighbors, friends, and family lash out against one other. I am not your mayor. I'm just a person who lives in Jasper like the rest of you. *All of us* have a lot to feel sorry about. What happened a month ago is unexplainable. We don't know how it happened. We don't know what to do. A couple of weeks ago, we were caught up in life's meaninglessness of leather seats and vacancies in cycling classes. Now, we have been equipped with an unprecedented degree of fear and foreboding. I know. I know you're scared. It's okay to feel fear. Our loved ones. Our wives, husbands, brothers, sisters, aunts, uncles, sons, daughters. They're not dead. We know that much. When will they wake up? I don't know. The CDC is working on something, and now the government has quarantined our town. For all we know, this could be a global pandemic. The safest thing for us to do is not let this restriction get the better of our humanity. There is no 'East' and there is no 'West' anymore. There's just *us*. *We*. *We* will work together and fight

The Town of Jasper

through this for our loved ones. *We* will keep them safe. Whatever we can do to ensure the future for them and this town is our top priority until this passes."

People began to look around and nod their heads in approval. Richard's speech sparked a fire. Richard looked at the onlookers and grinned. He had them eating out of his hand, and it was time to ignite the flame inside of them. Richard pointed to a middle-aged woman in the crowd.

"You there," he said.

The woman was dumbstruck by the spotlight.

"Me?" she asked.

"Yes. Please. Tell the town your name. Tell them the names of your loved ones who are still not awake."

The woman swallowed nervously. She became upset. She sported a Jasper football sweatshirt with the sleeves rolled up. She looked around her as everyone in the room listened.

"My name is Patricia Wagner. My son Jeremy and husband Phillip are dea…under".

Richard looked at her and smiled.

"Thank you, Ms. Wagner," he said.

Richard looked at a man in the crowd wearing a backwards ball cap and a plaid shirt. He was a thin, lanky fellow with a stubble beard.

"Sir!" he shouted as he pointed to him.

The man's pupils dilated and posture stiffened as Richard looked at him. The man spoke out loudly.

"My name…is Robert Grisham. My wife…and daughter haven't gotten up yet."

Richard looked at a young teenaged boy.

"How about you son?"

The teenager spoke confidently.

"Adam Laskey. Mom and Dad."

One by one, people started randomly shouting out their names and telling the town how many loved ones they had who had yet to wake up. Richard and the town listened to everyone's short biography of pain. After nobody else spoke out, Richard allowed a short moment of silence for the town to regain their spirits.

"My wife. My son. My daughter. The three people I hold most dear in this world," Richard said in a low tone. "I made a promise to them. That I'd do everything in my power to fix this. Or I'd die trying. My son gave this to me the night before it happened. Right before he went to bed."

Richard reached into his pocket and took out a piece of paper with a drawing on it. He held it up for the crowd to see. The drawing was of Richard, with a caption on top reading 'My Hero'.

Richard held back his emotions as he looked at it. Tears trickled down both cheeks as he blinked.

"Said he made it in art class that day. Forgot to give it to me when he got home."

The crowd looked at Richard and felt sorry for him. As if his loss was more significant than theirs. Richard put the drawing down on the table and looked at the herd of people. A feeling of motivation and a surge of energy boiled inside of him.

"I know this town will prosper more now than before 'The Incident'. Look around you. These people are your family. They have been all along."

Some of the audience began to clap and cheer. More people looked at their peers and nodded their heads. Richard felt his hands clenching the wood podium. He began to believe that they would listen to him. That they would follow him.

"When this is all over and we beat this thing, and our loved ones wake up. They're not going to wake up to the old Jasper.

The Town of Jasper

They're going to wake up to the NEW JASPER! A Jasper where everyone is equivalent!"

The crowd roared in excitement.

"A JASPER OF EQUALITY AND ALLIANCE!"

The cheers of the crowd grew louder and louder.

"They will wake up, and look at the faces who made it that way. The citizens here. The citizens who, starting *tonight*, will swear their allegiance to this new community and the future of EACH AND EVERY ONE OF ITS LOYAL RESIDENTS!"

Richard couldn't hear himself think over the outbursts of cheers, cries, and chants. From that moment on, Richard went on to become Jasper's most recognized and reputable people, from helping each person with small chores to implementing law and order that was deemed fit by the majority. Along with his charismatic attitude that wore off benignly on the residents, he made them feel safe and gathered a sense of hope that was all but diminished. They trusted him more and more each day to do the right thing and to do right by them. No one ever questioned his leadership capabilities or his decisions to rebuild and foster the community. He took the podium in the town hall that night and set a precedent of strength and change that would establish Jasper for years to come.

The Safe Zone

Present Day 2016
Five Years After "The Incident"

Richard entered a private room where his two children were being kept. His hands were bloody and badly bruised from his interrogation with the prisoner. He walked up to where his son slept and reached to grab Joseph's body. Richard's hands remained wrapped around Joseph's forearm as he hummed the same melody his wife would to make sure their children would fall asleep in peace. He sat down and leaned his back against the bed. He rocked his body back and forth as he caressed Joseph's dangling arm, getting blood on his son's hand. After no more tears could be shed, Richard began to think about Diane and how she would not want to see him like this. He thought about his father and how he would handle the situation. He got himself up off the floor and wiped his face with his tremulous hands. He regained his composure and placed his son's hand back on the bed. He wiped Joseph's arm with a towel and kissed his forehead. He straightened his clothing and let out a sniffle. He opened the door and walked into the hallway, making his way to the gymnasium. On his way to the big room, he ran into Benjamin.

"Richard," he said. "One of them is outside. He won't come in unless he sees you."

"Okay," said Richard as he walked towards the main entrance to greet his friend.

He saw Richard in the main room and got out of the vehicle filled with supplies. The man was dressed in ragged clothing that covered his face. He greeted Richard like a spy delivering information.

"Hello, my friend," said Richard. "Welcome."

Edmund showed some of his face by removing the apparel that covered it up.

"It's okay. You don't need it, here."

Reluctantly, Edmund removed the clothing and showed his entire pale face. Feeling like a new kid at school, he looked around, inspecting the foreign place.

"The supplies are in the trunk. I'll wait in the car and…"

"No…" Richard said. "Come inside."

Edmund thought about the offering for several seconds. Knowing his friend would not take no for an answer, he began to cover his face again.

"Without it," said Richard.

Edmund looked at Richard like he was crazy. But Edmund trusted Richard, and he knew he would not make him do something if he knew it would put him in harm's way. The two walked inside the safe zone together.

Inside Richard's private room, where his two children slept, he and Edmund looked upon them. Edmund could feel the weight of the atrocity that pushed down on Richard's shoulders. He felt helpless, wishing he had some magic power to wake them up.

"I'm sorry, friend," said Edmund sympathetically. "But I'm glad you showed them to me. They're beautiful."

"They are," said Richard. "They're gonna love getting to know you. Especially the girl. She's going to have hundreds of questions."

Edmund laughed out loud.

"Hopefully I have some answers," he said with a smile. "I should be on my way."

"Before you go. There's one more thing."

The gymnasium was packed with people attending to their loved ones. Aligned systematically and neatly in rows, the victims slept comfortably on mattresses, blankets, or pillows. Richard entered the room with a feeling of remorse. Citizens of all shapes and sizes decorated the room, standing or sitting beside their loved ones and friends. People looked up at Richard and up again in shock of Edmund. Some people stared and whispered, as the presence of the albino man was almost surreal to them.

"I don't know how to explain it," said Richard to Edmund.

Edmund looked around at everything. At the victims, their loved ones, and the ones staring at him. He saw what the once proud and prosperous community has been reduced to.

"There's so many children," Edmund whispered in sadness.

"There were more," said Richard.

"How have you done it?" asked Edmund.

"Done what?"

"How have you dealt with this for so long? The pain and misery?"

"The only way I know how," stated Richard. "I keep moving forward, and I try not to think of the people I love and the person I've become. How about you?"

Edmund did not say anything as he gaped at the horrific scene in front of him. He did not look at Richard when he responded.

"Along the lines of those same reasons, son of my father's savior. I guess you were right, after all."

"About what?" asked Richard as he looked over at Edmund.

The Town of Jasper

"We really are alike. I should be on my way," said Edmund with a slight sense of fear and sorrow.

"I'll walk you out."

"No," said Edmund. "Stay here. Be with your people."

The two shook hands before they parted ways. Richard saw Edmund off down the hall and looked back into the gymnasium. Most of the people were praying, and others rested beside their loved ones. Benjamin went around touching victim's foreheads with holy water, saying prayers for each of them. Richard stood at the forefront of a sea of bodies, feeling the exhaustion catching up to him. Near the center, Richard saw two little girls, Aden and Jacen, reading *The Cat in The Hat* to their mother and father, who were both victims of 'The Incident'. It put things into a certain perspective for Richard, and it agitated him. He made his way over to them, walking through the middle carefully. The two little girls, both with golden blonde hair, no more than six and eight years old, shared the book with each other and took turns flipping the pages and reading them.

"Hi, girls," said Richard.

They both stopped reading and looked up at Richard and blinked rapidly. Their tender faces reminded Richard of his daughter. He could see the innocence in their eyes and the sisterly love that has been forged since the atrocity.

"What are you ladies reading today?" he asked.

"Cat in the Hat," said the eight year old, Jacen.

"Oh, I love that one," Richard whispered excitedly. "Mind if I sit and listen?"

"Okay," said the six year-old, Aden.

Aden brought the book up to her eyes. Her older sister helped balance the book by holding on to the right side of the cover.

The small effort of teamwork made Richard happy. The sight was adorable as Aden read out loud. Richard looked to his right as he sat, at the two little girls' mother and father. He thought about how proud they'd be seeing their children the way they were. How strong they were.

"Oh-oh!" Sally said.

"Don't you talk to that cat.

That cat is a bad one,

That cat in the Hat.

He plays lots of tricks.

Don't you let him come near.

You know what he did

The last time he was here?"

The eight year old flipped the page, and the two took turns reading. Richard listened to them read and read, and it formed a therapeutic sentiment inside him. He sat on the floor and listened to the rest of the story as he relaxed. As the story progressed, Jacen began to read.

"And the ship and the fish.

And he put them away.

Then he said, 'That is that.'

And then he was gone

With a tip of his hat."

The girls put down the book and looked at Richard. Richard smiled at them, not knowing what else to do. He wished he could do something more.

"Fantastic job, girls. You both read really well," he said. "I wish I could read that well."

"You want to read the next one?" asked Aden.

"I have to go say hello to some friends, but I'll be back," Richard said.

The Town of Jasper

Richard reached into his pocket and looked around playfully. He took out several pieces of flavored bubble gum. Jacen's eyes lit up as Richard tossed the pieces to them.

"Don't tell anyone," Richard whispered to the smiling girls.

About ten feet away, the Blackman's held each other's hands as they stood over their son. Richard came up from behind them and put a hand on each of their shoulders. They looked behind him, but said nothing. The three of them looked at the handsome child named Nicholas. He was only twelve.

"It could have been him. They could have killed *him*. And everything would have been for nothing," said the boy's mother, Janice.

"But they didn't, and they won't. He's here; he's right here," said Richard, as comforting as possible.

"He is," said the boy's father, Martin. "But what happens when he wakes up and we're not."

Richard did not have an immediate response. He looked at the boy as he slept and began to think of something to reassure or hearten the two of them.

"You have my word. No one is going anywhere. And when he wakes, he's going to see the two of you," said Richard.

"They killed *children,* Richard," said Janice appalled. *"Why children?"*

Martin held his wife as the thought of it made her stomach spin. She felt ill and light-headed as Martin grabbed her tightly.

"What are we going to do about them?" asked Martin.

Richard released his grip from the two of them as they continued to fix their gaze on their only child. Richard whispered between them.

"We're going to find them, and we're going to deal with them," said Richard.

The two nodded their heads slightly, acknowledging Richard's violent and sadistic decision. Richard began his walk away from them.

"I'll give you two your peace," he said.

Richard made his way to a man kneeling beside his wife. Elon knelt beside his life partner Marissa, as she slept on an air mattress. Elon was an African-American man and retired literature professor. He was on both knees, saying a prayer. His eyes were closed as he whispered the prayer to himself. Richard towered over him and watched. Once the man finished his prayer, he opened his eyes. He noticed Richard standing behind him and he staggered, almost ashamed.

"Richard. I'm sorry I didn't…"

"Please…don't apologize," said Richard. "How you doing?"

"Fine," he said. "Well, ya know. I'm fine. I'm good," Elon said unconvincingly.

He was fidgeting and stumbling over his words. He was nervous because he wasn't a people person. He used to be before 'The Incident'. He was especially edgy speaking to the likes of the town's leader. Richard got on both of his knees next to him and looked at Marissa.

"My sleeping beauty," said Elon with a smile.

"That she is," said Richard respectfully. "How long you two married?"

"Twenty nine years," said the man. "We married young and never looked back. I got through everything with her. Financial troubles, my addiction, her illness…"

The Town of Jasper

Elon caught himself explaining his most deep and harnessed secrets and stopped himself from going on any further.

"I'm sorry. Look at me, pouring my guts out. It's not becoming."

"You don't have to be," said Richard. "What was she sick with?"

"She has cancer," said Elon. "She was diagnosed before 'The Incident'."

"Everyone fights a battle behind closed doors," said Richard. "Most of the people on the outside never know you're fighting them."

Elon nodded his head in agreement as he touched his wife's cold hands.

"I'm just afraid she's going to wake up one day, and I'm going to be wrinkled and grey."

Richard had no response to Elon's remark. The science behind why they didn't age was something Richard could never explain.

"We always worked it out. We always had balance," said Elon.

"You're a lucky guy. And she's a lucky woman to have a man by her side, no matter the situation. That's what keeps things together," said Richard.

"Yeah," said Elon. "I just want her…back."

Elon smiled now as he thought of a pleasant memory of how life used to be.   "We'd go dancing every Friday night. We loved to dance. It was something we just did," he said.

Richard looked at Marissa. She was a good-looking woman, with her hair extended to her shoulder blades. He pictured the two of them tearing up a rug on Friday nights. He pictured how happy they were before everything happened.

"My wife, Diane, and I never had the dancing thing down. She was pretty good, but I'm so uncoordinated I'd always step on her feet," Richard said.

Richard's comment made Elon laugh. Something he hadn't done in forever. Richard was always good at alleviating unpleasant situations. He could turn smug into smirk like no one else.

"It's not for everyone," said Elon comically.

"Well, sometime soon, the four of us will go out one Friday night and you can teach us a thing or two about the balance of things," said Richard.

Elon acknowledged Richard's optimistic request with a smile and a nod as Richard lifted his himself up off the floor. He patted Elon on the shoulder and walked away to leave him with his wife of so many years.

Richard looked at the floor as he walked, trying not to step on anyone's hands or feet. Before he could evade, he accidentally knocked into a woman who was also not paying attention.

"Oh, I'm sorry," said Richard.

Shameful, the woman quickly avoided him.

"I'm sorry," she said as she hurried off.

"Wait," said Richard.

The woman turned around and looked up at him. She had striking blonde hair and stood about five and a half feet.

"It's Olivia, right?" asked Richard.

"Yes," she said in a very low tone.

"How are things? Are you doing okay?"

"Fine," she said. "Thank you."

The Town of Jasper

The woman walked away and attended to her daughter, Shannon, who lay on the floor on a mattress. Richard walked up to her as she knelt beside her. Richard stood up as he looked down.

"She's beautiful. What's her name?"

"Shannon."

Nothing was said after that. Richard looked at the girl and saw his own daughter, Victoria. He looked down at Olivia, whose sadness and remorse had taken a toll on her mental state over the years.

"Where is her father?"

Olivia shook her head and looked at Richard. She had glowing blue eyes that could knock a man off his feet.

"I'm not sure," she muttered.

"I'm sorry. I don't know why I asked that. Forgive me," said Richard.

Olivia didn't make eye contact with Richard as she almost drifted into tears. She had much regret, and she was constantly reminded of her choice every time she saw her daughter.

"You come see me if you two ever need anything," Richard said.

Olivia nodded her head, and Richard let her be. He saw Ron and his wife, Kathy, in the corner. Kathy was holding a little girl's hand. It was the same little girl Ron rescued on the morning of 'The Incident'. Now eight years old, the girl held Kathy's hand and didn't say a word. Richard approached them and he greeted Kathy first. Kathy greeted him with a hug.

"Hi, Richard," she said as they locked arms around each other's backs.

Richard looked at Ron and they both exhaled. Ron's two children, Alyssa and Zachary, slept on the floor on top of blankets and pillows. Ron whispered to Richard.

"What are we going to do with the prisoner?" he asked.

Richard did not want to discuss the plan in front of Kathy. Richard gestured by looking down and away. Ron looked over at Kathy.

"Hey, hun. Can you give us a minute?"

"Sure," she said. "Come on, sweetie, let's go find your mom and dad."

Kathy held the little girl's hand and they walked off, giving Richard and Ron their privacy to discuss dire matters.

"Gather The Council. We'll have a meeting to discuss an approach."

"When?" asked Ron.

"Tomorrow. We need to plan for another attack. It's coming," asserted Richard. "I'll go see Edmund and the Fillmores alone and upon my arrival back; we'll set things in motion."

Ron agreed with him as he always did. Ron had become Richard's right hand man over the years. One of the few men Richard really trusted. A long moment of quiet followed as the two stood.

"There's something else," said Ron. "Someone came to the house a little while back."

This caught Richard's utmost attention. Richard was unaware of such a thing and another problem was the last thing he needed right now.

"He asked about what had happened, the incident, and he asked about you," said Ron. "He was a detective. We thought he was coming to help."

"What did you tell him?" asked Richard.

The Town of Jasper

"I told him nothing."

"What did he want to know about me?"

"He knows you're in charge. He wants to find you, and he's been looking for you for a long time," said Ron. "Said he interviewed other people and no one would give you up."

"You think he's working with *them*?" Richard asked.

"Not likely. I had to let him in. He had the proper identification, and if the government hired him, that means there's still hope they haven't completely given up on us."

"Maybe," said Richard. "Why does he want to find me?"

"I don't know. He probably thinks you have the most clear perspective of everything that happened and what is happening in here," said Ron.

"What does he look like?"

"I don't know. He was wearing a ski mask."

Richard became stressed and placed his hands on his hips. It was another thing he had breathing down his neck. He became angry at the fact that someone was tracking him.

"Who else has he spoken to?"

"Ford, I believe. I heard Nancy Ringwell spoke to someone. Could be a rumor. Walter Cavill was in an altercation with someone not too long ago. People on his street said it happened in his house with someone they didn't recognize. Maybe it was him."

"Possibly," said Richard. "What was his name?"

Ron thought for a moment to try to remember if the detective ever mentioned anything about his identity. Suddenly realizing it, he shook his head.

"He never did," said Ron. "I'm sorry, Richard, I shouldn't have agreed to meet with him without letting you know. He showed me his badge, and I thought maybe he was trying to help."

Richard remained silent about the matter as thoughts raced through his head. The situation was troubling him, and he was displeased no one was telling him about it.

"What are you going to do?" asked Ron.

"I'll deal with it when the time is right. We have other dire matters to focus on," reminded Richard.

Ron looked down at his children and began to nod his head in shame and disgrace. He shut his eyes and took a breath.

"It was a lie," Ron stated. "My daughter had an eye exam with the doctor to see if she would ever be able to see again. The doctor called me up and told me that her results were in. He wished he had better news and a way to make it turn. My mind twirled and everything was out of focus. I heard the doctor say the words 'never' and 'ways to deal with the situation'. I ended the call and put the phone down on the table."

This was something that had bothered Ron over the years. A dark cloud that constantly followed him around like a curse. He wished he could take it back, but he couldn't. Ron continued with the story, and Richard could tell it was eating away at him.

"My wife came down the stairs in a panic and with anxiety. She knew I was on the phone with the doctor. She rushed up to me and when she looked at me for an answer, I froze," Ron said as he fell into a deep stare. "I froze, and she asked me if everything was going to be all right, and I stood there with the phone in my hands and the words *she's going to be fine* came out. It was like it wasn't even me saying it. She held her hands over her mouth and cried. Then she threw her arms around me. I don't know why I did it, but I did. I lied to her. I lied to my wife."

"It was a good lie," said Richard.

"Is there such a thing?" asked Ron.

The Town of Jasper

Richard paused and let the question soak. He crossed his arms as he looked down. The gymnasium was still and quiet as Richard reflected.

"One day I told my son I'd give him twenty bucks to rake the leaves. He probably cleared out every leaf on our grass," Richard said with a smile. "When he was finished, I gave him the money and he took it. I told him you earned this money. He told me he was happy to do it, and that he didn't want it. I told him to take it and that hard work pays off. So, he finally took it. Later that evening, I heard footsteps in the kitchen where I kept my wallet. I saw my son put the twenty dollars back into my wallet and sneak away back to his room. So, later that night before he went to bed, I asked him. I said, *Joseph, what are you going to do with the money?* He looked at me and said he was going to save it, so he could buy a new baseball glove."

Richard looked over at Ron, who glanced back at Richard for a split second. He looked at his children again and placed his hands in his jean pockets.

"There is such thing," said Richard.

Ron didn't have a response. His silence was the acknowledgement Richard needed. It was also what Ron needed. Richard uncrossed his arms and ran his fingers through his hair.

"What did you see that day in the convenience store?" asked Ron.

"I saw a man willing to do wrong for the right purpose. I saw a father who'd do anything to keep a roof over his family's head. The same person I see now. Someone willing to do different wrongs to protect the same people he loves."

"I never told her," Ron stated. "What happened that day."

This, too, troubled Ron. Richard had no response for his old friend. Just silence to let him speak his mind.

"It doesn't make me feel good or bad...something in between," Ron said.

After Ron finished venting about the past, he knew there were current dire matters that had to be addressed.

"Something is coming, Ron," Richard stated.

Ron knew all too well of the danger Richard was inferring. It made him afraid to hear it. It woke him up and made him realize what he'd have to do and what could happen.

"I know," Ron said calmly.

"People are going to die. And if something happens, I know that I can rely on you God forbid..."

Richard looked at Ron like he had never looked at him before. It made Ron somewhat uneasy but also full of pride. Knowing that Richard entrusted him with his family's lives made Ron respect himself and Richard more. Richard looked at both children situated next to each other on the floor.

"Would you die for me?" asked Richard.

Ron, off guard and perplexed, did not know what to say. He did not want to answer too soon to show that he was untruthful. He managed his composure and looked at Richard, who was still looking down at his children. Knowing he would want nothing but his full integrity, Ron felt the words come out of his mouth.

"No...But I will *kill* for you."

Anonymity of Sin

Two Years After "The Incident"
April 2013

Two years had passed since the day of 'The Incident', and Sutherland has gotten nowhere. With countless approvals, paperwork, and liability forms to sign or wait on, he finally had clearance inside the wall. The brake pads squealed as Sutherland pressed his foot down on the brake pedal. He pushed the lever into park and turned off the engine. With a crack of his back and adjustment of his leather jacket, the detective was on his way towards the front gate of the wall. Guards with automatic weapons surrounded the wall and walked up to the detective slowly, with their hands out.

"Stop right there, sir," stated one guard firmly.

The guard was an African-American man with a short buzzed haircut and a bulky body. His puffed out chest and deep voice provided the cliché characteristics of a hardcore army soldier. Sutherland held up his jurisdiction papers.

"Detective Jack Sutherland. I have been granted access by the Federal Government of the United States into the quarantine zone."

The brawny guard walked up to Sutherland with his hands held on his belt and snatched the paper out of his hand. The guard examined it briefly and looked at the other soldiers at the front gate. He provided a nod to them and handed the paper back to Sutherland.

"Open it up!" shouted the guard.

The gate slid open slowly as Sutherland stood and watched. With each passing second of the gate opening, Sutherland felt a deeper sense of relief and accomplishment. Finally, he would get inside and start his case. He shoved the paper into his pocket and began to walk into Jasper. He looked at the guards surrounding the wall, who eyed him firmly. After he got ten yards inside the wall, the gate closed loudly behind him, causing him to jolt. Sutherland stood and studied the area for a moment. He breathed in the air and felt a certain freedom inside the walled off community.

Detective Sutherland finally started to walk forward amidst falling awe to the lonesome and forlorn scenery of the once flourishing town. Sutherland reached for his notepad tucked inside his leather shoulder bag, which was a gift from his now ex-wife for their tenth anniversary. He yanked it out and checked the information he scribbled down. Trying to find it among the scribbled mess, the name of the person was written on top of the yellow piece of paper.

Benjamin Frye

The sun managed to peak its way through the clouds and glistened the painted windows of the Jasper church. The sunlight from outside dimly lit the inside of the Lord's house. Inside, a tall gentleman in his late twenties with long black hair sat on one of the long benches facing the front. Benjamin Frye's eyes were closed, whispering a silent prayer to himself.

Detective Sutherland's footsteps were noiseless as he walked inside the church. He stood in the back center of the church for moment and thought about saying a prayer. With a look to his left, locating Benjamin, Sutherland decided against the useless plea for help from the Almighty. He placed the grey ski mask over his face and walked forward. The creak of the wooden bench directly behind Benjamin made him break away from his prayer and open his eyes. Benjamin did not look back, as he did not want the detective to know what he looked like.

"Good evening, Detective," said Benjamin, whose dull voice echoed throughout the church.

Detective Sutherland looked at the back of Benjamin's head.

"I hope I didn't interrupt anything," stated Sutherland.

"No worries. I was almost done."

Sutherland gathered himself and the supplies necessary to conduct the interview. He sat his notepad on his lap and clicked his pen. He looked up at the back of Benjamin's head again and placed the pen against the notepad.

"I'm going to ask you a series of questions. Please answer them to the best of your ability, as it is vital to my research and your compensation," Sutherland stated.

"Did you bring them?" asked Benjamin.

"I brought them," replied Sutherland. "Before I begin. Do you have any questions for me?"

"Are you here to help us? Did you find a cure?"

"No. A cure hasn't been found yet."

"Oh…" said Benjamin sadly. "What a shame."

"Can we begin?" asked Sutherland.

"Yes. Take it away, Detective."

"Do you have any immediate family who are victims of 'The Incident'?"

"No, sir. Just close friends."

"Do you know of any medical conditions they have?"

"Nothing that stands out. I know one of them had frequent migraines. Another had a slight lisp."

"And yourself? Any medical conditions before it?"

"None."

"And after?"

"None."

"What is your role here?" asked Sutherland.

"I am responsible for conducting and organizing the big events, meetings, et cetera. I have also implemented the rationing bylaws. I am also the stand in for Father Paul here at the church when need be. I have attained an abundant following over the last couple of years, which I do pride myself on."

"What are the names of the people in your following?"

"For the sake of anonymity, I'd like to keep their whereabouts and identities confidential. I hope you can respect that, Detective."

Sutherland wrote quickly and never found himself looking up at Benjamin. He questioned and wrote at the same time.

"What did you do that brought me to you?" asked Sutherland.

"When communication was cut off, I saw no other way. So I walked up to the front gate and pleaded my case. I told them I'd do anything to help. I told them my name and what I do here, and that I wouldn't leave until they brought me someone who would listen. So, finally, after hours of waiting at the front gate, a representative approached me and told me to be in this very spot, on this very day, at this very time. And so, here we are," said Benjamin with an eerie benevolence in his voice.

"What has it been like since 'The Incident'?"

"Initially, it was chaos. Old rivalries among the town at each other's throats. Panic. Fear."

"Have their been any suicides or violence?"

The Town of Jasper

"None. A lot of depressed people, as you can understand. But no deaths."

"And what about the victims? Have they experienced any abnormalities in their health?"

"Not to my knowledge. Everyone here is in good health and safe."

"Do you think that will change?"

"I know it will change," said Benjamin.

The statement finally made Sutherland look up at the back of the back of Benjamin's head. He stared at him for a moment, wondering what he meant by the statement.

"Can you elaborate on that statement?" asked Sutherland.

"This place is dark, Detective. The people don't see it. Their absence will make us define ourselves, soon enough."

"And who are you all?"

"Not who we are. Who we will become," stated Benjamin eerily.

The dark truthfulness and reality of Benjamin's words opened up Sutherland's interpretation and outlook of the closed-off town. Things were steady for the community. For the time being.

"Do you believe things will get better here?" asked Sutherland, eager to hear Benjamin's answer.

"Things aren't going to get better here. Not until the wall comes down. Until that happens, things are going to get worse before they get better. But you already know that, Detective."

Sutherland sat back against the wooden bench. The well-spoken interim pastor was truthful and direct. Sutherland soon realized the brutal truth wasn't something he wished to hear so early on in his investigation.

"Where are the victims being held?"

"They're in the hospital."

"All of them?"

"All of them."

"You say things will get worse here. Why hasn't 'worse' happened yet?" asked Sutherland.

"Because of him," stated Benjamin

"Because of who?"

"He made believers out of us."

"Who is he?"

"Richard…"

"Richard who?"

"Richard Morrissey, Detective."

Sutherland wrote as quickly as he could. He was attaining more information than he could process, but he did his best by jotting down scribbled notes. His handwriting was illegible to everyone other than himself.

"He is in charge here?" asked Sutherland.

"In charge? Well from a dogmatic perspective, yes. Richard has delegated equal responsibility vital to the community's survival."

"So it's a democratic society in here?" assumed Sutherland.

"When it wants to be," said Benjamin.

"Where can I find this Richard Morrissey?"

"Again. Detective. I must keep the citizens within this wall…"

"Confidential," said Sutherland, finishing Benjamin's sentence.

"Yes," said Benjamin.

"Do you believe he is doing a sufficient job as the man in charge?"

"All depends on your opinion of what sufficient is."

"Do you think he is this town's savior?"

"I think God and only God is this town's savior. He and his representatives."

"Who are his representatives?"

"The one's who aren't blind. The one's who can hear his call for help."

"Elaborate, please."

"Necessary actions will be taken to ensure the community's survival. In order for things to turn around for the better again."

"Elaborate again".

"It's about time I finish my prayers, Detective. I believe I have provided you enough information," asserted Benjamin.

"That depends," said Sutherland.

"Excuse me?" asked Benjamin.

"That depends on what your opinion of 'enough' is," said Sutherland.

"I do thank you for your time. Leave the box by the door and see your way out. I do hope to see you again. Hopefully next time we both have better news."

Sutherland looked at the back of Benjamin's head with a snarl and got up off the wooden bench. He packed his leather bag with his supplies and threw the strap over his shoulder. He reached over and picked up the large brown box packed with what Benjamin requested. He looked back at the figure of Jesus against the wall and decided again not to recite a plea for assistance.

Benjamin closed his eyes again and recited his prayer in a whisper. Sutherland dropped the box on the ground loud enough for Benjamin to be rudely interrupted. The box of black cloaks rested against the front wall as Sutherland walked out of the church.

Benjamin remained focused and finished the ending of his prayer. Silently, he whispered to himself.

"And in the end. When it is finished. It will be us who they will thank."

Leave of Absence

Present Day 2016
Five Years After "The Incident"

Sutherland's hands shook as he flipped through his paperwork and files. He had a cup of coffee beside him, surrounded by an empty office. His face was haggard and body exhausted. He hadn't gotten a full eight-hour night of sleep in months. His manhunt for Richard Morrissey had turned him into a borderline insomniac. He sipped on his coffee and rolled his sleeves up. A representative dropped by his desk and dropped a file down on it. Sutherland looked up haphazardly at the man.

"More photos from the hospital. I'm turning in for the night. You should too," the man said as he walked away.

Sutherland woke up like he just got a shot of adrenaline. He flung the file open and began flipping through photos. He flipped and flipped and saw the faces of the victims. He looked at each photo for about five seconds and flipped to the next one. He came across a photo that made him stop and stare. He went cold as he stared at the photo. He placed the other ones down as he looked at the photograph. His hands began to shake again as he held it with both hands. The photo was of a little girl. His little girl. As the tears began to rush down his face, he remembered the reason his wife and daughter left him. He remembered the day they stormed out of the house. He remembered it all. He looked at the photo again and put his hand over his mouth as he became more hysterical. The little girl, Shannon, had dazzling blue eyes and soft blond hair. He finally stopped crying and looked up at the ceiling. He flung the photo on his desk and opened up a drawer aggressively. He took out an orange vial and popped the cap. He slid some pills into his mouth like they were M&M's. He then took out a bottle of whiskey in the same drawer and poured an unhealthy amount into his coffee cup. He slugged from the cup and struggled to swallow. He fumbled around his pockets for something until he found it in his shirt pocket. He pulled out his lighter and ignited the flame. He snatched the photo off his desk and touched the bottom of the photo against the flame. The photo slowly burned in his hands as he sat back and watched it disintegrate.

The next morning, drunk and inebriated, Sutherland's face planted on his desk as drool drizzled off his lips. A foot kicked him hard on the leg. Sutherland barely managed to open his eyes as the foot kicked him harder. Sutherland woke up from his intoxicated state, with the bottle pretty much killed on his desk. Captain Larson kicked him again, this time hard enough to hurt him.

"Wake up," he asked nastily.

Sutherland took his face off his desk and came to. The room spun as he blinked out the dizziness. The detective looked up at the captain and the other few men who had checked in early. He said nothing to them as he looked at the mess he made on his desk. He snatched the bottle quickly, as if no one saw it already and looked for the top.

"Clean yourself up, and get your ass into my office," demanded Captain Larson.

Sutherland leaned back into his chair and sighed, knowing he had screwed up. Upset about the way he'd been carrying himself, he got up off his chair and attempted to stand up straight. The heavy boozing played with his head as the room spun for a minute. He lost his balance and placed his hands on the desk. He swallowed hard as he looked at a stray capsule. Tempted to pop it in his mouth given the early morning stress, he fought the urge and covered it up with paperwork and files.

Inside the bathroom, he splashed his face with cold water several times until he woke himself up. He turned off the faucet and looked into the mirror. Pale and weary, Sutherland looked like a borderline homeless insomniac. He straightened his collar and cleared his throat. He wet his fingertips with the running water and brushed his hair back, attempting to neaten it. He sniffled and cleared his throat again and walked out of the bathroom.

The detective walked into the captain's office. He shut the door and the sound of it made the captain look up and stop what he was doing.

"Sit," requested Captain Larson.

The detective stood, standing up until the Captain Larson gave him a dirty look. Finally, the Detective gave in and took a seat. Captain Larson stared at him for a few moments with a snarling, unforgiving look that he usually gave Sutherland. The detective, exhausted, returned a similar gaze. The two had not been seeing eye to eye on the investigation for the last year.

"You're out of time," said the captain. "It's finished."

"That's bullshit. You gave me the extension!"

"I gave it to you believing you would actually put it to good use! Instead I'm getting reports that you're beating the hell out of people and knocking on the doors of brothels!"

"I'm doing my fucking job!"

The captain leaned on his desk with his forearms. He looked directly at Sutherland and shook his head.

"What did I tell you when you came in here and *begged* me to take this case?"

Sutherland said nothing and tried to act oblivious to what the captain was talking about. Captain Doyle looked at Sutherland, awaiting an answer.

"I don't..."

"I said, IF YOU FUCK UP IN THERE, I'D PULL YOUR ASS OUT! Now, I have Washington up my ass because they've attained Intel that the man on the inside is a deranged alcoholic with an ugly history."

"What the fuck are you talking about?" asked Sutherland angrily.

Captain Larson plopped a file in front of Sutherland.

"Olivia Collette...formerly known as Olivia Sutherland before her ugly divorce. Moved away after things got ugly at home with an abusive husband. Called him a pill-popping psychopath with bipolar issues. Said he was a danger to her daughter."

"I never touched her!" Sutherland shouted.

Captain Larson looked at him, disgusted, and closed up the file. He pushed the wheels on his chair back and sat back.

"Doesn't matter. Word got out like I knew it would, and now D.C. is questioning not only your sobriety and mental health, but also this department's judgment as a whole. I should have never given you the green light. I knew you had the issues, and I did it anyway. It was my fault," stated the captain.

"You gave me the green light because you knew I could get the job done!" screamed Sutherland.

The captain got up and flailed his arms out to his sides. He looked at Sutherland with a questioning expression.

"It's been five years! They aren't awake! We still don't know what the fuck happened! What job did you do?"

The Town of Jasper

The detective said nothing. Stubborn and pissed off, he took a deep breath and looked down at the captain's desk, avoiding eye contact with him.

"You're off this. You're taking a leave of absence until further notice. Give me the badge."

The detective became defensive and angered with the captain who failed to empathize with his ugly situation.

"You can't take me off this. What about the town?"

"It's over. They're going in, and they are cutting their losses. This has gone on long enough. The NSA doesn't want a rattled beehive in their country anymore."

Sutherland grew uncomfortable and very uneasy. He was out of time on the case, and the person he wanted to protect along with the town of Jasper was now in jeopardy.

"I need to…."

"Did I not make myself clear?" Captain Larson shouted. "You. Are. Finished. *Jasper*. Is finished. Look at yourself. You can't even pull yourself together. You're a goddamn disaster. It's only a matter of time before you lose yourself completely. I've looked the other way for far too long because you were a good detective. But now I've shifted my eyes, and I see a man incapable of taking care of his business, let alone himself."

"No…" said Sutherland.

Stunned at the fact that his affirmation was rebelled against, Captain Larson rose out of his chair and leaned on the desk as he spoke to the detective.

"You can't stop it. The fate of the town that once was is inevitable. And I wont stall anymore so you can go on some suicide rescue mission to save the family that left you and track down some crazed recluse!"

"Fuck you, Rory," snapped Sutherland.

"Always way over your own head. What are you going to do? Go in there and solve everything? Your investigation doesn't mean a *damn* when the planes fly over! It'll be over in minutes."

Sutherland drew his firearm out of rage and pointed it at the captain. Desperate and distressed, the detective had nothing to lose anymore, and he had been pushed past the edge. Captain Larson walked backwards slowly and hit his back against the wall. The detective, ready to spew his superior's brain against the beige drywall took another small step forward and stopped.

"What am I going to do? I'm going to go in there and finish what I started. And when I come out of there with them, pray I don't walk back into this office and finish *this*," he said with a strict tone.

The detective yanked the badge off his shirt and threw it on the table with his firearm still raised at the captain. After some moments passed, the two exchanged a final stare of disagreement. The detective lowered the weapon and walked out of the door heatedly. Captain Larson watched him exit the room with a look of discontent and irritation.

The Town of Jasper

Persona Non Grata

Present Day 2016
Five Years After "The Incident"

It was early enough in the morning for it to be dark and light out. However, the day would rise relatively soon, and time was precious. Richard and a few men packed his truck with resources and ammunition. It was brisk outside, and the cold air seeped into their bones and joints.

"That's all for today," Richard said to the men.

The night sky was foggy, and the moon hid itself from Jasper. Richard closed the door to the car and turned on the high beams. The blinding rays lit up the area around the car, and Richard began his route to see Edmund.

The car's engine roared moderately as Richard felt a certain peace and quiet that he hadn't heard in years. It calmed his nerves and lessened his anxiety as he placed his left arm out the window as he always did when he drove. The road was pitch black, but the car's beams provided light several hundred feet in front of him. He drove slowly, looking for more traps and non-coincidental roadblocks. Fortunately, he came across none as he made his way up the path into the 'Keep Out Zone'.

He parked his truck in the usual spot where he always met Edmund and waited for him. With the car lights off, there was no light whatsoever surrounding him. He stayed close to the truck so he wouldn't get lost in the darkness. He looked around for Edmund, who was always very punctual and prompt. Richard didn't see anyone or anything around him. Finally, a figure appeared to his left.

"Richard..." said Edmund.

"I have more of what you asked for," Richard said.

Edmund inspected the cargo and said nothing. That usually meant he approved of it.

"Why did you come alone?"

"My men need rest."

Edmund smiled nervously.

"Something is happening. Something terrible. Isn't it?" asked Edmund, reading through Richard's lie.

"Something is," said Richard.

"You're going to kill people," said Edmund.

"Yes," said Richard.

Edmund became concerned and troubled. He did not fully understand the reasoning and motive behind 'fortunate' people's actions. To him, it was so much simpler to come collaborate and bind everyone together as one. He was all about strength in numbers. Richard was about strength in people.

"Should we do this?" asked Richard, referring to the trade.

"Yes. We shall," said Edmund with a worrisome look at Richard.

A band of Fillmore Whites removed the goods from Richard's trunk and took it back to their camp and shelters.

"What do you need this time?" asked Edmund.

"Nothing. This one's on the house."

Edmund looked at him, unaware of the phrase.

"I'm confused."

"It means I don't want anything in return," said Richard.

"Why are you doing this?"

The Town of Jasper

"Because you are a friend. And come tomorrow...this might be the last time."

Edmund's concerns worsened. He didn't want his friend hurt or killed. They had formed a bond over the months, and Edmund trusted him as much as his own people. Edmund looked up at the sky, leading Richard to do the same.

"Storm's coming," said Edmund.

The two looked up at the foggy clouds above as the chill of morning froze their bones.

"Life's biggest curse," said Edmund as he gaped upwards.

"I thought you liked the rain?" asked Richard sarcastically.

Edmund chuckled. He always admired Richard's sense of humor. He slowly adapted to sarcasm each time Richard visited.

"Giving you people you care about and then taking them away," said Edmund. "They come into your life, and then they get taken from you at some point or another. The biggest curse life has to offer is the people whom you care for in it. There you came through my land that day a threat, here you are today my friend, and now here you go a man who might not see the day after tomorrow."

"There's no way around it, Edmund. It needs to happen. I tried reasoning. I need to *save* the people I love."

"I never said you were wrong. I just wish there was another way."

"So do I," said Richard.

A few Fillmore Whites reached for the weapons in the trunk. Edmund shook his head at them. The men stepped away from the truck, obeying his command. Richard looked at Edmund puzzled.

"You'll need them," said Edmund.

Richard nodded.

"Edmund. If I-uh…"

The sound of an explosion from the distance stimulated Richard's mind as he looked in the direction of where it was coming from. He looked at Edmund, who nodded with extreme concern. Richard extended his hand to Edmund, who grabbed it tightly, hoping it wouldn't be the last time. Richard pulled Edmund towards him and gave him a hug. For the first time, Edmund showed emotion in front of another human being as he felt his chest and throat cringe.

"You aren't like anyone else, Richard," said Edmund.

"You either," Richard replied.

"You're going to make it, son of my father's savior," said Edmund as he held Richard tightly.

"Or I'll die trying," Richard whispered.

Sutherland's side arms were loaded and his bulletproof vest attached tightly around his chest. He drove down the main road, heading toward the entrance to Jasper. It was very early. Early enough for it to be both light and dark out. The day would rise soon, and time was precious. He prepared himself for resistance from the guards, but he had a plan. He also had a Plan B. Dressed in his police uniform, he stepped hard on the gas and accelerated further. He would arrive at the front entrance in minutes.

Everything spun around his head from the interviews, his past, his partner, his wife, and his addiction. He let it all out by punishing the gas pedal. Droplets of rain began to hit his windshield, and he heard thunder roar like the king of the jungle. Finally, he arrived at the gate. There were several guards on patrol. The wall at the entrance stood about forty-feet high. Two brawny men held their hands up, ordering him to stop the vehicle and turn

The Town of Jasper

it off. He watched the two guards approaching his vehicle and the guards atop the wall with rifles. He did not turn the car off; he opened the door and walked towards them.

"Not another step, Detective," said one of guards with his chest puffed out.

"What's the meaning of this?" asked Sutherland.

"I'm sorry, we can't let you in any further," said the other guard sternly.

"Why not? I've had clearance inside the wall before."

"Sir…Please get back into your car," said one of them demandingly.

"I have jurisdiction in there," said the detective. "I'm trying to help resolve everything and get the wall down."

"The wall is coming down today, sir."

Sutherland looked at them, taken aback.

"They woke up?" Sutherland asked excitedly.

"No, sir. They haven't."

Sutherland's high hopes were burned to ash and stepped on. He knew what that meant. He knew that meant the end for Jasper.

"When are they coming?"

"Sir. Please get back into your car. You will be in harm's way. We thank you for your duty."

Sutherland's body went numb, and his heart dissolved. He felt weightless. He had failed.

"Okay, then," he said as he walked back to his car.

The two guards watched him all the way back to his vehicle that was still running. Sutherland got into his vehicle and closed the door gently. He looked ahead at the two men reverting back to the wall. The front wall had a gate that would allow authorized personnel and resource trucks in and out when they were still providing them. He opened the glove compartment and saw his old friend in the small orange vial. He wanted it, badly. It taunted him, inviting him to pop it open and swallow two, maybe three at once. It taunted him again. Sutherland closed his eyes tightly and clicked his seatbelt on, fighting his demons with all his inner strength. The urge was like an itchy mosquito bite on his ankle. Sutherland slammed the glove compartment closed and kicked the gas pedal with his right foot. The car's tires whistled and engine hummed as it headed towards the front gate at an increasing speed.

The two guards, completely shocked by what was happening, fumbled for their side arms. By the time they got them out and raised, Sutherland's vehicle was in front of them, heading for the front gate with no sign of stopping. All of the guards opened fire on Sutherland's vehicle. Bullets pierced the vehicle in all directions as Sutherland ducked down in front of the wheel. The gate was just fifty yards away as the marksman shot at his windshield, shattering the glass. Shards of glass and debris hit the detective's face as he gained speed. Bullets whizzed by his head, missing him by mere inches from behind. He was now ten yards away as the incoming fire intensified. A bullet grazed his right arm, causing a flesh wound, but he was unable to feel it with his adrenaline pumping. Five feet away from the gate, Sutherland screamed at the top of his lungs. The car crashed into the gate, sending the metal entrance flying several feet in the air. More gunfire ensued as they aimed for his tires. The vehicle was fifty yards or so within the wall. Sutherland weaved left and right so they couldn't get a clean shot at the tires. Now closing in on a hundred yards inside, the guards fired off wild shots, and one managed to hit his back right tire. The vehicle wobbled and shifted to the side as the next bullet hit the front right tire. With all the vehicle's momentum traveling on its side, it eventually rolled over.

The vehicle tumbled violently a few times until it finally came to a screeching halt. Upside down, the wheels on the vehicle spun, and smoke began to emanate from the hood. Unconscious, Detective Sutherland's vision was blurry as he found himself upturned inside the vehicle. He coughed as his arms dangled helplessly. He could smell smoke, but wasn't sure where it was coming from. He wasn't sure if he was in pain due to the shock he was in. He slipped in and out of consciousness as the vehicle began to heat up.

Outside the vehicle, the engine caught fire. The marksman on the wall aimed down his sights on the scope and saw the inferno from the vehicle. Looking for the detective to squirm out so he could finish him off, the other guard ordered him to stand down. The marksman looked down below at the wreckage of the wall.

"If he isn't dead already, he doesn't have long. We need to get reinforcement down here for repair," shouted the other guard.

The marksman looked out from atop the wall at the flame-engulfed vehicle. A few moments later, the vehicle exploded, creating a thunderous sound and display of incredible detonation, which sent small burning car parts flying in all directions.

James D. Gianetti

Proditor

Present Day 2016
Five Years After "The Incident"

When a new queen bee is available, the workers will kill the reigning queen by "balling" her, colloquially known as "cuddle death": clustering tightly around her until she dies from overheating.

At daybreak, Richard rushed into Town Hall, where Ron Carlisle greeted him. Richard was apprehensive and frenzied, rushing up to Ron.

"What happened? Is everyone safe? I heard something from the entrance of the wall," asked Richard hectically.

"Everything is fine. Our scouts said a vehicle drove into the wall, and it was shot down by the guards."

"What about the driver?"

"Whoever it was, they died in the explosion."

"There's no time for that matter right now. Is everyone ready?"

"Yes. The Council is all there. The plan is a go."

"Good," said Richard.

"You sure you don't want to…"

"No…"

Ron nodded his head in approval, knowing Richard knew what he was doing.

"Okay, then," said Ron.

Ron would conduct The Council meeting while Richard and two of his best men would head to the barn to retrieve his wife.

The Town of Jasper

Ron needed to stay, in case of a pending attack in Richard's absence. Also, Richard wanted to recon the barn and count the amount of Redeemers so he could pinpoint exactly who they were. Ron and The Council were tasked with conducting a comprehensive attendance report while Richard was gone; therefore, they would find out exactly which people were involved in the group of extremists.

"I need a minute," said Richard as he walked quickly into the bathroom.

Richard mulled and thought over and over about the plan. He checked his pistol's clip. It was fully loaded, just like the last three times he checked it. Time was running short, and he knew another strike was coming. His prisoner was most definitely dead by now from starvation, and the Redeemers he knew were under the impression that he told him everything he needed to know. He placed his gun in his holster and adjusted his knife in its sheath. He walked over to the mirror and stared at himself. He saw the wear and tear of the several years decorated on his face. He was no longer the man he used to be. He had done things that made him fearful of his own self. He had become the necessary sinner Jasper needed in its time of dire straits. The necessary monster that his loved ones needed him to be. He looked away from himself and held in his stomach fluids. He thought about the prisoner, and asked himself how many more he'd have to kill to save his people. A malicious thought to say the least, Richard believed in thinking up the worst possible scenarios, especially now. He always prepared himself for the worst possible outcome, because in Jasper, the worst possible outcome was always the likelihood. With the dark thoughts, Richard purged his stomach fluids into the sink. He spit and dry-heaved until the knock on the door disrupted his purge. He looked at the door with his sleep-deprived eyes and rushed out of the bathroom, headed outside towards his vehicle.

Accompanying Richard to the barn would be Dallas and a young man named Ian Pratt. Richard started up the engine while Ron walked up to the passenger's side door and looked over at him.

"Everything will be done when you get back," he said.

With a nod from Richard, Ron took a step backwards and the truck pulled away. Ron watched them for a moment and walked back inside where he was noticed an angst ridden Benjamin, standing in the main lobby.

"Where is Richard going? Is he going after his wife?"

"Yes," said Ron. "Is everyone inside?"

"Yes. We're all ready. Is everything okay?"

"Everything is fine. We need to be very precise with our record keeping of citizens. Is everyone in the Safe Zone ready to be accounted for?"

"Yes. I handled the matter personally," said Benjamin.

"Good," said Ron as he opened the door to The Council's room.

The members of The Council looked at Ron take center seat, wondering where Richard was. Some of them looked around.

"Where is Richard?" asked Kendrick.

"He is on his way to find the Redeemers," said Ron.

Banter and chitchat amongst The Council progressed after the comment. Ron put his hands up, trying to gain their attention.

"Listen closely," Ron said. "He is doing some reconnaissance to find out how many of those bastards there are. In the meantime, we need conduct a comprehensive record of how many people are here and who they are. Therefore, we will know who they are exactly. We can end this conflict tonight."

The Town of Jasper

"Where is he doing this reconnaissance?" asked William.

"At the barn on Dickinson."

"How does he know they're there?"

"They're there," said Ron.

Richard drove up Dickinson Street, headed for the barn house. He parked his vehicle a few blocks away. The three of them got out of the vehicle and paced furtively towards the rear of the barn. About twenty-five yards apart from each another, the barn house was in sight of them at their respective angles. Richard gave the hand command to stop and kneel. They observed the outside of it and saw no sign of human activity. After Richard scanned the area thoroughly, he gave the command to move forward. The three men made their way unnoticed and behind a nearby patch of trees. They were only fifty yards from the barn house. The barn was owned by Patricia and Galen Vanderbilt. Unfortunately, Galen passed away of cancer and Patricia was a victim of 'The Incident'. Richard looked over his tree to devise the most strategic way to snatch and grab.

"Safeties off," he whispered to the two men who were now only feet away from him. "Let's move."

They paced forward, making little noise and heading for the barn house. Richard would take the front, and the two others would take the side and rear. Now only twenty-five yards away, the three men broke their formation as planned. The area was quiet and empty. It concerned Richard, thinking they might get ambushed. He took cover against the barn and looked around as his heart raced. The coast remained clear as Dallas and Ian checked the sides and rear. There was a small patch of woods at both sides of the barn, which Richard meticulously and rigorously checked. The windows were fogged up and making it impossible to see inside the barn. Knowing time was running short and they were possible sitting ducks, Richard rushed up to the barn door and noticed the lock on it. He checked his surroundings once more as Ian and Dallas joined him at the front.

"It's all clear, boss," said Ian.

Richard inhaled and pointed his gun at the lock. He pulled back the trigger as the lock exploded. He pulled the double-sided doors open and immediately raised his weapon, ready to fire at the first thing that moved.

To their surprise, the barn was empty. There was also no sign of Richard's wife. The three men continued to check every corner with their guns raised. Panicking, Richard began to accept the fact that Diane wasn't there and that the prisoner lied to him. The inside of the barn house began to spin, and Richard nearly fainted.

"They're not here. What should we do?" asked Dallas.

"We need to get out of here. This is a trap," said Ian.

"Boss…"

"They're not here…" said Richard gently. "We need to get back."

"What?" asked Dallas, who didn't hear him.

Richard looked at them with fear in his eyes. Fear the men never saw in Richard.

"We need to get back!"

Inside The Council room, Ron remained at the helm, assuring everyone that the plan would work. The Council was somewhat offended, due to the fact that they were uninformed and unaware of the secret plan. They were also oblivious to the impending threat that headed towards them at that very moment.

"When I get word from Richard, we will move forward with it."

"Any idea when that's going to be? We are vulnerable here with him gone," said Matilda.

"Should be soon," said Ron.

A group of people stampeded down the hall towards The Council room. They removed their weapons as they got within a hundred feet of the door.

"We need to be patient. Just a little longer," Ron continued. "We're going to be fine."

The group of people opened the door to The Council room and barged inside. Ron, along with the rest of The Council, looked up in astonishment and inquiry. The group of people stood along the back borders of the room with knives and blades in their hands.

"What is going on? Why aren't you in your quarters?" asked Ron.

With that, Benjamin stood up and walked towards Ron.

"What's going on here?" Ron asked

"The culmination of our righteous mission," said Benjamin.

The group of people, including Flynn, Burt Ryloth, and Earl Pike, walked up behind each member of The Council and placed their blades against their throats.

"No," said Ron as he nearly choked on his words.

He looked at Benjamin, who now shifted his body towards the hostage council.

"Today the wall will come down, and we will bring back Jasper. Richard will not find us at the barn," said Benjamin. "He will find that we are here. As we always have been. And in the end. When it is finished. It will be us who you will thank."

Benjamin, leader of the Redeemers, nodded to the group, holding their blades against The Council's jugulars. All at once, they slit their throats, sending their blood squirting and spouting sloppily across The Council table. Ron nearly collapsed as he witnessed the murders. He became as fearful as he was on the day of 'The Incident'. A feeling he wished to never again feel. Benjamin drew his pistol out quickly. Knowing he would be killed, Ron drew his but was shot several times in the chest and torso by Benjamin, who had the quicker hand. Ron flew backwards and hit the wall hard, sending his gun flinging out of his hand. Benjamin looked around at The Council as they bled out.

"No hesitation. No uncertainty," said Benjamin callously.

The group of Redeemers rushed out of the room, ready to finish the genocide which they started.

The gas pedal pressed against the floor of the car as Richard sped towards the school. He got on his walky-talky.

"Ron! Evacuate the building! Ron!"

The silence on the other end made Richard bang the top of the car.

"Shit!"

Dallas got on his COM to signal the men on guard.

"Johnny One, come in. Evacuate the building. Again. Evacuate the building."

The man on the other end of Dallas' COM came in with a choppy signal.

"You want us to evacuate?"

"Yes! Get everyone out! Rendezvous at point F. The Redeemers are in the building!"

"On it!" shouted the man on the line.

The Town of Jasper

Inside the school, people evacuated and ran around in a crazed riot. They carried their loved ones in their arms or in wheelchairs. The gunman tried to maintain order while trying to find where the Redeemers were.

"Everybody outside to the rendezvous point! Get everyone out!" shouted one of the gunmen.

People ran outside as the Redeemers, dressed like regular people, approached the gunman.

"Get outside quickly, they're here," said one of the gunmen to Benjamin and the group of them.

"Very good," Benjamin said as stabbed the man in the stomach.

The gunmen let out a gasp as Benjamin plunged the blade deeper into is abdomen. The other guard saw Benjamin and, with a panic, lifted his weapon up at him. Before he could fire off a shot, a Redeemer stabbed him in the back. The Redeemers picked up the weapons and began to act as the guards. They made their way into the main lobby, evacuating everyone out of the school.

"Everyone get to the rendezvous point!" shouted Benjamin as he waved people out.

Outside, the storm brewed and brewed into what looked like a hurricane. It would hit Jasper in less than fifteen minutes. People scattered out of the school towards the rendezvous point, which was Town Hall. This would allow the Redeemers to gather them all in one place and kill every last victim. The people struggled to carry their loved ones into the heart of town as they ran away from the school.

Richard mounted the curb to the school as more and more people poured out. Richard ran out of the vehicle and into the building. Benjamin greeted him with his gun in his hands.

"Richard! Thank God, you're safe!"

"Where are my kids?

"I saw someone carry them out. They're headed towards the rendezvous!"

Richard bolted away from him.

"Richard! Ron is gone," said Benjamin sadly.

Richard looked at Benjamin for a moment without much time to process an emotional response.

"Make sure everyone gets there safely!" Richard shouted.

Benjamin made his way quickly outside as Richard checked the gymnasium of the school to make sure all the victims had made it out. The gymnasium was completely empty. He ran as fast as he could towards the room where his children were and kicked down the door. Both of his children were gone. Like a gazelle, he ran outside en route to the rendezvous.

It began to rain outside, and the droplets hit Richard's shoulders. Thunder rumbled in the distance, causing the ground to slightly tremble. Richard got into his truck and sped to Town Hall to meet up with the remaining residents.

As the people of Jasper vacated and relocated, three planes began their prep to bomb the town and cut the country's 'loose end'. They would make their descent in less than an hour. Operation S.H.A.D.O.W. was a go.

/ The Town of Jasper

Crossfire

Present Day 2016
Five Years After "The Incident"

The storm raged on directly above Jasper, with rain coming crashing down and the winds fast enough to sway Richard's truck. The howling winds and vicious downpour were negligible to the echoing sound of the thunder that shook people's bones and lightning that provided an Armageddon-like vibe.

    Richard floored it as the truck battled the severe weather. The windshield wipers made a loud squeaking noise as they rapidly moved left and right. Richard drove down Penston Street, which had wooded areas on the left and right. Richard's gun was placed on the passenger seat next to him with his peripherals constantly glued on it. In the distance, Richard saw a few men on both sides of the road. Two on the left and one on the right. He slowed down, but still traveled quickly. He rolled his window down, figuring them to be a few stragglers who fell behind en route to Town Hall. As he rolled the window down, the men opened fire on his truck. The bullets shattered the windshield, causing Richard to put his arm up to block the shattered glass. He maintained control of the vehicle with his right hand as he swerved wildly. He looked over the steering wheel and saw the man on the right side with his gun raised. He swung the wheel in his direction as he ducked and pressed his foot on the gas. The truck hit the man dead on, sending him flying back. By chance, Richard was not hit by any bullets. He reached for his gun that fell on the floor on the passenger side. His pulse raced, with everything happening in what felt like slow motion. Richard got his fingertips on the gun and picked it up.

One of the men raced towards the passenger side door with his gun raised. Richard pointed his side arm at the open driver's side window and fired off a single shot at the man's head as soon as he saw him. The man shot backwards as the bullet killed him instantly. Richard got out of the car in a frenzy and saw the third shooter to his left through the downpour. The man fired off a wild shot, hitting the truck. Richard raised his gun quickly and shot the man down with two accurate shots to the man's chest. The man fell to the ground with Richard approaching him. The man moaned and groaned as he looked up at Richard, who pointed his gun and fired off a shot that killed him. Without hesitation, Richard holstered his sidearm and grabbed a sledgehammer in the back of his truck and walked over to the man he hit with his truck.

On the ground, the man's back and ribs were broken. Richard looked down on him with the sledgehammer in his hands held securely.

"Where are the rest of them?" Richard screamed. "Where is my wife?"

Unable to produce a word from the amount of pain the man was in, Richard swung the sledgehammer down harshly against the man's core. The first swing paralyzed the man. The second and third swing shattered his torso and spine. Richard got into the truck and sped down the road headed for Town Hall, knowing time was running short.

Everyone made it to Town Hall safely. Every able and willing person gathered the victims inside as best they could. Everyone was completely unmindful to whom the Redeemers were, and had no idea they were among them. Benjamin orchestrated everything in

The Town of Jasper

both Richard and Ron's absence, having everyone escorted outside once all the victims were safe indoors.

Everyone gathered outside in the brutal rain, which started to become a safety concern. Richard sped up to the outside of the building and scratched the brakes still. He rushed out of the car. The people outside looked at him, bothered by the fact that his car was battered and that he looked slightly mangled himself.

"Is everyone inside?" he shouted.

People nodded their heads and shouted yes. Benjamin gave a nod to his men who were among the crowd, and suddenly, the Redeemers broke away from the pack and circled around them. A dozen of them rose their guns at the crowd, ready to take out every last one of them. Benjamin pointed his gun at Richard's leg and put a bullet in his thigh. Richard screamed in pain as Benjamin picked him up by his collar. Everyone looked on in dread and dismay, as Benjamin had his arm around their leader's neck and gun dug into the back of his head.

"Everyone stand still!" shouted Benjamin.

A few men went to grab or point their weapons at them, but Benjamin ordered them to do otherwise.

"Don't try!" he yelled. "The wall is coming down today!"

Benjamin gave another nod to two men, signaling them to go inside and burn the Town Hall to the ground. Everyone stood together with their hands slightly raised, perplexed at Benjamin and the others. As the two men made their way inside to wipe out the last of the victims, there was a roaring, thunderous sound of something in the sky. It was not the thunder or lightning. Three planes soared above the dark grey clouds. Unable to see them through the fog and clouds, their shadows could be seen hovering above them, headed in their direction. Everyone looked up in astonishment, due to the fact they hadn't seen or heard a plane in years. A few thought it was rescue, maybe a resource drop off of some kind. Then unexpectedly, objects dropped down from them. The bombs hit the ground, causing a massive quake beneath everyone's feet.

People screamed and began to panic in horror. They scattered quickly for the entrance to retrieve the victims. The Redeemers opened fire on the crowd amidst the aerial attack. Everyone ducked as bullets flew everywhere around them. The large group of people ran towards town to find shelter and cover.

The Redeemers shifted their attention to the planes, leaving them vulnerable. A few townspeople aimed down their sights and began shooting at the Redeemers.

Gunfire ensued as lighting, thunder, and explosives began to rain down like hell on Jasper. Men cried out to everyone to find cover and safety as the battle of Jasper began. Redeemers and townspeople took cover and shot at each other wildly. During the chaos, Benjamin grabbed Richard and used him as a human shield as he ran to take cover behind his truck. Bullets hissed by and sprayed in all directions. Benjamin backpedaled, pulling Richard along with him. Knowing he had one chance to survive, Richard timed his footsteps with Benjamin's and placed his right foot behind Benjamin's, causing him to trip and fall backwards. They both hit the ground hard, with Richard on top of Benjamin. Richard turned around and got on top of Benjamin, who tried to raise his gun. Richard swatted the gun out of his hand, sending it flying several feet away. Richard broke Benjamin's nose, by delivering a harsh head butt. Richard clenched his fist and struck Benjamin several times in the jaw.

The Town of Jasper

The shooting continued as the planes circled back around. Buildings began to give, and some caught fire. People ran through the streets wildly, as the Redeemers shot some of them down.

A few members of town, along with Gary Ford, took cover behind the post office and opened fire on a few Redeemers headed their way. One of the Redeemers hit the ground after being hit in the neck. One of the Redeemers, a woman, shot at Ford and the others and hit Ford in the shoulder.

"Son of a bitch!" shrieked Ford as he got up in rage and sprayed bullets at them. Ford emptied his clip and mowed down the remaining two Redeemers. He threw the weapon down as more people ran towards him in a hurry. One of the women was Olivia Collette, who rushed up to Ford with her daughter in her arms. He escorted them inside the diner across the street.

Olivia led the people into the diner and through the kitchen. She led them towards the basement one by one. Once everyone was downstairs, Olivia walked down the wooded staircase with her daughter, Shannon held tightly in her arms. The group of people all cluttered around something.

"What?" asked Olivia.

She walked towards the attraction that the people surrounded and saw a woman lying unconscious on the floor. It was Diane Morrissey.

The planes made their second pass and dropped some more explosives down in the direction of the battle. The street cracked and busted out, spewing stalactites. Some people fell down from the impact. Buildings and stores sustained massive amounts of damage.

Richard and Benjamin wrestled on the ground. Richard had no time to think about the fact that one of his most trusted allies was actually his worst enemy. Richard gripped his dirty, bloody hands around Benjamin's neck and squeezed with all his strength. A straggling Redeemer came up from behind Richard and aimed his weapon. What the Redeemer didn't see was the man running full speed at him to his left.

Ron Carlisle tackled the man like a linebacker. However, the Redeemer was able to fire his shot off and graze the side of Richard's ribcage. Ron and the man fumbled and fought for the gun, as Benjamin got on top of Richard and dug his fingers into his wound. Screaming in pain, Richard tried to take a few swings at Benjamin, but was unable to connect hard enough. Without another option, Richard grabbed Benjamin's forearm and sunk his teeth into it like a vampire. The blood sprinkled out of Benjamin's arm, causing him to release his hand from Richard's flesh wound.

Richard heard a gun shot from the other end of the truck and was unable to see what happened. He feared the worst for Ron. Benjamin leaped at the gun he dropped and clutched it with both hands. Richard reached for his as well, and the two began to roll over with their guns pointed at one another. With his side gashed and cut, Richard was slower to the draw as Benjamin rolled over and took aim at Richard. Several bullets pierced through Benjamin's body as Ron Carlisle appeared from the other end of the truck just in time. His shirt was unbuttoned, showing his chest with bruises and flesh wounds from where the bullets hit his Kevlar vest. He helped Richard up, who winced in pain. The weather was in its prime, sending debris, branches, and countless objects flying in all directions.

"We need to find cover!" shouted Ron.

"Stay here! Guard the hall!" screamed Richard as he limped quickly ahead.

The Town of Jasper

He looked in the bed of his truck to try to find anything of use. In the corner, there was a smoke grenade. He grabbed it and headed north.

In the center of town, the shootout continued. Redeemers scattered, shooting at everyone that moved. Richard took aim and fired off a few shots but was unable to see if he hit anyone through the wreckage, smoke, and rain. He took cover behind a post box and poked his head over it. There was a group of people being fired at across the street. Richard made a dash for them as the planes turned around to make their third pass. Richard fired off a few shots as he ran towards the panicked crowd. He met up with Officer Gary Ford, who provided most of the protection.

"How many?" asked Richard.

"I'm counting seven," said Officer Ford.

"You hit?" asked Richard as he looked at officer Ford's shoulder.

"I'm good," said Ford.

"We're in a bad place here, they have the upper…"

The planes flew over, dropping down more explosives dangerously close to them.

"Down!" shouted Richard as he jumped on top of Officer Ford.

A few cars exploded and flipped over. Half of the strip mall across the street came crashing down. Smoke and fire engulfed the street as Richard came to. He looked up at the planes that headed in the direction of the 'Keep Out Zone'. Richard looked on and prayed for Edmund and the Fillmore Whites. A couple of men got up, their ears ringing from the blast, and found themselves in the crossfire under fire. Richard screamed out to them, but they couldn't hear his holler. They looked like two chickens with their heads cut off before they were viciously shot down.

"We have to move!" shouted Officer Ford.

Richard saw smoke in the horizon. It was coming from the church. Richard got behind cover as he looked out at it. He turned to Officer Ford.

"Cover me!" Richard shouted.

"What? Where are you…?"

Richard beamed out into the middle of the street, which was swallowed up with smoke and fog. Officer Ford got out from his cover and fired off a few shots in the direction of the remaining Redeemers. He managed to take one out as Richard made a break for it. Richard also fired off a few rounds during his trajectory. Richard reached the other side and was out of ammo. He unsheathed his knife as he hustled onward. A Redeemer ran up to him through the mist, causing Richard to violently collide with him. The Redeemer, a middle-aged bald man with more girth than Richard, hit him in the head with the end of his rifle. Richard fell to the ground as the man let out a scream and pointed his gun at Richard's face. Richard grabbed the barrel of the gun and pushed it away. The gun went off and missed Richard's face by inches. The bullet grazed Richard's ear, taking the lobe off. He grabbed the man's collar and pulled him towards his blade. Richard plunged his blade into the brawny man's chest. The man's eyes bulged as Richard dug the blade deeper and deeper until the man was finally dead. The big, bald man fell off Richard, who got himself up with his ear gushing blood. He looked up at the again coming from the church again and ran towards it.

The sound of thunder, weapons firing, and the planes overhead made Jasper feel like a hellish war zone. Buildings collapsed, trees

The Town of Jasper

fell, people were being shot down, and Ron stood helpless, guarding Town Hall. He heard people screaming for help, the same way he did on the day of 'The Incident'. He held his gun tightly and tried to block out all the violence and agony. Finally, Ron made a call and abandoned his post ready to flank the remaining extremist.

Ron sprinted through hell and looked around at the once proud community reduced to rubble. Dead bodies littered the streets and gunfire rang out like an out of sync melody. Across the street, by the convenience store, Officer Ford and a few men were pinned down. Ron couldn't tell where the Redeemers were firing. His eyes watered as the smoke and heat from the flaming buildings got into them. He squinted and pointed his gun, ready to fire at anything coming his way. He heard Ford's voice screaming out, so he followed in that direction. More gunfire ensued, and he did not hear Ford's voice after it. His heart thumped and banged against his chest as his face went cold. His forehead began to sweat profusely as he could hear men close by. Impossible to see even five feet in front of him, Ron felt alone. Feeling like he was being hunted, Ron felt a cold sweat down the back of his spine. He heard footsteps all over but didn't want to fire and hit one of his own. He walked forward with his knees bent and made it all the way across the road by the convenience store. A few Redeemers were lying dead on the ground near the area of the convenience store. Up against the sidewall of the store, Officer Ford rested up against it, with a bullet through his cheek and neck. Ron rushed to feel Ford's pulse. Ron wrapped his dirty fingers around Ford's jugular and did not feel a pulsation. Officer Ford was dead.

"Don't move," a voice behind him said.

Ron slowly turned around to face the ender of his life. Behind him, Dallas pointed a gun at his head.

"Shit," Dallas said with a sigh. "Where's Richard?"

"I don't know," said Ron.

In the distance, the 'Keep Out Zone' was an inferno. The planes veered off, done with their task. The town, completely ravaged and destroyed, was subjected to a sinister-like chaos and assault, which made it look like something worse than the underworld.

Richard rushed towards the church, which was up in flames and half torn apart. Father Paul was still inside. The blaze was so significant and prevailing that it caused an explosion that sent a chunk of the roof collapsing inside. Richard feared his friend did not survive inside the inferno.

Without thinking twice, Richard made a dash inside the burning church to save his friend. The fire and the flames burnt the hair off Richard's arms as he hurried towards the confessional. The church was completely destroyed, with the windows shattered and wooden benches going up like logs in a fire pit. He leaped over debris and burned his hand on the piping hot wood. The confessional had a ton of debris in front of it but was still manageable to get through. Richard leaped over a large piece of wood but lost his balance, causing him to crash down on shards of glass and tiny, sharp chunks of wood. He pushed his chest up with both hands but did not see the beam come crashing down directly above him.

The massive wooden beam trampled his back, crushing him. He was trapped under it, with what felt like a broken back, and felt the weight of everything through the wooden beam. There was no way he could move, let alone get the large piece of wood off of him. This was it for him, he told himself. This was how it ended. In such a familiar place, where he always found shelter and serenity, was also going to be the place that buried him. He looked over at the confessional as the church became more and more engulfed with the only friend of the devil. He tried to move forward, but the bullet wound, the brutal heat, and the punishing object that dominated atop him prevented him from doing so. Amidst all the wreckage and ruin to the church and to himself, Richard did not even feel the jagged-edged piece of wood, sunk deep into his side.

The temperature soared within the house of God as Richard felt himself drift away slowly. He began to wonder where he'd go in the aftermath of all he had done. Would God open his arms and make an exception for his necessary sins? Or would Satan step down and give him the throne? Richard could see the bright light and gradually began to accept and welcome it more with each passing second.

But suddenly, he felt the massive beam become lighter on his back as it lifted off him. Was he dead? Was this all in illusion? As the wooden beam was being taken off his back, Richard reached for his gun. Two burly hands clutched tightly on the back of Richard's burnt shirt. Richard grasped the handle of his pistol as he was aggressively turned on his back by the mysterious figure. As he rolled over, Richard aimed the gun upwards at the man and yelled in rage. Detective Sutherland quickly deflected the gun out of Richard's hands, sending it soaring several feet away. Richard managed to throw a left hook amidst his significant wound. The blow hurt Richard more than Sutherland, but his knuckles struck Sutherland's jaw fairly well.

Richard scurried on the ground for his gun, and as he did so, Sutherland fumbled to draw his out of his holster. Richard squirmed and crawled towards his weapon and leaped for it. He clasped it with both hands and took aim at Sutherland from the ground. Sutherland drew his gun as quickly as he could but saw Richard already had his gun drawn at him. Sutherland leaped out of the way as Richard fired off his last two shots. Both bullets hissed by Sutherland, missing him by mere centimeters. Richard reached for his knife and barely managed to get to his feet. He saw his foe getting up from behind a burning church bench and he hurled himself on him. Sutherland's knees buckled and he fell to the ground. Richard grasped the handle of his knife, ready to stab Sutherland to death.

The two tussled on the ground, deflecting each other's hands and arms. Sutherland grabbed Richard's collar and pulled Richard's head towards his elbow. The impact of Sutherland's elbow against Richard's nose nearly broke it. Richard managed to shake off the blow to his nose and punched Sutherland a couple of times in the jaw. Unable to get a good look at Sutherland, Richard raised his knife and brought it down as hard as he could towards Sutherland's chest. Richard let out a yelp of agony and violence. The detective's quick instincts and reflexes saved his life, as he caught Richard's wrist swinging downwards. The two struggled and grunted as they fought for control of the knife. Sutherland found it difficult to breathe with Richard's knee digging into his stomach. Richard clenched his teeth as he used all his strength to plunge the blade into Sutherland's heart. Sutherland began to lose stamina as he looked up at Richard's face, which was mangled and covered in ash. However, portions of Richard's white face were visible, which caused Sutherland to realize.

Richard pressed down on the blade as he looked into Sutherland's eyes. Gradually, the two men stopped struggling with the knife as they both eventually fell into a state of awe. Richard and Sutherland looked at each other's nearly unrecognizable faces for the first time in five years.

Detective Sutherland looked into the eyes of his old partner and best friend. Richard looked at him, wondering if it was a mirage. Without time to process or emotionally comprehend, Richard got off of Sutherland and fell on his back in extreme pain and agony. Sutherland went to help his friend, but Richard pointed towards the confessional.

"In the confessional! There's a man in there! We need to get him out of here!" screamed Richard.

With a little reluctance, Sutherland had no time to debate or dispute.

"Stay here!" he ordered to Richard.

He ran through the fire and avoided all falling debris as he jumped and dodged the bits and pieces of the church on the floor. He got inside the confessional and saw Father Paul unconscious. He grabbed the priest and carried him with all his strength. There was an exit door nearby, which Sutherland made use of by kicking it down. He rushed the priest outside to safety and set him down on the grass. The rain and wind calmed down as the storm began to pass. He hurtled back into the falling church to rescue his longtime friend.

In the same spot, he saw Richard crawling on the ground. A gigantic part of the roof came soaring downward. Sutherland leaped out of the way of the falling debris at the last moment. The section of the roof barreled down on the ground, which caused a blockade between himself and Richard. Knowing he only had one move to save him, the detective leaped through the flame-immersed barricade and rolled ineptly on the floor in front of Richard. More objects fell and ejected outward around them.

Sutherland jumped on top of Richard, covering his body from the impending heavy discharges from the walls and ceiling. The church was about to completely give any second. Sutherland turned Richard over and lifted him up in his arms. He made his way to the front exit, which was the only other feasible way out. Sutherland pushed through the bottomless pit and managed to get outside to safety.

He set Richard down next to Father Paul who slept on the grass with his eyes closed gracefully. The rain began to slow down as the storm began to pass. Sutherland took deep breaths as his lungs battled with him. Richard was on his back in front of him, with his eyes open. His face was burnt and body beaten and wounded. Sutherland looked down at him and saw him clutching the wooden object in his side. Richard looked at his old friend and smiled and then down at the object wedged into his side.

"Don't look at it," requested Sutherland.

"It's bad. I know. This way you don't have to lie to me," Richard said half jokingly.

"You'll make it. I just need to find…"

"No. No," said Richard struggling. "Please stay."

Sutherland halted and knelt down beside his friend. Richard held his head.

"You cheap shotting bastard."

"Cheap shot? At least I don't punch like a woman."

The two shared a mild laugh, which caused Richard pain in his side. Sutherland held Richard, who shoved his hands away.

"Where the hell you been? I told you to come visit me years ago," said Richard.

Sutherland laughed but also felt deep sadness. He didn't know what to say to him after so many years. The rain turned into a drizzle as the thunder hollered quietly.

"Don't say it," Richard said.

"I wasn't," said Sutherland with a slight chuckle.

"Yes, you were. It was rolling off your tongue."

The two exchanged smiles as the blood oozed out of Richard's ribcage. Richard sighed and raised his eyebrows.

"So," he said. "Tell me about your life over the last five years."

Sutherland showed his white teeth as he grinned. It was a defense mechanism for his bereavement and realization of the horrible truth.

"I got divorced," said Sutherland.

"Mutual separation?" asked Richard.

"Let's call it that. Sure."

"Definitely your fault," said Richard.

"Up yours," said Sutherland with a smile. He let the humor of the moment last a few moments. "You always were a shitty shot, by the way."

"Up yours more," said Richard with a chuckle that made him cough up some blood. "Do you still love her?"

Sutherland didn't say anything. He sat and pondered deeply, asking himself the question. Richard looked at his friend, awaiting an answer.

"Do you?"

Sutherland continued on with his silence, but Richard wanted an answer out of his friend.

"Do you still…"

"Yes," interjected the detective.

"Then make it right and fix it," said Richard.

"I can't," said Sutherland. "It's something that can't be undone. I can't turn it around."

"Everything turns around," said Richard. "Whether you believe it to be true or not."

"She's in here," said Sutherland. "I don't even know if she's alive."

"She's alive," said Richard.

"How do you know?"

"I don't know. But I just know," said Richard.

"I'm sorry you never got a chance to meet my family. It was my own fault. I know that now. We were just going through…"

"Changes. I know," said Richard painfully.

"Next time. We're there. All of us. Next time it will be all of us. I swear it," said Sutherland, rushed and frantic.

"Yeah. *Next time…*" said Richard, somewhat unconvinced.

Sutherland became overwhelmed with sorrow and grief as his friend began to slowly die. Richard's eyes began to shut.

"Hey, hey, hey," said Sutherland.

Richard swallowed and opened his eyes, which looked like it took a lot of strength.

"Just making sure you still give a shit," said Richard with a smirk.

"You asshole," said Sutherland softly and sadly. "You know, I got that dog. Thing chewed up my sofa."

"I told you to get the cat," said Richard with a half-smile.

Sutherland shook his head and could not laugh anymore. This was it. It was close. His throat began to close up and he blinked his eyes numerously to keep the tears in. Richard let out as big a sigh as he could.

"How did we get in a mess like this?" Richard asked, looking around him as best he could. "Where did it all go wrong?"

"I wish I had the answer," said Sutherland quietly.

The Town of Jasper

Richard breathed in and out of his nostrils loud enough for Sutherland to hear. The situation became more and more of an emotional burden for Sutherland as he tried thinking of topics to keep a conversation going.

"It was you," Richard said. "*The detective.*"

Sutherland looked at his friend, wondering how he knew that. The two friends let some silence pass as Richard's breathing intensified and got much heavier. Richard shut his eyes.

"After. I want you to go the old law office on Main Street. Inside the bottom drawer of the big desk there's a picture frame. You can't miss it. Have it delivered to my address when they wake."

"You're not going to do it yourself?" asked Sutherland, hoping for an optimistic answer from his friend.

"No," said Richard sadly. "I'm not."

"I still don't know," said Sutherland with a cracked voice.

"Still hung up on it after all these years?"

"I'm a detective," said Sutherland sadly. "I'd find out eventually."

Richard smirked with his eyes closed and it made Sutherland's heart melt.

"When I'm done. Reach into my right pocket. It's in my wallet. I don't know why I still carry the damn thing around."

Sutherland looked at his pocket. Richard bellowed in pain as the life drained out of him. Sutherland was too choked up to keep the conversation afloat.

"Why won't they just wake up?" Richard asked quietly. "What is it going to take?"

"I don't know," said Sutherland as tears dropped from his eyelashes like water from a leaky faucet. Richard began to fade farther and farther away now.

"Jack," he said, whimpering. "Tell me about your day."

Tears streamed down the detective's cheeks and nose and he wiped them off, not wanting Richard to see them. But the mourning could be heard through his voice.

"Nothing too exciting, really. Got into a car accident, got shot at, and saved your ass."

Richard's expression was monotone and dormant. His life slipped deeper into the horizon with each fleeting moment.

"You said you wouldn't say it," Richard said very softly.

The detective's face trembled, and his lips quivered as he began to cry out loud.

"Why?" asked the detective hysterically. "Why did you go in?"

Richard felt as light as a piece of lint as a bright light overcame him. It was time.

"Why did you?" asked Richard.

Sutherland's face trembled and shriveled up as the tears rapidly emptied out of his eyes. Richard showed a lifeless expression across his face as Sutherland broke down in front of him.

"I saw the fire. I..." said Sutherland through his crying.

"No. Not into the church..." whispered Richard.

Sutherland made a fist and placed it against his mouth as he tried to hold it together. Unable to holster his emotions and remorse, Sutherland began to weep and sniffle.

"Because no one else would," said Sutherland.

Richard smiled as he shut his eyes. Sutherland's eyes became red and his cheeks were soaked with his tears.

"We both had our reasons..." said Richard gently.

The detective wiped his wet eyes and cheeks with his left hand as Richard Morrissey slipped away. Sutherland looked at his friend and old partner, unable to fathom it all. His body began to shake as he sat on the grass beside Richard, knowing there was not a thing he could do to bring him back. He wept as he slowly reached his hand into Richard's pocket and yanked out his beat up, brown wallet. His hands shook in haste as he opened it. Inside, there were cards and some cash. His identification was tucked in the right side pocket. He placed his thumb up against it and slid it out carefully. The weightless card balanced between his fingers as he looked around for the name. In small black print, Detective Sutherland's heart stopped and body went dull. In small black print, it read,

Richard Morrissey

It never fully processed in his head as he held the card in front of until it slipped between his fingers. The card fell to the ground, but the detective's hazy gaze remained fixed on his fingers. His whole body went numb as a heat flash pulsed up his back. Completely blocking out everything around him, he did not see Father Paul looking at him upright. The priest looked at him neutrally and down at Richard's dead body. Sutherland looked over at Father Paul. The two sat in front of one another and exchanged looks of traumatism.

In the center of town, the fighting had stopped, and the smoke began to clear. The planes did not circle around again, and everyone got out from behind their shelters and covers. They walked into the middle of the street and looked down at the most unimaginable thing they had ever seen. Ron Carlisle walked towards an injured Redeemer. He knelt down and pressed his pistol against the man's forehead.

The large group of survivors looked down at the road through the haze and the smog. They looked at what stood before them. Some of them dropped their guns and weapons at the sight of it. Others fell to their knees and placed their hands over their mouths. Amongst the rage and ruin of the town that fell apart around them, the townspeople looked upon the most beautiful thing they had seen in years. Facing them, standing in unison, at about fifty yards away, the victims looked at them. Awake.

The victims looked around them at the massacre and devastation. They saw the dead bodies on the ground and the once gorgeous buildings collapsed to the ground. Like a nightmare, their town was completely desolated and destroyed. They looked with faces of dread and horror, unable to produce a word to describe it all. The two groups watched one another in the crossfire of the fall of Jasper. Ron clenched his teeth as he clenched the Redeemer's throat with his left hand and dug the muzzle of the gun into the man's head with his right. His finger pulled back gently on the trigger when the sound of a voice made him look up.

"Dad?"

Ron looked ahead and saw his daughter Alyssa among the crowd of victims. She looked directly at him in trepidation. Ron's mouth opened in shock as he fell off of the man he was about to kill. The gun slipped out of his hands as he crawled on all fours, unable to blink while he stared.

Gradually, the two groups got closer and closer together, as if they were approaching an alien race. Finally, they found themselves close the void that separated them and looked at each other's faces in wonder.

Olivia Collette walked outside of the diner, holding her daughter's hand with Diane Morrissey walking beside her. They looked in disbelief as the fighting had concluded. No one murmured a word or sound. The rain had stopped and the sun began came out of hiding from behind the clouds.

Behind the massive gathering of survivors and victims, two people walked down the road. Detective Jack Sutherland walked beside Father Paul, holding the body of Richard Morrissey in his arms. When they reached the others, Father Paul looked around in a look of horror and pain that could not be described.

Olivia stepped out into the street with her daughter to make sure what she saw was real. The detective looked at them, unable to comprehend it all. His daughter was upright and mentally stable. How could that be? *How is that possible?* Sutherland asked himself. Olivia returned a gaze and expression of exhaustion and spoil.

Diane Morrissey walked in front of Olivia, looking at the man in the detective's arms. Her face cringed as she shook her head, not wanting to believe it. In the span of the five minutes since her awakening, her reality became a nightmare. Sutherland looked at Diane with a degree of grief beyond measure.

For so long, the people only knew life without their loved ones. They always told themselves what they'd do or how'd they change if they ever woke. Now, after five years, after surviving, starving, sinning, killing, and pushing, they did not know what to do or what to say. The victims, as they stood, saw the townspeople of Jasper not for who they were, but what they had become. Just as Richard said they would.

James D. Gianetti

Things Always Turn

A week after 'The Awakening', the wall came down. The government made a promise to rebuild the town of Jasper brick for brick. They supplied food, water, and resources with the help of the Red Cross and countless charities. Loved ones were buried, and funerals and eulogies were held. The fire was put out, but the effects and results of the aftermath would live on with the townspeople of Jasper for eternity.

    A few days later, inside the Church, which began its reconstruction shortly after it burned, the wake for Richard Morrissey was held. Only half the church was reconstructed. It was a gorgeous day, and the sun shined down brightly on the incomplete half of the place of worship. They gathered inside of it. Every single person in town, to pay their respects to the man who saved Jasper. Ron Carlisle sat up front with his wife Kathy and two children, Zach and Alyssa. Everyone reunited with their loved ones as they sat silently. In the back, Detective Sutherland stood and looked at his ex-wife and daughter sitting up in the front. He looked at Richard's wife and two children, who all sat and cried. Sutherland had completed his task. He had done his job. *But for what?* he asked himself. He found his wife, his daughter, and his partner, but nothing had changed. His manhunt for Richard Morrissey turned on its side, and the cause of 'The Incident' remained a mystery. They were alive. They were awake. Without any reason to move towards something, Detective Sutherland felt useless. He felt alone. But, for the first time since he could remember, among all his dark thoughts, he did not feel the urge to find the small orange vial.

The Town of Jasper

Father Paul conducted a prayer out loud to the viewers and guests until something stopped him from going any further. He stopped his speech and his face drooped down as he observed what stood ahead. The entire church turned around to see what the priest was staring at. Their mouths dropped to the floor. People grasped the person next to them, as they became fearful and uneasy. The entire tribe of Fillmore Whites stood at the back of the church, quietly. Over a hundred of them gathered, led by Edmund, who stood at the front. Each of them had a basket of food, water, and flowers. Father Paul, along with the remaining townspeople of Jasper, looked at them in wonder.

"May we pay our respects?" asked Edmund.

The sound of his voice shocked the people who did not believe they could speak. Father Paul looked at Edmund and smiled.

"Absolutely," he said.

The Fillmore Whites walked around the church, handing their baskets of goods to each person. Everyone got something. The people looked at them in complete surprise as the Albino men and women distributed and provided. Father Paul felt happiness and joy, as he knew Richard had something to do with it all. Once everyone had something, Edmund walked up to Father Paul at the front of the church.

"You are Paul. The teacher of God's words," Edmund asked.

"Yes," said Father Paul. "I am."

"He spoke of you. Said you are one of the last great men in this world."

"No. One of the last is gone now," he said as he looked at Richard's casket.

Edmund walked up to the casket and placed a flower upon it. His eyes overflowed with tears as he felt sadness and loss.

"These are on the house," whispered Edmund as he placed his forehead against the casket.

Everyone got up to look as Edmund clasped onto the casket of his good friend and closed his eyes.

"Life's biggest curse," he whispered as his head remained on the casket.

Edmund waited a few more seconds before letting go. He did not wipe the tears away from his soaked face as he looked up at the priest. Father Paul gave him a proud nod and couldn't help but get choked up. Edmund walked off, as the remaining Fillmore Whites placed flowers on Richard's casket. Edmund walked up to Richard's children and knelt in front of them. Diane looked at Edmund's wet face and cried. Edmund wiped her tears with his fingers and rested his head against her hands as he clutched them. He looked up at his daughter, Victoria, and placed his hands on her cheeks and kissed her forehead. Her breathing was perfectly normal as she cried and sobbed. Joseph looked down as he wept with deep and dark sadness. Edmund got up and walked up to the boy. Joseph wept and sniffled as Edmund fell to his knees and took the boy's hands and held them gently in his. Joseph looked up at Edmund's ghostly face and looked directly into his red eyes without fear.

"The son of my savior," whispered Edmund as he pulled the boy in and hugged him.

Joseph cried into Edmund's shoulder as the leader of The Fillmore Whites felt a new extent of love for another human being.

"Me and my people. We will protect you until the end of time," whispered Edmund into Joseph's ear.

The Town of Jasper

After the respects were paid and the wake neared its conclusion, Father Paul began his concluding remarks. He stood in front of Richard's casket as he asked everyone to rise. The Church, packed with hundreds of people, stood up and listened.

"They told me he came in here during it all. The years after 'The Incident'. I was told he came here to confess his sins to me. He knew I couldn't possibly hear him or see him. But he came in here and made me feel like I was still with him. He did the same for all of you. He did things that can't be explained. Things you all probably had to do yourself, I'm sure. Thing got dark here, no question. We, the victims, only saw the aftermath. The very end. We still don't know how it happened or why. Was it a test? Was it a sign? It doesn't matter. It doesn't. Before me is a man of God. Like his father, a natural-born leader and a savior. A savior, whom I have known since he was a child. I looked after him like he was my own. In many ways, he was. I helped bury his father and now…we all owe our lives to him. For what he has accomplished. The things he did. Only now, we know how lucky we are to have had a man like him within the walls. Only now, I know how lucky I am, to have once cared for the man who walked into this church to confess his sins and save my life."

Later that night, after everyone left, Diane held Victoria in her arms as Joseph trailed her out of the church. Father Paul looked over the casket and said some prayers. Diane smiled at him. Father Paul smirked back at her.

"Tomorrow, I'll get some strong men in here and we can carry him to the car," he said. "It's supposed to be a beautiful day for the burial."

Diane smiled and nodded at Father Paul and walked down the aisle of the half church. Joseph did not follow his mother; instead, he looked up at Father Paul, who looked down at the boy curiously.

"Will you open it?" Joseph asked.

Father Paul looked down at the boy as his heart broke into pieces. Joseph stood in front of his father's casket with a picture he drew five years ago. The picture was of a man with dark brown hair and a brown leather jacket with the words 'My Hero' written on it.

A year after 'The Awakening', the town of Jasper had been restored for the most part and everything went back to the way it was. The victims awoke and were in perfect health. A degree of poetic justice, the hibernation had cured every one of their diseases, handicaps, injuries, and defects.

It was a sun-filled day with not a cloud in the September sky. Kathy Carlisle walked outside of the house in a rush with her two children behind her with their backpacks on. They shuffled into the car while Ron walked down the driveway to retrieve the paper. His wife reversed the car down the driveway and sped off.

A police officer passed by Ron as he read the news headline in the black and white. The officer's window was rolled down and gave Ron a friendly nod. Ron nodded back and smiled as he gaped down at the cul-de-sac. In the distance, the little girl from the day of 'The Incident' opened the door to her parent's car. The girl, now grown and maturing, placed her backpack into the car and sat inside. Her mother walked down the driveway and dragged a garbage pail. She noticed Ron through her peripheral vision and stopped to stare at him. Ron returned a similar expression of nothingness and looked away.

The Town of Jasper

Later that day, Ron walked inside the library to browse and kill some time. He paced up and down the aisles with a few books in his hands. There was a man in front of him as he walked up to the line at the front desk to check his books out. The man turned around.

"Hey, Ron," he said in a friendly tone.

"Hey, Dallas," Ron said. "Enjoying retirement?"

"Just passing the time," he said peacefully. "I'll see ya around."

Ron walked up to the front desk and placed the books down on the table. A woman named Martha checked them out.

"Find everything okay?" she asked nicely.

"Yes. Thank you," said Ron.

The local convenience store was on the same block. Ron walked inside the familiar store and walked into the back to retrieve a gallon of two percent milk. He walked up to the front and placed the gallon of milk on the counter. He reached for a pack of gum and threw it next to the milk. A man named Nick looked at him and smiled. Ron flipped through his cash and placed a ten-dollar bill on the counter. Nick looked at the cash and up at Ron.

"Keep the change," said Ron with a smile.

An hour later, Detective Sutherland strolled into the post office with a package. A package he promised to deliver for an old friend. The object was found under the rubble and wreckage of the law office after the destruction of the town. It took months of tracking and persistence on Sutherland's behalf to obtain it.

As he walked inside the post office, a couple walked out. Sutherland held the door for the joyous people who gave him a nod and smile. A man named Elon thanked the man as he and his wife walked outside holding hands.

Two days later, at six o'clock, that package arrived to its intended destination. The doorbell rang as the postman walked back to his vehicle and a woman opened the door. Diane Morrissey looked down at the brown box and lifted the package up with curiosity. She placed the package down on her kitchen table carefully and began to open it. The lids popped up off the brown box that weighed no more than two pounds. She placed her hands into the box and pulled out the object. The object was a small picture frame with a tiny piece of paper in the center. The small piece of paper had a phone number written down on it. Diane's phone number. The one she gave to Richard the day they met. There was a small note attached to the picture frame. On the note, it read,

You Weren't Just Another Number

Diane Morrissey dropped the picture frame on the floor and cried hysterically into her hands as she felt her life dissolve slowly out of her soul.

That same day, at six o'clock, inside a pearl white house, with a white picket fence and a big brown door, a woman prepared dinner. A seven-year-old girl recited math equations and solutions out loud to herself as she wrote intensely with her sharp pencil against a white blank page. A loud knock on the door caused the woman to stop stirring her pot of stew to find out who was paying her a visit. She wiped her hands on her red polka dot apron while her daughter dropped her pencil and ran excitedly towards the door. The little girl rushed past her mother and approached the door. She placed her fingers around the knob and pulled the door inwards. At the doorstep, the little girl saw a man. A man whose eyes glistened with wholesome joy at the sight of the small girl. A man whose tears

The Town of Jasper

gradually trickled down his face at such sight. A once scientific man who didn't believe in the nature of miracle or marvel. A man holding a leash attached to the collar of an aged, yellow Labrador Retriever. A man looking to start the 'what happens next' part.